THE
PROTEST

ROB RINDER

THE PROTEST

CENTURY

CENTURY

UK | USA | Canada | Ireland | Australia
India | New Zealand | South Africa

Century is part of the Penguin Random House group of companies
whose addresses can be found at global.penguinrandomhouse.com

Penguin Random House UK,
One Embassy Gardens, 8 Viaduct Gardens, London SW11 7BW

penguin.co.uk
global.penguinrandomhouse.com

First published in the UK by Century in 2025
005

Set in 13.5/17pt Fournier MT Std
Typeset by Jouve (UK), Milton Keynes

Printed and bound in Great Britain by Clays Ltd, Elcograf S.p.A.

The authorised representative in the EEA is Penguin Random House Ireland,
Morrison Chambers, 32 Nassau Street, Dublin D02 YH68

A CIP catalogue record for this book is available from the British Library

ISBN: 978–1–529–93475–5 (hardback)
ISBN: 978–1–529–93476–2 (trade paperback)

For Morris Mallinek and
'The Boys' of the 45 Aid Society

Prologue

It was a warm summer's evening in June, as the guests arrived at London's Royal Academy on Piccadilly for what purported to be the hottest night of the year.

The great and the good were here, chatting, chinking glass; old friends, new networking opportunities. A steady stream of waiters, dressed in black Nehru jackets, served elegant pink curls of smoked salmon on transparent trays etched like chessboards. Flutes of chilled champagne were stacked up like pyramids on black velvet-covered tables, and a small jazz band was playing to the right of the red carpet, just as the sun dipped low in the sky. There were sequinned jackets, high heels, nipped-in waistcoats, flowing trousers, pantsuits; the beau monde was out in force. Newspaper diarists circled, pens poised for any gossip. Benedict Cumberbatch, Taron Egerton: simply everyone was here.

This was Art, with a capital A. And the Max Bruce retrospective was one of the most exciting events to be held at the RA in almost a decade.

Natasha Fitzjohn fiddled with her platinum necklace, nervously scanning the cobbled courtyard, waiting for the main event to arrive. As curator of the exhibition, she had been working up to this moment for the past three years. But the painstaking diplomacy and relentless negotiations had finally paid off and she'd managed to secure the loan of Max Bruce's famous masterpiece *Primal Scream* for public viewing for the very first time.

A vast, imposing oil of the birth of a baby. It was regarded as one of the finest examples of the chaos of childbirth, motherhood and the earliest gasps of life. It was Bruce's first major work, and it had catapulted him to fame, and possibly infamy; and, almost as soon as it had been so well received, it had disappeared. It had reappeared some decades later, only to be snapped up by a reclusive Russian oligarch who lived in Surrey.

But here it was, at last, inside the gallery, awaiting the big reveal. Natasha smiled to herself; the only person missing was the artist.

'He's a bit late,' declared Alexandra Williams, checking the time on her phone. It was 7.28 p.m. Known as Lexi to everyone, she was Natasha's unpaid 21-year-old intern, who'd been helping with the exhibition. 'Doesn't it say six-thirty on the invitation?'

'I am sure he wants to make an entrance,' replied Natasha, with an irritated rattle of her bracelets, as she ran her hand through her sleek dark bobbed hair. She was an elegant, put-together woman in her early forties who bristled with ambition and focus. 'But it is, frankly, verging on rude, bearing in mind it's his party.'

Finally, an explosion of flashbulbs announced Max Bruce's arrival in the street outside. The conversation at the party lulled and all eyes turned towards the stone archway, the black-and-gold gates, as Max Bruce and his entourage walked into the court-yard. Natasha allowed herself the briefest of exhales. The 62-year-old Bruce crossed the cobbles, a symphony of primary colours in a red suit, yellow shirt and pale blue shoes. He was playing to the crowd, waving and posing like a peacock. Behind him were his two partners, commonly known as his 'wifies', who stood either side of him, creating the effect of a perfect bohemian throuple. Camilla, on his right, was the elder and first wife. A great beauty in her youth, she was now sixty years old and was working a fuchsia turban and a matching Zandra Rhodes kaftan, with scarlet nails and Andrew Logan mirror rings. Her signature ebony cigarette holder had been replaced with a lengthy vape. To his left was wifie number two, Elisa. Tall, thin, blonde, thirty-five years old, inscrutable, she was dressed entirely in black with red lipstick and dark glasses, looking every inch like a backing singer for Robert Palmer. Fanning out behind them, also posing for the photographers, was Bruce's ever-expanding brood of nepos, who mostly appeared to have come straight from the skate park. The oldest and best known of these was Loughton. Wearing a backwards baseball cap, with baggy trousers and bow legs, he stood next to his father and his mothers, two fingers together under his chin, as if he were auditioning for James Bond (which he might have been). For Loughton was one of those nepo children who seemed to chop and change and alter their careers without any transferable, or indeed obvious, skills.

'Loughton!' shouted the paparazzi. 'This way!'

Loughton pulled out a small sauce bottle from his trouser pocket and waved it at the press. Currently a famous graffiti artist, he was also flogging his new hot sauce range at Aldi, and he had clearly been told to use any marketing opportunity possible, even his own father's retrospective.

Max Bruce sailed through the crowd, to a ripple of applause. His thick white hair stuck up and his sharp dark eyes scanned the sea of faces, as he walked towards Natasha, who was standing at the entrance to the gallery.

'Over here! Mr Bruce!' yelled a photographer.

'Here, Max! Max!' shouted another.

Natasha smiled politely from the lectern at the entrance to the gallery. She stood in front of the microphone, waiting for the noise to die down. Eventually, she tapped her champagne glass and coughed.

'My lords, ladies and gentlemen, good evening. May I be the first to say what an honour it is tonight to be in the presence of the great . . . the brilliant . . . the extraordinary . . . Max Bruce CBE . . .' She paused, waiting for the cheers of acknowledgement at his newly acquired gong in the King's Birthday Honours list. 'Max Bruce . . . you don't need me to tell you, is Britain's greatest living artist, with a collection of incredible works housed in some of the most prestigious museums and galleries all over the world. And we are particularly proud, indeed honoured, and delighted, to have secured nearly all his works, here today. From the Met to the Tate, to Venice's Guggenheim – they have all travelled far for this first-ever Max Bruce retrospective.' There was more applause. Natasha smiled and surveyed the pleasingly glamorous crowd. 'There is one painting that I know you are all very much looking forward to seeing . . . *Primal Scream.*' There were loud whistles and cheers. 'Firstly, I would very much like to thank Mr Sergei Valutov for his extremely generous loaning of *Primal Scream.*

4

I know that after the campaign failed to keep the painting in the UK (or "save it for the nation") we were all a little broken-hearted at the thought it would never be seen again. But thanks to the huge generosity of Mr Valutov, we shall *all*, for the first time since it was painted over four decades ago now, be able to enjoy its extraordinary vibrancy, powerful imagery and its deftly intoxicating use of colour and paint. So, thank you, Mr Valutov.' She clapped gently to the left and to the right of the lectern. The crowd craned its collective neck, searching for the shadowy figure of Valutov. 'Sadly, Mr Valutov can't be here tonight – he is otherwise engaged – but we are eternally grateful for his bounteous generosity . . . Now, without further ado . . . I'd like to invite you all to follow me inside the gallery, where our president, Lord Armitage, will say a few words, as indeed will . . . Max Bruce.'

The excitement in the crowd was palpable. There was a certain amount of shoving and jostling as the guests surged forward, following the main party through the doors to the gallery and into the hall, and on into the large brightly lit side room, where the enormous canvas depicting the bloodied freshly born baby taking its first breath dominated the room. It was awe-inspiring, with its thick, heavy use of oils. Max Bruce's wives both stood still, side by side, their mouths ajar, as they took in the astonishing image. Some people applauded spontaneously, some just sipped their champagne and stared.

'Before we hear from our president, I'd like to invite Max Bruce to say a few words,' declared Natasha, extending her arm. 'Max Bruce!'

The guests applauded, they shouted, they cheered.

'Stop the war!' came a cry. 'Stop the killing!'

Everyone looked frantically around the room at where the chant might be coming from. Suddenly, there was an unholy, guttural scream as a young woman launched herself from the crowd straight at Max Bruce.

'STOP THE WAR! STOP THE KILLING!'

She screamed and, as she screamed, she sprayed a can of bright blue paint all over Max Bruce's face. She covered him from forehead to chin, his eyelids, his lips, even the lobes of his ears.

Everyone was too stunned to move.

'Lexi!' Natasha shouted from the side of the room. 'Lexi! What are you doing?!'

'Stop the war!' Lexi yelled, pummelling the air with her fist. 'Stop the killing! Stop the war! Stop the killing!'

A security guard stormed through from the back of the hall, scattering the guests, pushing them to one side. There was the sound of smashing glass as champagne flutes crashed to the ground. But it was the security guard right next to the painting who wrestled Lexi to the ground. She didn't resist, instead she raised her arms in the air. She'd made her point. Max Bruce had been Blue-Faced. Her work here was done.

The two wives were hysterical. Bruce laughed a little, he was incredulous, as though incapable of processing what had just happened to him. While Loughton swung his phone around filming the attack, his father wiped the blue paint off his face, using the back of his hand, dabbing the sides of his mouth with a white handkerchief that he pulled from his pocket. Meanwhile, the security guard dragged Lexi away through the parted crowd.

'Stop the war! Stop the killing!' she still shouted.

Bruce made his way towards the microphone set up in front of his masterpiece.

'Well, apologies for my appearance,' he joked. Everyone laughed. 'I know I like a blue as much as Picasso but—'

He collapsed to the floor. The guests laughed again. Maybe this was all part of the show? And then they stopped as Bruce began to roll around on the parquet, frantically tugging at the neck of his yellow shirt, his heels drumming the ground, his eyes rolled into the back of his head. He gurgled, he retched, he heaved, he vomited, he convulsed. No one knew what to do. Camilla was screaming, her hands clamped to her cheeks; Elisa was shouting for help, and Natasha and Lord Armitage stood near the lectern, rigid, rooted, white with shock, unable to do anything but stare.

It took less than a minute for the aging *enfant terrible* of the art world Max Bruce to die, in front of his two wives, five of his children, the press, the paparazzi, and the great, the good and their guests.

And no one could do a thing about it.

One

Adam Green woke up, tired, in his flat in Islington. It took him a second to remember where he was. He had lived in this modern conversion, just off Upper Street, where the walls were painted a subtle grey, his bathroom gleamed with black mosaic tiles, and his kitchen, confusingly, had no drawer handles, for over six months already. But still, every morning it took him by surprise. He'd woken up before his alarm and, as he sat on the side of his bed, scratching his dark hair and contemplating what might constitute the swiftest breakfast, his clock radio switched on.

'The art world has lost one of its biggest stars,' began the news at the top of the hour. 'Max Bruce was killed last night . . . in front of his family and friends at the opening of his hotly anticipated retrospective at the Royal Academy. And we are joined now from the scene, by our arts correspondent, Jenny Jones . . . Jenny . . . what a tragedy . . .'

Max Bruce? Adam had heard of him. He walked into the kitchen/dining room/sitting room of his tiny flat and turned on the television, where they were playing Loughton Bruce's video of his father's death with the final harrowing moments pixelated out for taste and decency and an early-morning audience. But the screaming, and the shouting, and the 'Stop the war!' chants were all perfectly audible. Next, there was footage of the protestor, a woman, being dragged away, frog-marched out of the place by two security guards.

What a way to die, thought Adam, staring at the screen while taking a pinch of fish food and feeding the bug-eyed goldfish his mother had given him as a flat-warming present. Having never expressed any interest in pets, or indeed fish of any kind, Adam had convinced himself that his mother's gift was some sort of early-warning alarm system, like a canary down a mine. If the fish died, it proved to her he couldn't look after anything, least of all himself. So he fed it religiously every day, if only to prove her wrong.

'What a terrible loss to the nation this is, and what a terrible way to die,' declared a woman – CURATOR, NATASHA FITZJOHN it said on the screen. 'The art world is much diminished in this country after what happened here. We are all in mourning, and in shock.'

In a voiceover the newscaster continued to explain quite how important an artist Max Bruce was. There was some early colour footage of him partying in the 1980s, a montage of his work with thick paints and bright colours, expressive hands, large faces, a close-up of the famous painting, *Primal Scream*, a head shot of the woman accused of the murder, Alexandra (Lexi) Williams – she looked young, defiant and scared at the same time. Then there was more footage of the party, the family's grand entrance to an explosion of flashbulbs, a few cutaways to Loughton waving his bottle of hot sauce, and one image of Natasha Fitzjohn smiling at her lectern and . . . was that the Stop the War campaigner, Lexi Williams, standing next to her? Also smiling?

So she had been working at the event? Not someone who'd come in off the street? Adam frowned at the screen, as he took a blueberry Pop-Tart out of his bare bread bin and slipped it into his shiny new Dualit toaster and spun the dial.

They cut back to the studio where Lisa Andrews, the normally sunny-looking newscaster, was sombre and sober-faced.

'Joining us now in the studio is our crime correspondent, David Grave. Dave,' said Lisa Andrews. 'A very sad day for the nation . . .'

'Indeed it is,' agreed Dave. 'Very sad . . . But this murder of Max Bruce is all part of the Blue Face protest that has been sweeping through the country over the past few months. A backlash against an illegal war that is still raging in Khandistan. The "Stop the war, stop the killing" chant that is so familiar to us all and particular to these protestors was heard at the event last night, along with the similar spray-can of blue paint that this group of protestors use. But this, as you know, Lisa, this is the first time that the protest has ended in the actual death of one of its victims.'

'Which begs the question, Dave,' cut in Lisa, 'was the Home Secretary just lucky last week when the protestor missed his face and ruined his suit by spraying it blue, or did he actually escape an assassination attempt?'

'Good question, Lisa,' acknowledged Dave. ' "The Lucky Home Secretary", as the Right Honourable Mitchell Hiddleston is now known, might indeed have been "the extremely lucky Home Secretary", for he was targeted by this very same group – and who's to say that his can of paint was not laced with something? And the protestors just missed?'

'Is that what the early suggestions are? That the paint was laced with something?'

'Indeed they are, Lisa. Police sources are claiming that the can used to murder Max Bruce was laced with some sort of poison.'

'Poison? Can you suggest, at these very early stages, what sort it might be?'

'This is pure supposition, Lisa. But there are speculations that it might be cyanide.'

Lisa turned to face the camera. 'Cyanide,' she repeated. 'Well, thank you, Dave. That was David Grave, our crime correspondent, and obviously, as this is a rolling story, we'll keep you updated with any changes.'

Adam sat down on the sofa (one of the only pieces of furniture in his flat), his piping-hot Pop-Tart on a small plate on his lap, staring even more attentively at the TV.

'We are now joined here in the studio by the leader of the Stop the War campaign, Cosmo Campbell.'

Adam looked up from his plate expecting to see a hirsute, unshaven character in a camouflage jacket wearing a vegan scarf. Instead, a young man in a suit and tie appeared on the screen who looked very much like he could be canvassing in Bristol for the Lib Dems.

'Mr Campbell, do you run a terrorist organisation? Was this in fact a terrorist attack in broad daylight, right in the heart of London's West End?'

'Er? What? No . . . Absolutely not.' Cosmo Campbell's youthful cheeks flushed with indignation. 'This is not the way we work as a group. Stop the War is about ending the killing, ending the war in Khandistan, and ending the slaughter of innocent women and children. We are a pro-life group, not pro-death. Why would we want to kill Britain's most famous living artist? Why would that help us? What would that achieve?'

'Publicity, Mr Campbell? Lots and lots of publicity. Which is presumably why you continue with your extremely dangerous Blue Face protest that has just resulted in the death of this country's most famous living—sorry, most famous artist.'

'A murder is not the sort of publicity we are after.'

'And yet . . . you persist? Even after the Home Secretary was attacked last week. Did your organisation want to murder the Home Secretary, Mr Campbell?'

'No, we did not.' Cosmo Campbell looked anxious. His top lip glittered with sweat under the studio lights. 'This is not the organisation that we are. We are a peaceful organisation. We advocate peace, not war.'

'But Max Bruce is dead, Mr Campbell. How do you account for that?'

'I can't.' Cosmo Campbell slowly shook his head. 'I just can't. It was not supposed to happen like this.'

'Was Alexandra Williams working for you?'

'No one works for our organisation. It is staffed by volunteers.'

'Did Alexandra Williams volunteer for your organisation?'

'Not that I am aware of.'

'Not that you are aware of . . .? Yet she had the spray-can of blue paint – your spray-can of blue paint. And she was shouting your slogans before she murdered Max Bruce.'

Lisa's tone was not hectoring. She was feigning surprise, her voice had gone up an octave, her forehead was furrowed (as much as it could since her most recent trip to Harley Street). She paused and waited for Cosmo Campbell to respond.

'Stop the War did not murder Max Bruce,' was his simple reply.

'Thank you, Mr Campbell.'

Adam started to flick through the channels. The Max Bruce murder was the top story on each and every one. There was wall-to-wall coverage, wall-to-wall talk, wall-to-wall usage of Loughton's video, which either he must have sold to the press or it had been lifted from his Instagram. There were outside-broadcast vans parked up on the verge in front of the Home Secretary Mitchell Hiddleston's country house, outside Reading, where the journalists – instead of having the Home Secretary or even, fingers crossed, his wife to talk to about how lucky he'd been to have escaped death by 'Blue Face'– had been forced to stand in front of a hedge, hunched against the summer drizzle as they speculated about whether Stop the War should be banned as a terrorist organisation.

'Who is Lexi Williams?' presenters were asking on another channel. 'And what exactly turns a seemingly normal grammar-school girl into a murderer? Is social media to blame?'

Adam was intrigued by the montage of images that were running across all the news outlets. Someone had gone into Alexandra Williams's social media accounts and had released a heady cocktail of images, mostly of Lexi (as all the press were now calling her) drinking 'heady cocktails'. Pink drinks, yellow drinks, large frosted glasses with paper umbrellas, shiny red cherries and slices of melon or pineapple. Lexi was now a loutish heavy drinker. She was photographed dancing on a table, sporting a very short skirt and a bikini top. There was one of her smoking an apparently hand-rolled cigarette. All those images that she had posted across her socials, craving likes from her friends, had now been weaponised by the media. Adam sighed. She was now a badly behaved party girl, who drank too much and, very possibly, smoked weed.

Sky News had her Twitter/X account as background for an interview with some of the guests who'd attended the party. Eat the Rich, Stop the War! Get Rid of them ALL were plastered all over the TV screen.

Adam shook his head as his Pop-Tart grew cold on his lap. Those photographs, those tweets, the Instagram snaps, the reels, the Facebook likes – they all combined to form an image of a normal young woman who'd had some fun in her life. Yet within less than twelve hours, these same images had been manipulated in an entirely different way. And it had all happened so quickly.

He turned over to GB News where the reporters were vox-popping people along Oxford Street, shoving microphones under their noses, asking what they thought of Lexi Williams.

'It's such a shock,' said one woman. 'I mean, what did her parents do wrong? It's like all these cases of people being addicted to social media. They're radicalised by it. It's a curse.'

'It's such a shame,' added another, nodding in agreement with her friend. 'It's all to do with the social media. All of it. It's all the media.'

'It really does make you think,' said the first.

'About what?' asked the reporter.

'Bringing back hanging.'

Adam switched off the television. He was late and, suddenly, he felt like he really needed a shower.

Two

Adam was hurrying down Chancery Lane, heading towards Stag Court, clutching a stack of briefs tied with the distinctive pink ribbons of defence cases, when a taxi pulled up in front of him at the corner of Fleet Street, and its occupant slickly exited, black court heel first.

'Adam!'

'Georgina!' he said, a little surprised to see his fellow colleague taking a black cab to work.

Although they'd both been members of Stag Court now for the past several years, and had started out as pupils together, he would personally never be quite that flash. But Georgina Devereaux came from a different school of thought, mainly private, and her career was flying: she had already made Junior Treasury Counsel, the youngest ever to do so. And they only appointed the brightest, the best, the fairest and the most ethical. On top of that she had charm, charisma, and a dress sense as sharp as her sense of humour. And great hair.

'Have you heard?' she began, a smile playing on her lips. She was clearly, and not for the first time, privy to something he was not.

'Heard what?' Adam's shoulders slumped a little. He really should get better at playing chambers politics. He'd much improved since his first couple of years, when he'd dreaded the endless 'networking events' he'd been forced to attend, where he'd spent most of his time with his teeth gritted, his hand gently sweating around the neck of a beer bottle, his buttocks firmly clenched with mortification, as he'd walked around desperately searching for subjects that might constitute 'small talk'. But not being familiar with summers in Tuscany, the boarding houses of Marlborough College, or that lovely little restaurant off the King's Road, he did not have the easy confidence of Georgina. Ever since Oxford, Adam had never really felt that he belonged in 'the room'. Any room.

'Morris is back.'

'Morris . . .? Morris Brown?'

'Yup.' She shook her auburn blow-dry and pursed her lips, pleased that her news had landed.

'*The* Morris Brown?'

'Yup.' She smiled and raised her eyebrows. 'He's back from Yale. He's been teaching some specialist course or other, I'm not quite sure what, and he's just written this book – well, not quite a book, a sort of pamphlet thing – about the explosion of youth crime in the UK and the reasons behind it. It's been reviewed in today's *Times*.'

She whipped out a copy of *The Times*, neatly folded, from under her armpit. Adam managed the swiftest of glances at the article where he noticed that some phrases and statistics had already been underlined in red pen. He sighed inwardly. While he'd been feeding his fish and munching on a tepid Pop-Tart, she'd already been way ahead of him, underlining passages in

The Times while undoubtedly drinking a spinach-and-celery smoothie after forty-five minutes of wall Pilates, or whatever that app was she'd flashed in front of his face last Friday.

'Everyone's terrified of him.' She grinned. 'Even Tony.'

Adam followed her over the road past a humbug-striped Tudor building and the court outfitters, Lipman & Sons, to a heavy black wooden door that led to a hidden cobbled lane beyond. Although just a few steps away from a busy Fleet Street, it was like entering into a hidden world of clipped lawns, fountains and ancient buildings with narrow back streets. This was a part of London steeped in a history and tradition that hadn't changed in centuries. Adam always felt a frisson of excitement as he walked down the lane.

Dressed in their crisp white bands and billowing robes, a barrage of barristers marched past Adam and Georgina on their way to the High Court. A couple were already wearing their horsehair wigs, but the others mostly had them clamped under their arms. Behind them came the clerks, wheeling their hefty trolleys across the old flagstone pavements, groaning under the weight of thick, heavy case files. Opposite the entrance to Stag Court stood the magnificent Middle Temple, where the first performance of *Twelfth Night* had been performed in front of the indomitable Elizabeth I.

Adam stopped and looked at Georgina.

'I doubt that,' Adam eventually replied.

'What?'

'That Tony's scared of Morris Brown.'

Chief clerk Tony Jones was not scared of anyone; in fact, he ran the place. Nothing happened in Stag Court without his say-so. If he asked you to jump, you'd ask how high. He distributed the cases, decided who could prosecute or defend what, and was in charge of socialising and networking events. Everything went through Tony. Bald, broad and brought up on the bombed-out playgrounds of the East End, he was as sharp as his suits, and his neck was as thick as his Cockney accent.

'I promise you, I'm not lying,' Georgina continued, pausing on the flagged steps of Stag Court, worn smooth by hundreds of years of busy lawyers bustling over the threshold. 'Apparently, Morris Brown's last junior had to leave chambers altogether he was so run down and exhausted. He ended up working on daytime TV.'

Adam stepped inside the narrow hallway and was surprised to see his ex-pupil master, Jonathan Taylor-Cameron, already standing in the clerks' room attempting some sort of small talk with Tony, who was sitting behind his desk, dressed in a white shirt with a scarlet tie and a sharp suit with a silver sheen. Jonathan had one hand on the desk and was laughing heartily at his own joke, head back, nostrils to the ceiling. Meanwhile, Tony's cheeks were puffing a little with boredom.

'Well, it all sounds very entertaining, Mr Taylor-Cameron. I'd like to say I wish I'd been there, but I imagine it's not my sort of a crowd.' He clicked the end of his Parker pen, indicating to Jonathan that he should move on.

Ever since his catastrophic divorce case, when Jonathan had been taken to the cleaners by his livid third wife, losing the house in the Dordogne, the pied-à-terre in Chelsea and the cottage in the Cotswolds, Jonathan had been touting for work with increasing desperation. His wife had also managed to persuade the court that she needed a hefty monthly maintenance cheque, on top of which Jonathan still had five of his children to put through some form of education. He'd thought that Freddie going to Durham University might have cut him some slack until he'd realised that universities were no longer free.

Added to his woes, Jonathan had made the fatal error of upgrading to a younger, thinner blonde version of his third ex-wife, with whom he was now struggling to keep up. Recently Adam had noticed Jonathan's louche, jaded, boyish charm had given way to a haunted, hunted look. He now went to the gym at 6 a.m., smelt of Tom Ford Tobacco Vanille and had a 'hairstyle', where the strands from the back of his head were brushed forward to hide the receding M-shape at the front. His paunch had also shrunk to its pre-expense-account proportions, but at least he was saving money at the florist.

Adam remembered those heady early days of working with Jonathan only too well, how he'd sent flowers out to Jonathan's various girlfriends and mistresses, making sure they all received the correct message – whose 'milky thighs' he was missing that week; it had been a task in itself. Although it was surely only a matter of time before those bills picked up again. If you married your mistress, as the saying went, you only created another vacancy. Jonathan had yet to marry Pippa, a 'gallery girl' who worked on Bond Street. She spent busy days multi-tasking – flogging paintings, organising facials and holidays in Gstaad – all in office hours.

'Adam!' Jonathan turned round to see his old pupil. 'How are you? Busy?' he asked, looking down at the pink-ribboned briefs.

'Aren't we always?' Adam smiled.

'Some of us are.' Jonathan nodded slowly and then glanced over at Tony and the pile of papers on his desk.

Tony's desk was piled high with incoming cases, some highly lucrative and some pro bono, but the truth, Adam knew, was that Tony didn't entirely trust Jonathan. Jonathan had been riding high since he'd won the Jessica Holby case, but ever since he'd drunk far too much at last year's Christmas party Tony had been holding back. It had been one of those evenings in which Jonathan had started recounting old war stories to anyone who would listen, as he'd propped up the bar in El Vino's just off Chancery Lane. Not only had he done appalling impressions of his clients – including an intricate array of regional accents – he'd finished the whole schpiel, with the line 'We all know that "no" secretly means "yes"' – to a resounding silence.

'Well, you certainly have your work cut out for you,' interjected Tony. 'Your new pupil is waiting for you outside your room, Mr Taylor-Cameron.'

'He is?' Jonathan rolled his eyes. 'I can't believe it's that time of year already – can you, Adam? There's no peace for the wicked . . . just a hefty prison sentence.' He chortled.

'*She* is,' corrected Tony.

'She?' Jonathan perked up.

'Miss Jackson,' said Tony. 'Stacey Jackson.'

'Miss Jackson . . . With the nice ankles? We interviewed a while ago?'

'I couldn't possibly comment on Miss Jackson's ankles, sir,' replied Tony.

'It's an innocent question, Mr Jones, an innocent question. People are so tetchy these days, honestly, Adam. There's no joy in the world today.' Jonathan rolled his eyes again. 'Wish me luck.' He headed off down the corridor in a cloud of expensive aftershave. He paused and turned round. 'Oh, Mr Jones, is Morris Brown returning today?'

'He most certainly is.'

'The old socialist returns.' Jonathan sighed loudly. 'If only one could afford to be one of those.'

It had just gone 8.45 a.m. and Adam had made a cup of coffee and was getting his feet under his desk, when there appeared to be a sudden drop in temperature and the normally busy, industrious sounds of Stag Court fell silent. It felt as if a north wind had blown through the building. The windows chattered and clattered with the icy blast. There was a rap on his door, it sprung open, and Georgina slipped swiftly in.

'He's here,' she whispered, her eyes wide, as she gripped the door handle.

'Who's here?' Adam whispered back.

'Morris Brown.' She nodded over her shoulder.

'Why are we whispering?'

'Because everyone is shit-scared of him.'

'Why?'

'Because he's brilliant and takes no prisoners, and he's a difficult bastard to please. He's one of the few who take on heads of government. And he fights the fight. All the time. And he's got this odd stare so you never know who he's looking at, which I'm pretty sure is a technique that basically means you have to be on it all the time, otherwise he'll catch you out. I met him once at a literary festival. I queued up for hours, I got him to sign his books.' She gave Adam a grin. 'He's talking to Tony now.'

Adam came slowly out from behind his desk and together

they both poked their heads out from behind the door and stared down the corridor. There was a glimpse of a pinstriped suit, and the murmuring tones of two men talking, and the gentle rumble of laughter.

'I wonder,' whispered Georgina, 'if I might ever get to work with him . . .'

Three

An hour later, Adam walked down the corridor towards Jonathan's room – the land that Tony's brisk, smart, upgrading makeover forgot. The door was open and as he approached, he could hear Stacey, talking her new pupil master through the last few weeks of her flat-hunting crisis.

'Quite a few of the places I've looked at have been really quite shabby,' she said. 'And they are very far away from here, and with the amount of rent they're asking, you'd think I was trying to live in a palace. I mean, London prices are something else, aren't they? In Manchester, there's plenty of relatively cheap accommodation, despite it having the biggest student population in Europe. I don't know what I'm going to do. What did all the other pupils do before? I'm crashing with a mate for the moment, but that can't last forever . . .'

Adam could see her eyeing up Jonathan's curling plaid wallpaper, the cracking dark leather swivel chair, the terrifying taxidermy of what was once the family Jack Russell, and the veritable jumble sale of silver photograph frames that cluttered his desk, all boasting some sort of 'Jonathan Taylor-Cameron achievement'. Rowing, shooting, riding, at a wedding, Ascot, with one of his many children — all taken in the last century, judging by the haircuts and the yellowing hue of the photographs. In fact, the whole place had the appearance of a jaded gentlemen's club that smelt of spilled claret, over-cooked grouse and ancient, post-prandial flatulence.

'Manchester?' Jonathan mumbled, an apparently unpleasant taste in his mouth.

'North,' replied Stacey, with an arched eyebrow.

'There you are, Adam!' proclaimed Jonathan, springing out of his chair with surprising enthusiasm. 'I am not sure if you remember Stacey? The new pupil. Can you believe out of those four hundred applicants that were so carefully sifted through, all those rounds of interviews and advocacy exercises, the pupillage committee found Stacey here? Gosh, she was only just telling me, in riveting detail, the story of her house-hunting in London.'

'Flat-hunting,' she corrected. 'I can't afford a house.'

Jonathan didn't bother to hide his irritation. 'Not yet, dear, no.' He smiled tightly. 'Anyway, Stacey . . . moving on. Or in. This is Adam, Adam Green, he's been a member of Stag Court for . . . er, a while, and he is your new mentor.'

'Hi.' She smiled broadly, possibly with relief.

'So, any problems . . . with stuff.' Jonathan rubbed his hands together. 'Anything that needs mentoring – he's the man. I imagine his door is always open . . . and all that jazz. Isn't it, Adam? Ready for some mentoring?'

'Always open,' agreed Adam.

'Good. In my day there was just a pupil master, now everyone's worried about mental health.' Stacey smiled tightly. Jonathan laughed heartily and then inhaled loudly through his back-teeth 'Great. So, now, Stacey, your first job of the morning, every morning, is a nice strong cup of coffee on my desk, with just the tiniest, the *briefest* amount of milk.'

He put his forefinger and thumb together, to show her just how tiny the amount actually was. Adam watched her as her bright blue eyes narrowed and she looked Jonathan up and down. It was obvious she was weighing up whether to tell him where to go, or indeed to go and get his cup of coffee himself. Instead she sighed loudly and turned to walk up the corridor.

'Every year they get worse,' declared Jonathan, with an exasperated throw of his right hand towards the door. 'This one's about as annoying as having spinach in the teeth, Adam. I would say as irritating as a three-flush floater, but you're probably not allowed to say that these days. So, spinach it is: no matter how hard you pick at it, it's still there. I honestly think you were perhaps the last half-decent pupil we had. Even then you weren't very good, but at least you were happy to get a cup of coffee. You hovered around in the shadows, waiting to be spoken to. This one starts conversations . . .' He gesticulated towards the open door again. He sighed. 'I seem to remember she had nice ankles. Do you remember the ankles, Adam?'

'I can't say I do,' replied Adam, a little disheartened that Jonathan only remembered his compliancy rather than his sharp legal mind.

Jonathan was being particularly testy this morning, which, as Adam remembered, was normally something to do with money.

'This has been a terrible morning: not only have they put VAT on Florence's school fees, they've increased the bastards – and the ex-wife wants a new car.' He looked at Adam. 'It makes you wish you could turn back the clock. Don't ever get married, Adam, and don't ever have children. They will bleed you dry and never say thank you. Is it too early for lunch? You know how much I like the fish-and-chip luncheon at Inner Temple.'

In fact, there was nothing that made Jonathan Taylor-Cameron happier than a Friday fish-and-chip lunch, a large glass of claret, accompanied by the familiar burling baritone of his fellow barristers.

'Unfortunately,' replied Adam, looking at his watch, 'it's Tuesday and only ten a.m.'

'Coffee?'

Stacey walked back into Jonathan's room, wearing a wide, fake service-industry smile, like an air hostess who'd just spat in your drink. Which she might well have done. For Jonathan's coffee was the colour of taupe and half of it had already sloshed over the side, filling up the saucer.

'Would you like a little biscuit?' she asked, holding up a small packet of custard creams.

Jonathan winced. He looked like he might actually throw up. He shook his head, and half closed his eyes, as if he were concentrating hard on nice things.

'So . . . what do you think of the Blue Face case?' asked Stacey.

Adam's heart sank. This was clearly going to be a marriage made in hell. He wondered whether he should take her aside right now and give her a few tips on how to deal with Jonathan, such as keeping out of his way, agreeing with him, and reminding him when he might have a meeting at the Garrick. But with her bright eyes and her quick manner, he suspected that she was one of those people who had to make their own mistakes.

'The what?' asked Jonathan, as he pushed his cup of coffee to one side and sat down at his desk. 'The blue what?' If he was hoping his imperious attitude might have caused her to take a step back (quake? quiver? or be quiet, at the very least), he was mistaken.

'The Blue Face case,' Stacey continued. 'The suspect is this girl called Lexi Williams who sprayed this artist in the face with a spray-can of paint laced with cyanide.'

Jonathan's heavy lids flickered as he listened to her voice with its Northern tones.

'It looks like it's an open-and-shut case to me,' Stacey said. 'She was caught red-handed, or blue-handed as it were – ha-ha-ha, that's a good joke . . . And then there are all these witnesses, plus the son's video. Loughton Bruce, the graffiti artist – d'you know him? I've seen his work. Anyway, that clearly puts her in the frame . . .'

'No case is open-and-shut, Stacey, unless it's a suitcase,' replied Jonathan. 'Now, if you please, I have something for you which is probably more your level: Bexley Mags.' He pushed a file towards her with his index finger as if it might be mildly contaminated. 'Shoplifting – smoked salmon from Marks and Spencer, Bluewater shopping centre.'

'And they're prosecuting?' she replied, with a laugh that made Jonathan wince again. 'Jeez, what with the cost-of-living crisis, shoplifting has gone through the roof. Why bother? No wonder the system is grinding to a halt and the prisons are full. Did you hear there are only something like seventy to ninety places left in the whole country? They're letting people out early. I saw it on TikTok last week. The prisoners were all celebrating, drinking champagne.'

'Yes, well,' Jonathan said, 'this was *seven* whole sides of smoked salmon, several packets of frozen prawn vol-au-vents, a bottle of Bollinger, and four boxes of their finest champagne truffles.'

'What was she doing? Throwing a party?'

'You could say that.'

'What are *you* doing going to Bexley, Jonathan?' asked Adam. Surely his mags days were over? Obviously Stacey would be doing all the work, would have to stand behind Jonathan in the magistrate's court: she had only just started her 'first six' (six months), and was therefore not qualified to do anything else; in her second six months she'd be on her feet doing her own cases, and Jonathan's work on top. But for now, she had to stand behind Jonathan.

'The accused's husband is a dear friend of mine,' he said to Adam. 'I'm helping him out. This is not the first time she's done this. She's a serial offender. She enjoys the thrill of stealing . . .'

'She's a klepto?' asked Stacey.

'A what?' Jonathan knew perfectly well what she'd said.

'A kleptomaniac?'

'Something like that.' He edged the file closer.

'I was hoping for a . . .'

'A bigger case?' Jonathan smiled and laughed a little and looked across at Adam. 'Don't they all! It's the old cab-rank system for you, Stacey, I'm afraid. You have to take what you're given, if you are free . . . and last time I looked, Stacey, you were most certainly free.'

'Of course, Jonathan. When is the case listed?'

'Tomorrow, I think?' He frowned 'Or quite possibly this afternoon. You'd better check. Oh, and while you do, could you possibly pop out and take in my dry cleaning?' He nodded towards an elegant suit jacket that was hanging off the back of his door.

'Your drying cleaning, Mr Taylor-Cameron?'

'Yes, Miss Jackson. My dry cleaning. It's important to look good in court.'

'We both know I can't do that. It's above my pay grade, Mr Taylor-Cameron. Well above my pay grade.' She smiled as she closed the door behind her.

Jonathan exhaled sharply at his desk. He'd normally slam his fist down on his leather-topped table in frustration, but Pippa had been making him use a mindfulness app to help with his anger management issues. It appeared to be working, thought Adam; a little, at least. But Stacey Jackson was definitely spinach in Jonathan Taylor-Cameron's teeth. As he left Jonathan to stew in his own furious juices, Adam checked his watch. Poor man. It was still another two hours till lunch.

Four

It didn't take long for the emails, memes, theories, suggestions, possible motives, gossip and the background around the Blue Face protest to start pinging around Stag Court, and indeed all the other Inns of Court in the capital. Over the next three days, it became the biggest story of the year, and barristers, much like journalists, began to talk and trade information back and forth. Adam knew it was no coincidence that the grubby hacks of Fleet Street had used to coalesce around Chancery Lane and the High Court: the two institutions were symbiotic. Each scratched the other's back and bought each other fine wines and tankards of ale in the half-timbered taverns of High Holborn.

'So?' asked Georgina, leaning over. 'What have *you* heard?'

She and Adam were standing next to each other by the new coffee machine that Tony had purchased for the main meeting room as part of a glamour drive, to impress the new high-end clients that he'd been cultivating as part of his plan to make Stag Court only 20 per cent legal aid. Someone had told him that a chic machine that could make proper lattes (other posh coffees were available) would help win more cases. But somehow he seemed to have inadvertently created a canteen in the main meeting room.

'That it's cyanide, for sure. A friend of mine at 15 Bedford Row has a friend who said that the police have tested the paint and it was definitely laced with cyanide,' replied Adam, pleased to be able to contribute for once. His phone had been buzzing with WhatsApps and Blue Face memes from friends and colleagues, each of them with a theory as to why a seemingly sweet middle-class girl from Gloucestershire would want to murder such a formidable talent, almost all of them different.

'Right, cyanide,' said Georgina, nodding, as she made herself a double espresso. 'I thought everyone knew that . . .'

'It's the internet that's done it,' came a voice that Adam recognised. 'She's been radicalised by social media and, according to Twitter, it's all to do with bad parenting and lockdown and being stuck in your bedroom in your own personal echo chamber. No one can believe it. Why would a nice girl kill Britain's greatest living artist?'

They both turned round to find Stacey standing in front of them, waving her mobile phone. Blonde curls, pretty smile, neat black skirt, white cotton shirt, files clutched to her chest with her spare hand. Adam smiled while Georgina looked her up and down, slowly.

'Stacey Jackson,' she said. 'I'm Jonathan's new pupil.'

'Are you indeed?' Georgina looked unimpressed.

'Yeah,' Stacey replied.

'This is Adam Green,' said Georgina. 'He was Jonathan's pupil a few years ago.'

'We've met.' She grinned at Adam. 'He's my mentor.'

'He is?'

Finally, something that Georgina didn't know.

'How are you getting on?' Adam asked.

'How did you survive?' Stacey said with a brief roll of her blue eyes. 'I mean, he's not all bad . . . obviously. But that room of his, it hasn't been cleared out since the last century. It's full of stuff – there's a dead dog that keeps staring at me. And it smells of aftershave in there. And you saw him try to make me take his dry cleaning! There are rules against that sort of stuff these days, I told him.' She laughed. 'Well, you know, I don't think he was pleased.'

'I used to take his dry cleaning for him,' admitted Adam.

'You did?' Stacey looked a little taken aback.

'And book his restaurants and send bouquets of flowers.' Adam's cheeks flushed with remembered embarrassment.

'Well, things were different back then,' Georgina chipped in. 'Also' – she smiled, very briefly – 'Jonathan may not be a judge, but he is a KC, and being a great barrister is not about having a First Class Honours degree from Oxford and a lofty Bachelor of Civil Law. It's about judgement, and he'll be judging your pupillage. You never know, he might end up in the High Court.'

'And there I was, thinking they were trying to make the judiciary less male, pale and stale,' replied Stacey, with a cock of her head.

Adams laughed a little. Georgina shot him a look.

'*My* gossip,' continued Georgina, ignoring Stacey and speaking directly to Adam, 'is that she didn't get bail. The family, Alexandra Williams's family, have turned down legal aid. Apparently they didn't like who they'd been given, and they have clubbed together, or are doing some GoFundMe thing, friends are chipping in for her defence, and they're doing the rounds, trying to find the best brief possible for her.'

She picked up her double espresso, smiled stiffly at Stacey and left the room.

'People will be starting a GoFundMe for you if you're not careful,' said Tony, looming in the doorway, his shaved scalp gleaming in the overhead light. 'We need a few more big cases from you, Mr Green. Some nice corporate stuff. Gross negligence. Like the other day, with Serpentine Water, after they dumped thousands of tonnes of raw sewage into the river – you did well, defending them.' He patted Adam on the back. 'Very well indeed. A nice little cheque. We need more of the same. I've got a few intros to come from some Harley Street practices, and possibly a big NHS hospital trust – they always need representation. I am thinking of organising a small networking event, building commercial relationships, which I would like you to come to. When I say "like" you to attend, I think you and I both know what I really mean.'

'Of course, Tony.' Adam nodded. 'I am happy to come to any networking events, building commercial relationships, that you organise.'

'Good lad.' Tony turned to Stacey. 'I'm not sure why *you're* standing around socialising, Miss Jackson. Those papers won't read themselves – and Mr Taylor-Cameron certainly won't. You don't want to let him down now, do you?' He pointed at his heavy gold wristwatch that he'd recently been presented with after twenty years of service at Stag Court. 'As my mother used to say, it's your own time you're wasting, and anyway, it looks like you've got quite a lot of work to do.' He glanced down at the files she was holding. 'Run along now. The pupils' room is at the end of the corridor.'

'The box room?' she demanded. 'With all the chairs?'

'Next to the cleaning cupboard. That's right. Plenty of space in there.' Tony folded his thick arms across his broad chest and waited for her to move.

'I was just going to . . .' She pointed towards the coffee machine. Tony didn't move. 'Um, see you later, Adam.' She walked quickly down the corridor, still clutching her files.

Adam felt his cheeks flush and looked down immediately at his shoes. Out of the corner of his eye he saw Tony's top lip twitch with irritation. Miss Jackson was a little too confident for Tony's liking. She'd better watch out, thought Adam. Tony's pet peeve was his perceived attitude of Gen Z: they didn't abide by the rules, apparently – or worse, they didn't appear even to know them, and some (which was possibly true of Miss Jackson) knew the rules and refused to abide by them. Either way, it was obvious that Tony would be coming down on Stacey like a tonne of heavy-duty case files, for there was nothing, *nothing* that Tony Jones disliked more than cockiness.

Adam slipped past Tony and into his room, closing the door. Unlike Jonathan's dusty, fusty mausoleum, or indeed the general chaos of plenty of the other barristers' rooms in Stag Court, most of which looked like they'd been recently raided by the Flying Squad, Adam's desk was neat, tidy, logical, uncluttered and devoid of personal mementos – save for the one wooden-framed photograph of him and both his parents, taken just a few weeks before his father had died. All three of them were gathered around a shiny red bicycle. It was Adam's tenth birthday. He was standing on a yellow, green and brown swirl-patterned carpet, gripping the handlebars, wrapping paper shredded around his feet, his chin in the air, grinning at the camera, through a massive mop of dark curls. He had no idea who'd taken the photograph. Perhaps his grandma had been there? Or a neighbour? But it was the last one of all three of them together. He stared at it often, not with sadness anymore. That tight, suffocating agony had dissipated over the years. In fact, the photograph made him smile. The demons were still there, the fight for justice was still what Adam thought about, the passion that coursed through his veins, but after a few years at Stag Court, he knew that in order to be able to fight the good fight, he might occasionally have to defend the likes of Serpentine Water.

Adam picked up a file and sighed with resignation. If Tony wanted him to defend botched Brazilian bum-lifts, he didn't have a huge say in the matter. He opened his laptop to go through his emails.

Suddenly his door burst open with an almighty swing, a clatter and a thwack as the door handle slammed into the wall.

'Adam Green?'

'Yes?'

Adam clung on to his own desk, his fingers turning white, as Morris Brown marched in and slapped down a file. The man was every bit as formidable as Georgina had described. His brown wispy hair was wild, thinning and sprouting in every direction, his eyes were wilder as they scanned the room, seemingly independently of each other. He was neither tall nor broad, more of a terrier than a barn door of a bloke. He was wearing a pinstriped suit that, even to Adam's untrained eye, looked immaculate, fine and clearly tailor-made. And he exuded an electric, kinetic energy, born from the sharpest and quickest of minds, which bored easily.

'So. What do you know about the anti-war spray-can protest?'

'Umm . . . Er . . .' Adam stammered.

'Come on . . .' Morris Brown clicked his fingers repeatedly.

'Only that the famous artist Max Bruce was murdered in front of his family, at the Royal Academy, and that the police have charged a young woman in connection with the murder . . . Oh, and it's cyanide poisoning,' Adam added, just to show that he was up to speed with the news and the gossip.

'Is it though? Cyanide?' Morris's right eye looked at him while the left appeared to drill a hole through his temple and into his soul.

'That's what they are saying.'

'Who are "they"? And what exactly are they saying?'

'The media . . .'

'Ah! The media!'

Adam's palms began to sweat. No wonder Morris had a reputation for winning nearly every case he'd ever taken on. You could barely form a thought without him making you doubt everything and anything you were about to say. 'According to the media, a girl who is involved with the anti-war protest laced a can of spray-paint with poison and murdered Max Bruce . . .'

'But is she responsible? The only thing we know for sure is that Max Bruce CBE, Britain's greatest artist, is no longer living. And . . .' He picked up the file from the desk and checked the name. 'Alexandra Williams . . . is the defendant. And, as of now, Adam, *we* have been asked to defend her.'

'The Blue Face case?' Adam was stunned. This was the biggest case of the year. With Morris. He felt a sudden surge of adrenalin. If there was such a thing as a legal hot ticket, this was it.

'I think we should try and avoid saying that,' said Morris. 'It's too much of a visual. I think we should tone it back and down – but yes. Alexandra's parents have been in touch. Apparently they googled me, and they found me via Nisha, who asked for you . . . personally. No idea why anyone would ask for you, personally. And frankly, you would not have been my first choice. I need someone dynamic and thorough and smart. More like Miss Devereaux, if I'd had a choice, but I don't . . . so I have you.'

He paused and looked round Adam's room.

'You haven't done much with the place, have you? Bit bare? Boring. Get yourself a pot plant or something. Something to look after. It's good for the soul, something else to think about other than yourself.' He tapped his temple with his index finger. 'I need you at the top of your game, Adam. This is a big case. Possibly the biggest of the year. Certainly one of the most high-profile. There will be a lot of press and a lot of media attention. Sir Max was a very popular figure. He's very well known, a household name, which is rare for an artist. And they will be throwing a lot of accusations around. Lots of theories. Lots of stories. Untruths. And we need to be ready. It won't be as lucrative as your Serpentine Water gravy train.' He smiled. 'But you know the ordinary citizen deserves justice, just as much as the big conglomerates. We're here to fight for the underdogs as well.' He tapped the top of the file. 'See you tomorrow, Adam. And oh . . .' He paused.

'None of your Poirot business.' Adam opened his mouth to speak. 'Your reputation precedes you, I'm afraid. We don't need any of that amateur sleuthing. Leave that to the police. OK? And Adam?'

'Yes?'

'You can sit down now.'

Five

Phone call

'Mum! Hi. Are you OK? It's the middle of the afternoon – you never call in the middle of the afternoon. You're normally playing cards with Anna Goldberg. Have you had a fall? Are you ill?'

'Oh no, dear! I'm fine. Fit as a fiddle – a well-worn fiddle, mind. Or, as my old mother would say: "I'm as well as can be expected." I'm looking forward to this evening. There's a speaker coming to the synagogue. They're coming to talk to us about putting on a play. I'm thinking of auditioning.'

'You are?'

'Only for a Jewish husband role.'

'What's that?'

'A non-speaking part!'

'That is the oldest joke in the book, Mum, it really is.'

'I know, but I love it. It still makes me laugh. Anyway, I'm not calling about that. How are you? How's that cough? Better? You need to look after that cough.'

'The cough's gone.'

'Gone? Are you sure? It's not totally gone, Adam. I can still definitely hear a bit of it in your voice. Gravelly. Scratchy. Did you use the Beechams I sent? I was a bit worried that they'd sit in that post-box thing of yours in your flat, you know – the cubbyholes – because I know you never check the post. Young people don't check the post. No one sends letters anymore now, do they? That's the problem. Just bills and catalogues. So did you get the Beechams?'

'I did.'

'And you used them, Ads? Did you? There's no point in sending stuff and you not using it.'

'I did.'

'That's good, that's very good. Debbie's son didn't look after his cough, and he ended up with bronchitis. All over his chest. He nearly went to hospital. Hospital, Adam! No one wants that.'

'I am sure they don't.'

'Anyway, Anna's visiting her brother near Swansea, so I was talking to Debbie, and we were discussing this murder, you know the one that's been all over the TV? It's been on *Lorraine*, *Good Morning Britain*, with that nice Jewish boy – what's his name? All over the media, and I said to Debbie I'd give you a call – seeing as you work with these people, you'd know whether that girl was guilty or not. Because from where I'm sitting, it looks like she deserves everything she gets. Have you seen it? Spraying that man in the face like that? The artist. Murdering him. In front of his family. His wife. Wives. He's got two of them, Adam. Imagine that? That must be tiring: most men can't cope with one wife. Those poor children. Nothing worse. Terrible.'

'I know.'

'Debbie says they should lock her up and throw away the key – that's what they're saying. That female columnist I like, the one who always makes a lot of sense in the *Daily Mail*, she agrees. I read it this morning. Especially as she tried to kill the Home Secretary – what's his name? That woman's a terrorist. And there'll be a recall on those spray-cans at B&Q, let me tell you. I mean, if you can put cyanide in them, what else can you put in them? They'll all have to come back. Who uses those paints anyway, apart from graffiti artists? In my day they weren't called artists, they were called vandals.'

'I've just been asked to represent her.'

'Who? The terrorist? You have? That's incredible. That's something to tell Debbie and Anna Goldberg when she gets back from Swansea. I couldn't be more proud, Adam. What a case! Everyone knows about it. Everyone's seen it on the TV. You'll be on TV! And you're going to make sure she's brought to justice.'

'I'm defending her.'

'Defending?'

Silence. Mum coughed. Cleared her throat. There was a rustle of a handkerchief. She blew her nose.

'Well, dear . . . everyone needs some sort of defence, don't they? Isn't that what you always say? Someone on their side no matter what? Good for you . . . for helping. Good for you. Is that Jonathan with the smooth voice your boss again on this one?'

'No, he's not my boss.'

'You've got a different boss? Is he nice? I hope he is.'

'I don't have a boss.'

'You're doing it on your own!'

'No, I have a lead on the case. I'm self-employed, Mum, I don't have any bosses.'

'Tell that to that Tony fellow I met with you – he sounds like a boss, and he certainly thinks he's your boss! So who's your boss on this one? Sorry, lead. Who's your lead?'

'My lead is called Morris Brown.'

'Is he good?'

'He's very good.'

'Is he nice?'

'He's a well-known advocate for protestors, especially environmental protestors.'

'Tree huggers? Oh, Adam . . . I do hope you know what you're doing.'

Six

It was an unseasonally chilly morning for July, just past 9 a.m., and Adam felt himself slowly sinking into the doughy back seat of the elderly Uber, his knees rising towards his ears. So many passengers, so many drunken backsides, the springs in the seat behind the driver had given up all hope. The Little Tree that swung from the rearview mirror also needed changing. The acrid smell of chemical peach was on the wane, barely combatting the heady high note of last night's chips.

Next to Adam, and looking significantly more perpendicular, was Morris Brown, knees straight ahead, files on his lap, dressed in another smart pinstriped suit, a white shirt and a navy blue tie. He was staring out the window through the snaking raindrops at the passing suburban streets, at the lengthy queues for the bus, at the few tardy children running towards the school gates, and at the drifting orange Sainsbury's bag billowing in the sharp breeze.

Morris knew this route well. 'Go left at the corner shop. Straight over at the roundabout,' he told the Uber driver. But Adam had never been to HMP Bronzefield in Ashford, Kent. It was a Category A top-security prison which housed both adult and young offenders and was the largest female prison in Europe. Adam was more used to the big Victorian red-brick buildings, like Wormwood Scrubs and Wandsworth, with their towers, thick walls and rolls of barbed wire. But the entrance to HMP Bronzefield looked more like a suburban motel, a Travelodge, with its low-rise modern glass-and-aluminium windows. A Union Jack flag flapped merrily outside.

Except there was nothing merry about Bronzefield, which kept some of the most dangerous female prisoners in the country, some infamous, some best forgotten – from Britain's youngest-ever female murderer at the age of twelve years old to the likes of Rosemary West. It was not the sort of place you got sent to on remand unless the Crown had charged you with terrorism or murder.

Adam shivered a little as he got out of the car. He would have thought he'd be used to entering these sorts of places by now, but somehow there was an aura of profound sadness and misery that emanated even beyond the gates. How on earth had Alexandra Williams ended up here?

'Adam, hi!' said Nisha Desai, with a warm smile. 'So nice to see you.'

Standing by the entrance to the prison, her dark hair frizzing in the drizzle, Nisha was dressed in a tightly belted Mackintosh, with a capacious bag slung over her shoulder, full of heavy files. She was clutching her mobile phone in one hand and an unused umbrella in the other.

Adam had grown extremely fond of Nisha over the years. She had instructed him on every high-profile case that he had ever been on, and he would go to the ends of the earth for her. They were good friends, and over the years they had not only developed a strong relationship but also a deep trust, mainly borne from the hours they'd spent sitting outside cells waiting to be let in to talk to their clients, or squashed beside each other on public transport, their elbows clamped together in the crush, attempting to read notes and briefs. He knew all about her solicitor husband, her two small children, and her house in High Barnet. He knew she liked to play Candy Crush on her phone, whenever it stopped ringing with new clients and new cases, most of whom were on legal aid. He had never met anyone who worked harder than Nisha and who also appeared still to care. Tony had been trying to get Adam to move on from Nisha, 'the patron saint of lost causes and public money', as he always called her, but she believed in Adam and often she really did come up with something extraordinary.

'How was your journey?' she asked. 'Did you go to Staines railway station like I told you to? Morris,' she nodded towards him. 'We have never met but I am a great admirer of your work. And I am reading your book! Or at least, I am trying to, but I am always so tired when I get into bed, I keep falling asleep.'

' "More soporific than Nytol." Ms Desai, I'd honestly hoped for a better review,' replied Morris, taking in the strikingly diminutive size of the solicitor, who was five foot at a push. The sensible kitten heel made little difference.

'Call me Nisha,' she replied. 'And that's not what I meant. It's work, children, having it all.' She laughed. 'It's exhausting.'

'I hear you've been made a partner in your firm. Congratulations.'

'I have. Thank you, Morris.' She looked across at Adam and raised her eyebrows. How did he know?

'And you've worked with Adam before?'

'Adam and I know each other well,' she confirmed. 'He's very thorough; he's very good. He's my superstar, in fact.'

'Let's hope your confidence in him is not misplaced,' replied Morris. 'Shall we?'

Slamming the doors of the Uber behind them, the three of them made their way towards the main entrance of the prison where there was quite a crowd of press and protestors. Adam was a little surprised. He had been expecting a few journalists maybe, a film crew perhaps, a couple of cameras using the prison as a backdrop for an update on the case. But protestors? There were about a hundred of them, some with handmade placards, one beating a drum, all raising their fists and screaming.

'Free Lexi! Free Lexi!' they were chanting over and over, in time to the beat.

Standing a few feet away was another group yelling, also at the top of their voices, 'Lock her up! Lock her up!'

The ones wanting to 'Free Lexi' were perhaps a little younger and a bit more likely to glue themselves to a road, or some railings outside a bank. But otherwise, there was little difference between the groups, expect for the slogans.

'Polarised Britain,' declared Morris to both Nisha and Adam, as he walked towards the crowd, pointing from one group to the other. 'That didn't take long.'

'Since she's been charged, #FreeLexi has been trending on social media, as has #LockHerUp,' said Nisha, trotting alongside Morris, trying to keep up.

'Excuse me – Morris Brown! Would you call your client a terrorist?' shouted a lone reporter, pointing a Handycam straight at the three of them as they tried to negotiate their way swiftly through the crowd.

'Mr Brown!' began the rest of the hack pack, latching on to his name.

'Mr Brown, did your client murder Max Bruce in cold blood?'

'Mr Brown, are Stop the War a terrorist group?'

'Why is your client in a maximum-security prison? Is she a danger to the public, Mr Brown? Is she a terrorist? Or is she just a murderer?'

The hail of questions came thick and fast as the three of them made their way through the crowd, blinded by flash-bulbs and the glaring light of the television cameras. Any notion that they might have slipped into HMP Bronzefield unnoticed was clearly foolish. It was almost a relief for them all to get inside.

As the main entrance door shut, the first thing that struck Adam was how modern the prison felt – strip lighting, a royal-blue fitted carpet, with matching blue chairs that were not nailed to the floor. It seemed to him more like an office block than a prison. As they passed through security, handing over their bags and files to be scanned, Adam was hit by the ubiqui-tous smell of disinfectant, cabbage and incarceration, as well as the usual background noise of shouting, screaming, arguing and door-slamming. Some things never changed.

'So, apparently it was your record of defending protestors that made Alexandra's parents so keen to have you on board,' explained Nisha to Morris, as they walked along the carpeted corridor towards the cell where Alexandra Williams was being kept in solitary confinement. 'I think it was your defence of the Newbury bypass protestors that made them really want to have you. That and all those pieces you've written in the *Guard-ian*, and some in *The Times*. Also, your recent appearance on

Question Time when you had that lengthy argument with Nigel Farage about the state of Britain. They mentioned that too.'

'Let's hope that my best days are not behind me,' joked Morris.

'I think it's the murder charge and the possible terrorism charge that has completely floored them,' added Nisha.

'I am sure,' agreed Morris. 'I think we are here?'

He turned towards the warden who had been walking alongside them, a large collection of keys rattling on his belt.

'Alexandra Williams?' Morris asked.

'Correct.' The warden nodded, selecting a large key. 'Any problems, we have a guard inside the cell and two outside. There's a panic alarm on the wall to the left of the door. We'll be straight in. All sharp objects have been removed from the prisoner. And I would also like to remind you not to leave anything behind – paperclips, pens, that sort of thing. Anything the prisoner might find useful. This is a category A top-security prison – all our inmates are presumed dangerous.'

He turned the key and pulled open the heavy door to reveal Lexi Williams sitting, slumped, her forehead on the table in front of her. She looked up as soon as they walked in and Adam was immediately struck by how young she was. Dressed in her regulation grey tracksuit provided by HMP Bronzefield, her thin mousy hair was scraped back off her face, tied up in a high ponytail. She was devoid of makeup and in the glare of the bright strip-light could easily have passed for about fifteen years old. There was a flicker of a smile as she appeared to recognise Morris Brown. But it was fleeting and her face rapidly returned to its set expression, that of clenched-jaw determination with a veneer of defiance, which was offset by her constant fiddling and chipping off what remained of her bright orange nail varnish from her short, bitten nails.

Adam stared at her hands. What sort of murderer had a manicure before setting out to kill someone?

'Alexandra,' began Nisha, settling down at one corner of the table, and taking out her files from her capacious bag. She pulled out her heavily chewed biro and placed it on top of the files.

'Lexi,' Lexi corrected immediately, as she battled to contain her emotions. 'My name is Lexi.'

'Of course.' Nisha smiled. 'May I introduce Mr Morris Brown and Mr Adam Green? They will be representing you.'

'Yeah, well, basically, we all know, like, what's going to happen.' Lexi sniffed and slid a little lower into her seat, her legs apart, her spine curved, her elbows on the table like a truculent teenager. 'I mean, it's not exactly Cluedo, is it? But it may as well be. Like, you've got me, in the art gallery, with the spray-can, and Max Bruce dead on the floor. Boom! Guilty as charged. I've seen *Law & Order*.'

'Now, Lexi, if I may,' said Morris, raising his hands. She sat up a little. Morris was the sort of man to whom everyone paid attention. 'Normally we would not meet until later, but we thought that since you were refused bail, and put in solitary confinement due to the potential terrorism charge, we should come and check up on you.'

'I consider myself checked!' She laughed.

'Anything you say in this room is privileged, which is a lawyer's way of saying "a secret",' Morris continued, unfazed. 'But between you, us and the good Lord, should you believe in Him – if you say you're guilty of the crime, then we cannot represent you anymore. I am sure you have seen many television dramas in which lawyers work hard to get a guilty person off the hook, but in reality it doesn't work like that in this country. So, if you have done it and you have killed Sir Max, then now is the time to tell us.'

'No comment,' Lexi said.

'OK, so why don't we start at the beginning?' suggested Morris with a click of his pen as he stared at her over the top of his half-moon specs.

'Are you talking to me?' Lexi asked, as she pretended to follow Morris's divergent gaze.

'Miss Williams.'

'Lexi.'

'Lexi,' repeated Morris, his hands steepling in front of his face. 'I know you think this might possibly be extremely amusing as you listen to your supporters outside, banging their drum, shouting to free you. And undoubtedly someone has told you that your Instagram page has gone through the roof, and you're very well liked on Twitter or X, and your TikTok is massive, or "viral", which I believe is the term, and you're practically famous, and it won't be long before you're asked to make cakes on the *Great British Bake Off*. But the thing is, a man is dead, and you have been charged with killing him . . . murdering him. There are also terrorist charges pending. This is a reality. IRL. Just so you know. This is not a drill, this is not happening online, this is not a game. This is happening to you . . . right now. You are being tried for murder and the National Crime Agency are investigating whether you are also part of a conspiracy to murder the Home Secretary as part of a terrorist organisation. That investigation is ongoing, and they would normally have concluded that before they charged you with murder – it's most irregular. But they seem determined to go ahead. I have never known them to do that before. So—'

'Yeah, well, I don't care.' Lexi yawned theatrically, her arms stretched above her head. 'I could murder a coffee.' She giggled. 'I don't mean literally, obviously. Murder!'

'No hot drinks, I'm afraid,' said Nisha, opening up her file.

Adam looked across at Nisha. For a young woman accused of murder and possible terrorism charges, Lexi was behaving very strangely indeed. Perhaps it was shock? This place was certainly out of everyone's comfort zone.

'Shall we try again?' Morris rested his chin on the tops of his fingers. 'You're from Stroud, Gloucestershire . . . That's a lovely part of the world.'

'Stroud! Lovely!' Lexi laughed again. 'It's the heroin capital of the UK!'

'Actually, the city with the worst drug problem in the UK is Birmingham, followed by Leeds and then London. And anyway,' said Morris with a quick glance down at his notes, 'your father, Andrew, is a company director and you were at a grammar school, so I can't imagine that culture bothered you very much. And you went on to Southampton University, where you studied politics and philosophy.'

'Except I never went, did I?' said Lexi, as one of her legs started to bounce up and down under the table.

'Lockdown?' asked Adam. She swung her head round; it was as if she'd just noticed him.

'What would you know about that?' she said, looking Adam up and down in his dark suit, blue shirt and dark tie. 'With your swish job and your nice house. I bet you spent most of your lockdown doing online quizzes with your chums and making sourdough with your wife!'

'Don't make assumptions about Adam,' interjected Morris. 'And I'm sure he's a terrible baker . . . What was your lockdown like?'

'Honestly,' Lexi said, 'quite lonely. Just me and my computer, in my bedroom. No lessons, no Freshers' Week. Why did I work so hard to get my A-levels when they didn't even let me sit the exams? What was that about?' She sighed loudly. 'I did two years of university, and I never met a soul. Well, we could go in for a term or something, I can't remember now, but by then it was so much easier to do lectures in your pyjamas, eating crisps in bed, so what was the point? All the lectures were recorded anyway. All you had to do was, like, watch them, and you could do it at three a.m., which I did, like watching the most boring TV show in the world. Do you know, I have a friend who was studying pathology, and, basically, she graduated having never been near a body. Not once. She can't get a job now as she's got no hands-on experience!' Lexi waved her hands in front of Morris's face, as if she were dancing jazz. 'Hands-on!'

Adam attempted to steer the conversation back to firmer ground. 'So, you must have missed hanging out with your friends?'

'Not really,' Lexi replied with a shrug. 'I was much more interested in how we were all being manipulated by the government to stay in and stay safe, or whatever they told us – to wash our hands, sing bloody "Happy Birthday", jab ourselves, take it for the team. "You young people, stop your lives so Gran can live a little longer, or for the NHS, and don't forget to bang on a pan while you're doing it." Do you know how many young men have died from the vaccine? Of heart attacks?' She paused, looking from Nisha to Morris to Adam. 'Let me tell you . . . hundreds. Hundreds and hundreds of them.'

'So, you spent a lot of time on the internet,' said Morris, scribbling away. 'What else did you learn?'

'Well . . .' Lexi leaned back again and sank even lower in her seat. 'The system is broken.'

'There are plenty who'd agree with that.' Morris nodded, pushing his specs back up his short nose.

'War is wrong and especially the war in Khandistan.'

'Did you join the Stop the War group during lockdown?' asked Adam.

'No.' She looked at him as if he were an idiot. 'That happened after, in my last year at Southampton. I had a friend who was involved, and he introduced me to them. So basically, I joined and I'm, like, glad that man's dead, and I totally meant to cover his face in blue paint, and I'd do it again in a heartbeat if it means there's one less capitalist bastard left in this world. Basically, he shouldn't have sold his painting to that wanker of a Russian oligarch. He's got blood on his hands; his palms are, like, dripping with the stuff.' She pushed her palms towards Morris's face by way of demonstration. 'He's worked with Putin, and we all know what that means. Dirty, filthy cash, and corruption is everywhere. Max Bruce was just as bad. They're all as bad as each other. They need to stop the war. Children are dying all the time, and for what? Dirty, filthy oil that's killing the planet anyway. Money corrupts the soul. It corrupts everything.'

'I couldn't agree more,' said Morris. 'That's a great speech, and I fully endorse your sentiments, but the only thing is, is it all worth your whole life?'

'My whole life?' she asked.

'Thereabouts,' confirmed Nisha, taking her pen out of her mouth. 'Twenty years, give or take. And that's without the potential terrorism charge.'

'Oh, well, who cares about any of that!' Lexi declared, lurching back in her chair, throwing her right arm in the air. 'The system wins again, and I'll be a martyr. A martyr to Stop the War! Someone's got to do it, and it may as well be me. Greta Thunberg started on her own and as she said: *No One Is Too Small to Make a Difference*. Now look at her.'

'Look at her indeed,' replied Morris, taking off his half-moon spectacles, with what Adam suspected was exasperation. 'Normally, Lexi, if you were a legal-aid case, your team – us, in other words – we would not be here. We'd meet at the plea and trial preparation hearing – the PTPH. But seeing as your parents have decided to pay for your defence, we are here, as a courtesy, really, I suppose, to them, as they are extremely worried about you, being in solitary. It's difficult, I know.'

'Have you done it?' Lexi looked at him.

'No, but I have represented many who have, and it takes its toll. So, I just want to leave you with the facts of your case at the moment. You sprayed the can, the can contained cyanide. Forensics have confirmed it is cyanide. They have swabbed your desk at the gallery, which was covered in cyanide, and your office drawer was covered in the poison, and they have found traces of cyanide in a vape refill that was also in your desk. Sir Max Bruce is confirmed to have died from cyanide poisoning. It is not looking good for you. So just to be clear once more: if you have anything you'd like to say, be it a declaration of guilt, or not, now would be a good time.'

They sat in silence for a second, staring at Lexi, who didn't move. There was a faint sound of chanting and the beating of a drum just audible through the sealed doubled-glazed prison window.

'Free Lexi! Free Lexi! Free Lexi Williams!'

She smiled at Morris, Nisha and then at Adam. 'See? It's already started . . .'

'What has?' asked Morris.

'The revolution,' she replied.

Seven

Back in Stag Court, Adam bumped into Tony Jones in the post room. He was scratching his shiny scalp in disbelief. He flapped out the piece of paper in front of him and squinted at it, as though he hoped the words on the page would change, disappear, or rearrange themselves in a different order.

'Unbelievable,' he said. He shook his head. 'Bertie Howard has recommended that Jonathan Taylor-Cameron prosecute the Blue Face case.'

Adam and Tony looked at each other. No one recommended Jonathan. Ever. For anything. You might just about recommend him to choose a bottle of wine at dinner: he was good with a wine list, and he was good with wine (he'd drunk enough of it). You might listen to his recommendation if you wanted to bet on a horse: he was a member of the Turf Club, and he was good with horses. But to suggest him to prosecute the most high-profile case of the year so far was baffling. Why? Why? Why?

'Bertie Howard is the last old member in the establishment.' Tony nodded, mainly talking to himself. 'I think I might cry, Adam!' he declared, somewhat theatrically. 'The defence and the prosecution of the highest-profile case this year, both in Stag Court!' He smiled. 'I am not sure what I did in a past life to deserve this, but I am pretty sure it was saving little orphans from terrible peril. Last time I was this emotional, Adam, was in 1990 when Mrs Thatcher was ousted, after she'd declared she was going to "fight on and fight to win". But those were tears of misery. Not joy. This is joy, Adam, pure joy . . . Oh,' he said, turning round. 'Talk of the devil.'

Jonathan breezed into the post room in a cloud of aftershave with a back note of Polo mint that he was clearly hoping would disguise the cheeky Marlboro he'd just chucked down a drain on Fleet Street. Adam noticed he was wearing one of his more expensive navy suits, which indicated he would be in court later that day.

'Who's the devil?' he asked, pulling his wad of post from his pigeonhole. Judging by the volume, it had been there for a few days. Pretending to look through his post, Adam listened as Tony launched into a schpiel that ended with him telling Jonathan that he'd been asked to prosecute the Blue Face case.

'What?' Jonathan's eyebrows flew up in the air. 'Are you sure?' He stared at Tony who was standing in the doorway. 'Bertie Howard said that? I know we're great chums at the Garrick, but I really wasn't expecting this. Did he say anything else?'

'Only that you know the art world well.' Tony's delivery was staccato, as he attempted to talk through his clenched teeth. Positivity was not something that came naturally to him.

'Did he say that? Good old Bertie! I suppose I *do* know the art world well. What with Pippa working in Bond Steet and all her lovely friends and all those exhibitions we've been to, gallery openings, pre-sales drinks at Sotheby's, Christie's. Yes . . .' He nodded along to himself. 'I agree with Bertie: it is my world. He's right. I'm perfect . . . I'm absolutely perfect.' Tony inhaled to say something, but Jonathan was so bathed in his own perfection he didn't notice. 'And don't forget "the Battle of the Bed", Tony – don't forget that. That was me. In my prime. A young whippersnapper' – he laughed at his remembered brilliance – 'helping out the artists.'

Jonathan put down his post and began pacing around the room, walking down Memory Lane.

'I'm afraid I am not familiar with "the Battle of the Bed", sir,' said Tony, with a slow, incredulous shake of his head. 'Are you, Mr Green?'

'No, I am not,' said Adam, trying hard to stifle his amusement. The vanity of Jonathan Taylor-Cameron was sometimes sublime.

'Really?' Jonathan put his hands on his hips in surprise and looked at them both. 'It was all over the media. These Chinese activists went to a gallery, the Tate , if my memory serves, and they bounced up and down on Tracey Emin's famous artwork. It was truly appalling behaviour. *My Bed* had just been nominated for the Turner Prize, and they bounced up and down on it like children, and they tried to drain the bottles of vodka. But the bottles were already empty. Terrible.' He shook his head. 'Anyway, so I helped dear Tracey and her gang with all their legal stuff. I had a girlfriend who knew them and who lived in a squat nearby – very bohemian, very pretty girl. She lives in Somerset now, four children. But I helped out all those artists back then. Pro bono, of course.' He laughed. 'Those were the days . . .'

'Well, it is thankfully not pro bono this time.' Tony put his arm around Jonathan's shoulders and gave his upper arm a strong, hard squeeze. 'It's CPS rates.'

'Jesus, Tony! CPS rates! I can't afford those. Have you seen the amount of bills I have to pay! I know, too many ex-wives, too many children – there's no need to point out the obvious.'

'But think of the profile. Think of the publicity.'

'Publicity?'

'I should think so. Max Bruce was Britain's greatest living artist. Even I've heard of him. And you, you lucky bugger, you've also got Georgina Devereaux.'

'Georgina?'

'Miss Devereaux. The best. I'm just off to tell her now. She'll be over the moon to be working with you. I know she will,' Tony said.

'Well, in that case . . . how can I refuse!' Jonathan chuckled to himself and ran a fingertip over one of his bushy eyebrows. 'Wait till Pippa hears about this. She's going to be all over me, the minx. I tell you something, Adam, my weekend away in the Cotswolds just got a whole lot filthier.'

He broke into a whistle as he walked back to his room, which was fortunate, as he didn't hear the shouting coming from Georgina Deveraux's room down the corridor after Tony delivered his news.

'It's like being led by a donkey!' Georgina declared a few minutes later as she walked into Adam's room and sat down, her head falling into her hands.

'I'm going to pretend I didn't hear you say that about our highly respected, esteemed colleague,' replied Adam

'I begged him, honestly, I did. "Isn't there anyone else,

Tony?"' she recounted. ' "Please . . .? Anyone but me. Anyone but Jonathan . . ." The man can't even speak – he's no Edward Marshall Hall or Jonathan Laidlaw – both of whom could turn a shopping list into the finest of arguments. Why didn't I say no to Tony while I still could?' She looked at her watch. 'Is it too early for a glass of tepid prosecco in a dishwasher-warm glass at the Wig and Pen?'

It was nearly 6 p.m.

'Half an hour?' Adam replied, looking at the accruing mountain of case notes on his desk.

'Sure,' she replied. 'That'll be just enough time for you to share the good news with Morris Brown that you are going to be handed the Blue Face case on a silver platter due to the risible opposition in the form of Jonathan Taylor-Cameron and his sidekick!'

Georgina picked up her laptop and her soft Smythson briefcase and three pink-ribboned files on some antisocial rent and eviction cases that she'd been asked to look into for Blyth Council. She'd told Adam about it before. It was quite a big case that she and Prudence had been working on together for a while. The council hadn't behaved well, but neither, indeed, had the tenants. However, now she had Blue Face to think about. Still, if anyone could handle all that pressure, thought Adam, it was Georgina. She really was impressive. No wonder she was the youngest ever member of chambers to become Junior Treasury Counsel.

Eight

It was Friday and Adam had been awake half the night, lying in bed listening to the drunks fighting just off Liverpool Road, his brain churning as he replayed the conference with Lexi at HMP Bronzefield in his head. There was something about the whole experience that made him feel uncomfortable. Lexi had looked so young and vulnerable in her prison tracksuit with her chipped nail varnish. And she had been so defiant, with all her arguments ready and waiting. Except none of them made sense. Why would a student from what was essentially a pacifist organisation murder someone? Yet the evidence against her was overwhelming. Even so, this case didn't smell kosher. Normally things would have progressed more slowly, but due to public pressure and the possible terrorism charges, everything had been expedited to the Nth degree. Things were moving very fast. And Adam never liked it very much when things were sped up too quickly. Detail often got overlooked, and to him detail was everything. The small things always counted.

He had wanted to discuss it with Nisha as they left the prison. She was always a good sounding-board, not least because she

63

was one of those people who really listened in interviews. A lot of people asked questions and didn't listen to the replies because they were too busy thinking of their next clever question.

But Nisha had had to run off straight after Lexi's interview. She'd jogged off up the road in her kitten heels (if it was possible to jog in a kitten heel) to Ashford station, saying it was quicker than getting a taxi. Despite the rain. Her phone had already been ringing repeatedly, and she'd had other clients to see – so many other clients. She'd had back-to-back meetings all day. Maybe he could call her later? He'd tried. She hadn't picked up.

So he'd come in early to Stag Court to read what few notes there were and watch Loughton's video again, and again. Frame by frame, in case he'd missed anything. And frankly – so far – Lexi was front and centre of the whole thing. There were some wide shots of the party, some zooms in and out of the *Primal Scream* painting, there were some close-ups of glasses of champagne. Loughton had filmed the condensation on a cold glass. It was very artistic. He'd clearly been planning to edit the footage into some sort of montage for his social media. There was Natasha Fitzjohn's speech and a sweeping shot of the moment when everyone searched for the oligarch who had loaned the painting. Valutov.

Adam smiled as he wrote down the name. He'd always thought that Bernie Madoff was a perfect name for a financial criminal who'd stolen other people's money. And this one was not so bad either. *Valuta* was Russian for 'currency' or 'money'. So, Mr Money-ov had loaned the painting but hadn't come to the party? Or maybe he had been there, watching it all unfold? Keeping an eye on his work of art. But no one knew what he looked like. Adam put the name Sergei Valutov through Google Images and came up with nothing.

He returned to Loughton's footage. Lexi was dressed up for the occasion, as any intern would be, with her orange nails, wearing a black dress with tiny blue flowers all over it. She was in the background, standing behind Natasha Fitzjohn for most of the event, right up until the moment she'd started to shout, 'Stop the war!' And then she'd surged forward, holding the can of paint in both hands, like an offensive weapon. Loughton had even managed to get a close-up of her face as she'd sprayed the paint. Adam froze the frame. Lexi's eyes were tightly closed, her brow was furrowed, and her wide mouth was grimacing, all her teeth on show. There was no getting away from the fact that she'd sprayed Max Bruce full in the face with blue paint. There was the shock on everyone's faces, and then the rugby tackle by the security guard. More shouting. And then Max Bruce's Picasso joke, and then his final collapse in front of his family and friends. The last few minutes were a gruesome watch.

Adam sat back in his chair. This was not going to play well with the jury, no matter what case he and Morris made on her behalf. But even so, there was still something that felt off-kilter for Adam. There was malice in Lexi's face but no intention. She didn't look murderous; in fact, she looked a little terrified of the spray-can itself.

He looked at his watch. It was gone 9 a.m. Perhaps Morris was in?

Morris's room was on the floor above. If the clerks were historically 'downstairs' and the barristers were 'upstairs', then Morris was lording it over them all, so much so that Adam had never had any need to go up there while Morris had been away, and now, as he approached the smartly painted shiny black door, it felt a little like hallowed ground.

He knocked.

'Enter,' came a deep voice.

Morris Brown's room appeared to be about twice, if not three times, the size of Adam's. It had dove-grey walls, a clotted-cream-coloured carpet, a large desk with a green-and-gold lamp, and three button-back leather armchairs in a neat row in front of the desk, behind which was a substantial bookshelf groaning with leather-bound tomes that, at a glance, appeared mostly legal; although on closer inspection there was a shelf of what were clearly expensive literary first editions. It had four sash windows with swag curtains and glorious views over the Temple Church with its Purbeck marble columns and Knights' Templar tombs. Consecrated in 1185, it was always full of shouting tourists, since it had featured heavily in Dan Brown's *The Da Vinci Code*.

'Beautiful view, don't you think?' said Morris, nodding towards the windows. 'On a summer's evening, if I have the windows open, I can hear the choir practising for matins. They create quite a magnificent sound for twenty-eight choristers, all dressed in their scarlet cassocks. Sometimes when I listen and close my eyes, I think I might have died and reached the Pearly Gates already.' He laughed. 'They'll have to carry me out of here in a box in the end anyway.'

'I am sure that won't be for a long while yet.' Adam laughed back, gauchely, moving from one foot to the other.

'You can never tell when your time's up, Adam. I'm sure Max Bruce thought he had a few more journeys around the sun left in him. But anyway . . . I've just got off the phone with Nisha. Lexi is still in solitary confinement pending the outcome of the terrorism investigation and whether the Crown decide to charge her. They are still looking at her computer and her phone under the terrorism act. It's a draconian act, that one. You're guilty until proven innocent. They're really going for it: throwing away the key – the lot. We need to try and find out where she bought the cyanide and prove that she's not part of a larger conspiracy.'

'Right.' Adam felt his heart sink.

'We've got our work cut out then.' Morris indicated towards the leather chairs.

'I can't help thinking that she's not our man,' said Adam, as he perched on one of them.

'I've been warned about you and your penchant for lost causes,' replied Morris, moving his tobacco-coloured wig off a pile of papers to the left of his desk. (Not that Morris was a smoker – although he might have been, the thirty or so years ago when he'd first been called to the Bar. It was just that barristers only ever really bought one wig, and that wig – all £500 of it, if you were buying one today – lasted for a lifetime, and it never got cleaned, no matter how hot and sweaty the trial, or how oily or greasy the barrister's hair was, or how many old pub bars it had been placed on. You could usually tell how long someone had been at the Bar by the jaundiced tones of the horsehair.)

'Is there any reason why you think it's not Lexi?' Morris asked, reaching for his spectacles.

'The method?' said Adam. 'Cyanide? It seems an odd choice for a philosophy graduate?'

'Women like poison.' Morris looked up. 'Women are seven times more likely than men to use poison to kill. But obviously, men are nine times more likely to kill than women in the first place, so there are more male poisoners than there are female. But given the choice, as Sherlock Holmes would say: "Poison is a woman's weapon."'

'But I think it's just not in keeping with her character? Also, where do you get cyanide from? How did she buy it? How did she get it into the can? Having met her, it doesn't feel like something she would do.'

'Feel? Think? Adam! I did honestly hope for a little better from you.' He sighed loudly. 'You're a barrister, not a therapist. You're not supposed to *feel* that your client is innocent, you're not supposed to *think* she didn't spray Max Bruce in the face with poison: you're supposed to present the facts. The facts, Adam. You deal in facts, not feelings.'

'I just don't believe that someone like her would or could do that. She's a pacifist.'

'She's the client, Adam. And what you believe and what you think don't come into it. We don't have to believe her. We don't have to like her. We don't have to feel anything towards her. Our job is to defend her. Put the Crown to proof. If the Crown are going to put her in prison for life they need to prove beyond reasonable doubt that she deliberately set out to murder Max Bruce. Feelings don't come into it.'

'Of course. Apologies,' said Adam. 'You're correct.'

'You'll find I mostly am,' replied Morris. 'And if you want to know *my* feelings about Alexandra Williams, should you want to ask my thoughts, I'll tell you. I don't think she is as nice and sweet and vulnerable as she appears.'

There was a stilted pause. The air hung heavy. In the silence, Adam swallowed and looked down at his shoes.

'You can probably go now, Adam.' Morris nodded towards the door.

As Adam stood up to leave the room, he noticed a painting to the right of the bookshelf. It was small, beautifully framed, with giant brushstrokes and bold colours. Morris followed his gaze.

'An early Max Bruce,' he acknowledged. 'I bought it after one of my first cases. I've been collecting contemporary modern art for a while.'

He looked down at a file on his desk. It was Adam's cue to leave.

Outside in the corridor, Adam exhaled. He'd had no idea he'd been holding his breath for that long. There was something about Morris that made you terrified of him and desperate to impress him all at the same time. Unfortunately, Adam knew he was only achieving the former. He knew he should have kept quiet about his feelings about Lexi. He knew that he had no real reason to doubt the video evidence, but there was something about it all that didn't quite fit. And he had to prove Lexi's innocence without incurring the ire of Morris. That was quite a tightrope to walk.

He returned down the stairs towards his room, deep in thought about who could possibly want Max Bruce dead. Who would benefit? How would they benefit? The Stop the War campaign had certainly not, if the headlines were anything to go by. Donations were down. Support for them was on the wane, and no matter how many panels, chat shows or phone-ins Cosmo

Campbell, the leader of the campaign, appeared on to deny the murder, his protests mainly fell on deaf ears.

Last night's *Question Time* had ended up in a shouting match with some of the hardcore Stop the War protestors invading the studio, demanding Lexi's release, only to have various panellists demanding that Mr Campbell and his organisation be banned, proscribed a terrorist group full of extremists capable of murder, and for Campbell himself to be put on a terrorist watch list.

'Ah, Adam! There you are!' came the booming baritone of Bobby Thompson. 'I've been looking for you everywhere. Do you want to hear some good news, for a change?'

'Always.'

'Come,' he said, opening the door to his immaculate room, with his clear desk, his neat laptop and his single row of red, black and blue biros. 'Do you remember the Sorokin case?'

How could Adam ever forget the case involving the violent Petrov Gang? His palms began to sweat at the mere thought of them and how threatening they'd been, and how close he'd come to losing his career. It was one of the worst moments he'd ever had in court, where he'd been accused of putting words into his client's mouth, coaching the defendant, Alexei Sorokin, who'd been accused of keeping guns – including the murder weapon – under his bed. Adam would never forget Alexei's terrified face and the fixed stares of the six heavily tattooed members of the Petrov Gang as they'd watched the court proceedings from the public gallery, as brother had testified against brother. He replayed the scene sometimes in his head during those white nights when he couldn't sleep. He remembered being asked to see Judge Wickstead. Had their complex history helped with Her Ladyship? He hadn't been able to tell at the time. All he remembered was the abject humiliation and terror he'd felt, that all his mother's sacrifices would be in vain as his job was put very firmly on the line. And frankly, if Bobby had not stood up for him, Adam knew he would have been disbarred.

Although Alexei had been freed after the court case, he'd been gunned down just days later on the streets of Walthamstow and had ended up in hospital – it had been touch and go. He'd survived. However, Adam had found it very difficult. Bobby had warned him that no matter how hard you tried or how much you wanted to, you couldn't protect everyone all the time and the cold, harsh reality of life sometimes won.

'Well, he just called me. Alexei.'

'You keep in touch with your clients?'

'Sometimes I do. If I think I can help – you know, later down the line. He was a nice boy in a bad situation. Gangs are the scourge of young men's lives. You and I both know that, occasionally, I try and do something for them.'

'So he's alright?'

Adam hadn't even dared keep up with the case afterwards. The Petrov Gang were not a group of people you'd ever want to mess with, and he'd had visions of being stalked by them after the case. He'd seen them, with their thick necks and tattooed arms, out of the corner of his eye many times ever since.

'Oh yes.' Bobby smiled. 'He's really well. After the shooting I got him into an anti-gang programme with a charity that I'm patron of, where they try and re-educate young people to get them back on their feet. So he did a computer science degree. At Middlesex University, and he's just got a job with TalkTalk.'

'That's great.'

Adam felt a huge sense of relief. It was brave of Alexei Sorokin to stand up to his brother Stepan and the Petrov Gang. It *was* possible to turn things around after all.

'That really is good news,' he added.

'I thought you'd like to hear that it was the right thing to do in the end. Talking of which . . .' Bobby rubbed his hands together. 'I'd like your help with a case I'm doing.'

'Anything,' said Adam immediately. Anything for Bobby.

'I'm glad you say that as I know Tony's after you to take on hugely lucrative cases involving hospitals trusts, I think. He mentioned them to me. But this will be pro bono, I'm afraid.'

'Great!' Adam lied.

He couldn't afford a pro-bono case. Tony would garrotte him in a side street off Chancery Lane and give his corpse to science if he accepted it.

'It's the British Army in Khandistan. You might have heard of the case. If you follow that sort of thing?'

'I think I might know about it?'

'It's a young lad being court-martialled for the murder of a ten-year-old boy in Khandistan.'

Adam sighed. 'I have heard about that. I've seen the photographs of the boy. It sounds like a deeply distressing case.'

'It is. It's not easy to defend. I've been doing it on my own, meeting the lad and listening to what he has to say, at the pretrial hearing and all that, but the prosecution has a junior and I really need your help.'

'You're defending the soldier?' Adam felt a little shocked.

'Absolutely,' confirmed Bobby. 'We are.' He patted Adam firmly on the back. 'It's good to have you on board, it really is.'

'How come you're defending him?' asked Adam.

'*We* are,' repeated Bobby. 'Read the notes.' He handed over a file. 'Oh, and by the way, it's in Aldershot in a military court.'

Nine

'A military court?' asked Georgina. 'Well, it's not much different from a normal one, apart from the jury being called "the board" and made up of servicemen, and three-quarters of the board have to agree on the verdict, and the judge is called the "judge advocate". But otherwise, it's the same sort of thing. It's normally in Bulford or Catterick. But Aldershot is good, and at least it's closer to Stag Court.'

Of course Georgina knew about military courts: she knew everything. Except how to eat a sandwich, apparently. Adam watched as she slowly dissected the tuna melt that she'd ordered for lunch, divesting it of all carbohydrate. Why had she ordered a sandwich if she didn't want any bread? was all Adam could think, as he watched her pull the thicks crusts off, pincering them between her bright red nails and placing them on another plate. His mother did the same thing. Ordered a sandwich and then complained about the bread. Why not just ask for a salad?

They were having a quick lunch at Fratelli's, the old Italian sandwich shop that also sold salads, filled baked potatoes and small, slightly dry pastries that looked like they'd been hanging around since the 1960s, when the cafe had been opened by two brothers – Sandro and Marco – from Naples. And it had been feeding hungry barristers, solicitors and clerks ever since. With its green-and-white-checked tablecloths and dark red chairs, it was the sort of place where you queued up and ordered and your food appeared in front of you a few minutes later on thick white china. It was also a good place for a gossip, as no one, except your closest neighbour, could hear a thing above the bubbling, hissing and screaming of the giant coffee machine, which sounded like a steam train screeching into Waterloo station every time anyone ordered an espresso.

'So you're defending?' Georgina continued, picking up a fork to start eating what remained of her sandwich. 'The case of the British soldier who is accused of murdering a ten-year-old boy.'

Adam stared at his cheese-and-tomato bap, slightly wishing he'd ordered something more exciting.

'That's tough,' said Georgina, picking up a slice of tomato. 'Is it just the soldier in the dock?'

'It appears so,' replied Adam.

'Well, good luck with that.'

'Don't you think our new pupil's great?' asked Adam, changing the subject. How he wished he'd told Bobby he was too busy – which he was. Too busy to want to eat his dry, unappealing roll, that was for sure.

'Stacey? She's alright, if you like that sort of thing,' said Georgina, her aquiline nose crinkling a little. 'She's not really my cup of tea – if I ever drank the stuff, which I don't. She's a bit pushy and annoying and thinks she knows everything, a bit of a smart-arse . . .'

Adam laughed out loud. 'A bit like someone else I remember when they first started!'

'Who's that?' asked Georgina, intrigued.

'You!'

'I was nothing like that!' Georgina looked genuinely affronted. She crossed her arms and leaned back. 'That's absolutely not true. And anyway, she's a terrible flirt.'

'Says the girl who had her pupil master, old Rory Parks, giggling like a schoolboy and eating out of her hand.'

'That was ages ago. And anyway . . . how could I help it if he fancied me?'

'So you're not denying it?'

'I'm not confirming it either. It's the not the flirting I find annoying, it's the lack of respect, the lack of fear. You and I were shit-scared when we arrived at Stag Court. Stacey, on the other hand, doesn't seem to give a shit. She refused to take Jonathan's dry cleaning. Imagine what would have happened if you'd done that? You'd have been castrated.'

'Isn't that a good thing, though? She's got balls.'

'More balls than you!'

'Well, I like her.'

'Well, good for you. I don't see her lasting long. Too sassy . . . Too stupid.'

They sat in silence for a second. Georgina sighed. 'Jonathan's very excited about the Blue Face case,' she said. 'Obviously we can't discuss anything. Chinese walls and all that.' She zipped her lips and raised her hands in the air in surrender. 'But we can't imagine what your girl is going to say. He's convinced she's guilty, and he's buying new cufflinks for the trial. I love his priorities. He's yet to read a file – he asks me to summarise them for him all the time – but he's worked out what he's going to wear on the court catwalk: the steps of the Old Bailey. He's just waiting to book his haircut, so he's ready for his close-up on the day. Fragrant and not a follicle out of place, that's our Jonathan.'

'Well, at least he likes you,' Adam said. 'I am finding Morris Brown very hard work. I'm sure he hates me, if he even thinks about me at all, which I am sure he doesn't. But you know how someone can bring out the worst in you? Or the best in you? They can make you feel cleverer and sharper and smarter, or they can make you feel like you know nothing, so that you start to doubt anything you think? You feel stupid. A novice. Well, that's Morris.'

'He famously has a difficult manner, that's all. He's so clever he doesn't understand why it takes us civilians so much longer to understand what he perceives as easy. I promise, I have a friend who knows the barrister who worked with him before. Apparently, he is the most brilliant person, kind and generous, when you get to know him. When are you going to stop being intimidated?'

'That's easier said than done.' Adam picked up his bap and stared at it. 'I can't even face this.' He put it back down on his plate.

'Listen.' Georgina touched the back of his hand. 'Why don't you come to this party tonight?' Adam immediately shook his head. 'Oh, come on! It's work. You can't refuse work. It's an "arty party".' She did the little quotation marks in the air. 'Jonathan's insisting I go – apparently for research. It's at Jean-Paul Norman's gallery. Max Bruce's dealer . . . It's in Hoxton, you'll love it.'

'Said no one ever.' Adam smiled.

'See, I made you smile. Oh, come on! We can go together, from work. We won't and can't discuss the case anyway. But it might be interesting to see "the art world" in the wild. It's background. It might be fun! I can't go on my own – I won't know a soul.'

Ten

Phone call

'Mum? Hi. This isn't the best time.'

'Are you busy, Ad? You're always busy. You're always working; it's not good for you. All work and no play. Is that fish of yours still alive?'

'Yes. I fed it this morning.'

'You should be careful with that. Did you know that you can over-feed them? Their memories are that short – three seconds, I think it is – that they forget they've eaten, and then they swim around the bowl and eat again and again. And then they die.'

'It's a myth that goldfish have a three-second memory, Mum.'

'Is it though? And in any case, how does anyone know? Have they asked them? How's work? Are you still trying to help that spray-can girl murderer? The Blue Face case?'

'She's been charged.'

'Well, they were all talking about it at the hairdresser's today. I went for a set on the high street, you know, with Lesley, who's been doing my hair for years. He said we should think about banning the lot of them.'

'The lot of who?'

'Those protestor people. What are they talking about? They're nothing but trouble. They nearly killed the Home Secretary.'

'I don't think *that* can of paint had any cyanide in it.'

'How do you know, Adam? Everyone's saying it's a lucky escape. They were showing the clips on TV again this morning and they had two people on the sofa talking about it – it was a heated debate, let me tell you. Kate Garraway had to ask them to stop talking over each other three times. I thought it might end in an actual fight.'

'Everyone deserves a fair trial, no matter what we think.'

'You always say that, Adam.'

'Do you remember what Grandad used to say? "Never forget how powerful it is to be innocent until proven guilty. If they don't have to prove guilt, they can do what they like to the innocent."'

'Your *zayde* was very scarred by what happened to him in Poland during the war . . . as we all were. But that doesn't mean the Blue Face girl is innocent. So, I thought I'd come over this evening to see how you are. I've shmaltz herring, cream cheese and platzels. Don't tell your goldfish we're eating his relatives. We could watch some TV, a film even? What do you think? I could be at the flat at about seven p.m., I could let myself in, lay up, and our dinner would be ready for you when you got in at about seven-thirty?'

'I can't tonight, Mum – sorry.'

'You can't work every night, Adam, you just can't, you'll

burn yourself out, like your friend did. Rupert? Was that his name?'

'It's not work, Mum. Well, it is, but I'm going to a party.'

'A party! Well, why didn't you say! A party . . . you must go to that. A party! Is it a birthday? Whose birthday? Is it a thirtieth? You're not far off that now yourself, are you? Whose birthday party is it, Adam?'

'It's an art party.'

'Well, I never! That's sounds very glamorous.'

'In fact, I should go. Georgina will be waiting for me downstairs.'

'Georgina? You're going to the party with that girl from work? The clever one with all the hair? Oh, Adam, you're going on a date with a colleague from work? I've told you before, I don't mind if she's not a Jewish girl. I'm sure she's lovely. I'm the only one of my friends who doesn't have a grandchild . . . Oh, you must go. You've got to go. A date with a colleague . . . Just wait till I tell Debbie at number forty-five.'

Eleven

The Red Square Gallery was down a cobbled side road, between Hoxton Overground station and the famous Columbia Road flower market. It had just gone 7 p.m. and it was a fine, balmy evening, as Adam helped Georgina navigate the road in her stratospherically high heels.

'Adam, I am so sorry,' she said, grabbing hold of his arm. 'I can walk perfectly well in these in Kensington, but I had no idea it was cobbles, cobbles, massive bloody cobbles out here. I mean, it's not as if I haven't been east before – I have, I've had Sunday lunch at Shoreditch House once – but this is a nightmare. I'm so glad you're here. This is SO not my world.'

As they got closer to the large red-brick warehouse, which was lit from below with huge scarlet spotlights, they saw that what looked like half the party were smoking outside. Young, glamorous, cool, wearing black, they were all talking in conspiratorial clusters, laughing, exhaling clouds into the sky and grinding their cigarette butts into the street with their heavy shoes. Adam and Georgina negotiated their way through the smokers to the door, where there was a girl with eyebrow piercings and a clipboard.

'Name?' she barked, barely looking up.

'Georgina Devereaux.'

Georgina smiled; the other woman did not. She took her time poring over the names on the sheet, which didn't appear to be written down in any logical or alphabetical order.

'There!' cried Georgina, pointing with the tip of her nail.

'Right at the end. You're not down as having a plus-one.'

'Pippa Trelawney said it would be OK?'

'Sure,' replied the Rottweiler with the clipboard. 'If you know Pippa . . .'

Inside, the cavernous room was rammed. Adam had never seen such a beautiful crowd of beautiful people. They all looked like they'd stepped out of the pages of a magazine, which, on closer inspection they mostly had. Models, artists, fashion designers; super-skinny women, high on Ozempic, studiously avoiding the passing trays of canapés; slick-looking young men in black open-necked shirts, with rows of silver chains hanging around their necks, knocking back jam jars of artisanal gin; they were all swirling around the gallery, clustering around the huge paintings hanging from the burgundy-coloured walls. There was Loughton who stumbled past, his nostrils frosted like a margarita glass. Both of Max's wives were in a corner, receiving guests, who were queuing up to shake their limp proffered hands and pay their respects. Camilla was swathed in diaphanous black silk, like a caparisoned horse in a funeral procession, while Elisa, also in black, was still channelling the inscrutable icy glamour of a backing singer in a Robert Palmer video.

'Oh my God,' whispered Georgina into Adam's ear. '*All* the witnesses are here. That's really bad. Just one drink and off, don't you think?' She plucked a jar of what appeared to be liquid and weeds and took a sip. 'What sort of drink is this?'

'Gin, lime and rocket,' replied the waiter. 'Or we have gin, ginger and watercress?'

'Georgie! It can't be you! Georgie Devereaux from school!' A pretty blonde woman came rushing through the crowd, her arms in the air, her Gucci handbag dangling from the crook of her elbow. 'Wow! It is you.' She pointed a thin finger, loaded with diamonds. 'This is totally amazing! What a coincidence. I haven't seen you since Val-d'Isère! Come, come and meet my new husband. Number two: let's hope this one's an improvement . . .'

Turned out it was Georgina's world after all, thought Adam, as he was left standing on the sidelines, holding a rocket-and-gin-filled jam jar, which looked like he'd been collecting tadpoles in the local pond. He could just leave. He could finish his drink and then leave. But the thought of going back to his empty flat and his memory-impaired goldfish was not that appealing. He could do some more work? But his mother was right, all work and no play . . . He decided to walk around the party and take a look at the art.

Up close, Max Bruce's work was spectacular. The big, bold brushstrokes and thick layers of paint piled on top of each other were extraordinary. The wild and varied use of colour made the canvases feel dynamic and powerful. They breathed energy and seethed with emotion. He must have been a very compelling person in life, if his works of art were anything to go by, thought Adam, as he stood in front of a canvas of a large vase of flowers. The rich colours, the tumbling petals were mesmerising. He read the sign: *DAHLIAS*. Painted just last year.

'It is beautiful, isn't it?' said a languid voice.

Adam turned. Standing next to him was a woman with long dark glossy salon-fresh hair, pale green eyes, dressed in a fitted black shirt and a tight black skirt. She was stunning and smelt of a heady fig perfume.

'Very beautiful,' agreed Adam, nodding his head. He imagined most people agreed with her. About everything.

'Belinda.' She smiled.

'Adam. Adam Green.'

'I think this is one of Max's best. I much prefer his later work to his early stuff. Although I'm in the minority. Have you seen the extraordinary paintings he's done with his iPad? It's very Hockney. Lots of glorious colours. Much more attractive than that dreadful *Primal Scream* painting, which I can't abide. I have no idea what all the fuss is about, frankly. Are you a fan?'

'Of Max Bruce? Um.' Adam paused. 'I am not that familiar with his work, to be honest. I've seen a few bits around. Are you?'

'I'm a buyer. It's my job. I buy expensive paintings for rich people who have no taste and who just want something to put on their walls. They like to know just enough about the artists so they can bore their friends about them at one of their dull little dinner parties.'

'Are there many of them?'

'What, dull little dinner parties?'

'No, rich people with no taste.'

'Thousands.' She smiled again. 'Which is fortunate for me.'

'Very.' Adam smiled back. 'What are all those red dot stickers on the frames?'

She looked a little puzzled. 'It means they're sold, of course. Have you never been to an event like this before?'

'Not often, no.' Adam took a sip from his jam jar. 'Well, never.'

'If you look closely,' she said, 'you'll notice they've all been sold. All of them.' She fanned her arm out. 'Literally *nothing* makes more money than a dead artist. And a murdered artist probably makes even more. It's the finite stock, you see. He's never going to paint again. I mean, look at *him*.' She nodded across the room at an elegantly dressed sixty-something man, with swept-back hair and thick black-framed glasses, who suddenly flung his arms around another female party guest, kissing her on both cheeks and laughing, throwing his head backwards. 'He doesn't look too upset about the death of his closest friend, does he?'

'Who is that?'

'That's Jean-Paul Norman, the owner of this place, the Red Square Gallery. He's been Max's sole dealer since the beginning. They were best friends at the Slade, only then Max became a famous artist, and Jean-Paul sold his work. He's done well, very well, making a hefty margin along the way. Fifty to sixty per cent.'

'What?' Adam was astonished. 'The gallery can make more on a painting than the artist?'

'Oh yes.' She nodded. 'And tonight, Jean-Paul Norman's made a killing. Oh, whoops.' Belinda laughed, lightly placing her fingertips on her ruby lips. 'That's a Freudian slip if ever there was one! Truth is, before his death Max Bruce's currency was on the wane. All it takes is a couple of poor shows in the auction house, a few paintings not making their reserve price, and then everyone catches a bit of a cold. I know Jean-Paul had to buy a few of Max's paintings himself just to keep the prices high. But now, obviously, he's printing money. I mean, look at those canvases selling at over £500,000 a pop. Anyway.' She paused. 'So, what do you do?'

'I'm a criminal barrister,' said Adam.

'Oh, that's a shame.' Belinda sighed. 'If you ever do divorce, here's my card.' She slipped it slowly into Adam's top suit pocket and pressed her manicured hand flat on his chest. 'Call me.'

Twelve

It was eight in the morning and Adam was sitting opposite Nisha on the train from Waterloo to Staines on their way to visit Lexi Williams in HMP Bronzefield. By some good fortune, they had managed to secure a double seat where they could look each other in the eye over an actual table, rather than the usual standing squash with Nisha stuck under Adam's armpit, which was their normal mode of travel.

'So what sort of party was it?' she asked, delving deep into her bag. Adam watched as she brought out a pair of nude court shoes, what appeared to be a packed lunch, and a flamboyantly beaded necklace. He was expecting Mary Poppins's hatstand at any second, when she finally brought out a fat file. 'Here,' she said, handing it to him. 'What?' she looked at the table, covered in accessories. 'I'm going to an event later.' She shrugged. 'What can I say?' She picked up the necklace. 'This is day-to-night jewellery, or at least that's what they said in the shop. It transforms any outfit.' She held it up to her neck.

'It does,' confirmed Adam. 'Very nice . . . It was an art party, since you ask, or that's what Georgina described it as.'

'You went with Georgina?'

'Nothing was discussed, obviously. It was her invitation. It was interesting to see all Max's family in the flesh, not on the video. His wives were there, together, side by side, creating a united front, with everyone commiserating. Loughton was wandering around . . . wasted.'

'You didn't speak to them, did you? They will be witnesses.'

'Of course they will be. But did you know that the agent, the gallery owner, makes between fifty and sixty per cent on each painting sold?'

'But that's more than the artist.'

'That's right – and do you know who stands to make a fortune since the death of Max Bruce? Jean-Paul Norman, his sole dealer since they were at art school together. He looked on good form last night, let me tell you. Very happy. Every single painting he had at his Red Square Gallery was sold. Little red dots everywhere. Apparently nothing makes more money than a dead artist, or so this woman I met told me.'

'You met a woman?' Nisha looked up from her file.

'Don't you start,' said Adam. 'You sound like my mother.'

'Well, you are nearly thirty,' declared Nisha.

'No, I'm not! God, you *are* my mother!'

'I'm your solicitor, Adam. I have enough children of my own to worry about without agonising about your nonexistent love life. Now . . .' She licked her thumb and placed a piece of paper in front of him. 'So, the terrorism investigation is still ongoing, though it is not part of our case, obviously. But this is the forensic report, with traces of cyanide all over Lexi's desk, her drawers and her hands, when they were swabbed at the police station. They have the spray-can and the vial of cyanide in a vape refill bottle in her desk drawer, and high-level traces in the ladies' toilets at the Royal Academy.'

'Did they swab her flat?'

'Yes, but nothing found so far.'

'So there's cyanide at work but not in her flat?'

'Correct. But the vape is definitely hers. She handled the spray-can, we know that. We have the footage. Our girl's in trouble, Adam.

'It doesn't sound good. We have a pre-trial hearing coming up and all we have from Lexi's original solicitor is her "no comment", so we must try and get her to talk to us today.' Nisha sighed wearily. 'The last meeting wasn't very successful, but I think maybe without Morris it might be a little easier. She was maybe giving him the big I am.'

'Or maybe she was just scared. Fear makes people do really strange things.'

'Either that or she's drunk the Kool-Aid and she genuinely believes she is some sort of Nelson Mandela character. Some sort of freedom fighter. It's like a warped form of narcissism. They're the "main character", as the young people say. I think today it's important that she understands how serious things are, and that she needs to start talking to help herself. No one else is going to help her dig herself out of this hole, least of all her followers on TikTok, who'll all be on to the next burning issue of the day as soon she is convicted. I've had her poor parents on the telephone all of Friday afternoon, trying to work out how they can help. Her mother, Hilary, can't stop crying. She's their only child.'

Arriving at the entrance to HMP Bronzefield, the atmosphere at the gates was a lot less febrile. The press had moved on, either waiting for further evidence in the case or concentrating their efforts on interviews with members of the Bruce family. There'd been thinkpieces on throuples – Max's wives had spoken of their sadness and shock on Radio 4's *Today* programme, and about how they wanted 'justice for Max'. But outside the prison there were only the die-hard campaigners who had bedded in. Literally. Opposing camps: clusters of tents were pitched on some scrubland to the left of the gates, with opposing placards propped up nearby, either freeing Lexi or locking her up. The chanting had stopped, for the moment.

Back inside HMP Bronzefield and Adam and Nisha were met with a significantly more subdued Lexi, sitting at the same table as before. She was still dressed in her regulation prison-grey tracksuit. Her scraped-back hair looked in need of a wash, and there was no more orange varnish left to be picked off her nails.

'Hiya,' she said. Looking up from her hands that were clasped in front of her on the table, she glanced from Adam to Nisha, a slightly glazed expression in her eyes. She'd been in solitary confinement for nearly three weeks.

'Are you alright?' asked Nisha, sounding more mother than solicitor.

'Yeah,' Lexi replied wearily. 'It's just weird. I am not sure how long I've been in here.'

'Twenty days,' said Nisha. 'And we're here to try and prepare for the court case. Where you will be pleading . . .?'

'Not guilty, obviously,' Lexi snapped.

'Great,' said Adam. 'We need to ask you a few questions to help with that.'

'Are there still people outside the prison?' Lexi asked 'I

spoke to my mum yesterday and she said there were loads — loads of people who still believed in me. Only I can't hear them anymore.'

'There are a fair few out there,' replied Nisha, placing her file on the table, and opening it. 'They're just a little less vocal than before.'

'That's important. Do you know what my socials are doing?'

'We haven't been tracking those, I'm afraid,' said Nisha. 'Now, if we could ask you a few questions . . . How long had you been working at the Royal Academy?'

'Three months. It was an unpaid internship, a work experience thing. It was hard work, actually. That Natasha Fitzjohn is one difficult woman. She wanted me in on time, all the time, and she'd have me working late most nights. And weekends. Sending out catalogues, updating mailing lists. I'm not sure what that has to do with art, but there you go.'

'Do you want a career in the arts? Is that why you applied to the gallery in the first place?' asked Adam.

'No!' She laughed. 'I'm an activist. I applied to the gallery as I knew Max Bruce was having an exhibition there, and I was going to help with the exhibition, get in on the inside, and then spray him. In the face. For Stop the War. I thought you knew all that? It's like a covert operation.'

'Just to be clear,' said Nisha, 'if you did kill Max Bruce and you confess it to us, we cannot represent you. We can't lie to the court, and if you change your mind, we'll have to walk away.'

'Don't be ridiculous!' Lexi exclaimed. 'I'm not a murderer. The whole point of Stop the War is that we are a pacifist organisation.'

'So what about the cyanide?' asked Adam.

'What cyanide? I don't know nothing about cyanide.' Lexi sat back, her hands in the air.

'We have the final forensic report, and the police have found cyanide on your desk at work, in the drawer of your desk, traces in your vape refill, on your chair, in the art gallery, and in the toilets. They are saying that you used the ladies' toilets to fill the spray-can with cyanide.'

'I don't know what you're saying, or what you're talking about – I know jack-all about cyanide. Is this what the police are saying?'

'Don't you remember them talking about poison when they arrested you?' asked Nisha.

'Look, they mentioned poison – I wasn't listening. It was all so quick. All I was told to say was "No comment." So I just said it over and over again, and then I was taken here.'

'I'd never normally ask this,' said Nisha, 'but did you put poison in the spray-can?'

'I didn't.' Lexi was beginning to get frustrated, irritated. 'Look!' She raised her index finger. 'I sprayed the old man in the face. That's the point of the protest, like a custard pie, a comedy custard pie, only it was blue paint. But I didn't kill him.'

Adam and Nisha sat side by side on the way back into Waterloo.

'She's not easy to like, is she?' Adam said, sitting back in his seat.

'You can say that again,' agreed Nisha. 'Do you think you should have a look at her social media, to see if there's anything we've missed? I know the media's been all over her tweets. Perhaps we should also talk to Cosmo Campbell about how they recruit their activists?' Her phone started to ring and she scrabbled about in her capacious bag. 'I should get this . . .'

It was already past 6.30 p.m. when Adam received a knock on his door in Stag Court and one of the young clerks handed him the file on the Ministry of Defence case in Khandistan. It was a hefty pile of papers and Adam sighed as he started to read the first page. Why had Tony reluctantly agreed to him taking on the case? But more importantly, why had he said yes to Bobby? He always said yes to Bobby. Maybe he should stop. He was not a desperate junior barrister anymore. He had got a few cases under his belt, he had a flat with a shiny silver toaster and some beers in the fridge. Perhaps he should stand up for himself? He stood up for other people all the time.

He winced as he read the notes. It was a brutal-sounding case. A ten-year-old Khandistani child had suffocated in the back of a tank. He'd been stealing medical supplies from the hospital, foreign aid, and a lance corporal had picked him up off the streets and shoved him into the tank as he hadn't known what else to do with him. He'd slammed the door shut, and had carried on with his orders to keep the fragile peace; having only just been at war with the very same people the previous day, he was now policing them. He'd ended up driving around with the boy in the tank until the boy had died of asphyxiation and dehydration. Why was Bobby defending this case? Even if the lance corporal had just been 'following orders', Adam couldn't use that, as you were not allowed to 'knowingly do harm'.

Sometimes defending, thought Adam, really did take its toll.

Thirteen

Phone call

'Hi, Mum.'

'Oh, Adam, I don't like the sound of that.'

'What?'

'Your voice. You sound very low. How was the party?'

'Oh, it was alright.'

'Only alright? How was the clever girl with the hair? Was she nice?'

'Georgina? She left with a friend.'

'Oh, Adam, a friend? Well, never mind . . . Is that why you're depressed? Because you sound depressed. Are you depressed?'

'No, Mum, it's not that. I've just been reading up on a case about the war in Khandistan.'

'Then I don't blame you. The situation there is enough to make anyone weep. Those poor people. When will it end? And all those young soldiers – dead. And for what? A bit more desert. A bit more sand. I can never understand these things. If only the people giving the orders actually saw the damage they were doing on the ground, then the world would be a different place. Get some women in charge, Adam, that's what I say. They'd get round a table, and they'd have a chat, and they'd sort it all out in a minute. What's the case?'

'The boy who died in the back of the tank.'

'I remember that. His photo was everywhere. Those huge dark eyes. What a tragedy. What a mess. Don't get too involved, dear. Seriously, it's not good for you. You need to take care and look after yourself. Life's about balance.'

There was a loud knock on Adam's door.

'Sorry, Mum, there's someone here . . . Come in.'

Stacey poked her heard around the door.

'I thought I heard your voice. It's gone eight-thirty p.m. Everyone else has gone. It's just you and me in the building, and I'm parched. Surely I can tempt you out for a drink? I thought working in chambers would be a fun, lots of chat, jokes, but the office, sorry, the rooms' doors are always shut. All everyone ever does is work. What do you think? Drink?'

'Is that a girl's voice? Is that the girl with the hair?'

'Mum . . . I'll call you back.'

Fourteen

A few minutes later, Adam found himself walking down Chancery Lane with Stacey Jackson.

'What do you fancy? Where do you fancy?' she was asking. 'You must know somewhere good. This is your hood.'

Adam had already vetoed the Wig and Pen, with its chandeliers, and its bright teal walls. There would be too many clerks in there from Stag Court, or even worse, Jonathan propping up the bar, telling stories while his lips turned the colour of the claret he was drinking. Even if this was just a nice quiet drink with a colleague, Adam simply could not bear the number of puerile jokes he'd have to endure tomorrow morning. Jonathan might have left school over thirty-five years ago, but old 'ragging' habits died hard.

'Here?' she asked, coming to a stop. 'I really fancy a strong cocktail.'

The Last Judgment, with its high-vaulted ceiling, black-and-white-checked floor and its great swathe of a bar, was one of those glamorous up-market bars that Adam had yet to frequent in his years at Stag Court.

'Oh, look,' said Stacey rubbing her hands together. 'Proper

drinks. Not like that Wig and Pen where no one's heard of an actual cocktail. What shall we have? What would you like? My shout.' She picked up the cocktail menu and ran her finger down the list.

'Absolutely not,' insisted Adam. 'Pupils never pay.'

'Oh, really? If you're sure? I think I'll have a Paloma. How about you, Adam? Do you want a Paloma?' Adam hesitated. What the hell was a Paloma? 'It's strong, with tequila. I promise you, you'll love it. Do you like tequila? Of course you do – everyone loves tequila. Go and grab that seat over there.'

Adam paid and went to claim a small table in the corner and waited for Stacey to come over with the cocktails. His mobile was buzzing on the table. He looked down. It was his mum again.

'Answer it if you want,' said Stacey, sitting down opposite and handing him his long, cold drink. 'My mum rings me every day. Do you think it's a Jewish thing?' She took a substantial sip. Adam looked at her, a little surprised. 'Oh, that's better,' she declared, looking up. 'Oh, I am too, Adam. Although I'm more *Friday Night Dinner* the show, rather than the meal.'

'Sounds fun.' Adam took a slug of his strong cocktail.

'Anyway, the phone thing? Do you think it's Jewish? My mum's relentless if I don't pick up. She just keeps calling and calling until eventually I have to pick up, and then she has this terrible habit of starting the conversation midway through, as if I know what she's talking about. She also never says who she is. It's like I'm supposed to pick up where we left off yesterday. She often says, "As I was saying," without even drawing breath. Cheers, anyway!' She raised her glass and clinked his. 'So, you're not taking it then? The phone call?'

'I don't think so. She'll only tell me what she's having for dinner.'

'Mine does that too! Right down to the snacks . . . This place is fun. Have you been here before? I always think you can't beat a good bar. I like a bar. In Manchester . . .'

Adam listened as Stacey talked him through her life and early childhood in Manchester. She was the eldest of three sisters, they were all very close in age, and the top floor of their house in Prestwich reeked of hairspray and perfume every Saturday night as they all competed for the bathroom mirror while getting ready to go out. She loved going out. She had a big gang of friends who she'd grown up with, and who she really missed now that she was down in London. They'd all stayed up north. She was the only one who'd gone south, and she found it all very different down here.

'No one's that friendly, are they?' she said, draining her cocktail. 'Fancy another?' she asked. 'Your shout again, obviously.'

'Of course,' said Adam, springing to his feet. 'Same?'

She nodded eagerly.

'So why did you become a lawyer?' he asked as he returned with the drinks.

'Well, to be fair, I didn't have a massive choice in the matter. If you have a mother like mine, which it sounds like you do, there are only about four things you can be: doctor, lawyer, engineer, or a disappointment – and bring total and utter shame on the family.' Adam laughed. 'You know what I'm talking about! Professions. Proper professions . . . Or black sheep. There's no in between. And since I was useless at biology and wouldn't know a knee from an elbow, the doctor thing was never going to happen. An engineer? Do I like bridges? No. There was only the lawyer thing left. So here I am. A barrister. And my mum is tickled pink. How about you?'

'My reason is a little different.' He paused. She's a barrister by default, he thought. That's a long way to go on charm and chutzpah alone. This was also perhaps not the time or the place to talk about his father's wrongful conviction and the subsequent taking of his own life. It was not a subject he'd ever discussed at Stag Court, and he was certainly not going to chat about it now over Palomas with Miley Cyrus playing loudly in the background.

'Bobby Thompson came to my school in North London and gave a lecture about the law and the justice system and the idea of fighting injustice, and I was hooked. I never imagined that I would be working with him this many years later.'

'I haven't met him yet,' Stacey said, smiling. 'But I've heard amazing things. He's a bit of a legend, isn't he?'

'He's a very nice man, and he's very loyal. He saved my career. I made this mistake – well, not really, but it sounded like I'd coached the defendant, and Bobby went into battle for me. I owe him a lot.'

'What's that bloke with the odd stare like?'

'Morris? He's so clever I don't think he understands that the rest of the world moves at a different pace.'

'He looks intimidating, that's for sure!' Stacey laughed. 'God!' She rolled her eyes. 'Let's not start on the rest of them . . . Tony's a bully . . .' she started.

'He's a nice bloke when you get to know him.'

'No he's not! In any other profession he'd be disciplined.'

'By who?!' Adam laughed. 'Also, I have to say, he might enjoy that.'

Turned out, Palomas were quite strong. Two drinks down and Adam and Stacey were laughing and sharing stories, mostly her observations about the rest of the barristers and clerks at Stag Court. Her impression of Georgina flicking her hair at the coffee machine had Adam in stitches, as did her take on Prudence and her dogs, and Gudrun Evans who never had a hair out of place.

'And as for Jonathan,' she declared. 'I mean, who is he?!'

'He was a very successful criminal barrister, who now has a lot of ex-wives and lots of children.'

'How many children does he have?'

'At least seven.'

'Wow.' Stacey sat back in her seat. 'Does the world really need that much Jonathan? Or spawn of Jonathan?'

'He was great in his day.'

'When was that? In the last century? Because that's where he's stayed. I mean, the dry cleaning, coffees with the little thimble of warm milk.' She demonstrated the 'thimble' with her finger and thumb. 'The flowers he sends. I've done three bouquets this week. Each one to a different address. How he finds the time and energy for so many ladies I don't know. Do you think Pippa knows what he's up to?'

'Probably. I'm pretty sure she was one of the bouquet women when I was his pupil.'

'How did you survive a whole year with him?' She shook her head and drank a little more. 'He's driving me to booze already, and I haven't even been here a month!' She waved her glass at him. 'One more for the road?'

Fifteen

Tequila. Tequila. Tequila. Three of them.

Adam was regretting his poor decisions, the subsequent headache and his dry rasp of a mouth, as he leaned against the Tube door on the Central line the next morning, heading towards Mile End. He had arrived earlier in Stag Court, only to receive a message via Tony to meet Morris at his house in Tredegar Square, just off Mile End Road.

'He must like you,' sniffed Tony, as he handed him the note. 'Almost no one gets invited there. I have, obviously. I go and have a Christmas drink with him every year. I sit and have a drink in his sitting room, and we discuss the year, the highs, the lows, and he gives me a bottle of whisky, an eighteen-year-old Macallan. It's a posh gaffe, but then again, it probably wasn't when he bought it twenty-five years ago.'

Adam turned the corner into the square and spotted Morris's end-of-terrace white stucco-fronted Georgian townhouse. He stopped for a second to admire it; it was indeed posh, elegantly proportioned and in immaculate condition. It had been loved like a child.

'Morning,' said Morris, as he opened the large black door

to find Adam standing on the steps. 'Sorry to drag you all the way out here, but I thought it would be a good way to really discuss the case as we're in court for the pre-trial hearing the week after next. Come in.' He looked Adam up and down as he closed the door. 'You look like you need a very strong cup of coffee. Late night?'

'No, not at all,' Adam insisted, running his hands through his dark hair, fighting a hideous clammy wave of anxiety, guilt and regret that was threatening to engulf him as he followed Morris along the corridor into his light, airy kitchen. He squinted in the sunshine that reflected off clean white surfaces, and the row of gleaming copper pans that hung on one wall in perfect ascending sizes. Opposite was a veritable library of well-worn cookbooks, each with dozens of pieces of paper sticking out, marking specific recipes. Adam walked over to a large sash window, which looked over a small, manicured garden bursting with roses.

'What a beautiful house,' he said.

'I've been here for decades,' replied Morris. 'How strong do you want your coffee?' He sparked up an ancient silver machine that wouldn't have looked out of place at Fratelli's.

A few minutes later they were sitting in Morris's drawing room, which had three double sofas, a few low tables covered in large art books, and a noisy golden carriage clock ticking away on the mantelpiece before a heavy gilt-framed mirror. It smelt strongly of Diptyque candles, like he was in a spa. Typical, Adam thought, the one day that he spent with the genius that was Morris Brown and he was not at the top of his game. He was furious with himself. He'd like to have blamed Stacey, but he knew that would not be fair.

'So how was Lexi?' asked Morris. 'Still enjoying her own notoriety?'

Adam described the difference in their client's appearance and her low mood.

'I spoke to her mother again yesterday. Hilary. Nisha gave her my number. The poor woman's in agony. She is saying the justice system is moving too slowly and she's desperate for her daughter to be out of solitary confinement. And I feel her pain. But with charges this serious, it's impossible. Her parents have asked us to apply again for bail, but it's pointless, it really is. Even if they are offering their house as assurance, with the terrorist investigation hanging over her you can forget about it. How did you get on at the party?'

'The party?' Adam felt a sudden rush of panic. Morris had specifically told him not to start digging around asking too many questions. 'Oh . . . the art party – I just popped in.'

'What did you see?'

'Lots of art, all sold, with the red dots.' Morris was nodding. 'Max's wives were there. They looked upset, as I suppose you would if your husband had just been murdered. The agent—'

'Jean-Paul Norman.'

'Yes. He didn't appear to be that distressed about his client's death.'

'Perhaps because he was making a fortune selling his old stock that he hadn't been able to shift in years at inflated prices, while taking his sixty per cent.'

'Exactly that. Surely that's a motive right there?'

'To kill off your one and only greatest asset and friend of over forty years?'

'He was losing money? He was desperate? Maybe he had

debts? He had plenty of opportunity. He was at the Royal Academy at the retrospective, standing next to Max for most of the party, according to the video.'

'In my humble opinion, this doesn't feel like a murder over money. Something like this, cyanide in the face – that implies contempt. Hatred, in the purest form.'

'Which brings us back to Lexi – she hated Max Bruce,' Adam continued. 'He was a symbol of the capitalist patriarchy.'

'Or was it a manufactured emotion, exacerbated by social media and her personal echo chamber? None of her arguments made sense when we spoke to her. I am not sure if Stop the War is a do-or-die cause like, say, the Suffragettes, who were prepared to be locked up and force-fed, and throw themselves in front of the King's horse, and blow up post boxes, and attempt to assassinate the Home Secretary. What did Lexi say when you discussed the cyanide?'

' "It wasn't me." '

'Ah, the old Shaggy "it wasn't me" line of defence,' said Morris with an amused curl to his lips. Adam looked at him blankly. 'The song? It came out in 2000. A bit before your time maybe. I suppose you're all Swifties now. Well, anyway, the Shaggy "it wasn't me" line of defence only works if we can suggest to the jury that someone else might have done it. That someone else planted the cyanide in the cannister and not Lexi. Also, the Shaggy line of defence is fairly useless when every single bit of press, film footage and social media clip has Lexi actually committing the crime. The terrible photos, the social media clips, and the forensics all point to her.' Morris sighed. 'Are you hungry? There's a great little cafe round the corner.'

*

A few minutes later, Adam was following Morris in his navy-blue cashmere coat and leather-soled brogues as he slowly walked around the square to the cafe. It was a ponderous pace, mainly because he appeared to know every single person on the route.

The postman was the first to greet him. There was a broad smile, a handshake and conversation about his children. His eldest daughter was about to have a baby. He'd be a grand-dad by Christmas. Next was the road-sweeper who'd worked the square for over twelve years. How was his brother? How was his back? He was then interrupted by a puce-looking lady with a heavy shopping bag and two children who were chasing each other around her ankles like Tom and Jerry. How was she? Had she managed to register with the local school? And on he went.

Adam was bewildered. Obviously Morris had lived on the same square for a while, but plenty of people could live next-door to each other in the capital and ignore each other for decades at a time.

Morris caught Adam's eye. 'I've been away,' he admitted. 'I haven't walked the square in a while. Here.' He opened a bright yellow door with a bell that jangled as it was pushed. 'Hello, Mrs Gessen. How are you?'

'Oh . . . my . . . goodness! Mr Brown, as I live and breathe! You're a sight for sore eyes!'

Mrs Gessen rushed out from behind her wooden counter and hugged Morris so tightly that the man practically disappeared into her ample chest and apricot-coloured tabard.

'Look at you!' she said, pushing him away. She had forearms like a bricklayer, from a decade of making flaky pastry, and a round, flushed, sweaty face from eating it. 'I am so glad to see you. So glad. How are you? How was America? How was the food? Sit down, sit down over there, with your friend. I bet you missed my food – all that processed muck they serve you there. I wouldn't feed it to my pugs. Shall I bring you over a spot of quiche? You like the Lorraine? Two Lorraines?'

'Oh, please, Mrs Gessen. Two quiches. I've been dreaming about these.' Morris turned to Adam. 'I promise you,' he said. 'They're the best in town.'

Warm and plump and wobbly, with the shortest pastry Adam had ever tasted, Mrs Gessen's quiches were indeed the best in town. Or at least just what one should order if one had been over-served tequila the night before. As Adam piled up his fork and sipped his glass of water, he could feel life returning to the arid wasteland that was once his brain.

'Do you know,' said Morris, dabbing his mouth with his paper napkin, 'I've been thinking. I might have made a mistake.' He paused. This was not something he said often. Adam stopped chewing. His fork in mid-air. 'The police are not going to interview widely, or dig too deeply – why should they? They have their suspect. Why do they need to look elsewhere? It's a nice fit. They have the son's video and a highly motivated establishment, government members, on their side. They attacked the Home Secretary, for God's sake. They'll be keen to make an example of Lexi. Anyone who is contemplating civil unrest and who thinks they can "stick it to the man", so to speak, will now know they cannot.' He sighed. 'We've yet to discover what's on Lexi's computer, but it is as open-and-shut as it gets – a three-day case max. But I think you need to do some digging, Adam. You need to go out and ask questions. Do we think this

21-year-old has the brains to have pulled this off? I don't. Talk to Nisha. We need to know who the prosecution is thinking of calling and then speak to everyone else. Everyone. It's obvious to me – well, both of us – that Lexi didn't knowingly commit murder. She sprayed him in the face, but had no knowledge that the spray was lethal. We now have to make it obvious to everyone else. Or at least make them doubt the narrative. So forget what I said.' He smiled. 'I was wrong. Be curious. Be Poirot. It's about time we engaged those little grey cells.'

Sixteen

Adam was sitting at his desk in Stag Court, with Morris's words reverberating around his less sore head. It was quite something that the notoriously brilliant Morris had put his faith in him, and Adam didn't want to let him down. He smoothed open the Blue Face file again (although he had to stop calling it that). As Morris had observed, it was emotive. The jury would automatically visualise those striking and graphic images they would have most certainly come across on social media, with Lexi's fixed grimace and Max Bruce's face covered in paint.

He went right back to Lexi's first interview and went through it line by line. There was not a huge amount to go on. She must have been terrified, sitting there with the duty solicitor, repeating, 'No comment,' over and over.

Adam turned the pages, then leaned back and closed his eyes as he realised he had to go with his instincts on this one. He was not a rooky barrister anymore. He had plenty of victories under his belt. He knew what he was doing, and he needed to trust what his gut was telling him.

He had another look through Loughton's video, taking in the shocked, open-mouthed faces of the guests, their wide eyes, their confusion, their terror. His heart skipped. He stopped the film. There. He rewound and leaned in. There she was, Lexi. He watched as she moved in and out of shot. He slowed the video right down. She left the frame, appearing to move to the right of the painting, *Primal Scream*, and then came back into shot a few moments later. He squinted. He replayed it again. Where did she go? She'd walked out of the shot with nothing in her hands and then returned with the spray-can.

Had it been stored inside the room itself? Had she hidden it in the gallery before the party? Was it not in her possession the whole time? Anyone could have tampered with it. Anyone at all. Adam looked again at the black dress with the blue flowers Lexi was wearing. She had no handbag and no voluminous sleeves in which to store the can. So she must have left it in the gallery. Overnight? For how long? Days?

He should call Nisha. This was 'doubt', surely?

She picked up immediately. 'Adam!' She sounded out of breath and out on the street, marching somewhere, her heavy, capacious bag slung over her shoulder. 'Have you been in court? Your phone's off.'

'It is?' He checked his mobile. It was. 'Sorry,' he replied. 'Where are you?' He vaguely tried to guess from the background noise alone.

'I'm on my way to Marylebone police station – an urgent call from a domestic abuse case. It doesn't sound very pretty . . . but . . .' She inhaled. 'I'm glad you called. I wanted to catch up with you as to where we are with Lexi. Have you got any further? I've had her poor mother on the telephone again, crying, asking if there's been any progress, asking whether, if they managed to get any more money, might things move a bit more

quickly? I tried to tell her that more money wasn't going to make any difference at all.'

'I've been looking at the footage and I don't think Lexi had the spray-can on her the whole time. I believe she hid it somewhere in the gallery, so it's possible it was tampered with.'

'But all the cyanide residue was found on her desk and in her drawer and in the ladies' toilets?'

'I know the forensics don't help us too much.' Adam sighed.

'That's an understatement.' She paused. There was a sound of her clicking heels on the road and a blast of a car horn. 'Alright! Alright! The man was *green*, the man was green!' she was shouting. The man definitely wasn't green, thought Adam, as he'd have heard the sound of the pedestrian crossing beeping in the background. 'Sorry about that,' she continued. 'I'm running late.' Wasn't she always? 'Anyway, what's worse, Adam . . . what's worse . . . is that I've got all the police photographs back from Lexi's flat, and it's full of melons.'

'Melons?'

'Cantaloupes. And they're all covered in blue paint. She'd been using them for target practice. They look very odd, Adam, let me tell you. Creepy. They are not going to play well, that's for sure.'

'Is that blue paint on the melons also contaminated with cyanide?'

'No, it's not,' she said.

'Well, then—'

'Well, then nothing,' continued Nisha. 'If Lexi used poisonous paint in her own kitchen she would have killed herself. Shit!'

'What?'

'I've gone the wrong way. I was so busy talking to you, I've gone down the wrong road. Anyway, I have written to the Crown.'

'O K.'

'I just find it extraordinary how little work the police have done on this case. They have barely spoken to anyone. They've gone with the idea that Lexi was caught red-handed, spraying the face of Max Bruce on film, and that's that. Case closed. I have always said this, Adam: the police really do lack imagination. I'd better keep my voice down as I have just walked into Marylebone police station.' She stopped then hissed down the telephone, 'But it's shocking how over-in-a-few-days they think this case is. I've been sent the basic statements from the witnesses for the prosecution and they're not calling anyone – well, hardly anyone. It smacks of arrogance. So, you've got free rein, Adam, to talk to anyone. They're not relying on the family, or anyone at the Royal Academy. It's O K for you to go and talk to them, as the prosecution isn't calling them.'

'Any of them?'

'Not one. Why bother when you have the suspect on film with the can in her hand? At least, that's what they're thinking. Lazy sods!'

She hung up.

Adam grabbed his dark suit jacket. It was still afternoon, and if he moved now, he would have plenty of time to get to the Royal Academy and walk through the whole crime scene, work out the logistics, and see if he could find out where and when Lexi had stashed the can and then work out a possible timeline for the crime. He was excited. Maybe there was some sort of a light at the end of this dismal tunnel after all?

He picked up his bag and opened his room door, only to come face to face with Bobby.

'Ah, Adam . . . Do you have any thoughts on the court martial?' he asked, looking up from the files he was holding. 'I presume you're up to speed on the notes. We're going to trial next week.'

'Oh! Sorry, I was just off . . .' began Adam.

This was all he needed, he thought. Why had he said yes to this Khandistan case? He'd never been in a military court. He knew nothing about the army, and he was already stretched and stressed as it was. He'd love to tell Bobby to choose a different junior, someone else. In fact, he'd love to ask why on earth he had picked this case, of all cases, in the first place. A British soldier killing a Khandistani child, asphyxiating him in a tank? It didn't look, or sound, like a case Bobby would defend.

But instead, Adam sighed inwardly. 'I've looked through all the files . . . and, um, well, it's a hard case, isn't it?'

'Aren't they all?' Bobby smiled. 'That's why we're here, Adam: to unpick the complex Gordian knot that is life.'

'I suppose so.'

'And this one is even more complicated than a knot, Gordian or otherwise. I think we very much have to consider the situation at the time, what was going on in Khandistan, the chaos, and the madness, the heat, the dust, how and why the young boy ended up in our boy's tank, and what the chain of command was at the time. There's quite a lot of legwork involved on this one, which is why I need you. You're a lot more nimble than I am!'

There was something so very warm and generous about Bobby, his manner, his demeanour. What could Adam do other than agree? He remembered vividly the day when Bobby had told him to stop playing the outsider card; that being popular in chambers and making friends was as important as being diligent and doing all the hard work. 'Being an outsider is not a virtue,' he'd said. Or something along those lines. Since then, they'd been friends. He trusted Bobby, and had always come to him for advice.

'I just never thought you'd want to defend a British soldier,' ventured Adam, immediately realising that this was perhaps a statement too far.

'And why would you say that?'

'Only, um, well, because you always defend the underdog,' he clarified quickly. 'I just thought that, you know, you'd be more likely to be on the side of the Khandistani child, that's all.'

'More likely, you say,' Bobby said slowly, still smiling, although no longer with his eyes. 'Maybe it's not about sides, Adam, but justice?' He nodded down the corridor. 'Let me show you something.'

Walking into Bobby's room, Adam glanced up at the clock on the wall; it was almost 4.30 p.m. already. He was really hoping to get to the Royal Academy before it closed. He wished quietly that whatever Bobby had to show him, it wouldn't take long.

Bobby went behind his neat, organised desk and opened a small leather box to the right of his computer. Taking out a key, he opened the long middle drawer in front of him and brought out a pile of letters and old photographs. They'd been sent from abroad, air mail: Adam could tell from the blue and red stripes around the edges of the envelopes. They'd all been addressed in the same large, looped writing, in thick black ink from a fountain pen. Bobby placed them on the desk and sorted through them slowly.

'So,' he said, picking them up individually and turning them over. 'It's all in here.'

Adam checked the clock again. He was pretty sure the gallery closed at 6 p.m. He moved anxiously from one foot to the other. Should he say something?

Bobby took out a faded photograph with a white border and placed it, somewhat reverently, on the table. He turned the image to face Adam. Adam leaned in.

It was a faded colour picture. The sky was pale grey and the grass a faded, dull green, clearly England. In the middle of the photograph was a young black soldier, dressed in full military uniform, complete with a regimental cap. His chin thrust towards the sky with pride and determination; he was saluting.

'You asked me why I am interested in this case and why we are defending it. Well, this man is the reason.' He tapped the photograph with his index finger. 'This is my father. Joseph William Victor Thompson. He left Turks and Caicos in 1962 to join the British Amy. Royal Artillery, Twenty-Nine Commando. He wanted to serve Queen and country, and he did . . .

'Here's another one.' He picked out a larger photograph where 'Gunner Thompson' (the name was printed along the bottom of the cardboard frame) was pictured looking a little less full of bravado, and a little more battle-weary, with two medals pinned to his chest. It had clearly been taken in a studio as it had that virulent blue background they'd used way back then.

'He earned those firing howitzers in Aden.' Bobby pointed

to the medals. 'He then served in the Far East, Germany and, of course, Belfast. He represented his regiment in boxing and running and he made friends for life. He was extremely proud of his connection with the British Army. He always used to say that he would be nothing without them. He helped run the West Indian Association of Service Personnel when he retired, which helps the community of servicemen who lost their lives in the Second World War and after that.'

'You must be proud of him.' Adam picked up the photograph. He could see where Bobby got his handsome looks from and his charming, wide smile.

'He first flew into Heathrow in the summer of 1962.' Bobby blinked rapidly with emotion. 'It was sunny, and the days were long, and he couldn't believe that the sun set at nine p.m. So late! In Turks and Caicos, of course, it disappears around six p.m. He wrote to my grandmother, saying, "They're liars, my friends. England is the land of the eternal sun. A sun that never sets." The evenings are golden, but when the winter came, he soon learned. He'd never been so damn cold in his life. His skin turned grey, and he shivered in his unform and wrote endless letters home begging his mother for thick socks! Knitted socks. And thick, extra-warm underwear!' Bobby looked down at the pile of letters on his desk. 'But he always said he wouldn't have changed anything. Even the racists – of which there were a few, but not many. And the couple that there were he dealt with individually. He loved the army, he loved his fellow soldiers, his band of brothers. The camaraderie, the loyalty, the deep personal friendships you make on tour, in adversity. He gave his heart and his soul to that institution. He always said that he was born in Turks and Caicos, but he was made in the British Army.

He died some seven years ago now. He lived long enough for them to unveil the African and Caribbean War Memorial in Brixton.' He looked up and smiled again at Adam. 'I sometimes find myself there, on a quiet Sunday afternoon, thinking of my dad, and all that he did. It's in Windrush Square.'

Adam stood in silence. He was deeply moved by Bobby's story, which went a little way to explain the man – loyal, rooted in tradition, and yet always ready to push at the boundaries. Both part of the establishment and yet at the same time wanting to bring it to task.

Bobby sat for a second, lost in thought, with a half-smile on his face, clearly reminiscing on conversations and memories past. 'So,' he declared, sitting up and patting the top of his desk, 'Gunner Thompson is the reason why we're defending Lance Corporal Danny Sutcliffe. The case may appear cut-and-dried, Adam, but this lad is being used as a scapegoat. There's a cover-up for sure that goes all the way to the top, and we're going to find it and expose it. These young soldiers have been taken for granted for long enough. They've been failed, exploited and thrown to the wolves. It's an injustice, and you know how much I hate that.'

'I do,' agreed Adam, with a quiet sense of euphoric relief. Of course Bobby would have his reasons, and of course they would be noble!

'I have some numbers I need you to follow up on.' Bobby scribbled away on a notepad with his blue biro. 'Here.' He ripped off the sheet of paper and handed it to Adam. 'They're some old contacts I have in the MOD. Give them a call, go and meet them. But be careful, Adam. Really careful. I can't stress this enough. This is a deeply sensitive case, as you can imagine.

The stakes are high. The food-chain is long, and no one wants us – you and me – to get to the top. If you want to kill a cobra, you have to slice off its head, and we really want the head, Adam, not the end of its long, slithering tail.'

'OK.' Adam picked up the scrawled piece of paper.

'Where were you going?' asked Bobby.

'Sorry?'

'When I bumped into you?'

'The Royal Academy.'

Bobby glanced up at his clock on the wall. 'If you run, you should make it. It closes at six p.m.'

Seventeen

About thirty minutes later, Adam sprinted down Piccadilly, his lilac-coloured tie flapping over his shoulder, his suit jacket billowing out behind him like a galleon in full sail. His face was scarlet, his skin was dank with sweat, and his lungs were killing him. He ran past the beautiful bookstores – Waterstones, Maison Assouline, Hatchards. He wished he could stop and browse, which was one of his favourite things to do. But he pushed on. He spotted himself in the opulent windows of Fortnum & Mason. He slowed a little to stare at the lavish profusion of macarons that arched into a giant rainbow in one window. On he ran past the piles of sugared almonds and the army of gingerbread men. If only he could stop. Fortnum's was his mum's favourite shop, and she made a hallowed visit to their food hall once a year, just before Hannukah.

Finally, he crossed the road to the Royal Academy, huffing and puffing his way through the archway and the black-and-gold wrought-iron gates. The same gates that Max Bruce and his entourage had walked through to an explosion of flashbulbs three weeks before.

'The Max Bruce exhibition, please.'

It was all he could do to stop himself from exhaling, puffing appallingly into the young woman's face. He'd made it.

She raised her left arm and checked her watch. 'You haven't got long: we close in forty minutes. Also,' her blonde head cocked to one side, 'there is limited access to *Primal Scream*, as . . . well . . . you know, due to . . . the incident.'

'I'm sure,' agreed Adam, still trying to catch his breath.

'So we'd ask you to respect the taped-off area and let the police do their work.'

'Are the police still here?'

'No.' She smiled tightly. 'They haven't been here for days now. Well, weeks, actually. In fact, they've barely been here at all . . . Such a sad loss to the nation. Everyone who works here is mortified.'

'Embarrassed?'

'Sad,' she corrected. 'Very sad . . . That'll be twenty-four pounds fifty, please,' she added, handing over a ticket.

Adam stood at the bottom of the marble steps, trying to imagine what the night of the party might have been like. Busy, bustling, old friends, glasses of champagne. It would have been a tight squeeze into the main gallery where *Primal Scream* was hanging. He remembered seeing and hearing the scrum on Loughton's video.

'The exhibition starts up the stairs,' called the blonde from behind the white Formica table, pointing with her index finger.

'Don't worry,' replied Adam, a little sheepishly. 'I have only come to see one work.'

'Oh.' She curled up her nose. 'You're one of those.' Adam

looked puzzled. 'One of the gawpers, who just comes in and takes a selfie in front of the painting, has a good look at the patch on the floor where he died, and then disappears. Well, you're lucky.' She shrugged. 'The place is empty. You've got the room to yourself . . . For your selfie.'

Adam hesitated, wanting to tell her that he was not one of those people. He was not a gawper, or a grief tourist who photographed misery for likes on the Gram. His interest was professional, legal; he was working on the case, and he was not even the sort who slowed down to have a look at an accident on the motorway. Who did that? Everyone but him, apparently. But he had forty minutes, and he'd better make the most of it.

He walked inside the hall of the gallery, and the painting on the opposite wall made him stop in his tracks. *Primal Scream* was enormous. Nothing like the *Mona Lisa*, which was so diminutive that when he'd gone to the Louvre, he'd barely been able to see it for the crowds, and the thousands of heads, and the iPhones on sticks all shoved up in the air. *Primal Scream* was imposing. It took over the room, it commanded your attention, it demanded it. Adam was lost for words. The raw energy, the burst of life, the miracle of birth. He was overawed. He now understood what all the fuss was about, why Max Bruce had been catapulted to fame overnight. Imagine painting something like that in your early twenties. How could you not be enthralled by something so vital, and so very human?

'It's beautiful, isn't it?' came a female voice right next to him.

Adam recognised her immediately from all the interviews on the television and from Loughton's footage.

'I am sorry to ask,' he said, smiling, exuding as much charm as he could muster, 'but are you the person who put the whole show together? What an amazing thing to do. It must have been hard work. How did you manage it?'

Natasha Fitzjohn looked a little taken aback at first, but she soon glowed with pleasure at such affirmation. Adam had read up on her in the files and knew she was in her early forties and had progressed through the ranks at exceptional speed. She was renowned for her sharp eye and brilliant diplomatic skills, and to have managed to get the reclusive Russian oligarch Mr Valutov to loan the painting was (or so he'd read) deemed the art coup of the century.

'What a terrible evening that must have been, especially after all your hard work,' he continued.

'It *was* terrible,' she said quietly, sitting down on the viewing bench in front of the painting. She shook her immaculate bobbed hair and smoothed down an expensive-looking maroon leather pencil skirt. 'I have never seen anything like it. Britain's greatest artist killed in front of everyone.'

'It must have been a shock . . . I am Adam, by the way. I'm one of the lawyers working on the case.' He offered her his hand. She hesitated for a second, and then shook it firmly.

'Natasha Fitzjohn.' She smiled broadly. 'Ask me anything, anything at all.'

'Do you mind?' asked Adam, indicating to sit next to her on the viewing bench in the middle of the gallery.

'Sure.'

Her expression was pleasant. Adam noticed how her dark makeup, her burgundy lips, almost matched the shade of her skirt. Her nails were painted a deep dark red. She seemed to be the personification of sophistication.

'You've worked here for a while?'

'Six years. Three of them curating just this exhibition. Before this I was at the National Portrait Gallery. That was a wonderful job, so many beautiful paintings . . .'

'I can imagine.'

'But this one' – she indicated in front of them – 'this painting really is special. I have loved it since I was a child.' She smiled briefly. 'When I saw it in books and photos, there was something arresting and moving about it.'

'Who's the baby?' asked Adam.

'That's the thing. No one knows. Max Bruce never said – and even when he was asked, he refused to tell.'

Adam looked around him. He looked down at the parquet floor and noticed that despite the clean-up, there were lines of blue paint lodged in the cracks. To the right of the painting was a chair. Black, metal; it didn't look hugely comfortable.

'Is that where the security guard sits?' asked Adam.

She looked over with evident disinterest. 'Oh, yes. It is.'

'Is he there all the time?'

'Mostly.' She shrugged. 'But, you know, he's human so he's allowed breaks . . . obviously.' She checked her slim gold watch. 'He's gone home now; he leaves a little early, if he can. To miss the rush on the Tube.'

'And Lexi, Lexi Williams, she was working for you?'

'Unfortunately.'

'How long, if you don't mind me asking?'

'Well . . .' Natasha sighed, trying to recall exactly when. 'March or April of this year, so a few months before the retrospective. She was an intern. We'd advertised the job in *The Art Newspaper*. We weren't inundated with applicants, as it was unpaid, but we needed some basic help to get the exhibition up and running: sending out invitations, asking for donations, organising all the shipping of the works. There's a lot of paperwork. She helped with that.'

'Unpaid?'

'Oh, totally unpaid! Most jobs in the art world are unpaid!' She laughed. 'Well, that's not entirely true: it just feels like it. Poorly paid, that's the term. Very poorly paid.'

'And she had radical views? Did you hear her talk about the Blue Face protest, or express any sort of political views?' Adam smiled, briefly, hoping the question didn't appear too pointed.

Natasha paused. She looked at the painting and then finally she turned to Adam. 'Well, she's young, isn't she? What's the point of youth if you don't squander it and have vehemently held political views? What's the quote? "If a man is not a socialist by the time he is twenty, he has no heart. If he is not a conservative by the time he is forty, he has no brain." Or something like that. Anyway, strong views and ideas are common in my world. Was she any different from anyone else? I don't know. Was she special or interesting? Definitely not.'

'But was she evangelical in her opinions?' Adam pressed. 'Was she radical? Did murder look like her style?'

'I wasn't aware she had a style,' replied Natasha sharply. 'Certainly not with those clothes! And what are murderers supposed to look like, anyway? Is there a murderous face? Murderous eyes?'

'Not in my experience.' Adam stood up, realising he'd probably asked too many compromising questions. 'Sometimes killers are attractive and charismatic, it just depends.'

'Who *does* stand to gain from Max Bruce's murder?' Natasha said. 'There's always his family. They're a very nasty bunch.'

Eighteen

It was just after 3 p.m. the following day when Adam finally made it back into Stag Court. He'd been defending a licensing case at the architecturally depressing Croydon Magistrates' Court. He was feeling quietly elated at having managed to defend a large bar group owned by a fearsome Rottweiler of a woman from Stoke, whose company had been caught selling alcohol to underage teens. But given that one of the experts in the trial couldn't tell the difference between a fake and a real ID, how was a barman in the half-light of a packed pub supposed to be able to tell the difference? The Stoke owner had been so delighted to have her licence returned that she'd given Adam a huge, suffocating hug on the steps of the courtroom.

He was starving as he walked up the steps into Stag Court. He'd yet to crack open his increasingly soft and soggy meal-deal sandwich, which smelt like a wet dog every time he opened his bag. Walking towards Tony's desk, his slight smile disappeared on seeing the vision that was Jonathan Taylor-Cameron, half perched, one leg swinging, his pale pink socks visible from below the leg of his Savile Row suit. Even from two feet away, he reeked strongly of the Marlboro Gold he'd recently stubbed out between the cobbles outside, and the fruity aromatics of his cheeky lunchtime Shiraz.

'Green.' He smiled wolfishly, shooting him with his index finger and a click of his back teeth. 'Looking forward to the case?' He rubbed his hands together. 'The Crown versus Blue Face . . . I hear there's going to be a massive media scrum outside the Bailey. I'm getting ready for my close-up.'

'You'll need a haircut then,' quipped Tony, pushing a pile of law books towards Jonathan's pin-striped backside, in the hope of edging him off his desk.

'What do you mean?' Jonathan frowned with indignation. 'I've just come from the barber's!'

'I'd ask for a refund if I were you.'

Adam glanced across and caught Tony's eye. It twinkled with amusement. He was clearly enjoying winding Jonathan up.

'Ignore him, Mr Green,' added Tony paternalistically. 'Anyway, how did the case go?' he asked as Jonathan removed himself from the table and marched off down the corridor, muttering to himself.

'Well.' Adam smiled. 'The judge found in our favour.'

'Excellent news, excellent,' said Tony, nodding. 'That's what I like to hear: another one for Stag Court. Lucrative as well, excellent news. That solicitor called for you, Nisha – the patron saint of lost causes – she said your mobile was off. She left you this message.'

He handed over a folded piece of paper, as Adam took his phone out of his pocket. It was indeed off. Again. He must have forgotten to turn it on after he'd come out of court.

'Thanks,' said Adam, opening up the folded paper as he walked down the corridor towards his room. Was there any reason for Jonathan to be so annoying? It was highly unprofessional of him to turn the Blue Face case into some sort of inter-Stag Court competition. He was prepared to wager that while Jonathan lunched with his chums in the hall at Inner Temple, poor Georgina was eating *al desko* and doing all the work.

He called Nisha's mobile.

'Adam! What's wrong with you? Since when did you become so hard to reach?'

'I'm sorry.'

'This is a quick one. I was thinking maybe we should find out a bit more about Mr Bruce himself?'

'I had an interesting conversation at the Royal Academy yesterday, and met the person who put the exhibition together.'

'The curator? Good! Natasha Fitzjohn. I mean, does Max Bruce even have a connection to the Blue Face protest? A visit to his studio might be helpful? Because frankly, the PTPH is fast approaching, and we need to come up with something. With all the Home Secretary stuff, they're keen to get this done as quickly as possible. And it's looking a little hopeless for Lexi at the moment. Check out the family. Talk to all Max's wives.'

'There are only two of them.'

'It's so typical of posh people: they always want more of everything. Why have one wife when you can have two? The studio's in Notting Hill.'

Adam grabbed a pen from his desk. 'What's the address?'

'You'll find it.'

*

The sun was finally shining when Adam arrived at Notting Hill Gate. It was a Friday afternoon, and the pavements were packed with tourists, all shuffling along the unfamiliar streets, staring up at signs, all searching for the same 'world-famous' Portobello Road, with its antiques market and mountains of second-hand clothes stalls, where fashion students competed to find the best pre-loved designer clobber. Adam followed them, also unsure of where he was supposed to be going, or indeed what he might ask when he got there.

Following the map on his phone, he walked past the rows of tiny Georgian cottages, covered in wisteria or climbing roses, all painted in bright pretty colours like boiled sweets. Then finally on the corner, opposite an antiques shop whose window groaned with treasures, he came across an imposing shiny black wooden door, and a wide oblong buzzer with the name BRUCE written on it in large capital letters.

He pressed it. No one answered the intercom, but the door miraculously opened.

Through the arched doorway was a cobbled courtyard. On one side was a tall building with two large windows that ran almost the full length of the upper floor, through which Adam could see the sky, skylights and the industrial metal girders that were supporting the roof. The old stable door was open, and it gave on to a staircase, down which rolled the heavy base of hardcore reggae music and the distinctly strong, sweet odour of marijuana.

'Hello!' Adam called out. 'Anyone here?' There was no reply. He started to climb the stairs, feeling awkward and out of place in his suit and tie and lace-up leather shoes. 'Hello!' he repeated as he came up the chipped white-painted wooden stairs.

'Up here!' came a male voice.

There was the sound of heavy boots on a wooden floor as they approached the top of the stairs.

'Oh,' said Loughton looking over the banister. 'Are you the dealer?'

'No, I'm the lawyer,' replied Adam.

'Oh,' said Loughton, looking a little disappointed. 'Well, you'd better come in then . . . Mums!' he yelled, over his shoulder. 'The lawyer's here.'

'A lawyer?' queried an imperious voice. 'Did anyone order a lawyer? I'm not sure we asked for one of those, darling!'

On the top floor of a converted mews house, Max Bruce's studio was something to behold. Light, airy, with high ceilings and expansive walls, it smelt of oil paints and turpentine, mixed with the marijuana, and was completely, overwhelmingly intimidating. Adam could feel his palms sweat, as he was taken straight back to being a self-consciously stiff teenager who appeared to have gatecrashed the coolest party in town.

There were glasses everywhere, half full, half-drunk, red wine, white wine; some were full of fag butts, others had been used to extinguish half-smoked joints. There were canvases propped against the walls. Some appeared to be finished, others had barely begun to emerge from the thick layers of paint that were smeared everywhere. There were two chaises longues placed perpendicular to each other to form a right angle, upon each of which was lounging a wife. They were both still dressed in black, like characters in a Chekhov play, each one holding a flute of what appeared to be champagne. Despite the sunshine and the stream of light pouring in through the skylights, the air hung thick with the fug of cigarette smoke.

'So you're a lawyer?' quizzed Camilla, peering out from beneath her black turban, which was tied at the front like a Quality Street.

'Not the dealer then?' Elisa slumped back onto her grey velvet button-back divan with evident disappointment. Her red lipstick was a little smeared.

'I love lawyers,' declared Camilla, sitting up and lighting a cigarette. 'They're such fun! Bossy, and in charge, and wearing those fabulous little wigs!' She exhaled a long plume of smoke that hit Adam straight between the eyes. 'How can we help?'

'Um, well, I'd like to talk about the other night, if that's alright?'

'Loughton!' Camilla snapped her fingers. 'Don't be so bloody rude, get the man a drink and a chair. What did you say your name was?'

Adam was given a high, hard stool to perch on and a mug of red wine, which he held like a cup of tea, without taking a sip, as he listened intently to Max's wives describe exactly what had happened at the gallery, watching as both of them expanded on how 'frightful' the whole thing was.

'It must have been a shock?' asked Adam, addressing his question to both of them.

Within a few minutes of Adam's questioning, both Camilla and Elisa appeared to relax, leaning back on their individual divans. Between sipping their drinks and lighting more cigarettes, and gazing up at the ceiling, as if in a therapy session, they shared with Adam what it was like to be part of the best-known, most bohemian throuple in the country.

'There's jealousy, of course there is,' acknowledged Camilla.

'But after a while one gets over that, doesn't one? One has to. Max was such a generous lover.'

'Oh, he was,' purred Elisa.

'We had very little to complain about. He was addicted to his work, obviously – most great artists are. But we had parties, so many parties. Loughton was conceived at a party, weren't you, darling?'

'So I've been told, a thousand times. Have you got any money? Mum?'

'I'm out of readies, darling,' Camilla declared.

'Mum?' he asked Elisa.

'Oh, it's there,' she replied airily pointing towards a bag on the floor.

Loughton sauntered over, rifled through Elisa's pretty beaded bag and pulled out, much to Adam's astonishment, four crisp fifty-pound notes.

'Thanks, Mum,' he said, folding the pink notes in half and shoving them into the back pocket of his baggy jeans. 'I just can't be bothered to go to the cashpoint,' he said, catching Adam watching him. 'I'm good for the money,' he added. 'I've got shitloads in my account.'

'Right,' said Adam.

'I'm an influencer.'

'I have never really understood what that means . . .' Adam was genuinely curious. 'How does it work?'

'Well, I influence.' Loughton shrugged.

'He gets paid for pushing products on social media,' interrupted Camilla, draining her flute of champagne. 'He's got someone who does all that boring stuff for him . . . Be a love, darling, and fill that up, will you, before you pop out?' Loughton duly obliged, while she held out her glass. 'He's doing very well at it, aren't you, darling? Very successful.' She nodded. 'And he has his sauce business.'

'Dragon Slayer.' He sniffed. 'I expect you've heard of it?'

'It's very hot,' hooted Elisa. 'In more ways than one!'

'It sounds it,' agreed Adam.

'He's considering branching out into the Deliveroo business, too,' announced Camilla. 'Posh delivery,' she added quickly. 'What's it called, darling?'

'Pukka-roo,' said Loughton. 'You know, as in pukka, meaning "cool"?' Adam smiled weakly. 'It's a working title,' Loughton explained. 'I've got meetings, backers, money. What I don't have is time. I'm time-poor.' He sighed, in huge sympathy with himself. 'What with all my art, my graffiti . . . and that. You're a barrister?' He looked Adam up and down and then sniffed. 'I was thinking of doing that. I quite fancy the standing up in court bit, although I'm not sure about the wigs.'

'No,' agreed Adam.

'Do you have any idea why she did it? That girl?'

'Well . . .' Adam smiled briefly.

'I mean, the thing is, I was quite pro them lot before – before they did that to my dad. I mean, who is pro-war? We're all anti-war, aren't we? And I thought the blue paint protest was clever. I followed them and liked their stuff. I've even retweeted them and put them on my reels. Not anymore. I hate them . . . I hate them so much for what they've done.'

'I'm sorry.'

'That's what everyone says. And it doesn't mean shit.'

Loughton kissed both his mothers on their cheeks and hurled himself down the stairs at a foot-stamping pace. Where was he going in such a hurry? Maybe the dealer was waiting for him further down the street? Adam continued to sit on the hard stool, while Elisa's head nodded in time to the music and Camilla's left eye closed slowly and languidly with intoxication. Perhaps he should leave? Maybe he was intruding on their grief, their mourning, such as it was. But then he remembered that both Nisha and Morris had trusted him to ask questions.

He coughed to clear his throat.

'Tell me, what do you know about the Blue Face protest? And did Mr Bruce have any dealings with them?'

'Cerulean,' said a man's voice. Adam turned. 'It's not blue. It's a certain type of blue. And they use the same cerulean blue each time. It's a trademark, a tag, I suppose . . . I'm Stan.' The man walked towards Adam and held out his hand. 'Max Bruce's assistant.'

Adam shook Stan's hard, calloused hand. The skin on his palm was rougher than a cat's tongue, toughened by years of graft. Dressed in a white T-shirt and ripped paint-splattered jeans, Stan was all muscle. He smiled briefly to reveal the sort of white teeth you only ever saw on a return flight from Turkey.

'Stan!' Camilla waved from her sofa. 'Do help us out. This man is asking us questions about the Blue Face gang. Did Max have anything to do with them? Stanny knows everything.' She was slurring a little. 'He's looked after Max for years . . . How many, darling?'

'Ten years.'

'There you go, ten years of getting Max's paints for him and rolling his cigarettes and making sure there's enough wine in his glass and getting rid of the models after he's painted them. Help the man, Stan. Help him!' She waved a finger at him.

Adam climbed down off the stool and put down his mug of wine.

'I am not sure why the gang chose him,' said Stan. 'Max had nothing to do with the war or Khandistan. He had no dealings with them. If he did, I'd know. I was with Max every day for the last ten years. My job was to organise things for him before he even knew he wanted them.'

'Pre-empt his thoughts?'

'Er, yes. I'd know he'd want an ochre oil before he did, and that was my job: to sort his paints, to keep the studio nice, to make sure the kids didn't use it as a dump, or a party flat, or whatever. So if the gang had contacted him, had blackmailed him, or bothered him before, I'd know.'

'Thank you,' Adam said. 'I am sorry for your loss,' he found himself saying. For the more Stan spoke about Max, the greater the melancholy on his face. 'I should probably leave,' he suggested.

'Let me walk you out.'

Adam said his goodbyes to the two prone wives and followed Stan down into the cobbled mews yard and out into the street.

'They're a mad lot,' said Stan, with a wry look on his handsome face. 'The question I'd ask myself if I was you is: who inherits Max's 26-million-pound fortune? That's what they say he was worth when he died, or was murdered. Twenty-six mil. That's worth killing someone for, don't you think?'

Nineteen

Phone call

'Morning, Ads. How are you? How's the cough? Getting better?'
'Yes, thanks, Mum.'
'Oh, that's a relief, Adam, it really is. I've been worried. I have. I had a long chat about it with Brenda Hoffman the other day. She's obsessed with her health now that she's lost the weight – and *kept it off*. That's the thing, to keep it off. I bumped into her in the chemist and she had a basket of vitamins, a whole basket stuffed to the top. They're so expensive, Adam. I watched her spend over sixty pounds in one go. Who needs all those things? What you should really do is eat properly. An apple. Some greens. I'm very old-fashioned like that, as you know – but that aside, Brenda Hoffman did give me one tip which I thought I might pass on. She swears by these vitamin C things, fizzy tablets. You should get some of those fizzy tablets, Adam – if you're short of the apples and the greens, that is. That's what she says. She hasn't had so much as a sniffle for months.'
'I'll do that, Mum.'

'I can send them to you if you want? Also . . . when are you having a holiday? You need a proper rest. And I don't count that mini-break thing you went on to Bruges. Bruges, of all places. I don't even know where it is!'

'Belgium, Mum.'

'Belgium! Who goes on holiday to Belgium? It's not even hot . . . Anyway, I thought I'd just give you a call – have you seen your artist friend's funeral is on the front page of the *Daily Mail*?'

'He's not my friend. He's the victim.'

'You know what I mean. It looks amazing, the funeral. Everyone was there. The wives, the children, Joan Collins, Lorraine Kelly. It's on the cover, and pages four, five and six. I haven't read it all yet. I'm on my way to the hairdresser's. I thought I'd save it for then and talk to Lesley. Lesley loves a funeral. He always says that everyone looks good in black. He's very interested in the case, Adam. He asks me all about it every time I go in. How's it going? Are you alright? Not working too hard?'

'I'm fine, Mum, I am. I've just got a lot on my plate.'

'Your plate is always piled high, Adam; it's a worry. You know what I'm going to do? I'm going to get some brochures together tonight, holiday brochures. Cruises, packages, that sort of thing. What do you think about Spain, Adam?'

'It's a very nice country.'

'Good, that's settled. I'll look for some brochures and send them over to you. Maybe I can come over at the weekend and we can go through them?'

'That's sounds great, Mum. I've got to go. Someone's knocking on my door.'

'Don't forget the fizzy tablets, Adam . . .'

Twenty

'Have you seen this?'

Adam found it impossible to hide his astonishment as Stacey walked straight into his room holding an open laptop by the corner, while simultaneously clutching what appeared to be a giant matcha latte from Starbucks in her left hand.

'You've got to see this,' she continued, laughing and shaking her blonde hair out of her face. She slapped the computer down on Adam's desk and looked for somewhere to dump her hot drink, before deciding to use a pile of files in front of her. 'OK here?' she asked, plonking it down before he could say anything. 'This is the best thing I've seen in ages.' She turned the open computer towards Adam and, bending over, started to scroll with her fingers. She was standing right next to him, her arm brushing against his. She didn't appear to notice how close she was, how much she was invading his space. Adam moved away. Her overfamiliarity was disconcerting. 'Come in closer,' she said. 'You can't see from there.'

Tentatively, Adam leaned slightly forward. She smelt of soap and lemons.

'Look!' she said. 'Look at the wifies!'

'What is this?'

'*Hello!* magazine. Online. Sit.' She pulled up his chair, and pushed her laptop in front of him. 'It's gripping. So, if you look through, you can see the whole thing, blow by blow. Max Bruce being buried at Highgate Cemetery along with all the greats. I looked it up. Karl Marx, Michael Faraday, Jeremy Beadle, whoever he is – they're all there. We should go, Adam, go and visit. I love a cemetery, particularly a Victorian grave. The rich ornate ones with archangels, and the shabby poor ones. "Even in death they were not divided . . ."' She paused. 'Anyway, look: the wifies are having a grief-off.'

Adam looked at Stacey, with her bright blue eyes and her fizz of hair, in total bewilderment. She was a few years younger than him, but her zest, her energy, the way she took nothing (or at least, very little) seriously and seemed to dance through life . . . it was so beguiling, charming, refreshing – and intimidating.

'Who's the saddest? Who's waving their handkerchief the most? Which wifie won, do you think?'

Adam scrolled through the photographs himself. Camilla and Elisa were both wearing large black hats with impenetrable black veils. Appearing in every photograph like a couple of gothic beekeepers, the only thing truly visible was each of their black gloved hands, which appeared to be clutching white lace handkerchiefs. There were more photographs of Max's myriad children, all in various stages of skater-park chic. Loughton was the only one who was dressed in a suit. He'd teamed it with a black shirt and tie and looked remarkably like a member of a boy band at an awards ceremony.

'Is that Pippa? Jonathan's Pippa?' Stacey squinted. 'It is! I recognise her. I saw her in the back of a taxi with him the other day and I never forget a face. She's wearing Alaïa. Wow.' She stepped away from the computer in admiration. 'No wonder Jonathan's broke – that's over two thousand pounds' worth of frock. Unless she bought it herself, of course, which is perfectly possible.'

'How do you know how much the dress costs?' asked Adam.

'It's Alaïa – everyone knows they cost about that much.' She looked at his confused face. 'I may be skint, Adam, but I can still read *Vogue*. Or even better, flick through someone else's copy.' She smiled and looked back at the screen.

'Who's that?' asked Adam. 'The man in pink?'

'I've no idea.' Stacey moved closer for a better look. 'Who wears pink to a funeral?'

'It's a bit bright,' agreed Adam.

'It's like they're celebrating the man is dead. Weird.' She looked again. 'No idea who that is. Oh, hang on, I think he's some sort of artist . . . Which one is your favourite nepo child?'

'I didn't know you were supposed to have one?' replied Adam.

Turned out Stacey was the font of all knowledge on the nepo children: she knew her Biscuit from her Jade, her River from her Wolf and her Wizard but mostly she appeared to know a lot about Loughton, and most especially about how badly his business was going. Brand Loughton, it seemed, had lost some of its lustre.

'That sauce – it strips anything, everything, even the enamel off your teeth and the silver off your stainless-steel pans. Never cook with it. I mean, God knows what they put into it. *No one* wants to buy it. It's always covered in those yellow discount stickers every time I go into Aldi. Also the name: Dragon Slayer, what the hell does that mean? It's hot enough to kill a dragon? Or it's making such a loss you need to kill your dad?

Which reminds me – the will's got to pay out soon, hasn't it? The twenty-six million? Or however much it is. I bet it isn't that much. They always throw these huge figures around, don't they? Fifty million, thirty million. And then you find the whole lot put together is a pathetic three million. Don't get me wrong, I'd love three million. But it's not fifty, is it? Are you alright, Adam? You haven't said a word . . .'

If he could get one in edgeways that would be good, he thought. She talked more quickly than his mother.

'How do you know all this?' he asked, incredulously.

'Twitter, Popbitch, TikTok, the *Daily Mail* sidebar of shame.' Adam looked at her with even more incredulity. 'Don't knock it, Adam,' she added, as she snapped the laptop shut. 'Life's not all books and briefs. You can learn all sorts of useful stuff on those sites. Like where the Duchess of Sussex gets her shoes – Aquazzura, since you ask.'

She walked off out of his room, leaving her cold matcha latte behind. Adam was about to pick it up and run after her. But what would he do when he gave it to her? No one wanted an old, cold drink. He could ask her out for another drink? He'd really enjoyed the last time, even if his head or his liver had not. That's what I'll do, he thought. I'll her ask out for a drink tonight. He was free tonight. He was not due in court until late tomorrow, and that was only a speeding case. The last time he'd done one of those, the police had never bothered to turn up and the magistrate had thrown the whole thing out, and it had been a gigantic waste of everyone's time and money. Tonight then.

He sat down at his desk feeling upbeat, breezy even. It was decided. He might possibly ask her to go back to the Last

Judgment, though he'd avoid the cocktails this time. His mobile went and he looked down at the number. He didn't recognise it. He hesitated.

'Hello?'

'Adam Green? This is Stan from the other day. Max Bruce's assistant. I was wondering if you were free tonight. For a drink, and a word?'

'Oh? Um . . . of course,' replied Adam, surprised by the sudden wave of disappointment that engulfed him. 'Where would you like to meet?'

Stan had chosen to meet at 5.30 p.m. in a well-hidden half-timbered pub in Soho, the Old Red Lion, in a pedestrianised side road off Wardour Street. Despite the golden light of a summer's evening and the gentle warm breeze outside, the place felt dank and a little dismal when Adam walked in. The brown carpet was tacky underfoot as he approached the bar. Its dark wood didn't shine, no one had buffed or polished it in months, and the air hung cold and inert. It smelt of spilled beer and brick-dust. This was clearly one those places that the gastro-pub developers had somehow overlooked. Adam squinted into the darkness. The bar was hushed and silent; the only real noise was the pinging and the bleeping of the fruit machine, as one afternoon boozer chucked away all his spare change in the vain hope of a win. What a weird place, thought Adam, with an involuntary shiver.

'Over here!' Stan waved from a hidden corner. 'I've got you a pint.'

Adam nodded and smiled and walked over, squatting down on the small stool, by the equally low-lying table that already had two empty pint glasses on it and a bag of half-eaten cheese-flavour crisps, which lay spatchcocked in the centre of the table like urban roadkill.

'You're alright?' said Stan, looking up as Adam sat down. He had Adam's crumpled business card in his hand and it looked like he'd been fiddling with it for hours.

'I'm well,' replied Adam. 'How was the funeral?'

Adam immediately regretted his question as Stan's face crumpled, his blue-white teeth glowing in the dark, and he started to cry.

'I'm sorry, I'm sorry,' he said, raising a hand. 'I've been here for a while, I've had a few, but it's just got to me that he's gone. I thought I'd come to his favourite pub and have a quiet pint and remember him.'

'This was Max Bruce's favourite pub?'

'It's real, authentic, full of proper working people. That's what he liked, that's who he was – nothing like those squawking women he was married to.'

'Camilla and Elisa?'

'He couldn't stand them, and they couldn't stand him. I could barely look them in the eye at the funeral. Frauds, the pair of them, with their crying and their flapping handkerchiefs and their stupid outfits, parading in front of the press, hoping for one of those looking-sad close-ups. I wanted to push them both into the grave after him.' He smudged a tear across his cheek with a big square hand. 'Anyway, I just wanted to tell you, really, that they are all after his money, and there's a lot of it. Quite a lot. It's all squirrelled away, of course – there's a big palazzo on the coast in Sicily. It was a wreck when he bought it, and he and I would spend months at a time out there, drinking bottles of wine, eating pecorino cheese and peaches and painting the place in our shorts. The frescos he did there were beautiful. Nothing like the stuff you see here. Delicate pinks, blues, lilacs. And then everyone else would come and join us for the summer, and then the fighting and the arguing would begin. Too much booze, too much sun, one of them wanting sex, the other one not. He'd disappear off to some local girl in the village when he'd had enough of them all, I think Maria was her name. But' – he leaned in, a pleading look on his face – 'don't listen to what they say about him. They'll say he's an ogre. But he's not. He rescued me from a rough life. My dad was a scaffolder from Epping. He used to beat me around a bit and I was desperate to get out. Max met me at a party and asked me to work for him and my life changed forever. Ten years.' He sniffed. 'Ten years I slept in that studio. Ten years I chose his paints, I washed his brushes. I still can't believe he's gone.'

'I'm sorry.' Adam took a sip of his pint. Stan might have had a few jars that afternoon, but there was no doubting his sincerity.

'It's all about the will, I think,' he continued. 'They're rinsing through the cash. It only pays out to his "legitimate" children, whatever that means. The ones that are actually his? Or only the ones he's got with his first wife? Because, as far as I know, Elisa isn't actually married to him. She says she is. But she's not. Bigamy is against the law. You don't need me to tell you that! But they like to annoy people by calling themselves "the wifies". But Elisa's children, River and Biscuit, are out of the will. It's a mess, isn't it?'

Stan put his head in his hands. Adam continued to sit there, waiting to see if he wanted to share anything more. After a minute, with his face still in his hands, Adam realised that might possibly be it. He got slowly up off his seat and made to leave.

'Um, excuse me,' he said as he walked past the bar. 'I'm not really sure what to do.' He indicated to Stan, who had now slumped sideways on the brown velveteen banquette, apparently asleep.

'Oh, don't worry about him,' the broad hirsute barman replied as he dried a pint glass with a tea-towel; the buttons on his white shirt struggled valiantly to hold the garment together. 'Stan'll be alright. I'll wake him just before closing.'

Back outside in the sunshine, Adam checked his watch. It was only just gone 6 p.m.: just enough time to get back to Stag Court, pick up some files on the MOD case, read the notes overnight, and take them on the train with him tomorrow to Bexley Mags for the speeding case.

Walking up the well-worn steps into Stag Court, he saw Morris coming towards him, dressed immaculately in black-tie.

'Good evening,' he said. 'Forgive the attire,' he added with a wave of his hand. 'I'm off to the opera. *Così fan tutte* – not one of my favourites, to be honest, but a grateful client bought me a ticket months ago. I didn't have the heart to tell him I'm a Friend of the Royal Opera already and I normally sit in a box . . . Anyway, anything to report?'

'I've just come from a meeting with Stan, Max Bruce's assistant . . .'

As they both stood in the archway, with various clerks and barristers excusing their way in and out of the building, Adam talked Morris through his meeting in the dark and dismal pub, and his recent afternoon spent in the company of the wives and Loughton at the studio in Notting Hill. He reported the amount of money in the will, all twenty-six million pounds of it, how it was only apparently being left to the 'legitimate' children, whatever that meant. He told him that there was a window when the spray-can had been left unattended by Lexi in the gallery, when it could have been tampered with – or even replaced? Like for like? Apparently it was a cerulean blue, not a normal dull blue, and the Stop the War protestors always used the same blue. Adam looked at Morris's impassive face for any sort of encouragement, or affirmation, a flicker of emotion, some sort of eye contact with either eye.

'Right.' Morris nodded, giving absolutely nothing away.

'So . . .' Adam hesitated. 'So it could be Stan from Epping, with the scaffolder father? Rough childhood, history of being violently abused. He was very keen to paint the others in a bad light, as it were . . . no pun intended.' Adam smiled.

'No pun made,' replied Morris flatly. 'And I completely disagree about Stan. Stan was happy with the status quo. Stan was living and working with someone he loved and admired. Why would he want that to stop? Money? Stan might get some money in the will, but enough to murder his mentor? Absolutely not.'

'Well, how about—'

'You're looking in the wrong place, Adam. You have to think about who would really want Max Bruce dead. This isn't a crime of passion. Passion is not expressed in a spray-can. This is fury, anger. I won't say injustice, as that would put Lexi back in the frame. But this person thought about what they were doing and planned it, carefully. It's difficult to lace a spray-can. Buy cyanide. It's precise. It requires finesse.'

'Well, Loughton's business is in the red, he owes money, and he looks like he might have a drug problem, so he probably owes more money elsewhere too . . .'

Morris simply looked at Adam and laughed. It was the most disconcerting noise, like a succession of loud hiccups. 'Loughton is not capable of thinking through anything that complicated.' The odd laughter continued. 'I imagine he finds reading off a menu is a little too taxing. Remind me why Nisha asked for you personally again? As I, frankly, have no idea.' He patted Adam on the shoulder, still laughing to himself. 'Keep up the good work. I'd better go, or I shall miss the curtain.'

Adam leaned against the wall outside the entrance and sighed. Why had he opened his mouth? Why had he proffered up so many theories – all of them, apparently, useless? Why did Morris make him feel so utterly talentless? He had that terrible feeling of butterflies at the bottom of his stomach, and a tightness in his throat. The anxiety of imposter syndrome. He could feel it rising up through his body, taking it over. The last time he'd felt 'the fear' was in the first few days of his pupillage, when Jonathan, to his huge surprise, had announced to everyone at the Wig and Pen that Adam had, in fact, gone to Oxford University. He'd chortled with astonishment. 'Unbelievable!' he'd said. 'How is that possible?' And now it was back again. The panic, the sweat, the nausea. He breathed deeply. Morris was a results man, he thought. Results . . . So he'd better get him some.

'Stacey!' he declared as he turned to go back into chambers. 'You're still here.'

She laughed. 'For my sins.'

'I can't imagine what those would be,' joked Adam, feeling his face flush with immediate embarrassment.

'My mum could give you a list.' She smiled. 'Are you coming back in?'

'Picking up some files . . . I enjoyed our drink the other night, by the way,' he ventured. Georgina was walking down the stairs, carrying what appeared to be her own dry cleaning.

'We should do it again?' suggested Stacey.

'Do what again?' said Georgina.

'Oh.' Stacey swung round. 'I didn't see you there.'

'Do what?' she repeated.

'Have a drink,' said Stacey.

Georgina looked from Adam to Stacey and then back again.

'I'm amazed you have time for any type of socialising, Stacey.' She said her name slowly, chewing on each syllable. 'What with all the work that Jonathan and I have been giving you. I hope you've managed to go through Alexandra Williams's bank account transactions, for instance. We need to know what she's been spending her money on.' Georgina smiled tightly. 'By tomorrow would be good.'

With an audible sigh Stacey turned round and walked back into chambers.

Twenty-One

On the way back from his speeding case the following day, which had been predictably thrown out of Bexley Mags due to the lack of police presence or evidence, Adam's mobile rang. It was Bobby. One of his contacts had come through, but the window of opportunity was tight, and he needed Adam to get to the MOD now, right away, before the Right Honourable Jeremy May changed his mind. He was about to board a plane for a low-level NATO meeting in Brussels, and if they left talking to him until he got back, he might have changed his mind.

'I know you can do this, Adam,' said Bobby. 'I have every confidence in you. Have you got the files with you?'

'I do,' replied Adam. 'I've been reading them overnight.'

'I'm lucky to have you.'

Bobby hung up and Adam smiled with relief. He had about forty minutes to read through the pages he had in his bag.

Crossing the bridge from Waterloo station and walking down Whitehall Court towards the Ministry of Defence building and its entrance on Horse Guards Avenue, Adam was struck by the sheer enormity of the building and the institution that it represented. Situated on the same piece of land as the old Whitehall Palace, it was the sort of dominant, monolithic building that was designed to make even the most confident of men feel insignificant. With its Doric columns, expansive steps and large statues of earth and water, it reeked of power.

Adam walked into the glass atrium where a few people appeared to be having stand-up meetings around high tables, while perched, half-buttocked, on stools. Some were smartly dressed in full military uniform; others were in suits staring at screens. Adam approached the front desk, where a bank of receptionists with headsets and microphones were fielding the endless bleeps of the switchboard. He stood there for a minute, craning forward, trying to catch someone's eye before he was finally acknowledged.

'Yes?' asked a florid middle-aged man, smoothing a few strands of hair across the top of his head. 'How can I help you?'

'I have a meeting with Jeremy May?'

'Lord May has already left the building.'

Adam felt a sudden wave of panic. He wasn't late. He was in the right place. Surely he couldn't have missed the one person Bobby had trusted him to meet?

'Are you sure?'

'Of course I'm sure, I watched him leave about five minutes ago.'

Five minutes?

'Do you know where he went? Or when he might come back? I could catch up with him? If I ran? Which direction?'

He checked his watch and the giant clock behind reception. It was 2 p.m.

'I'm sorry, sir, I am not privy to that sort of information.' The receptionist smiled and tugged at his lanyard. 'This is the

150

MOD, I'm afraid. Nearly everything here is classified information, especially the movements of our staff.'

'Of course.' Adam's brain was whirring. What would he say
to Bobby? The case was tomorrow. There was no time left. 'Of
course.'

Holding his files and anxiously scratching his head, Adam
made his way back towards the glass atrium entrance.

'Adam Green!' A booming voice came from the bottom of
the stairwell. Adam stopped as the sound of leather soles on the
marble floor came tap-tap-tapping towards him as he turned.
'Adam Green?'

'Yes.'

'Jeremy May.' Out shot a smooth, slightly tanned hand, with
clean, clipped, filed nails. It took hold of Adam's; the grip was
firm, hard, and the shake was brusque.

Jeremy, Lord May of Sevenoaks, was immaculately dressed,
in a dark hand-tailored Savile Row suit, a crisp white shirt with
a pale blue tie in a perfect Windsor knot, complete with dimple.
He was wearing gold regimental cufflinks, and his shoes had
been polished so beautifully Adam could see the man's teeth
reflected in the sheen at the tips of his toes. Jeremy May had
graduated with the Sword of Honour from Sandhurst, and it
showed.

'Lord May,' replied Adam, removing his hand from the
increasingly vice-like grip.

'Jeremy, please.' He slapped Adam hard across the shoulders
in a manner that was more threatening than matey. 'Shall we?'
He indicated towards one of the empty high tables and perch
stools in the atrium.

Two other men, dressed in less well-cut dark suits, hovered

and hesitated. Jeremy wordlessly raised a palm in their general direction, without even engaging in any eye contact. They took a step back. This was clearly a private meeting.

'So,' he continued, placing a large black file down on the round plastic table. 'I think this is what you might have come for?'

'Oh, yes, thank you,' replied Adam, making to pick up the heavy file.

Jeremy's palm slapped down hard. 'Don't open it here. It's all the communiqués, the comms between the commanding officers and the MOD from the end of the war. I hope you find it useful. I've signed an affidavit for you so that they can be produced in court without me – I'm sure Bobby will understand . . . I don't need to be involved. I'm not a fan of a courtroom.' He grinned briefly, or did he actually bare his teeth? Adam could not be sure. 'Your lot are always rooting for the underdog, aren't they?' He grinned again.

Adam knew exactly what 'lot' Lord May of Sevenoaks was referring to. He was clearly one of *those* – the sort of man who would 'jokingly' call him a 'Red Sea pedestrian' after a few clarets, and would also be absolutely outraged if Adam didn't roar with laughter at his sublime and original wit. As if he hadn't heard the same joke a thousand times before. His lot. That lot.

'Us barristers, you mean? We simply can't help ourselves,' replied Adam, looking him straight in the eye. 'We're obsessed with the underdog. That's our job.'

'Of course it's your job,' Jeremy acknowledged. 'Anyway, I hope you find this little affidavit and the file useful. Anything for Bobby, obviously.'

'Thank you.'

'His father and my father were in the army together. Did he

tell you? Old friends.' He tapped the top of the file with his fingers. 'Very old friends. And now, if you'll excuse me. I have a plane to catch.'

Jeremy turned towards his suited and booted sidekicks and they both walked up towards him to escort him out of the building, leaving Adam still perched at the high table.

Adam exhaled. He wished he'd said something cleverer to Lord May. Something rude, or smart, or some sort of witty retort. But he'd been so taken aback by the casualness of it all. The truth of it was that prejudice resided in the most unlikely of places.

Picking up the hefty file, Adam walked slowly through the revolving glass doors and out into the fresh air and the sunshine. Standing on the pavement, blinking in the bright light, he suddenly became aware that he was being watched. It was an odd feeling of the panic of being stalked, hunted down like prey, and it suddenly reminded him of the Sorokin case and the ever-lurking evil presence of the Petrov Gang. Across the road, between the swish of passing cars, Adam could see a red-haired young man staring at him. He was there, and then he was gone. Adam looked left, looked right, then suddenly, there he was again, coming towards him, weaving through the traffic. Should he run? Confront him? Ask what he wanted?

A silver Mercedes with blacked-out windows suddenly pulled up in front of him and the back window slowly opened. Adam closed his eyes. He was surely about to be shot. The Petrov Gang had found him, and they were about to take their revenge.

'Good luck,' said a voice. Adam opened his eyes. Lord May was sitting in the back seat. 'I forgot to wish you good luck,' he said. 'Break a leg, or whatever they say in court. Do your darnedest to get our chap off, will you? There's a good fellow. We're all in this together, aren't we?'

And off sped the car and Lord May with it. Adam breathed a sigh of relief and quickly looked around, checking across the road. But the man with the red hair had gone.

Twenty-Two

It was just past eight-thirty in the morning when Adam's fetid Uber stopped at the entrance to Aldershot, where a bright yellow sign declared WELCOME TO ALDERSHOT GARRISON, THE HOME OF THE BRITISH ARMY. A soldier in full uniform holding a clipboard strode up and tapped on the driver's window, indicating for him to open it.

'Morning,' he said breezily. He craned his neck in through the window and looked towards Adam in the back seat. 'Can I have your name please?'

'Adam Green.' Adam tried to sit up and edge forward from behind the driver's seat. 'I'm here for the, er, court . . .'

'The court martial?' confirmed the soldier, with a quick nod. His face was distinctly less sunny, as he looked down at his list of visitors. 'The court martial,' he repeated before he firmly crossed off Adam's name, running his pen over it three, four, five times. He took a step away from the car. 'Do you know where you're going?'

'To the court martial centre?' replied Adam. 'I have a map.'

'Right.' He didn't smile. 'We're just going to have a look underneath the car.' Two other soldiers, their caps pulled low

155

over their faces, approached with large mirrors on long metal poles, which they ran slowly under either side of the car, checking for bombs.

Adam sat in the back of the car in stiff silence. It was a few minutes before a hand was slammed hard down on the roof of the car indicating they were free to enter the base.

Adam stared out of the window as they drove up towards the car park, where he'd been told to meet Bobby. He'd never been on an army base before, and he was astonished at how expansive it was. Home to about seventy military brigades, with a population of over 10,000, he'd had no idea what to expect. There were nearly 4,000 resident soldiers here, 1,000 transitory ones, there were over 700 MOD staff, plus dependents, as well as military families. He passed a sports stadium, playing fields, a health centre, cannons mounted on large shiny black wheels, and a fighter jet posed on immaculate clipped grass.

Over to his right there was a large group of soldiers on a parade ground, marching, pounding the ground with their boots, their arms swinging as if one, in time to the music of a brass band. A French horn, trombones and trumpets all gleamed in the pale morning sunshine. Adam watched as they stopped, turned, and continued marching back in the other direction, in their khaki uniforms, their maroon berets pulled down hard, towards their right eye. Adam felt excited and yet intimidated at the same time. This was a world he knew next to nothing about.

The Uber dropped him off on the patched-up tarmac of a half-empty car park. And there was Bobby, standing outside the metal-mesh gates to Aldershot court martial centre. He was waiting right in front of a large red-and-pale-blue sign with the golden scales of justice stamped slap-bang in the middle.

The court session didn't start until 9 a.m., but Bobby wanted to run Adam through a few things before the judge advocate arrived and introduced him to the defendant.

'Sorry I'm late,' said Adam, breaking into a jog as he approached.

'You're not,' replied Bobby. 'Not at all. I'm early.'

Adam shivered a little, as he pulled on his robe in the car park. His wig was sticking out of the top of his half-open bag, which he'd placed on the ground. He looked over at the court martial centre. It was not as well maintained as the rest of the base. With its municipal architecture, metal railings and the white-wood-and-glass front door, it resembled a neglected village hall that only opened on Thursday afternoons for the weekly Alcoholics Anonymous meeting.

'I have never been anywhere like this,' he said.

'I can never quite get used to these places either,' agreed Bobby. 'I haven't been here for a while. The last really big case I remember here concerned a pilot who refused to fight in the Gulf War. It was interesting. His argument was not that he was a conscientious objector, but that the war itself was illegal. He lost the case and was sentenced to eight months in military prison . . . Shall we go in and find a quiet corner?'

They walked through the glass swing doors and into the strip-lit corridor lined with red plastic stacking chairs with black metal legs. Bobby made his way towards what looked like a coffee machine.

'Do you want one?' he asked. 'Before we go down and meet our boy? Black? White? I am not sure there is much of a choice.'

'White, please,' replied Adam, searching in his pockets for some change.

'Don't worry,' said Bobby. 'I've got it.'

They watched as the machine spat out a thin, white ribbed plastic cup, followed by what looked like a soil sample, a shot of tepid water, and a squirt of milk. A weak coffee aroma with a backnote of sour milk wafted up from the cup. Adam felt a wave of nausea catch the back of his throat.

'Thank you,' he said tentatively, as Bobby handed him the cup. It felt barely warm in his hand.

'You don't have to drink it, Adam. It looks institutional . . . Why don't we sit over here for a second.' Bobby pointed to two red plastic seats, side by side just opposite the coffee machine.

'Great,' said Adam, opening up the heavy file. 'So, you've read Lord May's affidavit and seen the files?'

'I have, I have.' Bobby nodded, giving nothing away, as he leafed through his papers. 'We've got Wickstead.'

'Judge Wickstead?' Adam heard himself fumble the words.

'No, Adam, the fashion designer Emelia Wickstead. My wife loves her clothes. But sadly she isn't a judge advocate general like Her Ladyship . . . Are you alright, Adam? You seem to have gone a little pale.'

Adam took a sip of his lukewarm coffee. He grimaced; he could barely swallow it. It really was as revolting as it looked.

'You're not worried about the Sorokin case, are you? That was a long time ago. Well, long enough – and anyway, I'm sure she won't remember.'

'Which bit do you think she won't remember? The bit when I was accused of putting words into the defendant's mouth, or the bit when you had to beg her not to report me to

158

the Bar council? Or the bit when she asked me into her room and then all but disbarred me . . .? I'm sure she'll have forgotten all of it.'

'Is this the first time you've had her since that trial?'

'Yes, it is.'

'She's a very fair judge, Adam, and she's honest as the day is long.' Of course she is, thought Adam. 'She's fair, balanced, she listens,' continued Bobby. 'You'll be fine. Anyway, it's a very different atmosphere in a military court. It feels less formal, mainly because the surroundings are.' Bobby looked up and down the corridor with its curling grey carpet squares. 'It's as if we've all been thrown together in a leisure centre off the Kilburn High Road, but oddly the jury are in uniform.'

The door to the building slammed shut and Adam and Bobby look up to see a slim elderly man in a brown pinstriped suit that glinted with grease patches; his trousers stopped a little too short of his comfy shoes.

'Mr Mann,' said Bobby, putting out his hand. 'Nice to see you again. Adam, this is Lance Corporal Sutcliffe's solicitor, Brian Mann. Brian, this is Adam Green, from Stag Court, who is working alongside me.'

'Nice to meet you, I'm sure,' began Mr Mann, proffering a clammy right hand. He shook Adam's hand softly and then coughed heavily into a well-used handkerchief he'd pulled out of his pocket. 'Good journey, I hope. You found the place alright, then?'

'Yes, thank you, Brian, I did,' replied Adam.

'Good, good.' He sniffed. 'Well, Lance Corporal Sutcliffe is in a cell at the end of the corridor.' He nodded, posting his handkerchief back into the pocket of his brown striped trousers. 'If you'd both like to make your way down here.'

Adam followed Brian Mann as he walked past him in a cloud of recent cigarette smoke and fermenting body odour.

Fifteen years. For murder. That's what Lance Corporal Sutcliffe was facing. 'Life' in a military prison. Adam had been to plenty of prisons but never to a military one. Well, there was only one – the Military Corrective Training Centre in Colchester, Essex. He knew prison for soldiers was tough. Adam had read up about it the night before. Up at 0600 hours, locked down at 1900 hours. Lights out three hours later. It sounded more like a prisoner-of-war camp, which ironically it had been. It had an 8 per cent reoffending rate, which was not surprising, as who would ever want to go back in there?

The stakes really could not have been any higher, thought Adam, as the keys clattered and the metal grilled door was opened by the guard to reveal a young man sitting at the table dressed in his military uniform, with cap, gleaming belt and shiny shoes. He leapt to attention as they walked in.

'Please, Lance Corporal – Danny. Please sit down,' said Bobby. The young man sat back down at the table and removed his cap, placing it next to him on the table. 'This is Adam, who is working with me. Adam, this is Danny.'

Adam was so shocked he could barely speak. Lance Corporal Danny Sutcliffe looked about twelve years old. He had pale eyes, a scattering of freckles across his nose, and was clean shaven, with the fresh, plump pink skin of a teenager. Adam was astonished that he'd ever been allowed to go to war, let alone be in charge of a weapon, or a tank. But according to his notes Danny Sutcliffe had joined the army six years ago, at the age of sixteen, and had worked hard and become a lance corporal, the lowest non-commissioned rank, one up from a private. His job had been to lead small teams, supervise privates and set an example. His duties could vary from gunner to mortarman, signaller to driver. And yet, on the fated day in question, he'd been in charge of a tank.

He looked terrified.

'Mr Green,' he said with a nod.

'Hello,' said Adam.

'Shall we sit down?' asked Bobby, scraping a red plastic chair across the floor. It made a desperate moaning noise, which augmented the tense and depressing atmosphere.

'So, I presume, Mr Green – Adam – you are across the brief?' asked Brian, in his nasal voice.

Bobby shot him a look. 'You presume correctly, Brian . . .' He paused and inhaled with irritation. It was obvious to Adam that Bobby and Brian were not the best of friends. 'So, Lance Corporal Sutcliffe, I just wanted to ask if you have any questions before we go into court?'

'Is my mum here?' he asked, his grey eyes darting from Adam to Bobby and back again. 'I really hope she is. I haven't seen her in ages. I'll be fine if she's here with me in court. She knows how to calm me down. I called her every day when I was in Khandistan, every single day. All I need to know is that she's here, even if I can't talk to her.'

'She is here,' said Brian, before coughing loudly into his handkerchief. 'I saw her earlier in the car park.'

Danny smiled. 'You did? That's good. Did she say anything?'

'No, she did not,' replied Brian.

'It's just her and me, you see,' he said to Adam. 'It's always been just her and me. Dad left a long time ago.'

'That's good to hear that she is here then,' said Bobby. 'A bit of moral support. Now, we've been through the process a few times, Danny, but just so long as you are sure what is happening. The prosecution will set out their case and call their witnesses . . .'

'They can say what they like,' said Danny, 'but it wasn't my fault. None of it. You ask any of the lads that were there, any of the band of brothers, the boys in my unit, and they'll tell you what happened. We were a good group of good boys doing what we were told. I miss them, I really do. Once you've been through that together you never forget them. We're joined forever . . . But I'm innocent, I swear. You have to believe me. I didn't do anything wrong. Nothing.'

'I know,' agreed Bobby. 'Trust me. Don't worry.' He leaned over and touched his arm. 'I'll see you in there.' He smiled.

Back out in the corridor, Adam and Bobby were sitting by the coffee machine waiting to go into court, when the wooden-and-glass door slammed again and two robed barristers walked towards them. Both men, both wigged, both smiling as if the scent of victory was only a few hours away. Not that either of them would be vulgar enough to mention the word 'victory', but there was something smugly confident about the pair of them as they wafted their way towards the coffee machine.

'That's Alexander Newbury and George Beaumont from 15 Bedford Row,' whispered Bobby. 'I have never appeared against either of them before. Newbury is supposed to be excellent, if a little verbose, and Beaumont – who knows. He's fresh off the blocks. Gentlemen,' said Bobby, getting out of his chair. 'Good morning.' He smiled. 'This is Adam, who I am sure you know – Adam Green. Oh, no, stop! I would wholeheartedly *not* recommend the coffee.'

Fifteen minutes later Adam was sitting next to Bobby in the airless courtroom, which indeed did have the feel of a hastily arranged meeting in a leisure centre. Devoid of panelling, galleries, throne-like chairs and carved jury benches, it was hard to believe that this brightly lit room that smelt of sour milk and boot polish could be a venerable enough venue to decide the fate of a young man. Adam watched as the jury filed in. Soldiers and officers. Adam was not well versed enough in the nuances of their uniforms to work out who was more important than whom. There were six of them in all, two women included. Each of their faces was entirely inscrutable. Unlike a civilian jury who itched and scratched, and moved around in their seats, looking up at the ceiling, mouths ajar, gawping, glancing around the public gallery, taking in their surrounds, this group – known as the board – all sat bolt upright, their hands on their thighs, staring straight ahead.

'All rise!' demanded a man in uniform.

Adam stood up and watched as Judge Wickstead swept in with her black silks billowing behind her, her wig perched on top of her immaculate blonde bob that framed the sides of her emotionless face. She had hardly changed since Adam had last seen her. She still had the same sharp blue eyes and a similar shade of red lipstick. Yet somehow her glamour was a little incongruous in such drab surroundings. She sat down behind the pale pine desk with a small crackling microphone and tucked in her long black gown, like crow's wings. Adam watched her survey the packed room. The board, the barristers, Bobby, and then, eventually, him. Not a flicker of recognition was visible on her face.

'Be seated,' instructed the uniformed clerk. 'And please may I remind everyone to switch off their mobile phones.'

No one from the board moved. In fact, the only person who did take out their telephone was Judge Wickstead, still the same large iPhone with a pink cover and little pugs all over it, as incongruous as it was when Adam had first seen it.

Almost as soon as they'd sat down, the double doors to the court swung open and Lance Corporal Danny Sutcliffe was escorted in and led to the other side of the room. He sat down at a table, with the board opposite, his pale grey eyes dancing around the room, apparently looking for his mum. A flicker of a smile ran across his face as he spotted her to the left of the board. Slim, with blonde cropped hair and dressed in a dark blue anorak, she nodded at him over and over, as if to reassure him. He nervously licked his lips as he glanced up towards the back of the court, at the rows of officers, sitting stiffly, their chests decorated with lines of medals. Behind them sat another group of men in civvies.

'Who are they?' asked Adam, turning and whispering into Bobby's ear.

'Spooks in suits,' he whispered back.

Lance Corporal Sutcliffe spoke once to confirm his name and for the rest of the morning he sat behind the desk, his hands in his lap, his legs parallel and his head bowed. His mother didn't once take her eyes off him.

Alexander Newbury opened for the Crown. He stood up and fluffed out his robe. He picked up his brief and then, somewhat theatrically, he placed it back down on the table. He had this.

Coming out from behind his desk, he approached the board and placed his soft, pale hand on the table in front of them.

'Late in the afternoon of 15 January of this year, a young Khandistani boy died of suffocation. It was an appalling death. Miserable and degrading by anyone's standards. He was stuck in the depths of a British Army tank, without food, water, light and, most importantly, oxygen, as it drove endlessly around the suburbs of the capital city, Khandi. Unable to shout out, unable to cry out, starving, thirsty, terrified, in fear for his life – rightly in fear for his life. Timur, for that was his name . . . Let's never forget his name. Timur died the death of a dog in the hot, hungry, thirsty, airless obscurity of a British Army tank.'

Alexander Newbury paused, leaving the bleak image to hang like a shadow over the courtroom. He picked up his glass of water and took a long glug as if to emphasise the fact that Timur could not. Adam glanced down to see Bobby's right leg moving rapidly up and down. He was annoyed.

'How did he get there?' Newbury began. 'Timur. Why was he there? Who put him there? I will show the succession of events that led to the tragic death – the murder – of this young man. I will show you, the court, how Timur was arrested at the main hospital for stealing medical supplies, medical supplies for his mother.' Newbury paused, as if to contemplate the importance of motherhood for a second. 'His mother, who was desperately ill at home. A mother of eight children – eight little ones – she needed to stay alive to look after all of them. Their father had been killed by our forces two years before. But Timur was caught stealing foreign aid and he was thrown into the bottom of a tank by *this* man, Lance Corporal Daniel David Craig Sutcliffe.'

Even the board moved this time. A couple of heads twitched and turned to look at the accused, who continued to stare at the table in front of him. He was rocking slightly in his red plastic seat, almost as if the description, the story that he was listening to, was too painful to hear.

'Did Lance Corporal Danny Sutcliffe care what was happening to Timur? Of course not! Did he look after his prisoner? No, he did not. Did he follow due protocol? Did he even follow the basic rules? Rules so basic, so fundamental to what it is to be a human being, you don't even need to be a soldier in His Majesty's Army to understand them.'

Adam could feel Bobby seething right next to him, bristling with anger and irritation. Bobby was normally a placid, measured soul, but Adam knew his blood was boiling underneath his benign-looking exterior.

'But!' Newbury raised a slim finger. 'But it is our case that Timur was *deliberately* killed. That Lance Corporal Sutcliffe intended to end Timur's life: he is guilty of murder. Timur did not die due to neglect. It was not gross negligence. It wasn't a mistake. This was the deliberate action of an angry man who wanted revenge. Revenge for the death of his friend, who'd been shot and who'd died in his arms the day before. They'd signed up together, they'd served together, and now Lance Corporal Sutcliffe's friend had been killed, shot by a Khandistani militant. Now he wanted revenge, and what better way to let off steam than to pick up Timur and drive around the hot, dry streets of Khandi until he died? And do you know the worst bit of all of this? The loss of an innocent life, of course. But what you must remember is that Timur, who went to find medicine for his mother, was young. Timur was not a burly man who could possibly have posed a threat to a trained sol-dier. No. Timur, who died of suffocation in the bottom of a British tank, was only . . . ten . . . years . . . old. A child. A child of ten who was murdered by a British soldier, in the blind fury of revenge.'

He stopped and turned to look at Lance Corporal Sutcliffe who now had his head in his hands and was shaking it slowly, as he rocked in his seat.

'Even if you are not sure that Lance Corporal Sutcliffe intended to kill young Timur . . . You're not sure he is guilty of murder . . . It is the Crown's case, in any event, that what he did was, at best, highly dangerous. It is not disputed that a young man died. If you are sure that any reasonable person would know – sorry, *should* know that placing a person in the bottom of an airless tank could result in his death, then we submit that you should find Lance Corporal Sutcliffe guilty of manslaughter by gross negligence. However, just to be clear: it is the Crown's case that Timur's death was no accident.'

Clearly distressed by what was being said in court, Sutcliffe looked up suddenly and there were tears prickling his pale eyes; his cheeks were bright red. His lips were clamped together as he stared at Alexander Newbury KC. He obviously wanted to shout, blurt out or yell something, but instead he just carried on shaking his head, as his nose started to run and silent tears poured down his cheeks.

'Your Ladyship,' said Bobby, springing to his feet. 'I think we might ask for a comfort break? My client . . .'

He didn't even need to finish his sentence.

'Absolutely,' replied Judge Wickstead, getting to her feet. 'Of course.'

'All rise!' declared the man in uniform.

The whole court watched in total silence as Lance Corporal Danny Sutcliffe was swiftly led out by two soldiers through the double doors, only for his loud cries of despair to resonate all the way down the bright strip-lit corridor.

Twenty-Three

It took fifteen minutes for Bobby and Adam to calm down their client, who wept openly on Bobby's shoulder, while Bobby patted him gently and repeatedly on the back. Adam had seen Bobby in many situations, but this was the most paternal he'd ever witnessed him. After a series of deep breaths, with Bobby holding him by the shoulders, staring him in the eye and talking to him calmly and telling him to trust the process and calm down and believe in justice, Lance Corporal Sutcliffe was finally ready to go back into court.

'Is the Crown ready to call its first witness?' asked Judge Wickstead, as she pushed back a stray blonde strand that had broken free of her wig.

'We are, My Lady,' replied Alexander Newbury, bowing his head obsequiously at Wickstead, who seemed to flinch a little with annoyance. It was going to take a bit more than overt kowtowing to ingratiate him with her, Adam thought. Newbury then turned to face and smile at the top brass, who were sitting upright in their seats, waiting for the takedown.

The energy in the court was nothing like he was used to. It felt ruthless, gladiatorial even. Maybe it was the uniforms, or the fact they were all senior officers. A gang together. These people were used to making life-and-death decisions on a battlefield, and that's exactly what they were waiting for.

'The prosecution calls Private Barry Evans.'

Private Barry Evans was a short, rotund, red-faced fellow, who looked of similar youthful age to Lance Corporal Sutcliffe. He was carrying his cap under his arm and appeared nervous as he entered through the double doors. He strained his head a little towards the top brass section at the back, clearly checking who was in court. He deliberately avoided looking at Sutcliffe as he swore on the Bible, before sitting down heavily in his red plastic chair. He confirmed his name and rank and nodded, indicating he was ready for Alexander Newbury KC.

'Private Evans, how long have you been serving in the British Army?'

'Six years, sir. I was sixteen years old. Straight out of school when I joined.' He nodded as if pleased with himself at getting his first question right.

'And did you sign up at the same time as the defendant?'

'Yes, sir, we did. We trained together. Here, in fact, at Aldershot. We met here . . . I didn't know him before.'

'When were you posted to Khandistan?'

'We went at the beginning of this year, sir – 6 January, I think, or thereabouts. Just before the end of the war.'

'And what was it like?'

'What was what like?'

There was a ripple of amusement in the court. Private Evans looked around, tickled that he'd made a few in the court smile. He was clearly one of the jokers in the company, one of the lads at the back of the class who'd left school with limited

170

options. Judge Wickstead glared her disapproval: she was not entertained.

'Khandistan?' Alexander Newbury gave a swift nod of apology to Her Ladyship, before spinning round to engage with his witness. 'What was it like when you arrived in Khandistan?'

'Well, we were at war, sir, so we were on a war footing. It was difficult. There was shooting – you know, combat, people getting injured, general madness. The base was O K. That was more or less secure. So we'd do a tour during the day, and then come back and sit around, eat, sleep, play a bit of football in the desert, that sort of thing.'

'Was the defendant there with you?'

'Danny? Yeah. He was there.'

'What was his job?'

'He's a lance corporal, so . . . er . . . just above me, but his job was to lead us a bit, set an example, and, er . . . be the sort of go-between between the corporal and the rest of us privates.'

'What was he like? Lance Corporal Sutcliffe?'

'Danny? Oh, he's a nice guy, one of the lads, loyal.'

'Too loyal would you say?'

'Objection,' said Bobby, wearily. 'Speculation. How would Private Evans know about Lance Corporal Sutcliffe's depth of loyalty? And to whom?'

'If you could keep your questions to your remit that would be helpful,' said Judge Wickstead, with a curt smile.

'Apologies, Your Ladyship,' said Newbury. 'Did Lance Corporal Sutcliffe have any friends in the unit?'

'Danny had lots of friends in the unit. He was a popular bloke.'

'Did he have any close friends in the unit?'

'His best mate was Private Keith March. They signed up together – they were at school together. I think they might have even lived in the same street.'

'And what happened to Private March, on 14 January of this year?'

'Well, he was shot. Shot dead. He died in Lance Corporal Sutcliffe's arms.'

'How did that happen?'

'We were in a close-combat situation. It was the last days of the war. The actual last day, in fact. We were trying to clear a market square. There were these Khandistani rebels in the surrounding buildings – we didn't know this at the time – and we'd been given the all-clear to move forward by another unit ahead of us. So we walked straight through the empty market, thinking it was safe and sound, and Keith – Private March – took one in the chest, and the first person on the scene with him was him, Danny.'

Barry paused and looked across at Sutcliffe, whose eyes were glazed, as he rocked in his chair, staring into the middle distance, seemingly reliving the whole experience. Adam glanced across at Bobby, whose face appeared crumpled with concern as he scribbled down some notes on the pad in front of him. Barry then looked up at the back of the court towards the row of officers and men in suits.

'Danny tore off his scarf thing around his neck and tried to stop the blood, which was pouring everywhere. Coming through his hands, through his fingers and the scarf – there was buckets of it. Danny was screaming for medics on his radio, and so was I, and so was Private Brooks. We were all screaming.'

'How long did you wait for the medics?'

'Fifteen, twenty minutes. We yelled, making calls on our radios. But they never came. It was too late. We didn't need them in the end. Keith bled out, while Danny held him. He died in his arms.'

'And how was Danny after that?'

'Gutted.'

'How gutted?'

'Objection!' Bobby put his hand in the air. 'Speculation.'

'Overruled,' replied Judge Wickstead. 'Continue.'

'How upset, do you think, was Lance Corporal Danny Sutcliffe after the death of his closest friend? His closest friend who'd died in his arms?'

'Well, how upset would you be?' replied Private Evans, his eyes narrowing at the stupidity of such a question. He leaned forward and grabbed the edge of the stand. 'Would you be happy if you'd carried the limp dead body of your best mate across your shoulders, and put it into the back of a truck, sat next to him all the way back to camp, and then watched him go home in a black zip-up body bag?'

'This is not a question for me,' replied Alexander Newbury. 'It's a question about Lance Corporal Sutcliffe. How upset was he?'

'How upset? Danny? His uniform was still covered in his best friend's blood when he went out the next day. How do you think he was? He was absolutely devastated.'

'No further questions, Your Ladyship.'

Adam watched as Alexander Newbury swept back to his desk, fluffing out his robe as he did so, like a strutting pigeon protecting his breadcrumbs in Trafalgar Square. There was something about Newbury that the normally dispassionate Adam seriously disliked. Three rows back, Adam could see Danny's mother was quietly weeping and dabbing the stream of tears on her cheeks with a crushed tissue. Of course, Adam suddenly realised: if Danny had grown up with Keith, if they'd joined up together and had been at school together, she would have known the young man too. She blew her nose quietly and then caught Adam's eye. He looked away. It felt intrusive to be staring at her.

'Your witness, Mr Thompson,' announced Judge Wickstead.

Adam opened up his file and placed it on Bobby's desk, should he need it. But Bobby pushed it gently to one side. Standing up slowly, he took his glass of water and drank from it, draining half of it, and then put it back down on the desk as appreciatively as one might the first pint of the night.

'Private Evans?'

'Sir.'

'Is it right that you fought your way into Khandistan? You and your unit. Side by side for two long, hard, gruelling weeks through the desert, carrying all your own supplies, sleeping out under the stars, in fear for your lives?'

'We did, sir, yes.'

'Is it right there were fierce battles, skirmishes and sometimes even close hand-to-hand combat?'

'Yes, sir, there was.'

'And you took casualties?'

'Quite a few.'

'There was shouting and chaos and dust and heat?'

'Yes, sir.'

174

'Where were you born?'

'Rotherham.'

'So this was possibly a little out of your comfort zone.'

'You could say that.' Private Evans let out a quiet, wry laugh.

'But you coped.'

'Yes, sir.'

'Why do you think you coped?'

'Because we were trained for it, sir. For years. I'd done enough training in the army before I arrived to know what I was doing.'

'Ah, you were trained for it . . . You were trained to live in desert conditions, trained to march with heavy equipment through the sand, trained by the British Army to defend yourself and to fight?'

'Yes, sir.'

'Did you train to be a policeman?'

'No, sir.'

'Did you train to be a peacekeeper?'

'No, sir.'

'And yet, when the war was declared to be over, which it wasn't, and still isn't, but when the war was *declared* to be over, that's exactly what you were asked to become. A policeman and a peacekeeper. That is what you and Lance Corporal Danny Sutcliffe were ordered to become, isn't that right, Private Evans? Policemen and peacekeepers? Something you were absolutely not trained for.'

'No, sir. I mean, yes, sir.'

'How did that come about? How did you learn about your new roles – those of policeman and peacekeeper?'

'We had a meeting.'

'A meeting? One meeting?' Bobby's voice rose with incredulity. 'Or were there several?'

'Objection!' Newbury leapt out of his seat. 'Private Evans was not in charge. How is he to know how many meetings there were!'

'Overruled.' Judge Wickstead smiled coldly. 'Continue.' She nodded.

'How many meetings did you have?' asked Bobby.

'We had one at the end of the war.'

'One meeting, at the end of a war that is still going on, to turn you from soldier to peacekeeper?'

'That's correct, sir.'

Private Evans glanced quickly towards the back of the court. Adam turned round to see a barrage of steely-faced officers staring back at him.

'Right. And during this one meeting, what did you learn?'

'That we were to be peacekeepers.'

'And what is a peacekeeper?'

'Someone who keeps the peace?'

'And what is that?'

'Law and order?'

'And yet you were surrounded by chaos, mayhem, fighting, looting. You were in the final death throes of the war, with your comrades being shot, men still dying, it was anarchy, and your new job – the job you were utterly unqualified for – was to keep law and order?'

'I was doing my best!' Private Evans sounded defiant, irate, enraged, even. His voice was raised, and his already-red cheeks were even more flushed.

'Was it just you doing your best?' Bobby's tone was so measured and calm.

'No, sir, we were all doing our best.'

'You were *all* doing your best . . . No further questions, Your Ladyship.'

As Bobby sat down, the atmosphere in the court shifted. Lance Corporal Sutcliffe looked over, a breath of hope on his young freckled face. Even his mother had stopped crying.

'Well done,' Adam whispered. 'I think the board were listening.'

'We'll see,' mumbled Bobby, leafing through the pages on his desk. 'Aren't they calling another private next?'

'I believe so,' said Adam, looking down at his papers. 'Private Brooks, who was also present when Keith March was shot. They are doubling down on the revenge theory that Danny was avenging the death of his friend. Hammering the murder not manslaughter.'

Alexander Newbury worked Private Brooks's testimony well. He described the shooting of Private Keith March from the lone sniper in the market, the terrible wait for help that never came, the long journey back to camp with the corpse on the back seat of the truck with Sutcliffe still holding his friend's increasingly cold hand.

'How did that feel? Waiting for so long?' asked Newbury, placing his finger on his soft lips in an attempt to look caring.

'Like we was abandoned,' replied Brooks, a tough-looking chap in his thirties who'd clearly been around the block a few times.

'Abandoned, you say,' repeated Newbury, a concerned

expression still playing on his face. 'And the next day when you went out on peacekeeping manoeuvres, did Lance Corporal Sutcliffe look like he'd come to terms with his friend's death?'

'Objection!' Bobby leaned forward on the desk.

'You may answer,' replied Judge Wickstead.

'I would say no. Negative, sir.'

'No further questions.'

Next, Bobby took Private Brooks back to the beginning, to their arrival in Khandistan as an invading occupying force.

'Is it right, Private Brooks, to say, at the very least, that the lines were blurred? That it was, and, indeed, still is, a situation so complicated and so difficult that some of the best minds and most distinguished politicians of our age have failed to sort it out?'

'It was hard, yes, sir.'

'Confusing?'

'Confusing, yes, sir.'

'I mean, if the Ministry of Defence can't make its mind up about the rules of engagement, how are you, Private Brooks, or, indeed, how was Lance Corporal Sutcliffe supposed to understand them?'

'With difficulty, sir.'

'And in all this madness and chaos, was there a protocol to deal with looters?'

'Looters, sir?' He scratched his head and looked up towards the back of the court.

'Local people stealing. I imagine there was some sort of advice given?'

'Well, just stop 'em, sir.'

'Just stop them. Of course. In the chaos and the madness, you were ordered to stop the looting . . . No further questions, Your Ladyship.'

As Private Brooks walked slowly out of the court, staring down at the grey carpet tiles as he left, there was some movement at the back as two men in suits and a further two in military uniform all slipped out of the back door. Adam watched them as they left. None of them looked particularly happy about the last few exchanges.

Bobby sighed deeply as he sat down, his shoulders slumping a little.

'I think that went well,' whispered Adam, trying his best to be positive. 'The spooks in suits looked annoyed anyway.'

There was whispering from the other desk, as Alexander Newbury and his number two, George Beaumont, conversed.

'My Lady, there is an issue of law.'

'Could the board please leave while I deal with this matter?' said Wickstead.

Bobby and Alexander Newbury approached the bench.

This seemed unusual. Was the prosecution not bringing out its next witness? After Bobby's strong performance with Private Evans and Private Brooks, there didn't seem much point, thought Adam. But surely that would be a tacit admission of failure on their behalf? Adam couldn't quite hear what was happening, but both parties appeared to be nodding in agreement. Bobby returned to his seat.

'I understand that the defence is calling Timur's mother,' announced Judge Wickstead. 'And I also understand that for security reasons, and due to visa requirements and travel restrictions, Mrs Tadishvili cannot attend until later next week at the earliest. So this trial is adjourned for two weeks.'

Judge Wickstead ordered the defendant to be returned to the cells, and the court rose as she left.

'Jesus,' said Bobby as he leaned back in his chair on the South Western train to Waterloo and closed his eyes. 'And Adam, let me be frank here, as a good Christian I never call on the Lord, but today I need all the divine inspiration I can get. There's something in this case that does not make sense.' He opened up his files. 'Jeremy May's statement is not really worth the paper it's written on. Despite his good wishes and kind regards to me and my family, it says nothing.' He pulled out a thick brown file. 'And as for these communiqués . . .' He opened the file, which contained little more than pages and pages of row upon row of thick black lines. 'Over half of this stuff has been redacted.' He sighed with exasperation.

'I thought we could use some of it. There are a few legible lines about the recruits being "young and green" which might be helpful from the files?' suggested Adam. 'They were out of their depth, scared, that kind of thing. Sort of continue what you started today?'

'True,' nodded Bobby. 'We can use that, obviously. But we need something else. The army is a closed shop. I should know. They stick together, of course they do. They're very good at covering for each other's mistakes. No one likes a snitch. I mean, look at all those spooks sitting there in court today.'

'Were they supposed to intimidate the witnesses, d'you think?'

'I don't know.' Bobby shook his head wearily. 'But this man's future is on the line. You know I can argue my way out of most things . . .'

'You can,' Adam agreed with a half-smile.

'But it's hard to fight for justice when you have one arm tied behind your back. We need to keep digging. Go through all these communiqués again, such as they are.' He passed over the heavy file. 'With a fine-tooth comb, we'll surely find the needle we're looking for.'

Twenty-Four

It was past 6 p.m. by the time Adam got back to Stag Court. Bobby had had to run off to a hastily arranged meeting with an old friend who'd served in Iraq, but he'd said he hoped he might have some information on the troops in Khandistan. Adam was sitting in his room, leafing through the piles of redacted communiqués wondering how he could possibly glean any more information from such a heavily censored source, when his phone rang.

It was Nisha. In a hurry as usual, asking him to come to HMP Bronzefield first thing the following day. She'd secured a meeting and had been called by Lexi's mother, who'd said that she was worried about Lexi's mental health, having been in solitary confinement for so long. She was also apparently willing to talk and she was ready and willing to discuss what had happened that night in the gallery.

'Her mother's exact words were: "She doesn't want to be a martyr to the cause anymore, and nearly a month in solitary is enough to break anyone." So we have a meeting tomorrow morning at nine a.m. Sharp. See you there.'

'Tomorrow? But I am snowed under with this court martial – I have six months of communiqués to sift through,' replied Adam. His tension levels were rising by the second. He knew he shouldn't have agreed to take Bobby's case.

'Who's leading?' asked Nisha.

'In Aldershot? Bobby Thompson.'

'Well, a man that brilliant (no disrespect, Adam) can manage his own communiqués. He doesn't need you at all.'

Why did people always say 'no disrespect', thought Adam, just before they said something that meant or did exactly that.

'It was difficult today in court,' he replied.

'I am sure it was, but I am also pretty sure that Bobby can manage,' Nisha said, somewhat curtly.

Sitting at his desk, with the windows open to the evening's summer breeze, Adam could hear footsteps and laughter coming up from the lane below, as other barristers and clerks left their chambers for the night. They were possibly off to see friends, have some dinner, or a drink in a pub on the way home. He sighed and looked at the pile of files on his desk. Why was everyone else capable of a work–life balance except for him? he wondered, pulling out the other increasingly hefty file on the Lexi Williams case.

Nisha was clearly not taking no for answer, and he owed her. She'd got him on the case in the first place – she'd insisted on him, even when Morris had actively wanted someone else. She'd got him most of his big cases; in fact, truthfully, she'd got him *all* of his high-profile cases. He could not afford to irritate her, and he certainly couldn't afford to let her down.

They'd been colleagues or friends ever since he'd been called to the Bar. Loyalty mattered.

There was a knock at his door and Georgina walked in.

'I thought I saw you coming back to chambers out of my window,' she said, standing propped up against the door frame, carrying her soft leather Smythson briefcase, her Burberry mac slung over her forearm, her normally swinging auburn hair a little flattened by wearing a wig all day. 'How was your day?' She walked into Adam's room and flopped into the seat in front of his desk. 'Mine was a right bitch!' she proclaimed, with uncharacteristic frankness. 'Prudence and I have been at it all day, in that shitty little courtroom, the seventies extension to Inner London Crown Court in Borough. The "chocolate box", or whatever the hell it's called.'

'The *what*?' asked Adam, with a laugh.

'That's what they call it, apparently. It's freezing in winter and boiling in the summer, and needless to say, today it was sweaty like a sauna. It's got these hideous low ceilings and the walls are made of breeze blocks all painted white.' She pulled a face. 'It stinks of drains, and last time we were there there was a leak, with water pouring through the ceiling. Some poor sod was trying to stop it by catching all the rain in a wheelie bin.'

'And it's called the chocolate box?' Adam was now seriously confused.

'Oh . . .' She waved her hand exhaustedly. 'It's called the chocolate box because the outside of said glorious building is clad with brown tinted glass, which looks like the cellophane wrappers of old Quality Street. Or something. Don't ask me, I never eat the stuff. I can't bear chocolates unless they're Charbonnel and Walker.'

'What were you doing there?'

'The Blyth housing case? Do you remember? Poor tenants and bad housing and criminal council behaviour.' She yawned. 'I am exhausted and we're back in tomorrow. Prudence will get us across the line, of course she will. Blyth Council are spending a fortune. I can't help but think the money could be better spent elsewhere than covering their backsides for having evicted some 'difficult' tenants who complained, and turned out to be right, about potentially lethal levels of carbon monoxide poisoning in their flats. Anyway, do you fancy a drink?'

'I have so much to do,' replied Adam, suddenly feeling overwhelmed.

'You've always got so much to do,' she said. 'My desk is piled high with stuff I haven't looked at yet. One drink won't hurt. You can come back here afterwards. I'll even go to the Wig and Pen if it makes it any easier?' Adam was still hesitating. 'Do you know what they say about all work and no play?'

'Probably.'

'It makes Jack Nicholson go insane in a snow-bound hotel in the middle of nowhere.' Adam looked confused. '*The Shining*,' she clarified. 'One of my favourite films ever. I used to watch it all the time in my flat off the Cowley Road when I was at Oxford.'

'And there was I thinking you never left the library,' said Adam, standing up and taking his suit jacket off the back of his chair. He evidently was going for a drink.

'I rowed as well, you know. Up every morning, with the lark, as they say. These hands were once calloused.' She waved a manicured hand.

'Not anymore,' replied Adam, with a laugh.

'Come on,' she said, linking her arm in his with an easy familiarity. 'I'll buy you a pint of Camden Pale Ale.'

'A half.' He smiled.

'A half.' She smiled back.

At just after 7.30 p.m. the crowd in the Wig and Pen was beginning to thin out. Most of the clerks and the trainee solicitors had already gone home, or gone on to their next event of the evening. The Wig and Pen, like most of the hostelries in the area, was rammed between 5.30 and 7.30 p.m. with post-work drinkers, but was mostly empty after 9 p.m. – except during the run-up to Christmas, when frankly, anything could happen.

Georgina came back from the bar with Adam's half and what looked like a stiff gin-and-tonic, which she proceeded to all but drain before Adam had got his glass anywhere near his lips.

'How was the court martial?' she asked, leaning back against the teal wall, her elbow resting on a geometric-print cushion that was plumped in the corner. 'I read about the case in *The Times* this morning. There were photos of the lance corporal. He looked about seven years old.'

'He doesn't look any older in the courtroom,' said Adam, putting down his glass. 'It is a difficult case.' He sighed.

'I'm sure it is,' agreed Georgina. 'Also, the other problem you have is the little boy who died—'

'Timur.'

'That's him. His photograph has been used everywhere. With his big eyes, and his long eyelashes, he's like the poster boy for Stop the War.'

'And the thing is, I have so much paperwork to look through, all these army communiqués, and tomorrow I have to go and meet Lexi again.'

'Your girl has finally agreed to speak, has she?' Georgina laughed wryly, before finishing off her drink. 'It's taken her long enough. Her defence case statement hasn't been served yet and we've only got days to go before the pre-trial hearing. And so far she's said nothing. Absolutely nothing.'

'I wouldn't go that far,' said Adam.

'The witness statements are pretty damning. No one disputes that she had the spray-can in her hand or that she used it. We're hardly calling anyone. Her initial interview reveals nothing, it's just a whole lot of "no comment" garbage. So far she's only got the "it wasn't me" defence. I think the Crown have spoken to Nisha, haven't they, and told her the shortlist they're calling? Which is really short! It's probably time for you to put on your Holmes act. Get yourself a pipe and a deerstalker and get out there!' She laughed. 'Oh, don't look like that, Adam – everyone knows that in another life you'd kill to be a private detective. Adam Green, PI. It has a certain ring to it, don't you think?'

'Ha-ha,' Adam laughed weakly. 'But I should really be helping Bobby. The last thing I want to do is let him down.'

'Oh, Adam.' She smiled, her nose crinkling as if she were talking to a child. 'That's really sweet of you. But I am sure Bobby can manage without you. He doesn't need you to hold his hand, or his pen, or do his homework. He's a big boy, and possibly one of the best. You don't get to head up all those charities, or speak at all those after-dinner events, or even visit schools if you aren't brilliant. He'll be fine without you. Who's for the Crown?'

'Where?'

'In your court martial.'

'Alexander Newbury and some other young barrister, George Beaumont.'

'Beaumont? From 15 Bedford Row?' She laughed. 'God! I used to go out with his older brother, Walter. He's good. Good-looking. Took silk last year. Bit older than us.' She smiled. 'I imagine the younger brother's quite good too. Diligent, if nothing else.'

Adam leaned back on his stool. He was feeling overrun with anxiety. His palms were beginning to sweat, his legs were jittery. *He* wanted to be the diligent one; there was nothing he disliked more than not being on top of everything, not knowing his brief, or doing something half well. One of the problems of being a perfectionist was not being perfect.

'Adam, stop worrying,' Georgina continued. 'You're looking super nervous. Bobby really likes and rates you. I've heard him say as much.'

'When?'

'Too many times to remember.'

She was just being nice, thought Adam, which was also worrying. He much preferred it when she was being acerbic, or superior, or talking in that posh shorthand that he could never quite follow.

'Bobby thinks that the soldier, Lance Corporal Sutcliffe, is being framed. He's convinced that he's being used as a scapegoat and that there's some sort of conspiracy with the military that goes right to the top.'

'Well, there probably is.' Georgina shrugged and rattled the ice in her glass, looking for one last drop. 'I have never known Bobby to be wrong, have you?'

'No.' Adam shook his head.

'But listen.' She leaned forward, a strand of hair falling across her face. She looked striking, beautiful even, in the evening light.

'Yes?'

'It's all about the Blue Face case, it really is. I know you want to help Bobby, but the one you should really be concentrating on is Blue Face.'

'I do wish you'd stop calling it that.'

'Well, everyone else does. I suppose it creates too much of a visual for you guys, doesn't it.' She grinned. 'In which case, I'll be sure to say it as often as I can. But seriously,' she added, 'it's all about the Lexi Williams case. The press are going to go berserk – everyone's talking about it already and it's only the pre-trial hearing next week. It's madness. Even Jonathan's putting in the hours. You know, I have never worked so hard on something that looks like it's going to be over in two to three days max. We can't discuss it in detail, of course, but if I were you, I'd concentrate on that. Bobby can survive a day or two without you.'

She stood up and swung her expensive mac across her shoulders and flicked out her hair, running her hands through it.

'Bye,' she said, leaning over the small pub table and giving him a kiss on the cheek. 'I've got dinner at Scott's – nice bit of fish. See you tomorrow. Good luck.'

She swept out of the pub, leaving Adam sitting on his stool, still nursing the remainder of his half-pint. He stood up and drained his glass. He sighed and walked out of the pub and back towards Stag Court.

It was on the verge of growing dark, and in the narrow lanes on the way back to Stag Court it was harder to see where he was going. It wasn't long before Adam had that sudden feeling of panic mixed with paranoia. He knew this wave of fear well. It was as if he was suffering from some sort of PTSD. All it took was a suspicion that he was being followed – the tiniest thing, something moving quickly out of the corner of his eye – and the fear came sweeping in. He sped up. He could hear his own shoes clacking, smacking the pavement, and yet his ears were straining to hear if there was any movement behind him. He could his hear his own breath, his own heartbeat thumping in his eardrums. He walked faster. The footsteps behind him sped up. He didn't dare turn around. What if there was no one there? What if all this was in his febrile imagination? Had the stress of the last couple of days taken its toll? Just a few more paces now. He could see the light in the doorway of Stag Court. The last few yards were too much as Adam broke into a run. Hurling himself down the cobbled lane, to the sound of his panicked breath and pounding heart, he skidded into the doorway, grabbing hold of the familiar stone surround and, as he did so, he turned, catching a glimpse of bright red hair and pale skin, just as a young man disappeared up an alleyway.

Adam punched the code buttons to the right of the door and ran inside the building, slamming the door behind him.

He recognised that face. It was the same young man who'd come rushing towards him outside the MOD.

What could he want? Adam leaned flat against the door, breathing heavily, his mouth dry, his chest hammering. What could he possibly want with him?

Twenty-Five

Phone call

'Mum!'

'Don't tell me you're *still* at work, Adam? You sound all breathy and panting – are you alright?'

'I'm fine, Mum, I'm fine. I've just run up the stairs.'

'Oh, you've got to be careful with that. D'you know what happened to Debbie at number forty-five's husband the other day?'

'She's got a husband?'

'Of course she's got a husband. Have I never mentioned him?'

'No.'

'Oh . . . Anyway, he was at Paddington station last week and he saw there was this free blood-pressure clinic – you know, one of those mobile NHS ones. So he thought, I've got a few extra minutes before my train – maybe I should pop in . . . have the pressure done.'

'Who does that?'

'Worried people, Adam.'

'The worried well?'

'We're all worried, Adam – I'm permanently on *shpilkes*. We can't help it, we're always anxious, we're all the worried well – until we are *unwell*, and then we are the worried unwell. Anyway, so Eric – that's his name – Eric has a suitcase and he has to carry the suitcase up the stairs until he finds the NHS unit, which he does, but by the time he's arrived he's so out of puff from the stairs that he's sweating and his heart is racing. And they do the test, and they tell him his blood pressure is through the roof and he might need statins, and to go to his GP immediately. He manages to get an appointment. How? Who knows? And the GP just laughs and says his heart is fine. It was the stairs and the suitcase that did it. Were you carrying a suitcase, Adam?'

'No, Mum.'

'I bet you were carrying all those files you take everywhere.'

'I've two big cases on the go at the moment. Of course I have files.'

'The Blue Face case?'

'Yes, that one.'

'How is that girl?'

'I'm going to see her tomorrow. But I am also supposed to be back in court with Bobby soon to defend the soldier in the Khandistani child case.'

'Oh, that case . . . that boy . . . What a mess, Adam. I don't know how you do it sometimes, I really don't . . . I am very proud of you – do you know that? I hope you know that. I am sure I don't say it often enough. And sometimes, I really wish your dad was around to see how well you've done.'

'Thank you, Mum.'

'I mean, the things you see. That poor little dead boy with the sweet face. I've seen his photo everywhere and it makes me want to cry, it really does, Adam. But that's my age. I cry at everything. Mostly adverts. I have to turn them down these days. The ones with the dogs are the worst.'

'Mum, I really should go. I have a lot of reading to do before I see Lexi in the morning.'

'Adam?'

'Yes?'

'Good luck, and don't work too hard.'

Twenty-Six

There were five days to go before the pre-trial hearing, and the crowd was back outside HMP Bronzefield. The pounding drum had been joined by more protestors waving placards and banners and homemade flags. They were infinitely more vocal than they had been before, Adam thought, as he and Nisha pulled up outside in the same decrepit Uber they had taken previously, although this time the driver appeared to have replaced the Little Tree and upgraded the jaded smell of sweet peach to a tangy sharp lime.

'You can tell there's been more press, can't you? It's been all over LBC, that James O'Brien, and Radio Five Live,' said Nisha, staring out the window. 'I mean, look at them all. I always thought that it took a long time to radicalise a crowd. But I think maybe I'm wrong.'

They shut the doors to the taxi and made their way towards the prison, as the 'Free Lexi' chanters did battle with the 'Lock her up' brigade. The once-green grass outside the prison had turned to mud, and the encampment of small tents and deckchairs and upturned crates was littered with empty water bottles, plastic bags and Styrofoam takeaway packaging. It was beginning to look a little like Glastonbury after they'd closed the Pyramid Stage and told everyone to go home.

Adam and Nisha passed through the now-familiar security and down the blue-carpeted corridor towards the interview room on the right. They were both deep in thought. This would be the last time they would have with Lexi before the hearing next week, and they really needed her to come up with some sort of explanation as to what had happened that night at the gallery. Normally, Adam thought, he would have had more time to dig around – more time to work out who Max Bruce's will was going to benefit, and quite how far in debt Loughton might be, despite his multiple careers, 'hot' hot sauces and influencing. But due to the possible terrorism charges, the whole case had been expedited, sped up. The main thing Adam needed to concentrate on was that he didn't need to prove Lexi's innocence, just an element of doubt.

The guard with a hip-load of rattling keys opened the door and Adam stopped. Lexi looked terrible. The defiance, the anger, the attitude, the brash, arrogant insolence had all disappeared; that teenage ability to laugh everything off and take nothing seriously, to act, and hang the consequences, were all gone. Every drop of energy and vitality had left the room. She appeared broken, crushed and practically lifeless. Her formerly bright eyes were glazed and her hair was slick with grease; she had surely not washed it since the last time they'd seen her. And the tracksuit she was wearing was now baggy in all the wrong places. The knees were distended, like large elephants' ears, presumably from hours spent lying curled up in the foetal position on her prison bed. She needed her mother, not a barrister.

'Lexi, how are you?' asked Nisha, her voice soft, gentle.

She placed her hand on the table, as if about to reach out and take hold of her client's. One of the prison guards coughed a warning.

Lexi's head moved to one side and her eyes squinted. 'Ummm,' she replied quietly. 'OK, I suppose.'

'We're here to help sort out a few last-minute questions for the hearing on Tuesday,' Adam began.

He was conscious he didn't want to hurry her, and yet equally worried that this was their last opportunity to speak to her properly.

'Tuesday? And then I'm out?' she queried. 'What day is it today?'

'It's Thursday,' Nisha said, smiling at her.

'So only a few more days to go?' Lexi's face brightened as she suddenly saw a shining light at the end of the long, dark tunnel.

Nisha shot Adam a worried look. She was clearly not across, or maybe she chose not to be across, what was actually happening.

'Until the hearing, yes,' said Nisha.

'The hearing?'

'Where we shall ask for bail again.'

'Bail. We're asking for bail . . . again. Do you think we'll get it?' Lexi asked.

'Obviously we're asking again, but because of the possible terrorism charges . . .'

Lexi slumped further into her seat, her shoulders rounded, and her gaze lowered.

'So,' said Adam with an enforced upbeat note in his voice. 'Just to reiterate, we're going with a not-guilty plea, obviously, and what I'd like to ask you, Lexi, if I may, is about the spray-can.'

'Is there still a crowd outside the prison?' she asked Nisha, ignoring Adam.

'Yes, yes, there is,' Nisha replied.

'How many followers do I have now?'

'Outside? About two hundred, give or take?'

'Online?'

'Oh, I'm not too sure. I haven't been keeping up with that.' Nisha smoothed down her notes and brought out her set of chewed pens. 'I am more of a real-life person.'

'Mum said it was over a million, and that I have a blue tick. Not that I care anymore. I am not being a martyr to that cause.' There was still a tiny glint in her eye, thought Adam. Her spirit was still there, only you had to look much harder to see it.

'Where did you get the paint?' he asked.

'B&Q,' she replied.

'Which branch?'

'Holloway Road.'

'Why there?'

'Easiest for me to get to. Look – I don't *know*!' She threw her arms in the air with exasperation. 'Just there, OK? It's just down the road from the Tube.'

'And the colour of the paint?'

'Oh . . . now *that*, that's very specific: cerulean.' She fluttered her eyelids, pretending to be pretentious. 'We're given the brand and the number of the paint so that we all have the same colour. Otherwise there would be no continuity of protest, would there? We're all part of the same group with the same aims. I can never understand those groups who throw soup or baked beans at paintings. It's either one or the other. Pick your lane. Pick your can! Are they part of the same protest? Who knows. It's confusing. And also, what a waste of food.'

Adam smiled to himself. He could hear his own mother complain about wasting foodstuffs by hurling them at art.

'Who gives you the brand and the colour of the paint?' Nisha asked, pen poised.

'Cosmo, Cosmo Campbell, he's in charge. He's the one who came up with the idea behind the protest. Blue is less threatening than red. Red is the colour of blood, obviously. So blue is more tame – and a bit a like a Smurf, and that "I'm Blue" song. Do you know that song?'

'No.' Nisha shook her head.

'Oh, anyway. So . . . we're making them look stupid. We're not killing them.'

'We've already established you have no idea where the cyanide came from.'

'Not this again!' Lexi sat up and spread her arms across the table. 'I have already said I have no idea about that stuff. Like, I didn't buy it, and I would not know what to do with it anyway.'

'Sure.' Adam was surprised at how quickly she took offense. But who knew what a month of solitary confinement did to a person. 'But forensics have traces of cyanide in your vape refill found in your desk.'

'I have no idea what you're talking about.'

'How far in advance did you buy the paint?' he asked.

'I don't know.' She looked at Adam, her face scrunched as she tried to think.

'The day before? A week before? A month before?'

'About two weeks before.' She nodded. 'I think. Maybe more. Three weeks?'

'Now this is important,' said Adam. 'What did you do with the spray-can of paint once you bought it?'

'Well, firstly, I bought three cans.'

'Why?' asked Nisha, pen poised again.

'That's what I was told to do,' replied Lexi with a roll of her eyes. 'Three cans. I used two cans to practise with at home, and one I took to work, and I hid it in my desk drawer in the office.'

'Tell me about the two at home,' asked Nisha.

'Those were both used up.'

'On the melons?' asked Adam.

'How do you know about those?' she asked.

'We have them here,' said Nisha, opening up the file and sliding out three large shiny photographs of five melons in a row in Lexi's small, cluttered kitchen, their yellow skin sprayed bright blue.

'Wow!' Lexi exclaimed, as she bent over the desk to look at the photographs more closely. 'There's my kitchen.' Her voice sounded a little wistful as she studied the images. 'The sink is full of washing-up. I should have done that before I left. I bet no one's done that, have they? It's all exactly as I left it. Those melons look weird. I remember doing those. Yup.' She looked up. 'So I did those, and then I took the extra can to the art gallery and put it in my desk.'

'How long was it in your desk for?' Adam looked at her intently.

'Oh, two, three days. That's right, I kept it there for three days, and then I taped the can underneath the security guard's chair in the main room, next to the big painting, *Primal Scream*, for easy access during the party. I couldn't walk around with it in my hand, could I? I had champagne to drink and guests to talk to. So I had to hide it somewhere.'

'How long was it under the chair?' asked Adam.

'It was there for two days,' replied Lexi.

'So the can of spray-paint was in the gallery for five days in total?' asked Adam. 'Five whole days?'

'Yup.' She nodded.

'And did anyone else know that you had that can of paint in the gallery?'

'No.'

'Not that you know of,' expanded Adam, scribbling on his notes. 'And when it was in your desk drawer, was it locked?'

'No.'

'Could you lock it?'

'No.'

'And could it – the spray-can – have been taken from your desk at any point?'

'Oh, easily!' Lexi exclaimed, flopping back in her chair. 'I put it there and left it there. Next to my vape. But, you know, I wasn't checking on it every twenty seconds. And if I went outside to vape, then the drawer was left open with the can in it.'

'And did you check on it, the spray-can, during those two days it was taped to the guard's chair?' asked Nisha.

'No.' Lexi turned to look at Nisha. 'To be honest, I was too busy with my job in the gallery. The party was just around the corner, obviously, and there was a lot to do. Even if it was a fake job, I still had to do it.'

'And the vape refill?' asked Adam. 'It's alleged that's where you kept the cyanide.'

'But I didn't, did I? Because I didn't buy the stuff . . . For the last . . . bloody . . . time!' Lexi stared at Adam with exasperation and irritation plastered all over her face.

'And on the day of the party?' Nisha chipped in. 'Was it simply a question of getting the paint out from under the chair?'

'Well, that took work,' Lexi said. 'I had to flirt with the security guard. I can't remember his name, but I would go down to the gallery and chat to him, because if I needed quick access to his chair, I needed him not to mind me sitting on the chair, or going near it, if you know what I mean? So on the night of the party, I said I felt a little faint. It was a warm night, lots of people in the gallery, and could I sit down for a second? And then, as soon as I sat down, I felt under the chair and ripped at the Sellotape and pulled the can out from under the chair and went for it.'

'Went for it?' Nisha sat back in her seat.

'Sprayed the man. You have to do these things quickly. You can't overthink them or security will grab you. That's what went wrong with the Home Secretary. The guy who did it bottled it at the last minute, and that's why he was sprayed in the neck and not the face.'

'As your barrister,' said Adam, 'I would urge you not to mention the Home Secretary. It is not going to help our case. And obviously, with the possible terrorism charges, it *really* won't help our case. At all. I am sure the prosecution will try and bring him up as much as possible and link your case to that of the Home Secretary, but I think we should avoid putting his name into the mix.'

'Right.' Lexi folded her arms. 'Shall I say this slowly? Again: I had nothing to do with the murder of Max Bruce. I'm a protestor, I'm not a killer, and I hate violence. I want to stop people from dying, not actually kill them. Got it?'

Nisha and Adam travelled back into London on a packed suburban train, both poring over their notes on their knees, flicking through pages, flapping them backwards and forwards, writing timelines and looking at photographs, searching through all the paperwork, at Lexi's first interview and their recent interview notes. What were they missing?

'Here's the B&Q receipt,' said Nisha. 'That well-known anti-capitalist company.' She ran her finger over Lexi's bank statements. 'She paid with a card at 2.35 p.m. on 28 May. Just under twenty-one pounds, so that's seven quid a can. And that was . . .' She paused. 'Exactly as she told us. Holloway Road B&Q, almost three weeks before the murder.'

'Right.' Adam nodded. 'Three cans?'

'I presume so,' replied Nisha. 'But give me a second and I can look it up online . . . B&Q . . . spray-cans . . . Oh, look, here we are: six pounds ninety-nine a can, and they have been discontinued.'

'I bet they have,' said Adam, as his phone started to ring in his pocket.

It was Morris, checking in about the meeting with Lexi. Adam talked him through the three cans and the practice run with the melons. He talked through the can being left in the gallery for five days, in an unlocked drawer, and for two of those five days its having been taped under the security guard's chair.

'That's progress, Adam, proper progress. Good work,' said Morris. 'There's a window of doubt five days wide. Now all we have to do is find out who tampered with the spray-can, because someone did, and it certainly wasn't our client. Everyone keeps telling me this case is going to be over in three days. I think you've lengthened it by a week, Adam, possibly more!'

'Thank you, Morris,' Adam replied. 'Nisha and I have been going through everything over and over, trying to piece together what happened.'

'I think you should go back to the gallery,' suggested Morris. 'I think we need to know what her desk looked like, the logistics of taking the spray-can into the gallery, and whether she could possibly have taped it to the chair without anyone seeing. Or maybe they did see? Ask around. Check it out, Adam: get sleuthing. I know I said I didn't like it, but now I do. Very much indeed.'

Twenty-Seven

The black-and-gold wrought-iron gates were glinting in the afternoon sunshine when Adam walked through the arches towards the entrance of the Royal Academy. As he crossed the cobbled courtyard, he looked up: the giant banners were still advertising the Max Bruce retrospective with detailed close-ups of the *Primal Scream* painting. The bloodied and crying baby's face, its wide-open mouth gulping its first breath, grasping life, showing entirely what it was to live. Adam stopped and stared at the banners flapping in the breeze which somehow seemed to enhance the image's vitality: the crumpled face, the shades of scarlet and burgundy blood, the noise of the scream. Did Max Bruce paint this image from an idea, a concept, a conceit? Adam shook his head. Surely the man had been there. How could anyone paint something so fundamental and visceral without being present at this, the moment of birth?

Adam found there was something deeply relaxing about walking up the stone steps and into the 250-year-old building, away from the bustle and the pollution of Piccadilly. Set up in 1768, run by artists for artists with an art school and a summer exhibition, there was something timelessly elegant about the place. A place to dream and think. Who on earth could plot a murder surrounded by so much beauty?

Yet on the night in question, someone had. Adam tried to imagine Loughton walking around the party, showing off his hot sauce, influencing people. How would he have known about the can of paint? There was no evidence he'd ever met Lexi, let alone found her can of paint and then laced it with cyanide. Surely nobody from the family could have known anything about it?

He walked into the almost-empty hallway. It had been packed that night, full of guests and champagne, all swirling around, jostling each other, trying to get to the front, to be closer to Max Bruce and his magnificent painting. He closed his eyes, tying to recall Loughton's video.

'You need to buy a ticket for the Max Bruce exhibition,' said the girl behind the white desk at the ticket office.

Fortunately, she was not the same young woman as last time, the one who'd implied he was a 'grief tourist'.

'The Pre-Raphaelites are free,' she added. 'But the Max Bruce is twenty-four pounds fifty, including a donation. Although Friends of the RA go free. Are you a Friend?'

'I'm looking for the curator, Natasha Fitzjohn? Or someone in security, maybe?'

'Oh.' She sat back and fiddled with the bolt through her eyebrow. 'Natasha's not here at the moment, but Steve is here. He does some of the security. He's mainly in the Max Bruce rooms. Do you want me to radio him for you? Who did you say you were?'

'I'm Adam Green, I'm a lawyer working on the case, and I'd really appreciate your help.' Adam smiled at her.

'A lawyer.' She raised both her eyebrows. 'For the Max Bruce murder?' She nodded in the direction of the exhibition room where Bruce had met his demise. 'It happened in there, you know. Can you believe it? There's still some of that paint on the floor. Health and safety have said it's not dangerous, but I don't want to go anywhere near it. I mean, I love a bit of true crime, me, but I never expected anything like that to happen on my actual doorstep. It's enough to give you the shivers.' She shivered by way of demonstration. 'Steve, Steve, Steve,' she said, picking up a walkie-talkie and pressing a button. 'Steve, Steve, Steve, this is Laurie, Laurie, Laurie. You're wanted at the ticket desk. Do you copy? Do . . . you . . . copy?'

There was a loud crackle as a security guard walked out of the large gallery room, holding a walkie-talkie under his chin. Adam turned and smiled at him but Laurie continued: 'Steve, Steve, Steve, do you copy?'

'I'm here,' said Steve with a wave.

'Ah, Steve! This is a Mr Green, and he's the lawyer working on the murder.'

'Right you are. Good afternoon, Mr Green.'

Steve rose up in his polished black shoes, to the balls of his feet and back down again. Dressed in a strainingly tight dark grey uniform, with silver military-esque buttons down the front and darker epaulettes on the shoulders, Steve had a round, damp pink face, a bit like a boiled ham. His hair, the same colour as his uniform, was neatly clipped at the back and heavily gelled in place, giving him the appearance of an unathletic 1950s schoolboy, or, indeed, Sir Keir Starmer.

'How might I be of assistance? Would you like to start with the scene of the crime?'

'Well . . .' Adam was a little astonished. He was expecting myriad questions and endless bureaucratic obfuscation, but instead he'd been given free rein of the gallery. He was also well aware that Steve might be a witness called for the prosecution, so he should tread very carefully indeed. 'Would it be possible to see the offices, where the suspect worked, for example?'

'The suspect.' Steve nodded gravely. 'Follow me,' he added, pointing forwards. 'Let's go up the back stairs.'

'Are these the ones the staff use all the time?' asked Adam, trying to keep his questions as breezy and as light as possible.

'Mostly, although Miss Fitzjohn is allowed to take the lift, as are senior members of staff.'

'But Lexi Williams?'

'Her?' He stopped and turned round, top lip curled. 'She was definitely not allowed to use the lift.'

As they walked up the well-worn marble stairs to the right of the hallway, Steve filled Adam in on his ten-year-long career at the gallery and how important his job was in the general scheme of things.

'I have to commute in from Ealing every day,' he said.

'Right,' Adam replied to Steve's shifting buttocks which were on the step above him, as they continued up the stairs.

'But obviously they value my commitment to the job, and the hours I have put in, my dedication to my duty and the security of the building – which is obviously very important – so they sometimes let me leave early.'

'Oh, that's nice,' Adam replied again to the buttocks.

'Particularly on strike days. That's how you look after your long-term employees, isn't it? That, and the free tea and coffee

I get in the staff canteen. I've got a special card that allows me that "perk", as I believe it's called?'

'Yes, "perk", that's the right word,' agreed Adam, thankfully to Steve's face this time rather than his backside.

'So, here's the main office,' he announced as he opened the double swing doors on to an open-plan office, which was entirely empty, save for banks of flickering computers with variously individualised screensavers: some had family snaps, of little children on holiday with pink inflatable flamingos and turquoise swimming pools; others had plumped for the generic Apple Inc. shots of hot air balloons over deserts.

'No one's here today. As you can see. They've gone on some office bonding course, after what happened,' said Steve.

Adam looked around, hoping for something to leap out at him. But it was just like any other office. There were eight metal-and-plastic desks, Anglepoise lamps, wheelie chairs. It all smelt of Pret a Manger wraps and Leon curry pots. The bins needed emptying, and there were piles of paper and post and exhibition catalogues on most of the desks.

'Do you know which desk was Lexi's?' asked Adam, scanning the office.

'That one.' Steve pointed. 'The empty one right by the door.'

'Do you mind if—'

'Be my guest. It's been cleaned and wiped down. Sit at the desk if you want.'

Adam did just that. He sat at the desk and opened the top drawer where Lexi had stored the spray-can and where the vape refill had been discovered. He checked and confirmed she could not have locked the drawer even if she'd wanted to. There were three drawers on one side of the desk, the top one deeper than the other two. He looked around the office: most of the drawers were shut but some, a few, were left half open. He looked up and down the office. So, in theory, the spray-can would have been easily accessible to anyone and everyone who'd walked past this desk.

'And how far is it to the gallery from here?' asked Adam. 'How long would it take for Lexi Williams to get down the back stairs and into the gallery?'

'A couple of minutes,' said Steve. 'Maybe less.'

'Do you mind if we take a look downstairs?'

'Sure,' said Steve. 'You're the lawyer.'

Adam followed Steve out of the open-plan office and into the corridor.

'Sorry . . .' said Adam. 'Where's the ladies' toilets?'

'The ladies'?' Steve frowned. 'The ladies' is just here.' He pointed. 'Opposite the curator's office.'

He nodded towards a large glass-panelled office, with elegantly framed paintings on the wall and a clear and immaculate-looking desk, lit by one single architectural lamp. It exuded sophistication, even through the glass.

Adam walked down the stairs behind Steve, retracing Lexi's steps, through the hallway and across the black-and-white marble floor and into the gallery, where he noted the police tape had been removed. The crime scene was now simply a slightly dull-looking patch on the parquet floor, where they'd over-scrubbed and stripped off the polish. Even if Adam looked closely, the blue paint in the cracks was almost impossible to discern.

'And this is where you sit and keep an eye on things?' Adam asked.

'Normally this room is empty,' said Steve. 'I'm only here keeping an eye on *Primal Scream* for this exhibition. I'm usually in the foyer, or sometimes, when we have a very expensive painting on loan, I'm there.'

'Right.' Adam nodded. 'So, your chair on the night of the murder, had been placed there . . .?'

'Two days before. When the painting arrived, so did the chair. But you know, she was here a lot, that Lexi girl, coming in and out, in and out, chatting away. I should have known something was up. But I thought she was nice, you know? She was young and sweet and chatty – very chatty.'

'And the chair? Tell me about the chair.'

'Miss Fitzjohn moved it in the morning, closer to the painting and the microphone, saying I needed a better view of it. But then Lexi came over and said she didn't feel well at the party and asked if she could sit down. Of course I said yes. I was standing anyway. She sat down for a second and then sprang up like a tiger and sprayed that poor man in the face. I mean, who would want to kill such a great artist? And in such a horrible way. It's affected us all. It really has. Most of us can't bear to be in this room, it's so upsetting.' He turned around to glance at the giant canvas. 'Although, frankly, I can't see the appeal of it myself. It's far too gory and graphic for my taste.'

Twenty-Eight

It was the day before Lexi's PTPH, and Adam was up early.

He'd taken a shower, using the last dregs of his bodywash, and, still wrapped in a towel, he wandered into his state-of-the-art kitchen devoid of cupboard handles, and opened the fridge. It was empty, save for a yellow plastic tub of Anchor butter, which was half used and streaked with peanut butter and garnished with toast crumbs. He looked down to the right: there were some beers rattling hopefully in the milk bottle section in the door, and there was one very hard bit of cheddar that was as dry and as cracked as an old man's foot. Adam slammed the door and sighed. Nothing. Again.

Turned out the only food in his whole flat was for the fish. Perhaps *he* was the canary down the coal mine after all, Adam thought, as he fed the fish a pinch of flakes. He'd be the one to die alone, eaten by rats, while this wretched fish would happily keep swimming round and round its bowl, with its big bug eyes, blissfully unaware its owner had copped it on the kitchen floor. He really did need to go shopping.

After a swift emergency breakfast of croissant and cappuccino at Paul's by Chancery Lane Tube, Adam thought he'd be the first into Stag Court. It had just gone 7 a.m. and he wanted to get a start on the communiqués for Bobby, before he was distracted by other things.

'Mr Green,' greeted Tony with a wave, almost as soon as Adam walked in through the door. 'You're in nice and early.'

'The early bird, as they say, Tony.' He wandered towards the post room.

'How are you?' asked Tony with uncharacteristic warmth. He clearly wanted something.

Adam stopped. 'I'm fine, just run off my feet, what with the pre-trial hearing tomorrow for Lexi Williams.'

'Oh, the Blue Face case.' Tony nodded. 'I think the whole of Stag Court is on tenterhooks for that one. Mr Taylor-Cameron's been putting the hours in for the Crown, that's for sure.'

'Good, good for Jonathan.'

'Not as many as his pupil has, obviously.'

'Of course,' agreed Adam. 'We've all been there. The dry cleaning, the red roses on the Rob Van Helden flower account.'

'Those are some posh flowers,' remarked Tony with a sniff. 'I sent them myself once. To the missus. Wedding anniversary, I think. She loved them. I had to take out a second mortgage.' He laughed. 'That's the least of it for Stacey.' He nodded towards the end of the corridor. 'She was in here at six a.m. most of last week, photocopying for Britain, as far as I could work out. You could fry an egg on that machine, it's so goddamn hot.' He paused. 'Court martial is gathering some momentum.'

'Is it?'

'It's very "controversial", apparently.' Tony drew some quotation marks in the air. 'Good for us, good for Stag Court.

We like a bit of "controversial".' He did the marks again. 'It keeps us "visible".' Again with the marks. 'I heard that Tory MP on the radio this morning while I was doing my teeth, on the *Today* programme. What's his name? Colonel John Perser, that's the one. Anyway, he was wanging on about this and that, soldiers and peacekeepers. It got quite heated for six-thirty in the morning. Did you hear it?'

'I can't say I did, no.'

'Got to keep up with the news, Adam. They said they're calling the mother, flying her over at the taxpayers' expense, apparently.'

'I am not sure how she is supposed to pay for herself?'

'You're not wrong there,' agreed Tony. 'Talking of money . . .'

Here we go, thought Adam. What had Tony got up his sleeve now? He smiled inwardly to himself: there was always something. Tony was not a man for small talk, a little chat. So much so that after several years at Stag Court, Adam still didn't know the name of his wife or how many children he had. He had a Staffordshire bull terrier called Princess – he knew that because the dog's photo was on Tony's desk. But he knew little to nothing else.

'I have a couple of case files that I've put on your desk.'

'Right.'

'They're nice and easy, Adam. A bit like that Serpentine case. Which was not long, or hard, or high-profile. But lucrative. That new flat of yours isn't going to pay for itself.'

'No, sadly it isn't; not that I spend much time in it. And I've no time to furnish it.'

'Curtains are overrated, Adam . . . Here's the thing!' Tony clicked his fingers as if he'd just had a lightbulb moment. 'This one doesn't have much paperwork. It's quick, it's easy. It's a private case of a doctor who—'

'Botched a Brazilian bum lift?'

'Oh, hello, Stacey, have you finally come out of your little cubbyhole?' said Tony, spinning round on his seat.

'Morning, Adam.' Stacey smiled over the large pile of photocopying that she was carrying. 'You're in early.'

'So are you.' Adam smiled ruefully, with a knowing nod. He'd been there before, doing all the heavy lifting, while Jonathan was ordering room service at Claridge's and dozing off on the ample cleavage of Allegra/Pandora/Emily. 'Jonathan working you hard, I see.'

'Jonathan?' Stacey raised her well-plucked eyebrows. 'He's a pussycat. After I refused to take his dry cleaning once, and buggered up his flower order twice, he's never asked me to do anything like that again. The real taskmaster is that Georgina.'

'Georgina?' Adam was genuinely surprised.

'That's the sisterhood for you!' She laughed and made as if to walk off. 'Oh, go on then, Tony: tell us.' She paused. 'What did your good doctor botch? Buttocks? Boobs? Lips?'

'Chin implants,' said Tony.

'Chin implants?' She smiled over her pile. 'Of all the things I could feel self-conscious about, I have never even looked at my chin.'

'One of the most popular surgeries of last year, he told me. Massive. All sparked by Instagram. Apparently, if you make your chin look bigger, then your nose looks smaller.'

'Unless they eventually meet in the middle,' said Stacey with a wrinkle of her nose. 'I read that happened to some royal family somewhere . . . Hang on.' She closed her eyes to think. 'The Habsburgs, that's right. They were so fugly, their noses and chins almost joined together.'

'That's impressive knowledge,' said Tony.

'TikTok,' replied Stacey.

Inside his room, surrounded by papers and files and piles and piles, Adam slowly worked his way through some of the Khandistan communiqués. Leafing through the redacted pages, he read what few lines or phrases remained. It was apparent just how bad the situation had been. It was also apparent just how much the papers had been censored. It wasn't clear how the chain of command was working, or if it was working at all. It was like trying to do a jigsaw puzzle with half the pieces missing. Adam was staring at the wall, deep in thought, when there was a knock at his door.

'Come in.' He looked up expecting Bobby to walk in.

'Adam,' said Morris, coming straight to his desk and sitting down opposite, placing another file on top of his collection. 'There's a lot of paperwork here.' He looked around, his eyes working independently of each other. 'Are you alright? This all looks a little worrying. You do know that the state of someone's desk is supposed to be indicative of the state of their mind? And this, this my friend, smacks of chaos.'

'I have got quite a lot on,' agreed Adam.

'So it appears.' Morris looked briefly sympathetic before picking up his file. 'Organising and prioritising is the key. Now – Lexi. We're in court tomorrow. Old Bailey Court Number One. One of my favourites, if you're allowed to have one. I always think of it as a silent witness to the changing mores in our society. I know books have been written about it, but I do always think it's special. Don't you?'

'I suppose so,' agreed Adam. He'd always found it intimidating for that very reason. Ruth Ellis, Jeremy Thorpe, Ian Huntley had all been tried there. Its notoriety preceded it.

'Anyway, to business. I think you've done a great job in finding a window of opportunity for the spray-paint to have been tampered with. That's good, although we should cast the net a bit wider.' He laughed. 'I'm pretty sure there will no surprises tomorrow. Nisha's done all the paperwork, and we'll just have to sit and listen to Jonathan. But I think in the time we have between the pre-trial and the trial we need to really look into anyone else who might have had issue with Max Bruce. This was a pre-meditated murder; it was planned with precision. You've looked into the family, or course. Probate has been sped through and the will is being read next week, I hear. But I can't help but think the answer to who killed Max Bruce is out there somewhere. We just have to keep looking.' He stood up. 'I think perhaps you should tidy your desk. See you tomorrow. Early. We should go and talk to our girl before she gets in the dock. It's an overwhelming experience, as you well know, especially if you've been in solitary confinement for a month. And she is young, with a volatile personality – we've seen that already. She'll need some reassurance. I'd rather it all didn't kick off in court.'

Adam felt sick as Morris closed his room door. If that pep talk was supposed to have made him feel better about the impending hearing tomorrow, it had had the opposite effect.

*

He sat at his desk for the rest of the day, working through lunch and well into the late afternoon. His neck was stiff, his back was aching, and his legs felt heavy and sore from hours of sitting at his desk, but at least now he felt he was entirely across what little evidence there was for Lexi's case. The police really seemed to have done the bare minimum. They had their forensics, their witnesses and very little else. He gave Nisha a quick call to check what time she was arriving.

'I'll be wearing my smartest frock,' she joked. She was on the station platform in Waterloo, about to take a train to Guildford.

'Why's that?' he asked, raising his voice above the background noise.

'The press, Adam, the press – it's going to be a scrum. It's the biggest case of the year. I think it's going to be mayhem outside the court.'

Adam was just packing up, mentally going through a checklist of what he needed for tomorrow. A clean shirt would be good, he thought, hoping he might catch the dry cleaners on the way home. Otherwise, it was the pink collarless one his mum had given him for Hannukah. His phone went.

'Oh good, I've got you!' It was Bobby. 'Drop what you're doing: I need you to go to the Special Forces Club now.'

'Now?'

'Now. Now.'

'But—'

'Adam, I'm sorry, I'm tied up, I can't get there, but my Iraq contact has come through. He's got some documents, *the* documents, he says, to clear our boy. He's going to meet you on the steps of the Special Forces Club in twenty minutes.'

'Where is that?'

'Knightsbridge.'

'What does he look like?'

'Don't worry, I've sent him your photo.'

Adam did his best not to panic. He grabbed his notes and papers and slammed his room door, hoping he might find a black cab easily on Fleet Street. As he sprinted up the lane, he wondered what he was letting himself in for. Was this legal? Where had the papers come from? What were they? Were they classified? Stolen? He stopped at the top of the lane, scouring the street for the golden yellow light of a cab.

'Taxi!' he yelled, waving his arm in the air. A cab pulled over with a high-pitched squeal of brakes.

He chucked himself onto the back seat, leaning upright and forward the whole way. Checking his watch, checking his phone, checking his watch again. Finally, they pulled into Herbert Crescent in Knightsbridge with a few minutes to spare. Number 8. There it was. A remarkably unprepossessing building: red-brick, white window frames, Victorian, steps and a shiny black door. You'd walk past it if you weren't looking for it. The only thing that indicated it might be a place of some importance or interest was the substantial CCTV camera beside the door. No one could come into or out of the building without being recorded.

Adam stood on the empty street. It wasn't cold, or dramatically dark, but he felt nervous. He stood away from the camera's gaze, not directly outside the club, and waited a few minutes. It was a quiet street, just behind Harrods, and every footstep echoed. Every time anyone approached, he looked up at them expectantly. Was this him? But no one would meet his eye. In fact, they mostly avoided looking at him at all. Ten minutes, twenty minutes, his nerves were not holding out well. Thirty minutes. And then his phone bleeped with a text. It was Bobby.

He can't make it. Sorry.

Adam sighed with frustration. At least he could go home. He'd missed the dry cleaners, of course. It was Mum's baby-pink shirt for tomorrow. Or maybe he could arrive in his white court tunic shirt with his bands already on. Or 'do a Jonathan' and arrive fully wigged and gowned and front page ready. What did he care, he thought as he walked towards the Tube; no one would be looking at him anyway.

And then suddenly, out of the corner of his eye, he saw him. The boyish face, the bright red hair. He'd followed him to here, from chambers to Knightsbridge, to the Special Forces Club.

A bolt of terror shot through him and Adam broke into a run. He legged it to the Tube, tumbled down the escalator, bumping into people, shoving them aside. 'Oi!' someone shouted, but he didn't stop, and boarded the first train he could find. The doors shut. He turned around, pressed his face flat against the glass. There was no one. Nothing. He scanned the platform again for red hair. Nada. He collapsed into a seat, looked up. He was on the train to Cockfosters.

Jesus Christ, he thought. I'm losing my mind.

Twenty-Nine

It was towards the end of July and the morning of Alexandra Williams's pre-trial hearing. As Adam and Morris turned left out of Limeburner Lane and onto Old Bailey road, the noise was overwhelming.

The drumming, the shouting, the chanting, it sounded more as if they were approaching a less joyful Rio Carnival than the steps of the Courts of Justice. Adam had expected a few bystanders, a couple of placards and some slogans, but not this.

The steps to the court were packed with a large crowd spilling out onto the pavement and into the road beyond. There were crash barriers trying keep the rival chanting groups apart, as well as rows of police in high-vis yellow jackets, who had linked arms to prevent any members of the crowd bursting out of their area.

There were bright lights and boom mics. Hand-held recorders and keen reporters – all panstick ready, smiling down up-close camera lenses while listening to producers barking orders in their ears. Outside-broadcast trucks were parked up on the pavement, with a few zealous traffic wardens circling like flies about the proverbial, issuing tickets.

In among the crowd, the most enthusiastic participants had blue faces. Like extras out of Mel Gibson's *Braveheart*, they screamed and shouted, spitting with vitriol and fury, jabbing the air with their fingers, their cheeks smeared with paint.

This was a mob.

Were they baying for blood? Whose blood? Lexi's? Adam wasn't entirely sure. But they were certainly raging, railing against a system that made them feel disenfranchised, forgotten and unheard.

Adam felt even more uncomfortable as he approached them. The atmosphere was tense, and it felt like most of the demonstrators had been bussed in from somewhere. It was coordinated disorder. They were the antithesis to the homespun haphazard campers who'd pitched their tents outside HMP Bronzefield, drinking their kombucha, while warming up a hearty chickpea stew. This lot had intent, they wanted to stir up trouble, and Lexi's court case was merely their latest excuse.

'Well, well, well,' said Morris, taking in the scene. 'I have done quite a few cases in my time, but never with this much interest. This atmosphere is febrile, and it's just for the pre-trial hearing. Imagine what it's going to be like during the actual trial. Let's hope the judge can keep control of the court.'

'It's Ms Justice Clare Peters. She's a stickler, isn't she?' asked Adam.

'Bluestocking, efficient haircut,' announced Morris. 'I'm sure she's good. Her voice is a little quiet. But let's see.'

As they got closer to the steps of the Bailey, with its impressive facade, and huge domed roof with the statue of Lady Justice on top, her golden arms outstretched, a sword in one hand and the scales of justice in the other, the noise grew louder, and the crowd was increasingly rowdy. The police were finding it hard to control them: they were being jostled backwards and forwards in waves, and some missiles were thrown, water bottles, a can of Coke.

At the top of the steps was Jonathan. Already gowned, although not wigged, he was exuding importance, standing next to Georgina, who was dressed in a smart black suit, her thick hair neatly tied back. She looked nervous, agitated, afraid, desperate to get inside. She smiled weakly as she spotted Adam at the bottom of the steps.

'Are you OK?' he mouthed up at her. He suddenly felt worried for her. He'd never seen her not in control or in charge. 'Are you OK?' he asked again, trying to give her some sort of reassurance. She nodded quickly, just as she was barged by a policeman and pushed behind a pillar. Adam lurched forward, trying to scramble up the steps after her, but he was stuck in the melee.

'Morris! Mr Brown!' shouted a journalist, pushing a reporter out of the way as she shoved her microphone into Morris's face. The problem with writing articles and being interviewed on programmes like *Question Time* and Radio 4's *Moral Maze* was that Morris was usually better known than most of his clients.

'Is Lexi Williams a terrorist, Mr Brown?'

'Was she part of the conspiracy to murder the Home Secretary, Mr Brown?'

'How many more people are on the Blue Face hit-list?'

'Should Blue Face be classified a terrorist organisation?'

'Is Lexi Williams a cold-blooded murderer?'

Morris held his bag in front of his face as he tried to force his way through the heaving pack of journalists and reporters who were blocking his way and shouting questions, while the hail of abuse grew worse from the crowd. Adam followed closely behind. He was barged and elbowed out of the way as he tried to get up the steps. Finally, they both reached the top and pushed their way through the ancient heavy doors.

'Good God!' exclaimed Morris, smoothing down his ruffled hair and tucking in his now less crisp white shirt. 'That was something else. Is Nisha here?'

Adam looked around the vast hall to see if he could find her. He glanced up towards the central staircase, with its ceiling of frescos, hand-carved coats of arms, and alcoves all lined with Sicilian marble.

The Old Bailey, with its eighteen courts and sublime architecture, was truly designed to make no one feel bigger than the law. Adam had grown fond of it over the years, with its maze of passages and corridors and rooms, its echoing halls and its entrenched traditions, the male barristers' robing room, which was vast and important and spacious, and the women's robing room, which was the size of a public toilet.

He'd got to know a few of the characters who made the place tick. The security guards whose unenviable job was to rifle through briefs and ladies' handbags, while everyone huffed with irritation and self-importance at being so inconvenienced. He'd chatted to some of the court reporters who worked for Court News UK, who'd spent decades 'grovelling' (as they called it) around the courts looking for the best stories that might make the papers. Cross their palms with a cold pint and they'd tell the most entertaining stories, from bananas full of cocaine, kidnap victims with sweets up their backsides, and endless MPs with their hands in the till or up their mistresses' skirts.

Crime, they swore, was more creative and interesting in the olden days. These days it was mostly murder. And bloody, gruesome murder at that. Just one look at the court listings for the Old Bailey published online every day told Adam this.

Court 3 – murder, a father beat his 10-year-old daughter to death and scalded her with a boiling-hot iron, her bones were broken, and she was found dead, covered in human bite marks.

Court 6 – murder, a stabbing in the park in Islington between two rival gangs.

Court 7 – kidnap and murder, gang- and drug-related violence in East London.

Court 10 – drugs and conspiracy to commit violent offences.

Court 13 – not sitting, but attempted murder, a stabbing in Hounslow.

The Old Bailey was the place where those who'd made some of the worst choices and the poorest decisions met with some of brightest and cleverest minds in the country. It was an oddly depressing place, and yet, at the same time, architecturally beautiful.

'Adam! Morris!' Nisha came bustling over, her kitten heels clicking along the black-and-white polished marble floor. She was, as promised, wearing a smart dress, which zipped up at the front and flared out around her shins. 'It's bedlam out there. I never expected it to be like that.'

'Extraordinary,' agreed Morris. 'Shall we go and see our girl before she gets into court? The queue looks like it's died down a bit.'

Adam joined Morris and Nisha in the security queue as they waited to go through the metal detectors and have their bags and files X-rayed. Morris dug out his keys and a mobile phone last stocked in the noughties, and placed them in the tray beside him, before walking through the metal arch. Adam followed suit.

What must Lexi be thinking? wondered Adam, as they searched his bag. Sitting alone in her cell, in the women's section, devoid of daylight, in a room so small you could almost touch all four walls at the same time, listening to the flickering of the fluorescent tubes overhead, or the shouts and the manic screams of her fellow-inmates as they all waited, rattling with nerves, to see which way the scales of justice would tip.

They walked down the first flight of stairs and then down again, passing guards and locked doors and yet more security.

The air smelt foul. Old, stale, with little oxygen, it hung heavy and thick with the sickly aroma of urine and bleach.

Finally, the guard opened a heavy door which led into a suffocatingly small cell. Lexi was sitting at a sticky table covered in scratches and half-hearted, half-desperate attempts at carving initials. Who would want to tag a filthy table in the depths of the Old Bailey was anyone's guess.

'Lexi,' began Morris as they all three stood in a row looking down at her pale, waxy face and her hollow, frightened eyes. 'We're going up into court in a minute where I think there might be quite a few people. Your parents will be there – your

225

mum and your dad – and of course we will. You don't really need to speak, just confirm your name, and then the court clerk will read out the indictment, the charges against you. And that's it, really. The judge will then give a date for the trial. It won't take long.'

'And you'll ask for bail?' Her eyes looked pleadingly at Morris.

'I will ask,' he said.

His expression did not emanate optimism. Adam knew the situation was hopeless. Lexi was facing a charge of murder and possible terrorism and there was zero likelihood of her being let out on bail, no matter how many houses her parents offered up as security.

'Listen,' said Morris, 'if you get scared, or nervous, or frightened, or overwhelmed, we can always ask for a break. Just keep calm.' He nodded.

'Keep calm,' Lexi repeated. 'I'll try and do that.'

Court Number One was packed when Adam, Morris and Nisha arrived. Jonathan and Georgina had yet to make their presence felt, but the public gallery was heaving and there was not a spare seat to be had on the green leather banquettes.

Adam looked at the row of high-backed leather chairs with their golden royal insignia stamps, the dark wood panelling, and the high white carved vaulted ceiling and remembered how intimidated he'd felt when he'd walked in here for the first time. The computers, the television screens, the microphones and the extensive array of religious books, all wrapped in velvet cloth for the witnesses to swear their oath on – his legs, he remembered, had turned to jelly. How someone with the life experience of Lexi Williams would cope with this was anyone's guess.

Opposite the carved wooden pediment, Ionic columns and the judge's throne-like chair was the dock. Raised above the rest of the court with a brass handrail and bulletproof glass, it was designed as if to force judge and defendant to look each other in the eye.

Above, in the gallery, some of the protestors from outside who had made it into the courtroom were packed in tightly together, hanging over the edge of the rails, straining, waiting to see the defendant come into court. A couple of the blue-smeared faces, Adam noticed, had managed to slip into the back.

'How are you today?' Raquel, the court clerk asked Morris. She was dressed in a tightly buttoned open-neck leopard-print shirt. 'Water?' She held up a jug.

'Oh, yes, please,' said Morris, his head down, looking at his files.

'Adam?' Raquel smiled tightly.

After a few years of coming to the Bailey, Adam had hoped that Raquel's antipathy towards him might have mellowed, but apparently not.

'Water – great. That would be very kind,' he replied, a little over-effusively.

Raquel frowned at him like he was an idiot, filled Adam's glass, and walked off in her red high heels. Jonathan swept in, his gown billowing, his nose in the air, like a bat on a catwalk. He wafted up to Morris and Adam, all smiles and pleasantries.

'I have never seen the gallery so full for a pre-trial, have you?' he said, his bushy eyebrows raised in surprise, and glee.

He chuckled, and a guff of his breath hit Adam straight up the nose. It smelt of Polos, stale red wine and cigarettes.

Behind him came Georgina, who appeared to be markedly more composed than she had been earlier. She half smiled at Adam before taking her position next to Jonathan.

'Lexi's parents are up there to the right,' whispered Nisha, sitting behind Adam. He looked up. He'd seen their photographs before but there, in the public gallery, their faces were stricken with worry. They looked diminished, cowed by their experience, exhausted.

And it had barely begun.

Thirty

'All rise.'

Judge Peters looked surprisingly short and stocky as she bustled into the courtroom. Adam had never been in front of her before, but he had always imagined, having seen her steely face on various websites and court reports, that she would be something of an Amazon. But no. She did indeed have what Morris had described as 'efficient' hair. Dark mouse in colour, neatly cropped, and barely visible from underneath her wig, it was sufficient to cover her head and was clearly paying lip service to the word 'hairstyle'.

As she arranged her robe and settled into her large, dark green leather throne, everyone sat still, quiet, as if they were holding their collective breath.

'Are you ready to proceed, Mr Taylor-Cameron?' She looked out across the courtroom. Her quiet voice was fortunately augmented by the microphone.

'I am, My Lady,' boomed Jonathan.

'Please bring in the defendant.'

The doors opened and in walked Lexi, escorted by two female police officers, who were handcuffed either side of her.

The court remained silent. All fidgeting ceased. Adam glanced up. Lexi's mother was clutching a white handkerchief over her own open mouth, and her father took off his spectacles and cleaned them on his lap. It was as if he simply could not watch his daughter being led to the dock.

Dressed in a clean (or new) pale grey HMP tracksuit, her hair in a ponytail, Lexi shuffled slowly towards the steps of the dock, which she was told to walk up and to remain standing, in silence.

'Miss Williams, you were charged with murder,' Raquel continued. 'That on 16 June this year you did murder Sir Maxwell Bruce OBE by poisoning him with the intention of causing his death. How do you plead – guilty or not guilty?'

Lexi anxiously glanced over to Morris who nodded slowly. 'Not guilty.'

There was a murmur of approval from the gallery above and what sounded like the weakest of cheers. Judge Peters looked around frostily.

'Please be seated. Mr Taylor-Cameron?'

Jonathan spun around on his feet with such a flourish that he might have been auditioning for a Saturday-night dance show. Judge Peters pursed her thin lips. This was only the pre-trial hearing. There was no need for such flamboyance.

'Your Ladyship has the summary already and will indeed know that the Crown's case is a simple one.' Jonathan looked up at the gallery and over at the court reporters who were sitting, pens poised. 'That Alexandra Williams murdered Sir Maxwell Bruce OBE at 19.50 hours on Monday 16 June 2025 in the exhibition hall of the Royal Academy of Arts on Piccadilly, London, by spraying poison all over the artist's face with the intent of killing him. In terms of evidence, we wish to submit to the trial that the murder was witnessed by a roomful of friends, relatives and . . . loved ones.'

'Who are you calling, Mr Taylor-Cameron?' Judge Peters asked sharply.

Jonathan sighed loudly with ostentatious sympathy and then proceeded to list the names of his witnesses: the arresting police officers and one of the two security guards who'd tackled Lexi to the ground.

'The Crown has forensic evidence to prove that the laced spray-can was in Ms Williams's desk at the gallery, and there were traces of cyanide in the ladies' lavatories, also in the gallery, and, critically, there were traces of cyanide found in a vape refill in Ms Williams's desk, which there is no dispute belonged to her.' He went on to name the forensic expert police officer he would be calling, before he added: 'The Crown will prove that this was no chance encounter, no mistake, no error. There is no doubt that it was a premeditated act.' He paused.

'And what would that entail?' Judge Peters asked.

'Photographic evidence, My Lady.'

'Photographic evidence of premeditation?' She looked quizzical.

'We shall show photographs from the defendant's flat where she had practised for this occasion many times over. She had spent hours perfecting her method, spraying the lethal weapon, on cantaloupe melons in her own kitchen.'

'Melons?' Judge Peters repeated.

Adam looked at the press bench. They were furiously taking down every word. Lexi's mother was clinging on to her husband's arm with both hands.

'We shall also prove motive. Digital evidence demon- strates that she was indeed part of the Stop the War campaign, that she had been in regular contact with the leader and get- ting instructions from the same group who had attacked the Home Secretary, the Right Honourable Mitchell Hiddleston.' Jonathan paused, as if waiting for applause.

'Is there anything else you wish to add, Mr Taylor-Cameron?'

'Only that we shall also examine the defendant's support for various other antisocial groups, and that I have furnished the defence with the used and the unused material.'

'Nothing else . . .? No bad character application?'

'No,' said Jonathan. 'No bad character application.'

He sat down. Georgina turned and whispered what appeared to be words of congratulations in his ear.

'He laid that case out simply and quickly,' muttered Morris, out of the side of his mouth.

'He did,' Adam agreed. Any notion that Jonathan would be sloppy or solipsistic was clearly not the case. He'd done his work, or at least Georgina had. They were a good team.

'Mr Brown?'

'My Lady?' Morris sprung to his feet.

'Is the defence planning anything further than the "it wasn't me" argument?' she asked, looking at the papers in front of her. 'Will the defence be calling any other witnesses?'

'In due course, we shall.' Morris nodded. 'It's something we are working on.'

'Very well,' said Judge Peters. 'Then I shall set the trial date for 4 September, if neither party has any difficulties with that?'

Adam had been at the Bar long enough to know that that was not a question. Of course no one had any problems with the date. It was set in stone, and it would take place in just over six weeks' time.

'My Lady?' asked Morris, raising his hand.

'Yes, Mr Brown?'

'If I might ask about bail for my client.' Morris got to his feet. 'She is a young woman with no previous convictions and no previous history. She is not a flight risk. Her parents have offered their house as security. If you might consider bail?'

'The defendant, Mr Brown, is accused of the most heinous crime there is. There is also a possible terrorism charge, which is still being investigated, and is live.'

'But she has been in solitary confinement now for five weeks, and at such a young age . . .'

'You can make an application in due course if the situation changes,' Judge Peters replied with a dismissive wave of her hand. 'But I'm afraid under these circumstances I can do nothing else other than deny bail. Take her back dow—'

The end of her sentence was drowned out by high-pitched screams as Lexi yelled, 'STOP THE WAR!' before she collapsed in the witness box, her legs buckling beneath her.

And with that the public gallery erupted. Banners, flags and placards came from nowhere.

'Free Lexi! Free Lexi!' the chanting began, as did the pounding and the drumming of feet on the courtroom floor.

Mr and Mrs Williams looked bewildered as they were surrounded by campaigners yelling to free their daughter. The blue-faced ones who'd been at the back of the gallery now surged to the front and were exceptionally vocal.

'Free Lexi! Free Lexi! Stop the war! Stop the war!'

'Order! Order in my court!' Judge Peters barked. 'Order!'

But the demonstrators simply shouted more loudly: 'Free Lexi! Free Lexi! Stop the war! Stop the war!'

A couple of toilet-roll streamers came flying out from the gallery, as if the Andrex puppy itself had been released in the courtroom. Adam had no idea what to do. Morris just stood there, watching the chaos. Jonathan looked wryly amused, and all Georgina could do was stare at Adam with her mouth slightly open, as if to say, Why aren't you controlling your client? Or her followers? Or both?

'Order! Order!' demanded Peters. 'Or I shall have the bailiffs evict you from the court.'

Lexi suddenly stood up in the dock. 'I'm not guilty, Your Ladyship,' she cried at the top of her voice. 'I'm not guilty!' Her arms were in the air and the female police officers struggled to pull them down. 'It wasn't me! This is a setup, this is wrong. I swear it! I haven't done anything. Please, don't put me back in solitary! PLEASE! Anything but that!' Her face looked desperate. 'I can't go back there!'

'Lexi!' her mother shouted hysterically from the gallery. 'LEXI! Lexi! My darling!'

'MUUUUM! I'm innocent, Mum – I didn't do it!' She was screaming up to the gallery as the two female police officers dragged her away. 'MUUUM! I swear on my life, it wasn't me!' she wailed. 'MUM! Mum! HELP ME!'

Thirty-One

Adam and Nisha were quick to get down to the cells to try and comfort the near-hysterical Lexi, who was shouting, screaming and hammering on the heavy steel door with her trainers. The noise and her piteous cries had also sparked the other inmates to kick off. The noise was cacophonous, and the atmosphere was intimidating, menacing and downright alarming as Adam and Nisha walked at speed down the corridor. A security guard pulled Adam to one side and shoved him firmly up against the wall. His nose was right in his face, and he could feel the heat of his breath on his cheeks.

'Oi!' shouted Nisha. 'Leave him alone!'

'Piss off!' snarled the guard. 'Now, listen here, you. You need to get your client to shut the fuck up.' As he spoke droplets of spittle sprayed Adam in the eye. 'Otherwise we'll have a fucking riot on our hands, and she'll have *that* on her charge sheet as well.'

A startled and petrified Adam tried to calm Lexi down, but she was having none of it. She continued shouting, yelling her innocence, and attempted to pick up the cell chair, with the intention of hurling it at the wall. It was fortunately bolted to the floor. But Nisha was brilliant. Years of dealing with children had clearly given her a skillset that eluded Adam. Within minutes of Adam leaving the cell, Lexi was crying in Nisha's arms and asking to see her own mother.

The days and weeks after the PTPH were, as Jonathan described them, a 'media shitshow' (although Morris's take of a 'media storm' was probably a politer and more measured depiction). Either way, the airwaves were buzzing with endless phone-ins, talk shows, news items and thinkpieces about 'the state of British justice', with in-depth discussions as to whether the public had 'lost trust in the law'.

A list of the usual suspects and troublemakers took to X/ Twitter and the non-terrestrial news networks and spouted a litany of unhelpful, incendiary words demanding the right to protest and demonstrate when and wherever they wanted, citing terms like 'democracy' and 'freedom of speech' as justification. Had Morris not been directly involved in the case he would most certainly have been dragged from television studio to television studio, to discuss the state of the nation and how 'the young' no longer respected the institutions or the establishment anymore.

'Jonathan is cock-a-hoop!' said Georgina, as she sat on her cardigan tanning her shins in the sunshine in the small park near Stag Court.

'Cock-a-what?' asked Adam, sitting cross-legged next to her.

'Pleased with himself. He's prancing around, to the Garrick and back, off to have dinner at White's, Blacks and whatever other gentlemen's clubs there are named after a colour. I don't think he's felt this relevant for decades. Even some of his children are talking to him.'

Adam and Georgina were having lunch together, insofar as either of them had any free time for lunch. But Georgina had insisted. It was a rare sunny summer's day in August, the skies were cloudless, and the park was nigh on empty due to the mass exodus of the school holidays. She'd dragged Adam out to appreciate a few rays – possibly the only rays they might see this side of spring.

'How is the florist account going, I wonder?' asked Adam, cracking open a cold Coca-Cola and turning his white, tired face towards the sun. From his previous experience he'd always noticed that the more successful Jonathan's career, the busier Mr Van Helden's delivery van.

'You'll have to ask Stacey about that,' replied Georgina. 'I know he's keen to keep me in my place, and remind me that he's leading, but not even Jonathan would get his number two to order his flowers. Although he did ask me to book a table for him for lunch the other day.'

'That's outrageous,' declared Adam.

'I just pretended I hadn't heard him.'

'He'd never ask you that if you were a man.'

'Do you think?' she said, shaking a large open packet of Tyrrells crisps at him. 'Sweet chilli and red pepper? It's practically one of your five-a-day. In fact, red pepper *is* one of your five-a-day . . . Vitamins.' She smiled.

'Vitamins.' He smiled back and helped himself to a small handful.

Georgina lay back in the grass and closed her eyes. Her thick auburn hair framed her face.

'There is something rather special about summer in the city, don't you think?' she said.

Adam wasn't really listening; he was just staring at her lying there on the grass next to him. He'd never realised there were so many colours in her hair. The way the sunlight was shining on it, he could see copper, gold, all the precious metals.

'Adam?' she asked, opening one eye.

'What?'

'Summer in the city?'

'What of it?'

'I like it – the place is empty, it's more relaxed . . .'

'And there are significantly fewer emails,' he added.

'Wow!' She propped herself up on her elbow. 'If only all the other Romantic poets had thought of that! "I wandered lonely as a cloud . . . with significantly fewer emails to deal with."' She threw her head back and laughed. 'Sometimes I despair of you, Adam! I really do! I have no idea what's going on in your head half the time.'

Adam laughed along, in the hope of disguising his embarrassment. He couldn't tell if Georgina liked him as a friend, or merely tolerated his presence since they'd started at Stag Court together and had had so many shared experiences. He liked her company. He liked her. She made him laugh and she was clever – really clever – and he'd always found that attractive rather than intimidating. Although she could be that too. He'd found himself thinking about her more these days. He was prepared to bet that *he* never crossed her mind.

She sat up and ran her hands through her hair and tied it up into a ponytail using an elastic she had around her wrist.

'How's your girl these days?' she asked. 'Have you seen her since "the riot"?'

'It wasn't a riot,' Adam said defensively.

'I'm teasing.' She smiled. 'Although if you read any of the newspapers they would beg to differ. "Courtroom chaos", or whatever they called it. Anyway, have you? Seen her?'

'Nisha has,' replied Adam. 'She was brilliant at dealing with her that day. I have never seen anyone so . . . compassionate. I think that's the word. She was so kind in that cell. I was useless, I didn't know what to do. It was terrible. Especially with that guard shouting.'

'You should have reported that guard,' declared Georgina, popping a few crisps in her mouth.

'What's the point?' Adam shrugged. 'He was as out of his depth as I was. I don't blame him really.'

'But it was assault.'

'Not really.'

'Anyway, your girl still doesn't appear to have much to say except, "It wasn't me." '

'The police have hardly done much digging either,' said Adam.

'There are more witnesses to your girl spraying her victim in the face than there were guests at the party,' replied Georgina. 'I know we're not supposed to discuss the case, but it couldn't be any simpler. Everyone saw her do it, and she doesn't deny it either. Jonathan's done a great job, even though I say so myself. He keeps saying, "Why over-complicate the case?" I mean, who are you going to call? The wifies? Like anyone will enjoy hearing from them! Although I do personally find them fascinating. I can't really work out whether they were both in love with him or not. Or was it just the fame and the glamour they were after? And all those mad children. Whose is whose? And don't they all call both of them Mummy? Or Mum? And I thought my childhood was complicated, with two sets of step-parents and five half-brothers and -sisters.'

'How many?' asked Adam.

Georgina never really spoke about her family or her background. Adam knew it was posh, obviously. Probably posher than Jonathan's. What Adam had learned over his few years at Stag Court was that the wannabe posh always talked about being posh, and the genuinely aristocratic kept it very quiet, only for them to suddenly come out with a bombshell such as Princess Diana was their godmother, or the Lord Chief Justice was their father's best friend, like it was common knowledge.

'Too many.' She waved her hand. 'And they're all much older than me. By about a hundred years.'

'Really?'

'We barely speak to each other – I couldn't pick most of them out in a line-up.' She shrugged. 'Anyway, the question I'd be asking myself about Max Bruce is . . . who hated him?'

'Well, it looks like there was a bit of a queue . . .'

'Who hated him more than his wives, his children and all of his friends?'

Later that afternoon, Adam sat at his desk going through the last few pages of the Khandistani redacted communiqués. He and Bobby were finally back at the court martial on Monday. They'd got news that Timur's mother's visa had been granted, and all her travel documents were in order, and she was expected in Aldershot first thing on Monday morning. But as he was reading his mind kept on wandering to Max's wives and his children. Loughton? Someone had laced the spray-can. Someone other than Lexi was responsible for Max's death.

On the pile of papers on his desk he saw, poking out from underneath the files on the dodgy doctor and his big chins on Harley Street, a copy of *Hello!* magazine, with photographs and coverage of Max Bruce's funeral at Highgate Cemetery. Georgina's words were still echoing around his head: who really hated Max?

Adam pulled out the magazine and started leafing through, past the pages of Coleen Rooney showing off her new kitchen, and some charity party where all the women looked as if they'd bought the same lips, hair, teeth and possibly chins from his surgeon on Harley Street. Finally, he found the photographs of the funeral. There were the wives weeping, clutching their handkerchiefs; there was Jonathan's Pippa, looking glamorous in her expensive dress; Loughton, looking smart and, for once, devoid of his hot sauce bottle. His face appeared to be genuinely grief-stricken, and there was a close-up of him crying on his mother's shoulder – one of them. Camilla. His forehand was pushed hard against her and he was burying his head in anguish.

He'd already looked at these photographs before, online with Stacey, but he hadn't noticed the stylish art dealer he'd spoken to at the art party. There she was, all décolletage and black netting. She was practically purring off the page. Adam glanced across to check that her business card was still on his desk. It was, propped up against a book. Adam turned the page. The spread seemed to go on and on. How could someone else's funeral be that interesting? There were some famous people looking sad, and Leo Woodall looking handsome, standing under a tree. More, slightly less famous people were also looking sad. Adam flicked the pages back and forth. There was one person who did stand out. In among the black, the hanky-clutching and the veils, there was one man who appeared in the background not so grief-stricken, or sad, and dressed entirely in pink. Pink jacket, pink shirt, pink tie.

'Knock-knock?' Adam looked up. 'And there I was thinking I was going to disturb you!' It was Stacey. 'The door was open.'

'It's too hot with it shut,' explained Adam. 'I'm just—'

'Reading *Hello!* magazine. I didn't have you down as one of those!'

'I'm not really. I was just looking at the funeral photographs again, to see if I've missed anything.'

'Oh, right.' She nodded, walking over. 'There are lots of wives shots. I remember those, and Pippa, obviously.'

'Obviously.' Adam smiled.

Stacey came and stood behind him, looking over his shoulder. 'There she is in her very expensive dress . . . It's like the ultimate Gothic fashion shoot, isn't it!'

'Except for this man,' said Adam. 'The man in pink.'

'Oh yeah.' She nodded. 'Well, he's an artist. That's his schtick, isn't it?'

'It is?'

'He always wears pink.'

'He does?'

'You know, like Geri Halliwell always wears white.'

'Right.' Adam was confused. Does she? Did she? Was Geri Halliwell a Spice Girl?

'I think he's called Martin Dyson. He's an artist and he only wears pink, as it's a celestial colour.' She tapped the photograph. 'There he is again.'

'Pink is a celestial colour?'

'Apparently.' She shrugged. 'He is never knowingly not pink. Even at a funeral.'

Adam nodded. 'Good to know. I'm not going to ask you how you know that.'

'Actually, I read that in—'

'Don't tell me . . .'

'The *Guardian*.' She grinned. 'Culture section on Saturdays . . . Anyway, I was wondering, if you're not busy, whether you'd like a drink? It's so hot, and I've had enough of running after Jonathan for one day.'

'What's he been asking for now?'

'Don't even get me started. I've got an encyclopaedic knowledge of nice restaurants with river views if you're interested, including a lovely Soho House pop-up in Windsor . . . You're paying for the drinks, obviously. Now I know pupils aren't allowed to.'

'Well, I owe you,' he agreed, picking up his jacket from the back of his chair. 'I'd never have found out who Mr Pink was without you.'

As Adam followed Stacey along the corridor, she explained that Mr Pink was, in fact, a well-known conceptual artist who had a large studio off Brick Lane, where he welded giant pieces of steel together to make kinetic sculptures, whatever they were.

'And that's art?' asked Adam.

'It most certainly is.' Stacey laughed. 'Very expensive art at that!'

'Oh, hello?' said Georgina, coming out of her room. 'I thought I heard laughter.'

'That was me, I'm afraid,' announced Stacey, with a shake of her blonde curls.

'We were just off out for a drink,' said Adam, feeling suddenly sheepish.

'Oh,' said Georgina flatly. 'I thought you were busy.'

'I am. I am.' Adam sounded defensive and added quickly, 'Would you like to come? Wig and Pen?'

'Sweet of you,' replied Georgina, smiling tightly. 'But I can't. Supper with Daddy.'

Thirty-Two

It was 9 a.m. and Adam was sitting in a cafe in a narrow street off Brick Lane, waiting for Martin Dyson to show up at his studio. His elbows were resting on the green-and-white-checked plastic tablecloth as he absent-mindedly stirred a mug of milky tea, trying to remember if he'd put any sugar in it. He didn't really like sugary tea, but sometimes it was what the body needed.

His drink the night before with Stacey had not been quite as agreeable as he'd hoped. As soon as he'd walked into the Wig and Pen he'd realised his mistake. Jonathan was propping up the bar with a few of his friends from 15 Bedford Row, and they'd clearly been at the Whispering Angel rosé for a large part of the afternoon. He and Stacey had managed one drink each, before Jonathan had decided to join them and invited another three of his buddies, whereupon they'd started trading old war stories and hooting with laughter at their own jokes, making any other conversation impossible. Jonathan had asked Adam three times how long he and Stacey had been going out; each time he'd slapped him hard on the thigh and had called him a 'dark horse', honking at his own hilarity as he did so.

Stacey had been the first to get up, amid of a roar of protest as Jonathan patted the chair next to him and insisted on buying her another drink. But she'd obviously had enough of being told the same story twice or three times over and having to fake either outrage or amusement depending on the punchline.

'See you later,' she'd said to Adam as she patted him on the shoulder.

Adam had stayed for one extra pint of Camden Pale Ale, for fear of being accused of walking Stacey home, or indeed inviting her back to his inhospitable flat with its hard cheese and fish food.

Now he looked up from his tea just in time to catch a symphony of pink entering the studio over the road.

A converted garage, large double doors, double height: from where Adam was sitting the studio looked like the sort of place you'd leave your car for an MOT rather than create art. Adam drained his mug. He'd definitely over-sugared his drink and it was not refreshing at all. It had coated his tongue with a sickly layer of sweet lactose, which he instantly regretted.

He crossed the road and knocked on the corrugated iron door. It was open. 'Hello!' he said, poking his head in. 'Hello?'

He walked tentatively through the doors. Inside it was nothing like Max Bruce's studio, with canvases and chaises longues and tables encrusted with layers of ancient paint. This place was a workshop, with wooden benches covered in bolts and nuts and screws. The windows were long side panels with a sort of plastic 'glass', which gave off a cold, pale blueish light, like an eternal winter. There were partially completed steel sculptures dotted around the room. Tall girders were welded together like human legs, and there was a sharp pin-like object on a plinth that spun on its point, seemingly with perpetual motion.

Adam shouted one more time, but his voice was drowned out by a spray of sparks and a screeching noise at the back of the room, where Martin Dyson was standing, wearing thick leather gloves, a blow torch in one hand and a protective visor covering his face, as he welded two blocks of metal together. Adam watched the fountain of sparkles that lit up the room like a Roman candle on Bonfire Night. There was something hypnotically beautiful about them as they launched in the air and then died on the concrete floor below.

'Can I help you?' Dyson flicked his visor up and looked quizzically at Adam. 'I don't normally allow visitors to the studio.'

His voice wasn't unfriendly; he just seemed a little startled to see Adam in the middle of his studio. In his early fifties, slim, straight nose and teeth, with a shock of salt-and-pepper hair and piercing blue eyes, he was a handsome man who must have been something of an Adonis back in the day.

'I am so sorry to bother you,' said Adam, stepping forward with a smile, 'especially when you are working, but I wonder if I might ask you a few questions.'

'Questions? About what?' Dyson pulled down his pale pink T-shirt.'

'Max Bruce.'

'That bastard? No, thanks.' He flicked his visor back down over his face. 'Thankfully the little shit is dead.' He flicked the visor back up again. 'Unless you've come to tell me he's resurrected like bloody Lazarus, I don't have much to add. I watched them bury him just to make sure it was true and not some sort of "fake news". It couldn't have happened to a nicer bloke.' He moved to put his mask back down.

'I saw you at the funeral,' Adam blurted out.

'You did?' He squinted at Adam. 'Who are you? What do you want? Are you a journalist?'

'No. I'm a lawyer. A barrister.'

'That's even worse. Making money out of other people's misery. You're all stains on society.'

'We, um, just try and uphold the law. Due process.'

' "The law is an ass." Dickens.'

'Well, sometimes, I suppose, it is,' agreed Adam cautiously. 'I'm trying to find out who killed him . . . Mr Bruce.'

'Sir Max Bruce OBE, or whatever he was? The list to off him must have been endless! Have you tried those wifies? Terrible name. Terrible women. They're a couple of old hags – all you need is one more and you've got the opening scene of *Macbeth*. Stirring their cauldrons, the pair of them. Either those two or the litany of spawn he's produced. Have you spoken to king of the half-wits, Loughton? He's thick enough to do something like that. He was stupid as a child, and now he's skunked his brain to shit and he can barely string a sentence together.'

'So you're not keen on the family then?' ventured Adam.

'No, they're a bunch of nepotistic, parasitic, spoilt morons. No, I don't like them at all.'

'Do you know them well?'

'I did. Very well. But now I avoid them as much as possible. Listen, why do you want to know all this?'

'I'm involved in the case, for the defence.'

'Oh, right.' He nodded. 'Well, in that case – do you want to come to my office?'

'That would be very kind.'

He indicated towards the back of the studio. 'This way,' he said, taking off his visor and gloves.

Adam followed Martin Dyson, dressed in his pale pink T-shirt and pink tie-dyed jeans, to a small door in the back wall, which opened into an office with a grey filing cabinet in one corner and pinboards on the walls covered in yellowed newspaper cuttings all featuring him: some were interviews, some events, and some were features including his apparent nomination for the Turner Prize. In the other corner from the cabinet was a large desk with a huge ancient Apple computer and numerous small kinetic black-and-chrome sculptures, all cluttering the space.

'I love these nineties city-boy toys,' he said, following Adam's gaze and setting off a row of silver balls, which ricocheted back and forth. 'They amuse me, and they're brilliantly designed. Here,' he added, removing a pile of elderly curled magazines from a chair. 'I'd offer you a mug of something if any of them were clean. My assistant is off this week, as you can see.' He indicated towards a dripping sink piled high with filthy chipped china. 'That's how I started – I was Bruce's assistant. Like Stan – have you met Stan? The poor sod. Imagine being in love with that monster for ten years.'

'He was in love with Max?'

'Oh yes, and didn't Max know it. The worse Max treated him, the more he loved him. I'm sure Freud would have a lot to say about that. Poor Stan – doesn't like himself, that's the problem. Anyway, so that was my job for the master that is – sorry, was – Max Bruce. The bastard. The thing is, when people treat you like you're a genius, you begin to think you are, and you end up treating people like shit. Your will, your way, your ideas and clever thoughts are gold dust – you are a colossus, the new Michelangelo, Leonardo, the second coming – and everyone else is a mere mortal with their paltry thoughts and their insignificant little lives. That's why the famous are so ghastly!' He laughed. 'They're infantilised. Their every whim is catered for. Have you ever been on a film set?'

'I can't say I have,' said Adam.

'The so-called stars are fed and watered and taken for "comfort breaks" like toddlers. No wonder they become monsters. The year you become famous is the year you stop growing as a person. That's why George Clooney, who became famous at thirty-three or whenever it was, is a nice, rounded individual, and Michael Jackson was forever six years old, creating Neverland in his garden and befriending a chimp. Anyway, Max became famous at twenty years old. He was fresh out of art school, which is why he remained a hard-drinking, pussy-chasing idiot, unformed, unkind, and a massive egotist. He consumed women who fell for the charm, and the boyish good looks and the idea that he was a loveable rogue, the *enfant terrible* – all those things.'

'And when did you start working with him?'

'Towards his mid-thirties I worked with him, or should I say *for* him – for about fifteen years, for my sins. I am not sure what I did in a past life to deserve that, but I must have been pretty terrible.'

'What did you do for him?'

'The same as Stan. Although, to be honest, our relationship was more fraught than theirs. I was out of art school myself and Max asked me to come and work for him. "Come and join the art world, come and work for me," he said. "I'll introduce

ROB RINDER

you to people," and to be fair, he did – that's why I stayed so long. But what he didn't say was, "I'll pay you jack-shit and steal your ideas." '

'He stole your ideas?' Adam was shocked. The more he learned about the art world, the more it confused him. 'How could he do that?'

'He could do what he liked: he was the famous one. He was, at the time, out of ideas. His star was waning, and he needed some new stuff, so he stole mine.'

'Sculptures?'

'I wasn't doing those then. I was interested in abstract stuff, playing around with ideas about stuff like . . . *Black Square*.'

'Oh,' Adam nodded, pretending he understood what Martin was saying. '*Black Square* . . . sounds interesting.'

'Well, Max clearly thought so, so he stole the idea. I was stupid enough to think it was exciting that he'd been inspired by my stuff, but then he did it again and again, and I realised that he was never going to credit me or anything like that. It was a one-way street, and frankly I have hated the man ever since.'

'Right,' said Adam. 'I can see why that would foster some sort of resentment.'

'Well, I'm glad he's dead, if that's what you want to know. Did I kill him? No.' He laughed. 'Look,' he said, searching on his desk. 'I even bought some of that cerulean paint.' He dug out a B&Q spray-can from under a pile of papers. 'Before they withdrew it from sale. I was going to do some sort of Blue Face sculpture, but then I thought better of it. Poor taste and all that. But I was sorely tempted.' He paused. 'But did I kill him? No. I couldn't be bothered. That would be an act that would require

251

effort. I have better things to do with my life. That girl's done the world a favour, frankly.'

'Yes, well . . .' said Adam slowly, getting out of his chair. 'Thank you for your time; it's much appreciated. Very kind of you.'

'Not to worry.' Martin Dyson smiled. 'To be honest with you, I ended up feeling quite sorry for the man in the end.' Adam paused by the door. 'The only truly great work he produced he did at the age of twenty. *Primal Scream*. It is an incredible piece. The birth of his daughter – I presume you know that?'

'I didn't think anyone did? Was it with one of the wives? Camilla?'

'No, it was way before all of that nonsense. Some poor student who was at art school with him. They had a daughter. I can't remember either of their names, but he ditched her, I know that. It was a liaison, I think is how you'd describe it. He treated her like shit. He never saw his daughter ever again, as far as I know. How sad is that?'

'It is,' agreed Adam.

'I told you he was a bastard!'

Adam walked out into the street and immediately telephoned Morris. Max Bruce had had a daughter who he never saw, and her birth was the inspiration for the painting *Primal Scream*. Morris sounded interested. At least it was new information.

'How long ago was that?' he asked.

'Martin said Bruce was twenty years old at the time.'

'So over forty years ago then?' said Morris. 'Did you get her name?'

'He couldn't remember either of their names,' replied Adam.

'That's disappointing,' mused Morris. 'The mother, coming back to wreak revenge. I keep saying it's a crime of fury, Adam, and that would make sense. But if they weren't married, she's going to be nigh impossible to track down. Keep digging, Adam, keep digging . . .'

Thirty-Three

There was an autumnal nip in the air, despite it being only the last week of August. Adam and Bobby were sitting on a white capped wall beside the car park outside the military court in Aldershot. Adam had the file of redacted communiqués out on his lap as he and Bobby were going through them one last time.

'Honestly,' said Bobby with a heavy sigh. 'What I wouldn't give to see these without all the heavy black pen. It's unforgivable really that these have been censored so heavily. I am fascinated how these big institutions never seem to learn. It's not the mistakes that bring you down, or the crime even, it's the cover-up. If they only said that hackneyed phrase – "Mistakes were made, and lessons will be learned" – then it would all be over much more quickly, and much less painfully. But instead we have to deal with this.' He fanned a piece of paper left and right, showing one side and then the other. Both sides were almost entirely black. 'It drives me mad.'

'I know,' agreed Adam. 'They were complicated to annotate too, because if you lost your train of thought, your concentration for a second, none of it made any sense at all. Oh, look,' he added, nodding at a taxi that had just pulled up in the car park, dropping off two scruffy-looking souls with a notepad, pens and a hand-held camera. 'The press have arrived.'

'Colonel John Perser has been called today,' said Bobby. 'And after his appearance on *Newsnight* and *Question Time* over the last couple of days, there's quite a bit more interest in the case.'

'Tony will be pleased,' replied Adam.

'I thought Tony was already quite pleased,' said Bobby. 'He's been smiling at me for weeks. Although I'm never sure what's worse: an irritable Tony or an obsequious one. They are both worrying!' He stood up. 'Come on, let's go and meet the solicitor.'

'Mr Mann.'

'That's him. Let's see if he has any updates on our boy.'

Walking through the now-familiar double doors and along the grey carpet-tiled corridor with the strip lighting, Adam and Bobby found Mr Mann standing by the coffee machine, waiting as his white plastic cup filled up with soil, tepid water and acrid milk. Adam could smell his five-day-old Lynx effect as soon as he approached.

'Morning, gentlemen,' Mr Mann said with a slow nod. 'Welcome back to the coalface.'

Bobby shook his hand energetically. 'How's our boy?'

'Lance Corporal Sutcliffe seems to be bearing up well. His mum's been to visit a few times, so I've been told, and he seems to be in good spirits. Well, better spirits than last time.'

The soldier could not have been at a lower ebb than when they'd last seen him, Adam thought to himself. The young man had been distraught. He wondered how he might cope having to look Timur's mother in the eye today as she sat in the witness box. Adam braced himself for what was surely going to be a tough day.

Inside the courtroom, it was already relatively full as Adam, Bobby and Mr Mann took their seats. In fact, as Adam looked around the poky low-ceilinged room with its municipal desks and elderly sound system, it appeared that the top brass was out in force. In front of the spooks in suits was a row of substantial-looking alpha males dressed in immaculately maintained uniforms with multiple chevrons on their sleeves and lines of medal ribbons on their chests.

'I see the big boys are out,' said Bobby, looking over his shoulder. 'They're here for Perser, I'd say. Everyone's keen to hear what he has to say. It all happened on his watch.'

The two barristers for the Crown, Alexander Newbury and George Beaumont, bustled in. They nodded at Bobby and Adam before taking their seats. They shuffled their papers and smiled at various members in the public viewing gallery, before leaping to their feet as Judge Wickstead arrived.

'All rise!' commanded the clerk in uniform.

Judge Wickstead appeared to be her usual frosty self, with her expressionless face and fierce blue eyes. The only difference was that her slash of red lipstick was now pink, which made her a little softer in appearance. Adam waited for her to make eye contact or register him. She did not, she simply stared straight through him as if he were a picture window. He was clearly of no interest to her whatsoever.

'Please bring in the defendant.'

Lance Corporal Danny Sutcliffe was escorted in by two other soldiers and was shown to the dock. Adam was pleased to see he did indeed look brighter than at his last appearance.

He held his head up this time, and didn't stare at the floor, and he even managed a small smile to his mother, who was sitting in the same place as before, still wearing her thin blue anorak.

'Are you ready, Mr Newbury?' Judge Wickstead asked the prosecuting barrister.

'I am, Your Ladyship,' he said, nodding. 'The Crown calls Ana Tadishvili.'

The room went totally quiet; all shuffling and coughing ceased. Adam had no idea what to expect, but it was certainly not the tall, rather elegant-looking woman who walked into court. Dressed in a long dark green hand-embroidered dress, with a purple pashmina wrapped around her shoulders, her dark hair was parted down the middle and tied back in a casual ponytail. She walked slowly, gracefully, glancing around the room, apparently taking it all in. She was followed by a diminutive man in an ill-fitting grey suit and white shirt, with thick round spectacles who, blinking rapidly, fiddled his way across the room towards the witness desk. He stood right next to Mrs Tadishvili and poured them both a glass of water. He was obviously her translator. As she was sworn in, her hand placed on a velvet-covered book, Adam noticed she had long dark burgundy fingernails. She spoke to confirm her name and remained standing, her translator right next to her.

'Mrs Tadishvili, if I may?' began Alexander Newbury. She nodded. 'Do you remember the night of 15 January of this year? Where were you?'

Ana Tadishvili started to explain to the court how unwell she'd been, how her house had been destroyed, and how she had found herself destitute and on the streets of Khandi, while civilisation had collapsed and lawlessness had broken out.

'What you probably don't understand, living over here,' explained the translator in immaculate English, 'is how quickly things fall apart. All it takes is one bomb to your house, and for your husband to be shot, killed by the enemy . . .' Mrs Tadishvili paused. Her voice cracked.

'Take your time, Mrs Tadishvili,' said Newbury.

'And then you're out on the streets with everyone else.' She turned slightly and addressed the board directly. 'You probably see a poor refugee standing here, from a war-torn country that is devoid of hope. But what you don't know is that I was a scientist, a physics professor at the University of Khandi. Head of department. Author of many papers. But none of that matters when your house is destroyed and your husband is dead, and there is no money, no food and no medicine. What is the use of money if there is nothing to buy?' She raised her fine dark eyebrows and looked across the room straight at Judge Wickstead. 'We are *all* only one terrible misfortune away from tragedy.'

Alexander Newbury cleared his throat. 'On the day in question,' he continued, 'how unwell were you? And what medication did you need?'

The story unfolded with Adam and Bobby both taking notes. Ana Tadishvili had a fever after receiving a wound to her leg when her house had been destroyed. It had got infected. The infection was travelling up her limb and she was becoming delirious. She needed antibiotics, and fast, otherwise she would die of sepsis. Timur, as the eldest, was dispatched to the hospital to find an old doctor friend of theirs who'd promised the drugs. But when he arrived it was chaos.

'How chaotic?' asked Newbury.

'Terrible,' replied the translator.

'I would like Mrs Tadishvili to speak, please,' said Newbury.

'I was too ill,' she answered, via the translator. 'I have no idea what the situation was like at the hospital. All I know is that when I recovered, I was told that my son was already dead.'

'How did he die?'

She pointed with her elegant hand. 'My son Timur was thirsty, he was hungry, he could not breathe. And this man did nothing.' She stared at Danny Sutcliffe. 'He did nothing at all. He carried on driving, while my ten-year-old son suffocated to death. My son was not a looter, he was a good boy from a good family. He studied hard at school. He wanted to be a professor like his mother. And now what? He is dead. He was treated like a criminal. He was ten years old, trying to find medicine for his mother. And then this.' She started to weep and, fumbling and shaking, she pulled a handkerchief from her pocket. She dabbed her eyes and sighed heavily. 'My beautiful son.'

'No further questions,' said Newbury, before he sat down.

Adam glanced over at Bobby. No one would ever want to come up against a grieving mother, ever. But had Alexander Newbury just left a hole in his prosecution large enough to drive a truck through?

'Mr Thompson, your witness,' Judge Wickstead said.

'Mrs Tadishvili, Professor,' began Bobby. 'Please may I say how truly sorry I am for the loss of your son Timur . . . My sincerest condolences.'

Ana Tadishvili looked directly at Bobby across the dreary municipal courtroom with such dignity and grace. It was quite something to behold. Her dark eyes were clouded for a few seconds as she slowly bowed her head and smiled gently at him.

'Thank you, Mr Thompson,' she said in clipped, clear

English. 'You are the first person to say this to me. I am grateful.'

There was a pause. Adam was shocked: she spoke better English than her translator. Bobby shuffled his papers. He looked up.

'I imagine the chaos and the tragedy of what happened to your family must be overwhelming. To lose your house, your livelihood, and indeed your beloved husband must have been terrible. No one in this courtroom could imagine such a thing, and to be injured, and unwell, with eight children to feed and clothe and look after . . . It is no wonder then that your son felt the need to run to the hospital, compelled to save his mother at all costs. Even if it involved looting humanitarian aid . . .'

'What is your question, Mr Thompson?' asked Judge Wickstead.

'Indeed, Your Ladyship, I was coming to that.' Bobby paused. 'However, if you were too unwell, Professor Tadishvili, delirious, as you said, battling an infection, a temperature, unaware if it was night or day, perhaps . . . how did you know that your son was placed in a tank and not killed some other way?'

'I was told by a neighbour, my doctor friend at the hospital, that is. He told me what happened,' said the translator.

'So you did not see it at first hand? In the chaos of war and false information, you were told this . . . by someone else?'

'I was.'

'And how did he – the doctor – come by this information?'

'He was informed by someone.'

'So he did not witness the crime either? He was relying on information from a third party?'

'He was.'

'You did not directly witness the crime, and your doctor friend – what was his name?'

'Dr Irakli.'

'Dr Irakli did not witness it either?'

'No.'

'No further questions.'

Bobby sat down. Adam looked across at Mrs Tadishvili's face; it was grim and pained as she tugged at her purple pashmina, pulling it tight around her shoulders as she walked briskly out of the court, followed swiftly by her translator. She had travelled all this way, thought Adam, to get justice for her young son, and although it didn't look like it now, he knew Bobby was on her side. He really was. She would get her justice, concluded Adam, but perhaps not in the way that she'd thought.

'Ready for the next one?' whispered Bobby to Adam. 'He's going to be a really tricky fish.'

A few minutes later and the tricky fish walked into court, dressed in an immaculately tailored dark suit, with a crisp pale-blue-and-white shirt and a navy-and-silver double-striped tie that clearly denoted he was the alumnus of some auspicious institution that Adam failed to recognise. A frisson of excitement and energy shot through the courtroom. The top brass at the back relaxed back into their seats, nodding to each other. It was obvious that 'their man' had arrived at last. Perser was here to finish it all off, clear it all up, and leave no doubt that the army had their murderer and he was very much bang to rights and the chaps further up the food chain could keep calm and carry on.

Perser looked smooth, confident, even a little tanned, as he strode towards the witness box. His golden cufflinks caught the light as he swore his oath loudly on the Bible.

'Colonel Perser,' began Alexander Newbury, 'how long were you on active service in the army?'

Perser looked at Newbury and Beaumont as he proceeded to tell the court of his illustrious career, which had naturally started at Sandhurst, where he'd sped through the ranks like lightning. He'd done two tours of duty in Iraq attached to special forces, and his final tour was in Khandistan, after which he had recently retired to spend a little more time in Herefordshire with his wife and three young children. He was now, of course, well known as an MP – albeit only briefly, as he'd lost his seat in the last election.

'What was morale like with the soldiers in the ranks in Khandi when you first invaded?' asked Newbury.

'Morale among the men was good,' nodded Perser. 'Excellent, in fact. The chaps were happy, they'd done well, they'd fulfilled their remit, and, you know, they'd broken through and defeated the enemy. We could not have done better. Mission accomplished.'

'And when the mission changed from that of occupying force to peacekeeping, did morale remain the same?'

'Absolutely. The boys knew their brief, even though the rules of engagement had changed – but the lads knew what they were doing. They totally knew what they were doing. We all made sure of that.'

'And did they follow their orders?'

'They did.'

'What happened on 15 January of this year? At the main hospital in Khandi?'

'Well, there was a riot and looting. A United Nations aid package had been delivered to the hospital full of much-needed medicine and drugs, for all the patients inside the hospital.'

'Were these important drugs?'

'Oh, they were vital. This was the first consignment they'd had in months and it was desperately needed. Crucial supplies that were being stolen by a mob.'

'Did you order Lance Corporal Sutcliffe's unit to intervene?'

'Not personally, no. I was in London at the time, in meetings. But they were there, the unit was there anyway, guarding the UN trucks. That was their job. Those were their orders.'

'Was Lance Corporal Sutcliffe under orders when he picked up Timur and placed him in the back of the tank?'

'Absolutely not.'

'There was no policy he could have been following?'

'No.'

'No protocol?'

'No.'

'Was he acting alone?'

'He was most certainly acting alone. He was supposed to be keeping the peace, preventing the looting of invaluable drugs and supplies, not picking up civilians. Those were his orders and that was that. Anything else is dereliction of duty. Pure and simple. A total dereliction of duty.'

'No further questions, My Lady. The Crown rests.' Newbury nodded and then sat down.

While Danny's mother slowly shook her head in disbelief,

an intangible wave of relief swept through the ranks, spooks and brass, all the way to the back of the room. Newbury had done well; he'd let Perser make clear that the buck stopped firmly with Sutcliffe.

'Colonel Perser,' began Bobby, 'you were in charge of the operation in Khandistan, were you not?'

'Not overall, I leave that to the mandarins in Whitehall, but the day-to-day, the military tactics, yes, I was: that was me,' he acknowledged.

'And when the tour of duty ended, and the war was declared over, and your troops then became peacekeepers, did they know what the new rules of engagement were?'

'They did.'

'How did they know?'

'They were briefed, of course, on the morning of the changeover.'

'They were briefed, once? That was it?'

'These are intelligent fighting men, they're all well trained. Once they have been briefed, they don't need telling twice.'

'Well trained in the art of war, but not in the art of peace-keeping, which I believe is a different skill, is it not, Colonel?'

'I am not sure I know what you mean.'

'Well, it is two different sets of training, is it not?'

'Usually, yes . . .' Perser sighed loudly and rolled his eyes with annoyance at Bobby's continued questioning.

'Two different sets of protocol.'

'Is that a statement or a question?' snapped Perser.

'In terms of protocol, Colonel Perser, may I ask a different question in order to help me to understand . . .? Lance Cor-poral Danny Sutcliffe was a witness to his fellow-soldier's shooting the day before the alleged incident. His friend Private Keith March took one in the chest, we have been told, and Lance Corporal Sutcliffe was the first on the scene and held him as he bled to death. And yet Corporal Sutcliffe was out on duty the very next day, the day of the alleged incident. His friend's blood, we were told, was still on his uniform, he had had no time to change it. Surely after your best friend dies you are allowed some sort of compassionate leave – leave enough to wash and change your uniform?'

'We're the army, Mr Thompson, not an HR department!' Perser chortled at his own joke, craning his neck around the court for an audience. The men in the room stared back blankly.

'I appreciate that you are the army, Colonel Perser, but even the army is not devoid of all sympathy or emotion.'

'No, it is not.'

'As you have stated, all the soldiers understood their limits and understood the new rules of engagement. After their single briefing they had gone from shooting to kill, and being shot at, to peacekeeping and trying to engage with the previously hostile community in order to rebuild the city.'

'That's correct.'

'And no prisoners were harmed, no rules were broken, and no civilian was poorly treated at all, let alone suffocated, during your tour?'

'To my knowledge, nothing happened.'

'Except this case, of course . . . To your knowledge, nothing else untoward happened at all in Khandistan, expect for this unfortunate incident with Lance Corporal Danny Sutcliffe.'

'Indeed.'

'How good is your knowledge, Colonel?'

'Pretty good,' he replied sharply.

' "Pretty good" . . . Then you will know exactly what year it was when the British Army last used this technique of turning an occupying power into a police force overnight, from war-fighting phase to peacekeeping phase, in twenty-four hours?' Bobby paused and waited for a reply. Colonel Perser said nothing. 'Shall I help you?'

'Do, please,' he replied, his voice dripping with vitriol.

'The last time the British Army used these tactics – the first and last time – was in Berlin in 1945. After the Germans surrendered at the end of the Second World War. How is it that the army are using tactics eighty years old? Granted, both societies were on their knees, but crucially, the first time these tactics were used the population was ready, willing and able to rebuild. But this time . . .'

'Berlin, 1945?' Colonel Perser shook his head.

'No further questions.'

Thirty-Four

On the train on the way back to Stag Court, Adam bought Bobby a can of Coca-Cola to celebrate the silent stony-faced stare that had followed Colonel Perser's cross-examination. The man had been seething as he'd walked slowly out of the courtroom, lips pursed, eyes fixed on the door.

'I am not sure I have ever seen anyone so furious,' said Adam with a laugh, handing over the can and a large fluffy chocolate-chip muffin to Bobby, whose face positively lit up. Bobby mightn't have been much of a drinker, but his fondness for sugary snacks and fizzy drinks very much accounted for his generous waistline and large, roomy suits.

'He was not pleased, that's for sure,' replied Bobby. 'I thought the victim's mother, on the other hand, was very dignified, and I was just sorry that I had to ask her those questions.' He grimaced a little. 'What an extraordinary story she had to tell. But I have to say that after all of that, our man is not off the hook.' Adam nodded in agreement. 'We need a proper smoking gun to shift the opinion of the board. They're a tough crowd.'

'They're hard to read,' agreed Adam. 'I spend a lot of time

watching their faces, to see what moves them. So far, it's very little. I assume we're not to call our boy?'

'Of course not, he's a total wreck. Goodness knows what damage he'd do his case . . .' said Bobby, opening his can with a click and a hiss. 'I'm wondering if we should call Lord May . . . What do you think? You've seen him more recently than I have. His father was a friend of my father's, as you know, and I have always thought that he might be on our side. Although his communiqués haven't been that helpful, he's been writing all those articles that are critical of what's going on in Khandistan, and he's been on *Channel 4 News* and *Newsnight*. Did you see him?'

Adam was flattered that Bobby was asking his opinion on such an important case, involving someone who so epitomised the establishment. But he wasn't too sure that he could share with Bobby exactly what he thought of the unpleasant little man, with his searing superiority, sublime arrogance and extremely shiny shoes.

'We could, I suppose,' said Adam, trying to sound even-handed. 'He might be useful; he might come up with some support for you. But he is still at the MOD and they do like to look after their own. From what I remember, he was quite clear he didn't want to come to court.'

'True, true,' said Bobby. 'They certainly do look after their own. Let me mull that one over. But we need something a little extra, and fast, frankly. Otherwise . . .'

He was working his way through his muffin and his fizzy drink, leafing through his files on his lap and answering the endless pings on his telephone.

'I'm sorry,' he said to Adam as his phone vibrated yet again with yet another text alert. 'It seems that Colonel Perser's evidence has gone viral, whatever that really means, as has my line about Berlin and 1945. It's all over Twitter, apparently, or so a friend of mine tells.'

Adam picked up his phone and started to scroll. 'Well, "Berlin 1945" is trending, that's for sure, as are the words "court martial".'

'Is that a good thing?'

'I think it might be,' replied Adam.

'Good. It might encourage a few more sources to come forward,' said Bobby. 'When a story gets traction, you'll be amazed what comes out of the woodwork. Sometimes the bright light shone by the press can be extremely helpful.'

'At least Tony will be pleased,' Adam said.

Tony was delighted when Bobby and Adam walked through the door at Stag Court later that afternoon. He was all smiles and handshakes; obviously there was nothing he liked more than a bit of press for chambers. Sometimes, he announced loudly, the pro-bono cases were worth it after all.

'Good work, good work,' added Tony, nodding, handing Adam a brief for the following week. 'There's some other stuff for you.' He nodded towards the corridor.

'Thanks,' replied Adam, walking towards the post room. His pigeonhole really was full. There was a dull-looking preliminary hearing for the Harley Street chin doctor, whose notes he had yet to read. There was also a shoplifting case, and ones for soliciting, robbery and a possible arson.

Adam felt his shoulders sink. The court martial and the huge amount of paperwork that it entailed had truly eaten into his time. He felt sick as he stood there, flicking through all the papers, trying to quell a wave of panic. He couldn't be working any harder, he knew that, but still everything was piling up on his already-crowded plate. He suddenly understood why his friend Rupert had suffered such terrible burnout and anxiety, why he'd left the Bar, never to return. It was relentless. No sooner had you cleared one case, than there was another one waiting. And there was the Lexi Williams trial which was also due in shortly, and he and Morris were still trying to nail down her defence.

They'd tried repeatedly to work out what had happened the night of the party, but nothing was making any sense. Nisha had spent the last few days trying to track down Max Bruce's lost daughter – but despite all her contacts and tenaciousness she had a drawn a blank. Morris had not said anything directly to Adam, but Adam sensed that he was worried about Lexi's case, and they had yet to hear about the terrorism charges, which hadn't been dropped, so she was still in solitary confinement in HMP Bronzefield.

'Oh, hello,' said Georgina walking into the post room. 'I see your court martial is all over the news this afternoon.'

'Bobby had a good morning,' replied Adam, his voice sounding flat.

'You don't sound too excited about it?'

'Look at all this,' said Adam, his fist full of papers. 'It just never stops, does it?'

'No.' She smiled, pulling a pile out of her own pigeonhole. 'It does not. The trick is not to get too overwhelmed by it all, I say.'

'But how?'

'Balance, Adam, balance.' She looked at him and smiled. 'When was the last time you went to the cinema, for example?' He stood there, trying to think. What was the last film he'd seen? When had he last gone? He liked his football, he kept up with his football, he always watched Spurs, because of his late dad. But the cinema? 'When did you last go out for dinner? It doesn't have to be an expensive dinner? Even a pizza will do.'

'I can't remember.'

'Well, what are you doing at the weekend?' Georgina asked brightly.

'Me? Um, seeing my mum, probably. Friday night dinner. Saturday synagogue. That sort of thing.'

'What are you doing for dinner on Saturday night?'

'Let me think . . . It's probably me and the fish,' said Adam dryly. 'Oh, and a pizza, since you ask, and some Saturday-night TV.'

'Come out with me?' she suggested.

'You?'

Was Georgina asking him out on a date? He surprised himself by how excited it made him feel. His heart actually skipped a beat, and he smiled.

'Me and the girls,' she continued, as she looked down at the papers in her hands. 'We always have a proper night out on a Saturday – wine, vodka, gin, sushi, possibly a bit of dancing to blow the cobwebs away. You should come.'

'With the girls?' he asked.

'You could cope with a girls' night, couldn't you, Adam? Hang out with the ladies. Wine? Dancing? You're a girls' boy. They'll love you.' She squeezed his arm. 'Let me know.'

'This weekend might be hard,' he said suddenly. The idea

of a whole load of over-served posh girls all shrieking with laughter, going outside for ciggies, and gossiping about 'Hugo, Orlando and Jigs' filled him not with horror or terror, but inadequacy. He'd be playing conversational ping-pong all night, never able to get a word in edgeways, while they all talked about their hols in Tuscany and their summer in the Med.

'But you just said you were staying in with your fish?' She looked at him in bewilderment.

'I have to look through the Lexi Williams case for Thursday. We're back in on Thursday, remember?'

'I know we are, Adam. We have ten days, not that I am counting – but the case is as open-and-shut as it could be. It's going to take three days in court max, and then we'll all be home for tea.' She smiled sharply. 'And I, for one, can't wait for the whole wretched, boring thing to be over and then I can go back to my old life, and never work with that Jonathan Taylor-Cameron ever again. I won't have to listen to his casual sexism or breathe in his Marlboro Gold breath or smell his post-prandial red any-bloody-more. I think I might down a pint of wine to celebrate.'

'That bad, is it?' he asked, a little astonished by her outburst. Georgina never really complained about much. She was one of those tough, resilient types. 'I'm sorry,' he added.

'Not to worry. It'll all be over soon . . .' She walked out of the room clutching her post and stopped and turned. 'Let me know if you change your mind about Saturday.'

Adam walked back to his room, kicking himself for being so unadventurous. But a group of Georgina's friends were bound to be intimidating, with all their hair and confidence. He sighed as he sat down at his increasingly cluttered desk. All he could think of was Morris telling him that his desk was indicative of his state of mind, and if that were true, his mind was an absolute mess. He stood up and started to go through the piles of papers, moving them from one side to the other.

There was a knock on his door.

'Come in,' said Adam, looking up. 'Oh, hello, Stacey. How are you?'

'Busy, busy, busy, as always. How did you survive the drink the other night?'

'It wasn't too bad in the end. I think Jonathan had consumed so much wine that I am not sure he remembered us being there.'

'Oh, that would explain the lack of banter the next day from him – either that or his chronic hangover: he could barely open his eyes and *all noise* was pain. Even my stirring his milky coffee put his teeth on edge! Oh, by the way' – she walked towards him, waving a large brown envelope – 'this came for you just now.'

'Right.' Adam indicated that she should put it on the pile with all the other papers.

'When I said it came for you, it was shoved into my hand as I was about to walk to chambers.'

'OK,' Adam said. 'Put it there?'

'The man looked desperate, actually. He asked for you by name, and said you should read it right away.'

'OK.' Adam sighed.

'He said you should read it now, and then he ran off, up the street, like he was frightened to be discovered.'

'What did he look like?'

'Young, scared. Oh, and he had bright red hair.'

'Why didn't you say that at the beginning?' Adam leapt out from behind his desk and snatched the envelope out of Stacey's hands.

'I didn't want to sound gingerist,' she said weakly.

'What?'

'Gingerist, talking about his hair.'

'Oh, don't worry. Thank you.'

He sat down at his desk, ripped open the envelope and pulled out the papers. He put them down in front of him and turned over each page carefully. How on earth had the boy with the red hair got his hands on these? They were unbelievable. He checked, and checked. They were exactly what he hoped they were.

He grabbed his mobile and made a call.

'Bobby . . . Bobby! Are you sitting down? I think we've found your smoking gun . . .'

Thirty-Five

'All rise.'

A few days later, Judge Wickstead strode authoritatively into the court martial at Aldershot Garrison, robe billowing, jaw set, a steely look of determination on her face. Her bright blue eyes scanned the packed room. Every spare chair was occupied, every bench was full; there were plenty of people standing, leaning against the wall, right at the back. The atmosphere was tense, the air was loaded with expectation. Word had clearly got out that Lord May, returned from his low-level NATO talks in Brussels, was going to take the stand, and everyone was keen to hear what he had to say.

Wickstead sat down with a swish of her gown and smiled at the uniformed clerk.

'Please bring in the defendant.'

Lance Corporal Danny Sutcliffe paused at the entrance to the courtroom. His grey eyes were wide open, his lips parted as he looked around at the substantial crowd. He appeared shocked. He clearly hadn't expected so many people; he blinked in the bright light.

'Are you ready?' Bobby whispered in Adam's ear.

'I am,' Adam confirmed. He felt a rush of excitement as he brought out his heavy file from his bag and placed it carefully on the table in front of them both.

'Mr Thompson?' said Judge Wickstead, looking at Bobby and then briefly at Adam.

Her gaze was glacial. This was the first time she'd acknowledged him in the court. He was tempted to nod, but didn't dare.

'The defence calls the Under-Secretary of State for the Armed Forces, Lord May.'

Although Jeremy May MP was wearing civvies – a smart charcoal-grey suit, a navy tie and a white shirt, with gleaming, glistening shoes – he positively marched towards the witness box as if to authenticate his previous military credentials. He nodded sharply to various uniformed officers. He only just managed to stop short of saluting them.

Adam glanced over his shoulder to see one of the spooks take out a slim notepad and a small, sharp pencil. Cocking his head to one side he was evidently prepared to listen intently and take notes. While Lord May swore on the Bible and confirmed his name, Adam watched Danny's mother shuffle and twitch in her seat, her top teeth digging into the flesh of her bottom lip. She was the epitome of anxiety.

'Lord May,' began Bobby. 'First of all, I would like to say how extremely grateful the court is to you for giving up your valuable time to come here today.' Lord May smiled graciously. 'We all know how very busy you are, with NATO and the defence of our nation.'

'It's my pleasure,' he replied unctuously.

'How long have you, sir, been Under-Secretary of State for the Armed Forces?'

'Almost five years now.'

'Five years is a long time at the helm. And as such, were you in charge of the Khandistani war and of our response to it?'

'I was. Not the daily running, obviously, as I was not on the ground.'

'But the overall strategy?'

'Indeed.'

'And as such, you received regular updates on the progress of the war and the progress of the eventual peace?'

'I did.'

'And did you read these updates?'

'Of course I did.' Lord May chuckled with exaggerated incredulity and looked around the court. 'When one is a minister, Mr Thompson, one of one's responsibilities is to read what one receives in one's red box. That is, after all, one's job. And a very important aspect of it too.'

'And you always did your job?'

'What a question, Mr Thompson! Of course I did.'

'Were you aware of the incident of 15 January of this year? The one that took place with my client here, Lance Corporal Sutcliffe, and the alleged victim ,Timur Tadishvili?'

'I was not immediately aware of it, but I did become aware of it later, quite a lot later, after the event.'

'And why is that? Was it not in your dispatches? Did it not appear in your red box?'

'Not to my knowledge.'

'Why might that be?'

'Maybe it wasn't important enough? How should I know?' Lord May shrugged.

'But it's important enough now. It appears to be very

important now. It is, indeed, a court-martial offence,' Bobby remarked.

'Things change, Mr Thompson. What you don't understand is the chaos of war. Many things happen at the same time, and not all of them get reported or written down until much later. There's a lot going on. All I know is that it is a grossly dangerous thing to do, to place someone at the bottom of a tank with little to no oxygen.'

'How do you know that? Has it happened before?'

'I could not possibly comment.'

'It seems there was quite a lot going on,' said Bobby, opening up the file on his desk, and stacking the pages with a brisk tap on the table as if to exemplify quite how much of 'a lot' there was. 'Were you across all of it?'

'To my knowledge, I was across everything.'

'Then, Lord May, you'll be able to explain to the court here exactly what a "wetting" is?'

'A wetting?' Lord May hesitated, his small eyes darted around the room, and there was an audible shift of energy at the back, as a few rows of suits and uniforms all sat up, paying attention.

'Yes,' Bobby said, looking down at his papers. 'A wetting.'

'I am not sure I'm entirely across that term.'

'Oh.' Bobby looked up in feigned surprise. 'Really? So not quite across everything then?'

'Apparently not,' Lord May replied, his voice dripping with sarcasm.

'Let me help you out here, if I may?'

'Please do.'

'A wetting was a way of dealing with looters . . . Shall I go on?'

'Please do.' May shook his head in irritation.

'The idea being, if you rounded up the looters, put them into trucks, or tanks, or any other vehicle, and drove them to the edge of town, forcing them into the river, and leaving them there, it would take them a significant amount of time to climb out of the river and, sodden, make their way back into town. A whole day even. Isn't that the idea, Lord May?'

'I couldn't possibly comment.'

'Which would be a whole day when they would *not* be out looting. The soldiers would thereby be controlling the situation, curtailing it. Would that be an accurate statement?'

'I could not really comment.'

'Was "wetting" a tactic of the British Army?'

'No.' Lord May's cheeks flushed and he frowned with fury. 'Absolutely not!'

'Then why is it referred to frequently in these dispatches?' asked Bobby, waving a few sheets of paper to the court.

'I am not sure what dispatches you have there.' May laughed derisively. 'They could be anything.'

'These are your dispatches, your communiqués, Lord May; the ones from your red box, the ones you read.'

'How did you get those?' His eyes narrowed. 'Those are not the ones I gave you!' He spat. 'Or your colleague.' He waved dismissively towards Adam, as if he were trying to shoo him along somewhere.

'No, the ones you gave us were redacted. These are not.' Bobby showed the pages to the court and handed a copied folder over to both Newbury and Beaumont with a flourish. '*These* are not covered in thick black lines that render them unreadable. *These* reveal the true level of concern for the situation, for the conditions that the soldiers were working under; a situation, if I could remind the board and Your Ladyship, that employed a protocol that had not been used by the British Army since Berlin in 1945. May I read some of these dispatches to you, Lord May, to see if you recall anything? If you recall, to the best of your knowledge, any of these reports that were sent to you and placed in your red box?'

'My Lady, I am not sure this is legal!' Lord May threw his arms in the air, looking around the court for some sort of backup, some sort of support. The suits? The uniforms? But none came. 'These are confidential papers – they're not for civilians. Members of the public can't read these! They're top secret, only for those with clearance.'

'For important people?' ask Bobby.

'Exactly, for important people only . . .'

His last comment hung in the air. There was a long pause. Judge Wickstead looked as if she was thinking, indeed absorbing what he'd just said. Or maybe she was just enjoying his discomfort, playing it out for a few extra beats. Adam certainly was. He fought hard to refrain from smiling. He'd disliked May from the get-go.

'In a democracy, Lord May,' began Judge Wickstead, 'unfortunately, the "important people" have to answer to unimportant people occasionally. For it is the public, the civilians, who elect the important people, and who, more importantly, pay for them. There is no such thing as government money; it is taxpayers' money. It's the money that comes out of the pockets

280

of private citizens. For which the government of the day is accountable . . . Mr Thompson, please continue with your line of questioning, but I do urge caution. Keep everything relevant to this case and this case only.'

Judge Wickstead nodded at Bobby and then at the board. Alexander Newbury opened his mouth as if to protest and then slowly shut it.

'Thank you, Your Ladyship. I shall be cautious.' Adam slipped Bobby a piece of paper. 'I only have a few questions, which are taken from your communiqués, Lord May. Sent from the front. In the last days of the war. And the beginning of the peace. From Khandistan to you. On 10 January – and I quote: "Our boys will not be qualified for this. Our boys are soldiers, and you now want to make them peacekeepers. This is not their job. When are the real peacekeepers coming? Where are the professionals?" On 15 January: "We need some guidance. Our boys are out of their depth. The situation on the ground is chaos. The lines are blurred. We are reduced to crowd control. Some have resorted to wetting the looters to stop them. We need a coherent policy. Please advise." On 16 January: "We can't carry on like this, the situation is out of control. It is desperate." To which you, eventually, reply: "It sounds like it is total chaos, I agree. If this does not stop soon someone is going to get seriously hurt." Do you recognise that as your reply, Lord May?'

Bobby handed over a copy of an unredacted communiqué to the court clerk, who gave it to Lord May.

'I do,' he replied flatly, barely giving it a second glance.

'And someone did get seriously hurt, didn't they, Lord May? You knew what was happening. You knew exactly what was going on. And yet you did nothing . . . There is dispatch after dispatch here, asking for advice, for help, for proper peace-keepers, policemen, and still you did nothing.' Bobby picked up sheet after sheet of paper and waved it at the court. 'You were told, you read your red boxes, so you say, you knew exactly what was going on, and still you did not act. No help. No funds. No reinforcements. You hung them out to dry . . . Lance Corporal Danny Sutcliffe is not guilty of murder or manslaughter, sir – you are!'

Adam felt a rush of adrenalin and euphoria. Bobby had nailed it. How could Danny Sutcliffe have acted dangerously with intent to kill when this was common practice? Those further up the food chain, Lord May included, must have known what was going on. There was a moment of silence before the court erupted. There was cheering, applause and the stamping of feet as the regular soldiers standing at the back put their hands together and roared their approval. Lance Corporal Sutcliffe stared over at his mother. His young face was pink, his grey eyes were clouded with tears. Lord May looked furious.

'I really must ask everyone to be silent!' shouted Judge Wickstead. 'Silence in court! This court must come to order!'

Finally, after two or three minutes, the soldiers calmed down and the court came to order.

'Mr Newbury,' said Judge Wickstead with a weary voice. 'Your witness.'

'We have no questions, Your Ladyship,' said Alexander Newbury.

'Lord May,' Judge Wickstead said. 'You may step down.'

Lord May walked slowly out of the courtroom. His face was rigid, his hands made fists by his side. He looked neither left nor right. Adam could smell his rage from across the room. He shoved the double doors open with the palms of his hands and they smacked against the walls before swinging back again. The whole court remained silent after his exit. All Adam could hear was the subsequent slamming of the front door to the building.

Thirty-Six

'Mr Newbury?' said Judge Wickstead, ignoring Lord May's dramatic exit. 'Are you ready for your closing speech?'

'My Lady,' replied Newbury, getting slowly to his feet. Adam couldn't help but think he looked decidedly less ebullient than when they'd first met. In fact, so did Beaumont.

Alexander Newbury KC ran through his case, reminding the board of the evidence from Timur's mother, from Lance Corporal Sutcliffe's friends, his fellow soldiers who had been beside him that fateful day, when he'd taken Timur off the streets of Khandi and driven him around for hours in the well of his airless tank, with no food, no water and no regard for human life.

'A young man's life was lost, before it had barely begun,' he concluded. 'Lance Corporal Sutcliffe knew what he was doing. He was intent on avenging the death of Private Keith March, his best friend, his best friend whose blood was still fresh on his uniform. He had a motive and he acted on it. None of us want to be here, none of us want to stand in judgement on a fellow soldier, but Lance Corporal Danny Sutcliffe did not have permission to act in the way he did. He acted out of malice. I remind you all that it is our case that he intended to kill this young boy. Even if you do not find that he formed the intent to kill Timur, this case is not over. What Lance Corporal Sutcliffe did was dangerous, sufficiently dangerous to cause death. He is culpable and he should be held to account. I invite you to find Lance Corporal Danny Sutcliffe guilty of murder, or in the alternative, manslaughter. Thank you.'

Newbury bowed his head to the board and then to Judge Wickstead and sat down. His number two, George Beaumont, grabbed Newbury's shoulder and gave it a congratulatory shake.

Bobby leapt out of his seat. Adam knew he was keen to keep the energy and the motivation from his cross-examination with May. He'd spotted a light at the end of the tunnel, and he wanted to guide the board towards it.

'Who was Lance Corporal Sutcliffe,' he began, 'if not a scared young man in a very difficult situation, at the bottom of a chain of command that had abandoned him? You can see from the communiqués that the men on the ground were asking for help, for guidance. Every day they begged for some sort of road out of the muck and the mire, the dirt and the dust of the desert. But no one listened. No soldier has been put in the same position since 1945, and for good reason. How can you change from soldier to peacekeeper overnight? How can you become a policeman with no training? They tried their best. But their best was not good enough. But should you be punished for that? Did Lance Corporal Sutcliffe deliberately do harm? No. Did he set out that morning to avenge the death of his friend? No. Was he put into a situation that his senior officers had already taken issue with? Yes. Did our own

Under-Secretary of State for the Armed Forces, in fact, write in his own hand that "If this does not stop soon someone is going to get seriously hurt"? Yes, he did. They knew what the situation was, and yet they did nothing about it. Lance Corporal Sutcliffe did not stand a chance. The situation was hopeless. How could he have thought that what he was doing was dangerous when everyone else was doing the same thing? Wetting of looters and putting them into tanks was widespread. It was mentioned, as we've heard, in dispatches. Repeatedly. This young man should be applauded, lauded, for his courage and for fighting for his country, not sitting here in the dock. What he did was common practice. Therefore, it could not be dangerous. The danger comes from those who tried to hide it. The cover-up. Those who planned this should be put in the dock. It was failure by our country of those they put in harm's way, and not of this individual. I therefore ask the board to find Lance Corporal Danny Sutcliffe not guilty of murder and not guilty of manslaughter. Thank you.'

Watching Bobby lay out his case in the courtroom was a masterclass. Adam was beyond impressed. The inflection of his voice, his movements, his pauses and hand gestures were all something that other barristers should study, thought Adam.

Judge Wickstead summarised the case and the board retired to deliberate their verdict, and Adam and Bobby moved into a small room near the courtroom, where Mr Mann had organised some coffees from the machine and a plate of Rich Tea biscuits.

This was the moment that Adam always found most difficult. Had they done enough? How would the jury (or in this case the board) react? Despite his increasing amount of experience, it never got any easier. The tension was always palpable, and the wait was seemingly endless. Bobby couldn't sit down; he was pacing around the room, a ball of nervous energy. This one was obviously more personal than most, thought Adam, watching him. Bobby was normally much more laid-back than this. The ghost of his late dad, Gunner Thompson, clearly still loomed large. Mr Mann, on the other hand, appeared untouched, he simply dunked his biscuits into his coffee and made small talk about the drunk driving case that was due in court tomorrow, and where he might go on holiday.

Adam watched the clock on the wall as the hands moved slowly, each minute crawling past.

Suddenly there was a hard rap on the door. Mr Mann put down his coffee. Adam checked the clock. They'd been sitting there for thirty minutes.

The board had decided.

Back in the packed courtroom, there was standing room only when the defendant, Lance Corporal Sutcliffe, was led in to hear his fate. His fear was obvious, as Adam watched him cross the room, his head stooped, his shoulders rounded, his mother standing two rows back, wringing her hands, still wearing her thin blue anorak.

Adam felt terrible nausea as the board walked in. None of them so much as glanced across at the defendant, which did not bode well. A life sentence in a military prison was at stake.

'All rise,' the clerk demanded as Judge Wickstead strode back into court, all gown and heels and reapplied pink lipstick.

'Has the board come to a decision?' she asked, after sitting down at her desk. 'Have you reached a verdict on which you all agree?'

287

'We have, My Lady,' replied the spokesman, a well-turned-out young officer in a green uniform with a highly polished belt buckle that shone in the overhead light.

'Would the defendant please stand.'

Lance Corporal Danny Sutcliffe stood slowly; his legs were visibly shaking as he held on to the desk for support. He looked at the ground and closed his eyes. Adam could see his mother also closing her eyes as she appeared to mumble a prayer to whatever god she believed in, her lips moving urgently and silently.

'On the count of murder, how do you find the defendant, Lance Corporal Daniel Sutcliffe – guilty or not guilty?'

'Not guilty,' replied the soldier.

'And on the charge of manslaughter?'

'Not guilty of all charges.'

There was an audible gasp. It was over. Sutcliffe collapsed forward with relief, his head in his hands. His mother let out a sob, while some of the rank and file soldiers clapped.

Bobby turned to Adam and shook his hand firmly. 'Thank you for that,' he said quietly, his eyes watering with emotion. 'Good work, Adam. Really good work.'

Newbury and Beaumont both nodded across at Adam and Bobby, briefly acknowledging a job well done. Adam shuffled his papers, tidying up the files, as he gave thanks in his head to the young soldier with the red hair. What a brave whistle-blower he had turned out to be. Not only had he saved Danny Sutcliffe, but he had also unearthed the true scandal of how the soldiers had been left to swing in the breeze in Khandistan, unsure of their brief or how to handle an increasingly danger-ous situation for all concerned – soldiers and Khandistanis alike. He couldn't help thinking that despite his elation and his joy at seeing Sutcliffe's relieved and happy face, there was deep sadness too. A young boy had died, but the wrong person had been in the dock, that was for sure.

Judge Wickstead thanked and discharged the board, and ran through various formalities to draw the trial to a close. But Adam wasn't listening and neither was Bobby; they were both watching Danny Sutcliffe's face as he sat blinking, slowly coming to the realisation that his ordeal was over.

After Judge Wickstead left, the courtroom exploded with noise and chatter and some relieved and thankful laughter.

'Thank you, sir,' said Danny Sutcliffe as he walked over and shook Bobby's hand. 'Thank you with all my heart.'

'Thank this man,' declared Bobby, pointing at Adam. 'He's the one who found the communiqués.'

Outside on the steps Bobby avoided all the reporters who were weaving around, sniffing out copy: the last thing he wanted was to appear jubilant when there were so many other complex aspects to the case. He'd leave that to Danny Sutcliffe and his mum, who were standing side by side, tightly holding hands with smiles on their exhausted faces.

'Come on, Adam,' said Bobby, giving him a pat on the back. 'Let's get out of here.'

As they both walked down the few steps of the municipal court martial building to the badly tarmacked car park and their waiting Uber, they were accosted by Lord May, who leapt out of his ministerial Mercedes.

'Congratulations,' he declared, anger seeping from every pore as he gripped Bobby's hand and shook it very, very slowly. 'You total and utter shit.' He grinned. 'Consider that the only favour I will ever do for you. I know you always thought our fathers were good friends. Well, let me tell you a little secret. My father always despised yours. My father always thought yours was a bloody coward. A disloyal, despicable . . . bloody coward.'

Thirty-Seven

Sitting on the train, Bobby's mobile phone did not stop ringing all the way back to Stag Court. No sooner had he put it down on the shared table than it started vibrating again, much to the irritation of the middle-aged woman opposite, who rolled her eyes and sighed loudly.

It was extraordinary, thought Adam, as yet another call came through, how much everyone enjoyed a success. What was the saying? 'Success has many fathers, but failure is an orphan.' That and, judging by the phone calls, how incredibly unpopular Lord May actually was. His testimony had been all over the lunchtime news already. He had apparently 'stormed out of the court martial', having been 'utterly humiliated' in the witness box. His role in the invasion of Khandistan had been questioned and found lacking, but mostly the press were rolling with his comment about 'important people'. Who were 'important people', they were asking, and how did you become one?

Adam sat on the train scrolling down the news sites, listening to the reports, reading the paragraphs. It all sounded so dramatic as each journalist added their own spice and spin. Had

May really stormed out of court? Well, he hadn't gone quietly, that was for sure. May's furious face illustrated most of the pieces, sitting below headlines such as KHANDISTAN COCK-UP, or OUR BOYS HUNG OUT TO DRY, or KHANDI-HELL. Bobby's name was mentioned repeatedly, and there were photographs of a smiling Lance Corporal Sutcliffe. Adam couldn't help admiring how quickly the news had come out. Each agency was in a race against the other: first to file wins.

His phone bleeped in his hand. Even his mum had texted him. Well done, Ads! she'd written, followed by a strong-arm emoji and a heart-eyes emoji. Adam's mum was never one to scrimp on emojis: her philosophy was why stop at one when three or four would also do.

Walking back from Temple Tube, Adam and Bobby rounded the corner of Pump Court as chambers finally loomed into view. Standing on the steps just coming to the end of a celebratory cigarette was Tony, all grins and smiles and banter.

'Big day, big day,' he declared, flicking his butt across the lane in one practised movement. 'Mr Thompson, Mr Green, very well done indeed. One in the eye for the establishment, and one big notch on the bedpost for Stag Court.'

'I am not sure if it's a quite a notch on a bedpost. But I'll take it.' Bobby smiled.

'Anything to screw over that tosser Jeremy May,' said Tony. 'I can't stand the bastard.'

'I think there's a long queue of people who dislike him,' replied Bobby, putting his hand on Tony's shoulder.

'And almost all of them are in the army,' added Tony.

'It was mostly down to Adam, if I am being honest,' said

Bobby. 'His whistleblower, his unredacted files. They made all the difference.'

'Well, I never, Mr Green.' Tony nodded slowly, his mouth pursed in appreciation. 'A pint at the Wig and Pen for you. *After . . .*' he added. 'Just in case you think I am getting soft in my old age: *after . . .* you have a word with one of the clerks inside, I think it's Jessie, who's got some files for you on your botched chin doctor. The solicitor from Hayden Beswick came over this morning and delivered a whole load of patient statements about the state of their chins . . . Or something to that effect.'

Adam's heart sank. Could he not pause for a second to savour their success?

'Anyway, Jessie has the files,' said Tony, nodding inside.

Adam reluctantly walked on, leaving Bobby laughing and joking with Tony, who was keen to get any inside chat on the court martial. His rampant dislike of Lord May meant he wanted to hear a blow-by-blow account of his takedown.

It was indeed Jessie, one of the newer clerks, who had a stack of statements from Hayden Beswick. They had been sent by a keen young solicitor called Claire Smith, whom Adam had never worked with before, but who was clearly on top of her game, as it was a hefty pile that she'd delivered. He could still hear Tony and Bobby talking outside on the street, and Adam felt the smallest pang of jealousy as he wandered towards his pigeonhole. He would quite like to be part of the banter, but somehow Tony never really included him. As he stood in the post room, he wondered how long he'd have to wait to be truly part of chambers. When would Tony ask him a question that wasn't to do with work?

Adam looked at his pigeonhole. There was one solitary envelope propped up on its side. Holding the heavy files in one hand, he took it. It was handwritten and hand-delivered; it simply had his name scrawled on the small white envelope.

He put down the files on the small post-room table and ripped open the envelope. Inside was a photograph. It was small and not entirely in focus, and on the back of it was stuck a yellow Post-it note, with the words 'Thank you' written on it. He turned the photograph over to take a look. It was of a group of soldiers, a band of brothers, standing together in front of a tank in the sunshine, in what appeared to be the desert. Adam looked a little more closely. There was Lance Corporal Danny Sutcliffe in the middle, smiling, with an arm around Private Keith March. Adam recognised him from the photographs Bobby had showed him before the court martial, and on the other side . . . Adam smiled to himself. Wow. There he was. The whistleblower. With his bright red hair, grinning at the camera, his hand shielding his eyes from the glaring sun. No wonder, Adam nodded. It all became clear. Of course. Danny had been saved by one of his own. Adam smiled and quietly put the photograph in his pocket. Better to say nothing, he thought. Why get anyone else in trouble?

'Adam!' said Bobby, poking his head round the door. Adam jumped out of his skin. Guilt written all over his face. 'Are you OK?' Bobby looked confused.

'Fine, fine,' he said quickly. 'You just gave me a fright.'

'Are you busy?' asked Bobby.

'Right now . . .? No.'

Although obviously that wasn't true – there were the botched chin job statements to read, Blue Face was about to open and he and Morris were nowhere near saving Lexi Williams from a lifetime in solitary confinement, and, on top of that, he had still not texted his mum back.

'Can you spare a moment and come to my room?'

'Sure.'

Adam followed Bobby along the corridor, half wondering to himself if he should share the photograph with him. But the fewer people who knew about the leak the better.

Bobby opened the door to his room and invited Adam in.

'I just wanted to say thank you for all your help with the court martial.' He opened a cupboard in the corner of the room and brought out a new bottle of whisky and two cut-glass tumblers. 'I am not a big drinker, Adam, as you know, but I would very much like it if you would raise a toast with me to Gunner Thompson, the man who inspired me today, and indeed who does every day. I have had this bottle a long time. It was given to me by a grateful client. It's a thirty-year-old Laphroaig, a single malt.' He cracked it open and poured out two large glasses with a fat glug.

'Here,' he said, handing Adam a glass. 'To Dad.' He clunked his heavy crystal glass with Adam's, and they rang like bells.

'To your father,' replied Adam, taking a sip, and thinking of his own.

How he wished he was still alive, so he could tell him what he was doing. Share his news. Maybe he'd be proud of him? Adam wondered what that would feel like, as the hot liquid burned the sides of his throat in the most delicious way. It was excellent whisky.

'Can I show you something?' asked Bobby, with a wide smile.

'Of course.' Adam nodded, taking another sip of the golden liquid.

Bobby opened the middle drawer of his desk, using the same small key from the same leather box that he'd used before.

'I don't normally get this out,' he said. 'I don't like people who show off very much. But I feel it's only appropriate, especially after Jeremy May was so rude. Here,' he said, taking out a small box which he opened slowly. He placed it on the desk and turned it around. Adam looked down at a silver medal in the shape of a cross with a plain dark blue ribbon attached to it. 'It's a George Cross,' said Bobby. 'It's awarded by the British government for "acts of the greatest heroism or of the most conspicuous courage in circumstances of extreme danger". It's my father's.'

'How did he win that?' asked Adam, overawed, as he bent over to admire the simple silver medal.

'It's a delightful irony.' Bobby smiled, taking another swig. 'He saved the life of a man called Anthony May, who was stuck in a hut that was on fire. My father saw the flames and broke in, and pulled the man out, giving him the kiss of life. That man was Jeremy May's father.'

Thirty-Eight

On Saturday morning, Adam lit a *yahrzeit* candle in memory of his father's death, and as he always did at this time of year, he went to synagogue with his mum. They had lunch (soup), and then he kissed her goodbye before he trailed around Brent Cross trying to buy some cushions and a rug for the flat he could barely afford and had no time to furnish. Eventually, after undergoing an existential soft-furnishings crisis, he gave up and returned home with little more than two saucepans for his tins of Heinz soup and a kettle for his collection of Pot Noodles. He fed his fish, worked endlessly through his notes for the Blue Face trial that was due to start on Thursday, and thought about how much fun Georgina might be having with her raucous friends out drinking vodka/wine/mojitos while he sat on his sofa working his way through a cheese-stuffed-crust pizza, while watching Saturday-night TV wondering when *Strictly Come Dancing* might finally start.

'You're cutting it fine,' declared Nisha, as Adam ran into the Caffè Nero just around the corner from the Old Bailey at

8.45 a.m. on Thursday morning. 'I was just about to give up on you and send out a search party.'

'Sorry,' Adam puffed. 'The bus was delayed, and then cancelled, so I had to run all the way.'

'Breathe . . . breathe, you'll be fine.' Nisha smiled, picking her capacious bag up off the floor. 'I did buy you a cappuccino, but I'm afraid I've drunk it. Can you hear the crowd already?' she said, cocking her head to one side. 'It sounds like it's going to be the same sort of bunfight as the pre-trial. Shall we see if we can slip in the back? I am not sure I can face the drums and the protestors with the blue faces, and those journos and the paps.'

'The paps?' asked Adam.

'Oh, yeah.' Nisha rolled her eyes. 'The whole Bruce family is here. The wives, the children, the lot. There have been gangs of teenage girls traipsing past, hoping to catch a glimpse of Loughton – at least, I presume it's him. I have already seen Jonathan stride by, with that poor Georgina trotting behind, lugging all the files. He looked more than ready for his close-up, new bouffy hairdo and everything.'

'Morris is meeting us inside.' Adam was still trying to catch his breath. Just his luck, the most important case of the year and he'd already got sweat seeping from every pore. 'He called me very early this morning. He had some Radio 4 interview car outside his house, and he was just doing a quick interview with Emma Barnett before he came over here. Nothing about this case . . . Or at least, that's what he said.'

'He's very in demand, isn't he, Morris? I didn't catch that, I'm afraid – I am more of a Radio 6 Music person myself in the morning, I find it makes me a lot less angry,' said Nisha. 'Shall we go?'

Nisha and Adam walked past the Bailey on the other side of the road. It was chaos, exactly as they had both predicted. The drums, the banners, the protestors with painted blue faces were all there, but their ranks had been swelled by screaming teens and banks of paps, who were falling over each other trying to get snaps of Camilla, Elisa, Loughton and the rest of the nepos as they all posed together looking (as the newspapers would assert later) 'solemn and sad', while the eldest daughter, sixteen-year-old Biscuit, 'worked her curves' on the steps of the court. The police were doing their best to contain the scrum, while Adam and Nisha slipped in through the side entrance, passing through the usual airport-like security.

On the second floor, Adam met up with Morris in the robing room. With its long slatted benches and clattering lockers, it was not dissimilar to the old changing rooms in any red-brick Victorian school. Morris had already been downstairs to the cells to have a few last moments with Lexi before she was brought up to Court Number One.

'I just wanted to see her myself,' said Morris, adjusting his wig and straightening his white bands below his neck. 'I know you and Nisha have been to visit a few times without me, so I just needed to look her in the eyes before we kick off. Mainly so I can tell her parents that she's alright. Her mother, Hilary, has been on the phone nearly every day. I thought we should try and have lunch with them, Adam, at the break? Take them to the public canteen.'

'Of course,' he replied, tugging the cord on his red cloth kit-bag with his initials on it.

It was an unusual move by Morris. The last thing Adam wanted to do was to sit down with the weeping relatives at the beginning of a trial. There was clearly a very kind side to him, thought Adam. No wonder half the square had hung around to say hello when he'd come back from the US.

Court Number One was packed by the time Morris and Adam arrived. Nisha was already there waiting, talking to the court clerk, Raquel, who was dressed in a tight-fitting red frock under her robe, which she had left mostly unbuttoned down the front, and cinched with a wide belt that she'd teamed with a pair of stratospherically high heels – it was an outfit that surpassed all the other outfits that Adam had seen her in before. Even Morris noticed.

'Crikey,' he whispered to Adam as he put down his files on the desk. 'Raquel is looking well.'

'Good morning, Mr Brown – and how are we today?' she practically purred as she poured him a large glass of water.

'Very well, thank you, Raquel. How's your mother?'

'Still poorly.' She smiled. 'But thank you for asking . . . Adam?' she asked brusquely. 'Water?'

She couldn't still be holding a grudge from the time he'd asked her about her text messages, way back during his first ever case involving the death of DI Cliveden? But there it was. It was obvious she'd rather have spat in his water than pour him a glass. She smacked it down on the table; a small amount sloshed over the side.

'What have you done to annoy her?' asked Morris.

'Who knows,' Adam said, shrugging, as on the other side of the courtroom a harassed-looking Georgina walked in behind a suave Jonathan, who stood an overly long time behind his chair as he surveyed the public gallery, checking for 'faces' it might be worth giving a little smile to.

Max Bruce's wives were at the front. Out of mourning at last, Camilla sported an emerald-green jacket with a fuchsia lipstick, while Elisa was still channelling the look of a Robert Palmer girl, with slicked-back hair, a black bandage dress and scarlet lips. She was hiding behind a pair of large round mirrored sunglasses, despite there being not a ray of sunshine in the courtroom.

The crackle of walkie-talkies and the buzzing of bailiffs announced the arrival of Lexi. The room fell silent as the doors opened. Adam craned his neck to try and catch her eye and give her a reassuring smile as she was led in. Dressed in a white shirt and blue skirt, she looked demure. Her hair was still tied back. She was led up to the dock behind the bulletproof glass. She scanned the gallery, looking for her parents who were sitting in the far corner, tucked in tight against the curved wooden carving of the panelled ceiling. Her mother gave her the briefest of reassuring smiles.

'All rise,' announced Raquel, as the diminutive, stocky Judge Clare Peters, with her efficient hair, minimal makeup and inscrutable manner, walked slowly towards her throne. Adam watched as she took her chair with a flap of her robe, her eyeline matching Lexi's. Judge Peters placed a small square of black cloth on the desk in front of her. This was a murder trial and, previously, when they could enforce the death penalty, judges had used to wear a black cloth on their head to symbolise the severity of the situation; however these days the cloth had been replaced by a small black square. Judge Peters cleared her throat and did not look across the court. But Lexi most certainly did. Her hard stare worried Adam. She did not look contrite at all; in fact, there was a determined look of confrontation on her face, which did not bode well.

Before the trial could begin, a jury had to be selected, and Raquel ordered them in and then told them to line up and wait to be spoken to. Sixteen men and women of different sizes, ages and ethnic backgrounds were ushered along, some more enthusiastically than others. Some were clearly intrigued, as they gawped at the gallery. Others couldn't get out of the courtroom quickly enough. The idea of spending the next few days or even longer with this lot was enough to make them want to run for the hills.

'The thing is,' began one woman with more plums than Waitrose, 'I've got a holiday about to be booked next week in the Seychelles. It's the trip of a lifetime and I simply can't miss it.'

Judge Peters was having none of it. Mrs Plum would have to miss her holibobs. One by one they were spoken to and she listened to their litany of excuses as they attempted to wriggle out of their civic duty. 'Having to work' only raised a sigh and an eyebrow. 'A business trip to Dubai' elicited a shake of the head. 'A driving test' made her frown. Only one woman who had to care for her elderly mother was released, and another young man who had a small business selling handmade sourdough door-to-door was also let off, as he was the main breadwinner – a joke that even managed to raise a smile from the bailiffs. But mostly, the more they squirmed like worms on a hook, the less Judge Peters was likely to let them go. Finally, after an hour of back and forth, twelve jurors – good and true – were picked and told to take their seats for the trial to begin.

Adam was half hoping for a break before they got under way, but Judge Peters was ruthlessly efficient, and immediately announced that the court was in session and the jury were sworn in.

'I must remind you that this is a very high-profile case,' she said, looking fiercely over her half-moon glasses. 'Anything you have read, or heard, or seen so far about the defendant or indeed the victim must be discarded and ignored. You must only listen to the evidence heard in this court of law and you must not discuss this case with anyone outside this court. They have not been privy to the privilege and the evidence that you have, and they may seek to persuade you one way or the other . . .'

The jury nodded that they were not prejudiced in any way.

Judge Peters nodded back. 'Proceed!'

Thirty-Nine

Jonathan Taylor-Cameron stood up and bowed towards Judge Peters and smiled briefly at the jury. He took a sip of water, adjusted his wig a touch. He was playing to the gallery, thought Adam, briefly irritated. He'd been by Jonathan's side enough to know the little flourishes, the spins he did in his expensive shoes, as well as the picking up and the nonchalantly putting down of his briefs. Which he duly did, just before he approached the jury.

'On 16 June of this year, the famous, beloved artist, the most talented man of his generation, was brutally murdered in front of his friends, his family, his wives and his dear, sweet children. One moment he was celebrating one of the greatest achievements of his life, a retrospective of his finest works in one the most celebrated galleries in the world – the *Royal* Academy.'

Jonathan stressed the word 'Royal' so much that Adam half expected a band of trumpeters to enter the court, complete with heraldic flags and chainmail.

'The Royal Academy in the heart of London. But instead of celebrating with his nearest, dearest – his loved ones – he ended up fighting for his life, unable to breathe, poisoned in the very room where he should have been enjoying his ultimate triumph.

'Sir Max Bruce OBE was known to all of us. He was a national treasure, a great artist and a great man. He was mentor to many and an inspiration to the nation. He was brilliant, and kind, and a father to six children, the youngest of whom is just five years old. What an unspeakable thing to witness. What an appalling thing to happen to such a great man. Over the next few days, you, the jury, will hear how the gifted and philanthropic Max Bruce was poisoned, sprayed in the face with that ancient and reliable killer, cyanide. You will hear how he fought for his life, desperately clawing at his own collar, as he lay, gasping, dying, on the parquet floor.'

He paused and took a slow sip of water, just so the jury could ponder the image of Max on the floor, pulling at his clothes.

'You will hear how the accused, a young woman, Alexandra Williams, launched herself at him, spraying him viciously in the face with her fatal can of paint. Don't be seduced by her youth or her seeming naivety, for she stalked her victim for months. She joined the Royal Academy expressly to murder Sir Max Bruce OBE. Was she interested in art? Or did she take the internship – thereby denying a more worthy candidate – simply so she could carry out her crime? You will be shown video evidence of the accused, Alexandra Williams, carrying out the crime. You will hear of forensic evidence of the accused practising the crime in her own kitchen! You will hear of the contamination in her own workplace. You will see digital evidence of obsession and fanaticism, of an ideology that was so deep-rooted in the accused's mind that not only was she driven to murder – she planned it, practised it and executed it in front of Sir Max Bruce OBE's very own children.

'Before I proceed, I am going to show said footage of what is, in fact, agreed evidence of the event and the evening in question. It is not disputed that Alexandra Williams was there that night. And this footage was taken by Sir Max's son. Images a child should never have to film, especially of his own father.'

The giant television screens in the courtroom flickered into life.

The opening frames were noisy and chaotic. There was laughing in the gallery, which rapidly became shouting and screeching. It was much louder than Adam remembered it to be, mainly because he'd watched the video on mute in chambers. He always thought that sound distracted from watching everyone's faces. But the cries of 'Stop the war!' resonated loudly in the courtroom. Up in the gallery both Camilla and Elisa winced. There were the screams of the guests, the shattering of champagne glasses, and then the security guards were seen thundering through the crowd and tackling Lexi to the ground before dragging her away, still shouting. Then Sir Max made his Picasso quip with his paint-smeared face that he attempted to wipe clean, and then he collapsed, writhing in agony on the floor. Jonathan stopped the film a little before the end. He glanced up at the gallery; there was no need to watch Max Bruce's final death throes.

There was a shocked silence in court.

Jonathan paused. 'Ms Williams disregarded the safety of others, and the emotional fallout of such a crime was total. For she believed that she was killing for a cause. That she, and no one else, has the moral high ground, over the rest of us mere pond life . . . fools . . . who know nothing at all.'

He added quickly, just to hammer home his point: 'You will understand that the accused joined the Royal Academy for the sole purpose of committing a crime, and you will see that on the night in question Alexandra Williams poisoned Sir Max Bruce OBE without remorse, leaving six children without a father, two women without a partner, and this country . . . without a national treasure.'

Jonathan stopped and inhaled deeply, as if he'd been personally affected by the loss of such a magnificent artist, and, enjoying the utter silence and the intense gaze of his captivated audience, he walked slowly back to his chair.

Adam glanced across at Georgina, who was looking up at Jonathan. It was not clear how much of that opening speech she had written. Adam suspected it would have been most of it, but Jonathan had sure as hell delivered it with aplomb. Adam had heard that Jonathan had been good in his day – he must have been, otherwise he would not have been a member of Stag Court in the first place – and he had to admit he was impressed. As indeed were the jury, who all turned to look at Lexi, in a very different way from before.

Next to him, Adam heard Nisha's stomach rumble.

'Do you think she's going to break for lunch?' she whispered hopefully into Adam's ear.

'Would the Crown like to call their first witness?' asked Judge Peters.

'Apparently not,' replied Adam, under his breath.

He'd heard that Peters was one of those judges who thought that the system was a little too flabby, lackadaisical, too slothful in its attitude to work, and a little too long on lunch and breaks. She had a reputation for working her court hard right up to the 1 p.m. break. Adam sneaked a look at his watch. It was 12.33, quite late in the morning to be bringing in the first witness.

'The Crown calls Malcolm Davis,' said Jonathan.

Morris immediately looked down at his notes. 'The security guard,' said Adam, leaning over. 'The big one. He's on film dragging Lexi out of the gallery.'

All three of them watched as a burly bloke with an Action Man haircut in a tight-fitting sweatshirt that showed off his ballooning biceps, and even tighter trousers that left nothing to the imagination, walked into court.

'Mr Davis,' began Jonathan, after Malcolm had been sworn in and confirmed his name. 'Were you working at the Royal Academy on the night of 16 June this year?'

'I was,' he replied, with a twang of an Australian accent.

Jonathan waited for a second, clearly hoping for more. 'Why were you working there on that night?'

'I was employed.'

'For the court,' said Jonathan tightly, 'could you say what your employment is?'

'I'm a gym instructor,' explained Malcolm. 'But . . .' He raised a large forefinger. 'I am also a part-time security guard in my spare time. I am employed by an agency – Muscle Men – and we do private events. Parties, birthdays, weddings, that sort of thing, anywhere that might need some sort of security.'

'And you were hired as security on the night in question?'

'I was . . .'

'Do please continue, Mr Davis, and explain to the court what you were doing that night.'

'My job that night was to mainly make sure that no one came anywhere near the big giant painting.'

'Were you briefed about anything else? Any other security threat?'

'Er . . . no.'

'So the attack came out of nowhere?'

'Yeah, totally out of the blue. But I heard the shouting and the yelling, and then I saw her, the defendant , spraying the old man in the face with the paint, and then instinct kicked in and I ran towards the perpetrator, and I took her down and then dragged her away from the victim.'

'Did she resist you taking her down?'

'No, she flopped over and made no attempt to resist capture at all, like a rag doll.'

'And you had a good view of what happened?'

'Bird's eye,' he confirmed.

'No further questions,' said Jonathan.

Judge Peters turned to look at Morris and Adam. Was she as nonplussed as Adam? All Jonathan had managed to prove was that Lexi had sprayed paint in Max Bruce's face. Something that the jury knew already as they'd just seen the footage.

'Your witness, Mr Brown.'

'Quite a sharp-eyed bird then, Mr Davis,' said Morris, a touch of humour bubbling through his voice. 'For according to the video we have all just seen, you were at the opposite end of the room when the incident happened, and yet you've informed us that your job was to look after the painting, and there was only one artwork in the room. What happened?'

'Well, that's because of that girl, there . . .' He pointed at Lexi.

'Ms Williams?'

'Yeah, well, she'd been flirting all evening with the other security guard, who'd given her his chair. He fancied her, right? And that night, she took him for a right ride. He thought he was in there, so he told us to go up the other end of the room, while what she was really doing was getting her can from under his chair, and didn't fancy him at all. She was using him, playing him for an old fool!'

'How would you know all this, Mr Davis?'

'It was obvious – bleeding obvious, OK? When you've been in security as long as I have, you get to see these things.'

'Obvious to you, a security guard hired for one night only, who spent the entire evening guarding the wrong end of the room? The opposite end of the gallery to the major artwork and the VIP guest?'

'Yeah, but I saw what I saw.'

'How long have you been in security, Mr Davis?'

'Eighteen months.'

'No further questions,' said Morris before he sat down.

Judge Peters inhaled and flared her nostrils. 'Let's break for lunch.'

Forty

The hallway outside Court Number One was bustling with all the people who'd been squashed into the public gallery watching the case. The wives, Loughton and the other nepos were all wandering aimlessly around looking for someone to organise lunch.

'Has someone booked somewhere?' Adam heard Camilla ask into the ether, with a hopeful and yet majestic wave of her hand. Eventually some sort of PR/PA type came scurrying through the melee and announced they had booked a dear little brasserie for lunch *en famille* around the corner.

As the crowd thinned, Adam spotted Lexi's parents standing by the staircase, looking like a couple of lost souls. They both had their hands clasped anxiously in front of them, as they scanned the crowd for a familiar face.

'Mr and Mrs Williams?' asked Adam. They both smiled weakly. 'Come this way.'

Adam ushered them towards the lifts. The doors opened on a silent group of people all avoiding eye contact, all observing the very specific sign on the wall: DO NOT DISCUSS CASES IN THE LIFT.

Downstairs, lunch in the public canteen at the Old Bailey was not what would traditionally be referred to as a fine-dining experience, with its bright lights, plastic trays and skinny sandwiches in airtight boxes, packets of crisps, cans of fizzy drinks, and small wicker baskets of electric-green apples so shiny they looked like they were made of wax. It was sometimes frequented by jurors trying their level best to spend their £5.71 per diems, while they waited to be called. It was an airless, joyless place that smelt of stale clothes, like a jumble sale. It was all a far cry from the plates of buttered asparagus they served in the barristers' mess on the fifth floor. But Morris was making a point of being kind to Lexi's parents, who were desperate to find out how he thought the case was going, and whether they might lift the appalling terrorism charges that loomed, like the sword of Damocles, above the head of their terrified daughter.

'I'm not sure the security guard said much,' ventured Hilary, staring at her cheese-and-pickle sandwich, the white bread already curling at the edges. She was obviously too anxious to eat it. Her thin hands were shaking, and her manner was twitchy. Adam noticed that she had bitten off most of her fingernails.

'I agree with you.' Morris nodded enthusiastically. 'He added very little indeed to the proceedings.'

'And you did well with the cross-examination,' she added. 'Didn't he, Andrew?'

Andrew had not even pretended to get any lunch; he'd bought himself a milky coffee in a Styrofoam cup, which was going cold in his hands.

'Yes, very,' he replied. 'What is happening with the terrorism charges?'

Morris explained he was expecting them to be dropped, as there was not enough evidence to connect what had happened to the Home Secretary with the death of Max Bruce. Adam felt a chill run down his spine. Standing in line, also buying a cup of coffee and a small packet of shortbread biscuits, was Judge Wickstead, looking chic in a dark suit and a burnt-orange silk shirt, tied in a pussy bow under her chin. One side of her sleek blonde bob was tucked behind her ear.

'Adam,' she said as she walked past, clocking him with her steely-blue eyes. He nearly choked on his Coke. Should he stand up? Sit down? 'Congratulations on your court martial.'

'Thank you, Your Ladyship,' he mumbled.

'I hear it was all your work.'

'I wouldn't go that far,' he replied quickly. 'Bobby did all the heavy lifting.'

'You gave him plenty to lift, apparently.' She smiled. 'Morris,' she added. 'Always good to see you.' And off she went, the metal tips of her heels click-clacking across the floor, as Adam fought hard to calm his furiously beating heart. It was as if she'd crept up on him deliberately to give him a fright.

Morris looked at Adam, his eyebrows arched questioningly. 'She appears to have you in her sights.'

Fortunately there was no time for an explanation, as they were due back in court, where Jonathan called the police forensic scientist.

Adam glanced up at the gallery and noticed that none of the Bruce family were in their seats. Either lunch was taking a little longer than expected, or, having posed for pictures already, they didn't feel the need to run the gamut of protestors and press on the Old Bailey steps again. Not that their seats weren't taken. This was the sort of trial that people queued up for, with no spot knowingly going cold before another backside occupied it.

Dr Malone, the police forensic scientist, arrived blinking on the stand. A small, fragile, elderly-looking man in rimless spectacles, his head moved continuously, as if he were constantly interrupting his own train of thought.

Jonathan did his best to settle him down, asking him some basic questions about cyanide and traces of it, and how much of it had been in the paint.

'Where else did you find traces of cyanide, Dr Malone? Where else did you swab?'

'Well,' began the doctor, 'we found traces of the poison at the Royal Academy, at the crime scene, in the ladies' toilets – the basins *and* a cubicle – under the suspect's fingernails, on her palms, and on, in and around her desk, and also in the vape refill in her desk drawer.'

'Would this be consistent with Ms Williams having handled the poison?' asked Jonathan, with a little sideways look at the jury. Were they concentrating on this?

'It would.'

'Where was the most contaminated area?'

'Under the chair in the gallery.'

'After that?' Jonathan smiled at the jury, and nodded in a way that indicated that that would of course have been the case.

'Her desk.'

Jonathan looked pleased. 'So, just to reiterate: the second highest concentration of poison was in Ms Williams's desk, along with the vape refill?'

'Yes.'

'No further questions.'

Adam didn't dare look up at the gallery. He knew that Hilary would have her head in her hands, and Andrew would be staring like a stoic into the middle distance. He could see Lexi slowly shaking her head, rocking back and forth, both arms wrapped around her body, self-soothing.

'Dr Malone? You are a forensic specialist, are you not?' Morris asked.

'I am, sir.'

'From your in-depth report' – Morris was flattering him – 'I notice there are no traces of the poison in Ms Williams's flat, the apartment that she was living in, at the time of the murder?'

'Yes, that is correct.'

'Would that strike you – an expert such as you are – as unusual?'

'How do you mean?'

'That if you are handling a poison, indeed filling a spray-can with poison, that there is no trace of said poison in your house? Surely you would have brought some of it home with you? On your clothes? Your shoes? Your skin – and yet, in Miss Williams's flat there was nothing. That is odd, surely?'

'Maybe.'

'How would you, as an expert, account for that then?'

'I can't.'

'You can't . . . You can't account for there being no traces of forensic evidence in Miss Williams's flat – none at all. Thank you.' Morris made as if to sit down, but then he stopped and turned back. 'One last question, if only to humour me. How many other people and places were swabbed by the police when they investigated this crime?'

'I am not sure I know what you mean.'

'It's a simple question, Dr Malone. Who else did the police take samples from?'

'Just Miss Williams, and her desk and the toilets and the gallery itself.'

'So no one else was tested? No one else was swabbed? And nowhere else was tested either?'

'No.'

'So, the cyanide could have been found on lots of other desks and under lots of other people's fingernails – but no one knows, as no one was tested?'

'Possibly.'

Morris scratched his neck and moved his wig with exaggerated bewilderment. 'So it could have been anyone at the party? Or anyone who worked at the gallery who had the cyanide?'

'In theory, yes.'

'In theory . . . yes. And I would suggest also in practice . . . No further questions.'

The police had a done bad job of investigating the murder: they'd got their suspect, and they had not made any effort to look anywhere else. All Morris and Adam had to show was doubt.

Adam dared to look up at the gallery again. The mood among Lexi's supporters appeared to have lifted a little. Hilary's head was no longer in her hands, and Andrew was sitting straight, although still not looking at his daughter.

It was advantage Morris.

Or at least that's what Adam felt as Jonathan called his last witness of the day.

PC Elena Bishop took the stand and said her oath with a level of complacent self-righteousness that Adam found worrying. Dressed in her dark police uniform, her silver buttons brightly polished, she reeked of jobsworth and paperwork and parking tickets – the sort of person who'd tell you off for accidentally dropping a crisp packet on the pavement and would watch and wait while you bent down to pick it up. She looked around the court and up at the gallery with a contented smile on her round face.

'PC Bishop, you were one of the first police to search Ms Williams's flat on the day of the incident, and it was you who were charged to look at her computer?'

'I was. I am a computer expert. That's my job and that's what I was given charge of.'

'Right,' said Jonathan. 'And could you tell the court what you found?'

'Nothing. Nothing at all.'

She looked surprisingly delighted to share such news. Adam wondered where this cross-examination was going.

'And her telephone?' asked Jonathan.

'Nothing either.' Her voice sounded all sing-song and nursery-school teacher, but somehow Adam knew something else was coming. He glanced across at Georgina who was looking intently at the witness, waiting.

'Is that unusual?'' asked Jonathan.

'Oh, very.' She smiled, pursing her lips with pleasure.

'What would that suggest to you? As an expert?'

'As an expert,' she repeated, enjoying the phrase, 'as an expert, that would suggest to me, in my experience, that it was a professional job, the sort of thing that I would, as an expert, expect to see in a terrorist organisation. It suggests to me that it was someone who knew what they were doing. They were cleaning their equipment, destroying their tracks.'

'So it was a professional job then? A professional hit?'

'Objection!' Morris leapt out of his seat and Adam almost joined him. 'Leading the witness!'

'I agree,' said Judge Peters. 'Mr Taylor-Cameron, you must be careful how you ask these questions.'

'I apologise, Your Ladyship. I really do . . . apologise.'

'Please ignore the last comment,' Judge Peters directed the jury.

Adam listened as Jonathan continued to suggest how very rare it was to have such a clean, pristine computer, all the time thinking that what Judge Peters had said – that the jury should unremember the fact that Lexi was a 'terrorist' and a professional one at that – would be unlikely. Jonathan had done it on purpose. It made him angry. He had to find out who'd murdered Max Bruce. No matter the brilliance of Morris, Lexi was looking at life behind bars.

'Oh, and while I have you here,' continued Jonathan, with an insincerity that made Adam's heart sink even further, 'can we have a look at Ms Williams's social media, which, oddly, despite her professionalism, she failed to delete.'

'She did.'

'For the court, we have images of her social media posts, which we'll pop up on your screens for ease of viewing. Here we go . . .'

Morris's head swung round; both of his eyes were focussed on Adam. 'What the hell is this?' he hissed.

Had they disclosed this? Had they said this was evidence they were going to use? Adam felt sick and panicked as he mentally skimmed page after page after page, after files, after notes, after sheets and sheets of paper. Had he missed something?

'So, if we look at the screen, Ms Williams goes by the name of @lexluthor189, which I believe is the name of Superman's arch-nemesis?'

'That is correct.'

'So, here are various statements that she's made, which are pro the Blue Face protest. I'll just flick through so you can get the gist . . .'

Huge images of Lexi's Twitter were beamed around the court. There were photographs of the Home Secretary with blue paint on his coat, accompanied by a litany of laughing emojis.

'And some anti-war slogans she has retweeted.'

Images of Out, Out, Out of Khandistan came up on to the screen.

'And could you read that out, Detective?'

' "It's time for them all to GO!" declaimed PC Bishop, as if auditioning for am-dram.

'Thank you, Detective – and who does that refer to? *Who* needs to go exactly? And what does "go" actually mean?'

'Well, "go" means "die" in the context of this tweet. And the people who need to "go" are "the rich". So "The rich must die." That's what she retweeted.'

'Objection!' declared Morris. 'Hearsay!'

'Overruled.' Judge Peters frowned. 'I am not following your argument, Mr Brown. The Crown provided the defence with these tweets some time ago, along with an application to rely on the hearsay statements that are made in them. The defence did not submit any objection. In addition to this, they were, and have been, all over social media and in the media itself for weeks. I think, maybe, I might suggest we break for the end of the day and you might discuss this matter with your junior, Mr Green, and perhaps, we can reconvene tomorrow. After you have your house in order.'

Forty-One

Men explode and women implode (as Adam had once been told by a psychiatrist), as the usual reaction to tragedy or something not going the right way. But Morris, as it turned out, just remained completely silent. He did not implode or explode or do anything. He did not move a muscle or even breathe (as far as Adam could work out) as they sat side by side in a black taxi on the way back to Stag Court.

It was only when they pulled up at the top of the lane that Morris finally spoke. He opened the cab door and slowly got out. 'Don't you *ever* do that to me again, Adam,' he said. Bizarrely, both his eyes seemed to focus fully when he was furious. 'You made us look amateur and unprepared. You have been so caught up with your feelings of innocence and your "hunches"' – he flicked a couple of livid-looking quotation marks in the air – 'that you have forgotten the basics, the paperwork, the paper trail. Your research needs to be forensic. You need to be accurate, and most of all, Adam, you need to use your brain, and not your heart, or your gut or whatever you millennials say. The law is dispassionate. If you lose sight of that, Adam, you will lose your head.'

He slammed the door, leaving Adam feeling as if he had just been administered six sucker punches to the head.

'Are you alright, mate?' asked the cab driver, looking at Adam in his rear-view mirror. 'Just torn you a new one, has he? Take your time. You look like you've had a tough day.'

In the back seat of the taxi Adam inhaled and closed his eyes. He had a long evening ahead of him, going through all the Crown's papers again, just to make sure he hadn't missed anything else. He couldn't understand how this had happened. His telephone rang in his pocket.

'Hello?' he said, expecting to hear the irate voice of Nisha on the other end, also tearing into him, reminding him that they had been served notice on the tweets weeks ago, that she had given him all the paperwork, and why hadn't he remembered it, or used it, or any of the bloody above? He gritted his teeth, braced for the onslaught.

'Adam Green?' It was a male voice.

Adam sat up and paid the taxi with his bank card. 'Yes?'

'I am sorry for calling you on your phone, but I am *that* annoyed about what happened in court today I had to call you.'

'Who is this?'

'Oh, sorry! It's Steve,' said Steve.

'Steve . . .?' Adam was racking his brains. Steve? Steve?

'Steve Graham, the security guard from the Royal Academy.'

'Oh, Steve! Hello.' Adam shut the cab door and began walking down the lane to chambers. 'How can I help you?'

'Well . . .'

Well, Steve had a lot to say about what had happened in court that day. He'd been listening to news of the trial on his portable radio through his earpiece in the gallery, something he normally reserved for special football matches, finals, that sort of thing – he was not unprofessional or anything, but what the other security guard had said about him in court, that he had been played like a fiddle and treated like a fool, had really got his goat. So much so that he'd spent the afternoon going through all the old CCTV footage, and he'd got something that Adam should come and have a look at.

'But haven't the police seen it all before?' asked Adam.

He was standing outside chambers, about to go in and face the music, or at least the blank faces of his fellow-barristers, as they would all pretend that they knew nothing about what had happened in court today. They were very adept at that. Avoiding the foul smell, anything a little tricky. It was that very English thing of ignoring the elephant in the room, even if it was sitting crossed-legged drinking tea right in front of you.

'The police!' Steve laughed. 'They've barely been here. Once they'd arrested that girl, Lexi, they almost never came back. They barely spoke to me, and I was right next to her when it happened, the murder – and the police haven't even asked me to come to court or stand in the witness box or anything. Instead they've asked that temp security guard. I mean, I've worked here for over ten years and I haven't been asked my thoughts at all.'

'That must be annoying,' Adam replied, trying to work out if Steve's nose was out of joint simply because he wanted to be in court, in the box, the centre of attention, mentioned in dispatches, or if he genuinely had something useful to say. 'Um, Steve?' said Adam as he spotted Georgina walking down the lane towards him. 'Can I call you back in a minute?'

'Alright, mate, but don't leave it too long: I'm off home in an hour.'

Georgina smiled as she strode towards him, her thick auburn hair shining in the afternoon sunshine.

'I would offer to buy you dinner tonight,' she said, halting on the steps to Stag Court, 'but I suspect you might be chained to your desk until dawn, self-flagellating, being flung scraps by Morris from afar.'

'You might find it amusing,' said Adam, 'but Morris certainly does not.'

'Don't worry,' she said, touching his arm. 'We all make mistakes. It's how we recover from them that counts.'

'Did you read that in a self-help book?'

'I might have done.' She raised her eyebrows.

'Except you never make mistakes.' He sighed.

'I do!'

'When? I can't think of one, ever.'

'Oh, come on,' she said, holding the door open. 'It'll all be fine. I promise.'

Georgina and Adam walked along the busy corridor where the banter and the laughter between the clerks and the secretaries stopped as soon as they approached.

'Oh, Adam!' said Stacey, walking towards them. 'I wonder if now might be a good time for some mentoring? It's been a couple of weeks since our last session and I thought—'

'Now is not a good time, Stacey,' said Georgina. 'If you

need a chat, I am pretty sure you'll find Jonathan in an excellent mood. In the meantime, Adam here is busy.'

Adam walked into his room and closed the door behind him. He'd had worse days in court, that was for sure, but this one might possibly rank in his top ten. He opened his computer to various terse emails from Nisha, where she'd re-sent the documents that had been served by the defence, along with a sharp note saying that the Crown's case had not even been that substantial, and that it was 'hardly Blue Arrow!' Adam remembered learning about the Blue Arrow case at Oxford, famously the most expensive case in British legal history, which had cost over £70 million in today's money, where four men had been convicted but their convictions were later quashed, as the trial was deemed to have been too complicated for the jury to have understood. Nisha was right: Blue Arrow this was not.

Adam logged into Twitter just to see if there had been any more activity on the @lexluthor189 account that he should be aware of. Lexi's account was still up, but it no longer appeared to be active or even live. The last few tweets had been the ones read in court earlier that day. He then made the mistake of putting #BlueFace into the search box, at which point his computer nearly combusted in front of him. The vitriol, the bile, the outrageous claims and counter-claims were something else – stop the war, the war is a conspiracy, it's fake news, down with the patriarchy, eat the rich, Max Bruce deserved it, free Lexi, lock her up, the wifies are lizards, the establishment is corrupt, who's first against the wall, art is a capitalist construct, who wants to cover Loughton in his own hot sauce and lick it off . . .

There were photographs from the steps of the Old Bailey,

where the wives were looking fragrant, posing and pouting. Loughton had been snapped from every possible angle. There was Jonathan, frequently posted along with #wanker, and then there were a few of Georgina accompanied by various fire emojis and some heart-eyes. There were a couple of wags who insisted she could defend them anytime! Or that it was worth doing time just to meet her! Adam did have to admit she looked beautiful on the steps of the Bailey.

His mobile rang on his desk.

'Are you on your way?'

'Steve?' He'd forgotten to call him back.

'Yes – I'm waiting for you here, otherwise I'd be halfway to Green Park Tube by now, before changing at Victoria for my District line train to Ealing.'

'I'm on my way,' said Adam, picking up his coat off the back of his chair.

This had better be good, he thought.

Steve Graham was waiting for Adam in the hallway of the Royal Academy as he ran up the steps and through the revolving door. The place was busy – there seemed to be quite a few people still milling around, and a small queue waiting to get into the Max Bruce retrospective, which, given that there were only forty minutes remaining before the gallery closed, seemed to be cutting it fine.

'There are quite a few people here,' remarked Adam as he shook Steve's firm, solid hand.

'It's the trial effect, isn't it.' He sniffed, looking at the punters as if they were gatecrashers at a wake. 'Just when we thought we'd got rid of all those rubberneckers and influencers, now they're back, photographing themselves in front of the painting all over again. Anyway . . .' He rolled his eyes and shook his head, his stiff gelled Sir Keir hair not moving an inch. 'You haven't come to see them though, have you? A busy man like yourself . . . Follow me.'

Adam walked up the well-worn marble back staircase to the side of the hall, giving Steve and his hefty backside a little more room than last time. Adam supposed that if you spent most of the day sitting down next to a painting, you needed a big seat.

'One more flight of steps,' puffed Steve, as he looked over his shoulder. 'Nearly there.'

It felt odd for Adam to be back in the gallery. He'd watched Loughton's video so many times he felt as though he knew the place like the back of his hand, but the difference between an image and reality was almost diametrically opposed. The place was much bigger, and there were many more passages and side doors. Steve unlocked the door to a room on the third floor with one of the many keys he had on a ring, and pushed it open to reveal a bank of computers with numerous flickering blue-grey images of the gallery below.

'This is where the magic happens, isn't it, Sergei?' Steve said.

In the darkness, his pale, angular face uplit by the strobing glow of the computers in front of him, was Sergei. He didn't shift his gaze from the screens.

'It is, Steve,' he replied, in a heavy Eastern European accent.

'Sergei's from Poland. He's been here, what? Two years?'

'Two years, four months and two and half weeks. Not that I am counting.' Sergei laughed dryly, his eyes still not leaving the moving images.

'Did the police come up here?' asked Adam.

'No,' replied Sergei. 'No one comes up here. Ever.'

'You would have thought the police might have wanted to see the footage from the night of the murder?' suggested Adam, pulling up a chair and sitting down in the dark.

'I have very bad angle in that room,' admitted Sergei. 'As it is normally hallway and not gallery. That big painting is not usually there. It was only for the exhibition. Other cameras in gallery are much better.'

He leaned forward and flicked back and forth from one room to another, demonstrating to Adam just how slick the security system was around the rest of the gallery. He could see faces, expressions, and there were plenty of good angles on the paintings.

'This one.' Sergei shrugged, flicking back to the large gallery and the image of *Primal Scream*. 'This one is bullshit. That's why the Russian oligarch insist that Steve sit there all day, to give extra security to priceless painting.'

'Anyway, you're welcome to see the attack, if you want,' said Steve. 'Sergei's lined it up for you.'

Adam sat and watched the grainy footage, which was filmed from one security camera high up in the ceiling pointed down towards the other end of the room at the painting. Adam hunched over and squinted in the darkness. Sergei was right: Loughton's film had captured the attack much better. The colours were brighter, and the faces in sharper focus, and the blue paint being sprayed happened right in front of him, with a close-up of Lexi's contorted face, plus the ripple effect of Max Bruce collapsing and dying on the floor in front of his own masterpiece while Lexi was dragged out by the security guards was fascinating. She was kicking and screaming, being pulled along the floor on her back in her black and blue-flowered dress, but not one person was looking at her. They were gripped by what was unfolding in front of them, as Bruce tugged at his shirt and rolled around on the parquet floor.

'I see what you mean, Sergei,' said Adam. 'It's not very clear.'

'As I said . . . bullshit.'

'But that's not what I asked you here to see,' said Steve. 'It's this. Play it, Sergei!'

They all three sat in the dark, staring at one screen that flickered and jumped.

'Tell me I'm not an idiot,' said Steve, pointing towards the chair in front of and to the right of the painting. 'Watch.'

They watched in silence as Lexi came into the gallery and seemed to look around, stood by Steve's chair, and then left again. Then a few minutes later another woman came in and sat down and looked at the painting. She walked up to the painting, stood extremely close to it, and then touched the bottom right-hand corner – caressed it, even.

'Stop, Sergei. OK,' said Steve. 'If you look at the timeline on that, it's gone seven p.m. so the gallery is shut. The other thing I will say is that you are not allowed to touch the art. That's against the law.' Adam wasn't sure if that was actually the case, although he understood what Steve was saying.

'Who is that then?'

'If it's not Miss High and bloody Mighty herself,' said Steve. Adam looked at him, none the wiser. 'She bloody loves that painting, there's film after film of her sneaking in and sitting there staring at it.'

'Who?' asked Adam.

'The boss. Well, not the actual *actual* boss, although she acts like she is – Ms Fitzjohn.'

'The curator.'

'That's the one.' Steve nodded. 'And look at this!'

Adam, Steve and Sergei all watched as Ms Fitzjohn picked up the chair and moved it to various places around the gallery. It was like she was furnishing her own sitting room. Adam sat back in his chair. He'd run all the way across town to watch Ms Fitzjohn being houseproud before a big party in the gallery, one she'd spent months putting together. Surely that wasn't unusual?

'There!' Steve's pink finger jabbed the screen. 'There's Lexi!'

Adam watched as Lexi sat down on the chair next and seemingly, while occasionally looking up the security camera, slowly placed an object underneath the chair, took out the tape from her bag and, within less than a minute, quickly scuttled out, her head down, avoiding her CCTV close-up. That was no surprise, thought Adam, feeling deeply disappointed. There it was: the can being put under the chair, stuck down with the tape. He checked the date: two days before the murder.

'Well, thanks,' said Adam pushing back his chair and standing up. 'Very kind of you to show me the footage.'

'No! Wait!' ordered Steve, his pink finger pointing. 'Take a look at this.'

Forty-Two

Adam arrived early at Court Number One, looking tired. He'd been up most of the night going through the Crown's printout of Lexi's Twitter feed, and examining the account himself while trying to avoid getting sidetracked. Obviously, he'd engaged with the platform before, but he'd never been one of those people who'd spent hours scrolling through stuff, liking other people's comments or, as far as he could work out, picking fights with other people. The world of activism, or at least the world that Lexi inhabited, appeared to be overwhelmingly binary – you were either for or against. There was no vaguely agreeing, or vaguely disagreeing. You were a vehement yes, or a vehement no; there was little nuance or argument, or acknowledgement of common ground, or indeed courtesy.

Adam sat quietly at the table in the barristers' mess, nursing a strong cup of coffee while leafing through the notes he'd made overnight. He was waiting for Morris, who'd suggested they should meet for a pre-trial coffee before they went back into court and started the cross-examination of PC Bishop.

With long wooden tables, oak-panelled walls and comfortable

leather chairs, the barristers' mess very much resembled a gentlemen's club from the previous century. Hot coffee, full English breakfasts and warm buttered croissants and jam were all available in the early morning. It was a place of quiet sanctuary, away from the hustle and the madness of the courts downstairs.

'Oh, hi! There you are. I bumped into Nisha downstairs who said you were here waiting to speak to Morris. Is he on his way?' Georgina stood by his table, dressed for court in a white shirt, bands, half-tunic, her wig tucked under her arm. She looked around the room at the numerous barristers all dressed the same, sitting at various tables, hunched over their papers, with wigs and bags beside them. 'I can't see him? Can you?'

'Not so far,' said Adam. 'But he said he'd be here at nine a.m.'

'Are you alright?' she asked. 'You look tired.'

'I've been up all night on Twitter.'

'Rather you than me. That's like disappearing down a rabbit hole of madness!'

'I can't even begin to tell you!' He smiled wryly. 'Do you want a cup of coffee?'

'Oh, don't worry. I was going to ask Morris something. But it doesn't matter now. See you downstairs.' She smiled.

Adam watched her go, smiling and nodding to various people as she left. It seemed everyone liked Georgina.

'All rise!' commanded Raquel a few short hours later, as Judge Peters walked into court and took to her padded leather throne.

The public gallery was as packed as before, but none of the Bruce family had decided to grace the front row with their presence this morning. Having made the front pages of every newspaper, including the *Financial Times*, they had clearly decided that their job here was done.

Lexi's parents were both there in the same seats that they had occupied the day before. Humans were such creatures of habit, Adam thought as he looked up at their worried faces. He'd noticed that members of the public often sat in the same seats every day for a trial. It was like they'd claimed their spot. Andrew and Hilary would be tucked in the corner under the carved arch for the rest of the trial.

PC Bishop was back on the stand, her big round moon face smiling at everyone, as if they might have missed her overnight. Jonathan danced around in front of the witness box, discussing some more of Lexi's supposedly incriminating tweets, which he showed on the screens in the courtroom.

'So other than these tweets, you found nothing else on her computer?' asked Jonathan.

'Nothing else. Totally wiped clean,' PC Bishop reiterated. 'Like new, it was. No search history, no nothing. She could have bought it yesterday.'

'No further questions,' said Jonathan, smiling graciously at the PC, whose ears went bright pink as a result.

'Mr Brown? Your witness.'

'Your Ladyship.' Morris nodded, rising from his seat, ostentatiously holding what appeared to be all of Adam's overnight research, which he then, just as ostentatiously, put to one side.

'PC Bishop . . . what exactly were you expecting – hoping, even – to find on Miss Williams's computer?'

'Searches for cyanide poisoning. Searches for murder. Or . . .' She paused. 'The private movements of Max Bruce, his family, his whereabouts? That sort of thing. Or how to put cyanide into a can, maybe? A detailed internet history.'

'Right . . . And let's, for the sake of argument, presume that Miss Williams's computer wasn't new – were you disappointed not to have found anything on it?'

'We were surprised . . .' she confirmed. 'But then again, as it was a professional hit, it was to be expected.'

'Sorry . . . you were surprised to find something you expected? I am a little confused.'

'We was surprised that it was a professional job, because she didn't look that much of a professional. But who can tell these days?'

'Who indeed can tell anything . . .' Morris turned to face the jury. 'Who's to say whether the computer was wiped? Who's to say whether Miss Williams did, in fact, *not* search for cyanide? And she did *not* search up "how to put cyanide in a can dot com". Should such a website even exist.' A small wave of amusement rippled through the court. Morris's eyelids batted briefly. 'Who is to say whether she did *not* look up cyanide, and did *not* find the website about putting it in a can, that she did *not*, in fact, set out to murder Max Bruce after all?'

'Well, er, no, maybe not?' PC Bishop looked confused. Had she just contradicted herself?

'Are you on social media, PC Bishop?'

'I am.'

'And how often do you go on it?'

'Quite a lot.'

'In the evenings, after work, that sort of thing?'

'Yes.'

'Is it possible to retweet something without reading it?'

'It is possible, yes.'

'As a computer expert, have you ever retweeted something without reading it?'

'Possibly.'

'I am sure you're not alone, PC Bishop. I am sure we have all done it.'

'I am sure we have.' She smiled in agreement.

'So perhaps Miss Williams could have reposted the tweet about "killing the rich" without even so much as glancing at the full tweet below? She could have seen the tweet and just pressed a button? She could even have pressed the wrong button? Or someone else might have used her account. No one knows.'

'It's possible.'

'Possible? Probable . . . No one knows at all.'

'No.'

'No further questions.'

PC Bishop walked out of the courtroom looking decidedly less confident than when she'd walked in. Morris had done a good job with very little to go on, thought Adam, hoping that he might be let gently off the hook, after the frosty journey the previous afternoon.

'That went better than expected,' said Nisha, leaning forward and whispering into Adam's ear. 'Have you been forgiven for yesterday yet?'

'I don't think so,' said Adam. 'However—'

He cut himself short. He'd been wondering whether to tell her, tell Morris, about what he'd seen on the CCTV cameras the evening before at the gallery. But the last thing he wanted to be accused of was 'sleuthing', or of being some sort of bargain-basement Sherlock, coming up with another useless reason why their girl couldn't have done it. The footage was grainy. He wasn't quite sure. He'd disappointed Morris enough without another tinpot theory. Adam needed to be certain before he showed anything at all to both Nisha and Morris.

'However . . . what?' asked Nisha.

'I'll tell you in the break.'

Jonathan was ready for his next witness and Georgina was passing him notes, jotting down some ideas as the detective was called.

DCI Ray Smith was a smooth-looking customer. He had thick, dark hair, a bit of a Tenerife tan, and a thick, dark moustache that he constantly stroked as if it were some sort of marsupial living on his top lip. He was wearing a brown suit with a matching tie, and a pale yellow shirt that was tucked in neatly around his slim waist. He stood up in the witness box, legs apart, leaning against the brass rail like he was about to order a pint in the pub.

'Detective Smith, how long have you served?' asked Jonathan.

Smith whistled through his back teeth as he stroked his tache. 'Eight, nine years.'

'And you have been to many crime scenes?'

'I have . . . Thousands of them.'

'Excellent.' Jonathan smiled, hoping the jury hadn't clocked Smith's dramatic hyperbole. 'Could you describe Ms Williams's flat for the court and explain anything that you found striking?'

'It was all striking.'

'The most striking . . .?'

'Oh – all the melons.' He paused. 'Rows and rows of them, all covered in blue paint.'

Adam and Morris had known this information was coming. They'd seen the photographs and read the police report, but when monitors flashed up the images of the bright melons lined up in a row, all covered in blue paint, the whole court gasped. They looked macabre. Frightening. They were the sort of image you could not get out of your head. Even if you closed your eyes, you could still see them, lined up, sprayed blue, the outline burnt onto the backs of your retinas. No amount of mind-bleach could get rid of them.

The gasp turned rapidly into chat, as everyone turned to their neighbour, expressing their shock and disbelief. Lexi's parents just stared, their faces drained of colour. Adam realised that perhaps they had not seen the photographs before, and that they were as shocked as everyone else.

'Order!' demanded Judge Peters. 'This court will come to order!'

The bubbling of conversation stopped.

'For the court,' continued Jonathan, after silence resumed, 'how many of these melons did you find?'

'We found sixteen cantaloupes, three honeydew, and one Galia.'

'All sprayed blue?'

'All of them had been sprayed blue with the same spray-paint that was used in the attack at the gallery.'

'So what would be your conclusion, Detective Smith, with your eight to nine years on the force?'

'That the accused had been practising using the spray and

getting it on target. Like a sniper at a shooting range, if you like, getting her eye in.'

'Practice makes perfect, as they say,' said Jonathan.

'Objection!' said Morris.

'Really, Mr Taylor-Cameron.'

'I apologise, My Lady.' Jonathan bowed his head. 'No further questions.'

Morris was up on his feet before Jonathan had had the chance to sit down.

'Detective Smith, you said just now that Miss Williams was using the same paint to practise in her flat as was used on the night in question?'

'I did.'

'Except it wasn't, was it? Because – according to forensics reports – the paint in the flat contained no cyanide at all, while the paint in the gallery was laced with it.'

'Well, of course, because if she'd used cyanide-laced paint in her own flat she would have killed herself.'

'And yet, here she is.' Morris indicated across towards Lexi. 'No further questions.'

As Morris sat down, Adam smiled at him encouragingly. He had managed to turn the idea of Lexi being some sort of assassin, training for a hit, using melon heads as targets in her bedsit in Archway, into a vaguely ludicrous idea. But even as he sat down the images remained on the screens. Rows and rows of bright blue melons. Sometimes she'd missed and the blue paint had dripped onto the sideboard, or trickled down the kitchen cupboards like little rivers of blood.

'That concludes the Crown's case at this stage,' announced Jonathan.

Both Adam and Morris frowned at each other: what was he playing at?

'Very well, this court is adjourned for the weekend, until Monday at ten a.m.' Judge Peters looked straight ahead at the dock. 'Take the prisoner down!'

Immediately the chants started at the back of the court. There was a hardcore gang of about fifteen, fists raised along with their voices.

'Free Lexi! Free Lexi! Free Lexi!'

'Stop the war!'

'Free Lexi! Free Lexi!'

'Order in the court! Order! Order in the court!'

Forty-Three

It was Monday at 7.45 a.m. when Adam walked into Fratelli's to find Morris sitting in front of a bacon roll with a steaming cup of black tea, bent over a copy of *The Times* finishing off the cryptic crossword, using a shiny golden Parker pen.

'I am sorry I'm late,' said Adam over the noise of the hissing coffee machine.

'You're not,' replied Morris, glancing up at the old black-and-white wall clock behind the counter and clicking the end of his pen, returning it to his top pocket 'I am just an early bird. I am partial to one of little Marco's bacon rolls in the morning when I can.' He nodded over at Marco, son of the original Marco, who was anything but little. 'And' – he tapped the folded newspaper – 'I always find that the cryptic helps focus my busy mind before going to court. Tea? Coffee? A bun?'

'A cappuccino, please,' said Adam.

'A cappuccino, please, Marco,' Morris ordered, with his finger in the air, before looking back at Adam. 'Or how to ruin a cup of coffee with too much milk and chocolate. Anyway.' He sighed. 'I just want to ask, before we go and see Lexi in the cells, if we're sure about putting her in the box today?'

'Absolutely.' Adam nodded. 'I think the jury need to know our girl and see what she is like.'

'That's my worry,' said Morris. 'That they won't like what they see.'

'But if we don't put her on the stand, it will look as if we have something to hide,' replied Adam. 'That we don't support our girl.'

'I am not sure it's as basic as that.'

'I can understand that you are not keen to call her to give evidence, but I think it's a risk worth taking. How else can we show that she's just a nice girl who had some issues during lockdown but who is not a murderer?'

Adam watched Morris from across the green-and-white tablecloth as his cappuccino arrived. He popped in two spoonfuls of sugar and stirred. He could see the intellectual battle writ large on Morris's face. His eyes, his frown – he was answering his own posed questions in his head.

'What are you worried about exactly?' asked Adam.

'That it will blow up in our faces. She is unpredictable. She is volatile. Of course she is. I understand that she feels cornered and is scared witless. But the situation makes me feel uneasy, Adam. I am a man who likes to know where he's going, I like to know how to steer the boat in an argument, and she feels rudderless. It's a risk, and I'm not fond of those.'

'But I think her passion and her youth will play well with the younger members of the jury, of which there are five or six. I have been watching them respond to her and they seem to like her. They are on her side.'

'And you don't think that she will alienate the older ones?' Morris asked, draining his tea.

'I think she'll win them over,' replied Adam.

'OK, then,' said Morris. 'Drink up and let's go and talk to her and see what we think.'

Downstairs in the women's cells section of the Old Bailey, it was unusually quiet, as Morris and Adam followed the guard to Lexi's cell at the end of the long, airless corridor. It was early on Monday, thought Adam, and some of the cells must have been empty; maybe there were fewer women this week. This time below ground the smell was more bleach than urine.

'Lexi!' said Morris as the guard opened the heavy steel door. 'How are you feeling?'

'Great!' she declared smiling from her cell chair, her right leg bouncing up and down. 'I'm excited. I can't wait to get at them.' Her fists were bunched, and her shoulders moved from side to side like she was sparring in a boxing match.

'Good.' Morris smiled weakly. 'It's not quite like that up there, obviously. You don't need to prove anything, of course. It's up to the Crown to prove their case; you don't need to do anything. But . . . are you really sure you want to give evidence?'

'Sure?' Her head turned swiftly, and she looked at Morris with puzzled bewilderment. 'Of course I'm sure! I'm desperate to. I've had to sit there and listen to them talking shit about me, biting my tongue, for days. They're a bunch of wankers! I can't wait. I can't stand them. It's my turn now.'

'Sure,' Adam chipped in, trying to calm her eagerness. 'The whole idea is that the jury get to know you and hear a bit about you, and all that . . . Our job – Morris's job – is to guide you through. Hold your hand, as it were. You don't need to say much, just answer the questions. Honestly, that's it. We can't rehearse you. Obviously. We are not allowed to coach you. But if you just answer the questions we put to you truthfully, and as simply as you can, then it'll all be fine.'

'Equally, you don't need to give evidence at all,' suggested Morris. 'But I do need to tell you that, if you don't, the judge might direct the jury to hold that against you.'

'But I want to,' she replied. 'It's my right to have my voice heard.'

'Of course,' agreed Morris, putting his palms up in surrender. 'And being a person of good character, you should have your voice heard. After all, you have nothing to hide, and you have told us everything.'

'I have,' she confirmed. 'The truth, the whole truth and nothing but the truth, so help me God!' she parroted with a three-fingered salute.

'Well, in which case then,' said Morris, smiling, 'you have nothing to fear.'

'We'll see you in there,' said Adam, with an encouraging smile. 'And don't forget to breathe.'

Forty-Four

'All rise.'

Judge Peters walked into court later on Monday morning with a determined look on her face. For along with the hundreds of articles about Blue/Melon Face over the weekend, with images of sprayed cantaloupes, there had been some criticism on social media on her management of the court process. There had been some talk – on an LBC phone-in chat show on Sunday morning – suggesting she possibly wasn't the best person for the job. Some bloke had even called in to opine that this was the problem with female judges: their inherent lack of authority. Adam had laughed as he'd listened, brushing his teeth and feeding flakes to his fish. That idiot had clearly never come across Judge Wickstead, who could turn a whole bench of barristers to stone with one flash of her steely eyes.

But Judge Peters had clearly taken the criticism on board and looked like she meant business this morning, plus there was more security in the court, and the bailiffs appeared alert and were scanning the public gallery for any signs of trouble. The atmosphere was taut and tense. Adam glanced up. News had clearly got out that it was the opening of the defence case.

Camilla and Elisa were sitting side by side, creating a united front, although Adam was relieved to see that none of the children were there. Why put them through an unnecessary ordeal, he thought. Although it was interesting that Loughton had passed up such a well-attended marketing opportunity, for the court was rammed with members of the press, their note-books and pens poised, ready to report on the trial of the year.

'Mr Brown? Are you calling your client?'

'Yes, Your Ladyship.' Morris nodded. 'The defence calls Alexandra Williams.'

Every head in the courtroom turned towards the door to watch Lexi being escorted into the witness box by two female police officers who, although not handcuffed to her, appeared to stick to her like glue. Dressed in the same white shirt and blue skirt she'd been wearing for the whole trial, her lank hair hanging loose, Lexi cut something of an apprehensive figure as she took the oath and confirmed her name.

Morris turned to face her and smiled, nodding a little for added encouragement, while Adam dug his fingernails into the palms of his hand and sent up a prayer.

'Miss Williams – Lexi,' began Morris, in the gentlest of voices. 'What was your childhood like in Stroud?'

'Normal, average.'

'Right – do go on.'

'Happy, I suppose. I was in the Brownies. I played football for my local girls' team. I even went to ballet class. I was busy. I had lots of friends. I used to go to the cinema once a week with my mates, and my parents sometimes. I'd go out. Hang out. Go to McDonald's. Although not anymore. I wouldn't be seen dead in the place. Oh – sorry!'

Morris smiled stiffly. 'And how was your lockdown experience?'

'Objection!' said Jonathan. 'How is this relevant?'

'Overruled,' replied Judge Peters. 'Let the defendant reply.'

'The same as everyone else's, I suppose. Long, boring, locked in on my own for hours in my bedroom. I didn't make sourdough, if that's what you're asking!'

A couple of people in the public gallery laughed. Lexi seemed pleased with the reaction. She looked to the gallery and grinned. Adam immediately began to worry.

'Did you spend a lot of time on your computer?' asked Morris.

'No more than anyone else.'

'Is that when you first came across the Stop the War campaign? On your own, in your bedroom?'

'Yeah, yeah, that's right. It just made a lot of sense to me, you know, stopping the war, stopping the killing,' she said.

'Stop the war!' shouted a lone voice from the balcony.

'Stop the war!' Lexi yelled back from the witness box.

Morris turned to shoot Adam an 'I told you so' look from below the witness box.

'Order! Miss Williams, this is the only warning I shall give you,' Judge Peters hissed like a snake, looking over her spectacles at Lexi. 'If you do not behave in my court, I shall have you removed.' She indicated towards the security guards standing either side of the main door. 'That is your final warning.'

'Sorry! Sorry!' said Lexi, putting her hands up. 'My bad.'

Morris continued his line of questioning, painting a picture of Lexi's growing interest in so-called fringe groups and ideas as part of her isolation during lockdown, living in a bubble and an echo chamber. His only problem was that every time

Lexi opened her mouth she found it difficult to stop talking. Perhaps it was an attempt to get her story across, or maybe it was the result of being in solitary confinement for so long. But the more she talked, the more she explained her 'vegan forever' diet and her passion for politics, the less appealing she became. Adam was watching the jury as their body language changed from one of engagement to disinterest. Even the younger members on the bench were leaning back and crossing their arms.

'The whole reason for joining the Royal Academy team was so that I could get closer to Max Bruce.'

'Right.' Morris nodded. 'So you did not know Mr Bruce personally?'

'God, no!' She laughed. 'He was chosen as he was super famous, a member of the patriarchy, and the cause would get publicity.'

'Your intention was just publicity? Not murder?'

'I'm a pacifist, not a murderer! I mean, I sprayed him in the face with some blue paint, but that was it. I put the can under the security guard's chair, I chatted him up a bit, so I could get easy access to the thing, and that was it.'

'Tell me about the cyanide?'

'I know nothing about that!'

'Where did you buy the cyanide?'

'I didn't. I wouldn't know how to. Where on earth do you buy that sort of stuff! And what would I do with it when I got it? I wouldn't know. Listen, I sprayed the man in the face to stop the war. Like, why would I want to kill him? I didn't even know him. My message is one of peace. I am a pacifist – why do none of you understand that? STOP THE WAR!'

'Miss Williams!' Judge Peters barked. 'You will sit and behave.'

'Oh, Your Honour – Judge. I am sorry. But I just don't understand what's going on here. This whole thing is so mad. The system is mad. What's wrong with everyone? It's so bloody obvious I didn't kill the guy. Why would I? I don't know him. I've never met him. It's just bonkers.'

Lexi paused, her face crumpled, she put her head in her hands, and then glanced up, looking Judge Peters in the eye.

'I just want to go home.'

'No further questions.' Morris sat down next to Adam.

Adam stiffened slightly. He knew that Morris was regretting his decision to go with Adam's idea. Lexi had not been good in the witness box, and now Jonathan was poised. Adam didn't even dare look; he could sense Jonathan's excitement from across the room. It was wrong to think of the legal process like a game of chess, but it did feel as if they'd just somehow managed to castle themselves.

Jonathan stood up and swooped like a vulture towards Lexi.

'Ms Williams,' he began. 'Alexandra, if I may.'

'Lexi,' she corrected him immediately.

Adam shook his head. Jonathan had wanted her to do that. It made her look contrary, picky, irritable, rude. He looked across at Morris, who was also braced.

'How did you come to be at the Royal Academy retrospective party on the night in question?'

'I was there on purpose. I was working, obviously.'

'It was planned. You intended to be there on that night?'

'Yes. Obviously.'

'And you intended to spray Sir Max Bruce in the face, as we

have accurately seen on the video footage taken from Loughton Bruce's smartphone?'

'Yes.' She nodded.

'And you did intentionally buy the blue spray-paint?'

Georgina passed Jonathan a note.

'Yes, I did.'

'And you bought it from B&Q on the Holloway Road?'

'Yes.'

'Indeed, you did.' He nodded. 'We have the receipt here. Exhibit 2.' The B&Q receipt flashed up on the screens. 'There we are, with your card details and the time and the date, nineteen days before the murder.'

'Yes.'

'And you practised with the paint in your flat on various melons, which we can see here.'

Up flashed the blue melon photographs. Again. Adam couldn't look. Jonathan was milking them for all they were worth.

'Yes.'

'And you will have heard that forensics have reports of cyanide on your desk, in your desk, in the ladies' lavatories, and in your vape refill?'

'I don't know anything about that,' replied Lexi, stepping back in the box with her hands in the air. 'I've never been in trouble in my life. You can ask anyone. I have never done anything wrong, and I don't know anything about any poison.'

'Oh? That's odd . . . Very odd. You have form with poisons, don't you, Ms Williams?'

Lexi puffed out her cheeks and looked over at Adam and

Morris, with confusion written all over her face. She had no idea what to say.

'What's this?' Morris mouthed to Adam. Adam replied with a shrug.

'I don't know what you're talking about,' said Lexi. 'I've never touched a poison in my life!'

'Oh . . . I think you do, Ms Williams. And I think you have.' Jonathan stopped and turned towards the front of the court. 'Your Ladyship, I have a legal application.'

Judge Peters looked across at the jury. 'We need to pause proceedings. I invite the jury to leave, and then I will hear your argument, Mr Taylor-Cameron.'

Adam looked across at Georgina as the jury filed out and the noise in the court, the whispering, grew. What was this? What was the Crown's plan? It was clear that Jonathan had something up his sleeve and that he had been waiting for this. Adam frowned across the court at Georgina, who resolutely refused to catch his eye.

Lexi stood in the dock looking confused at what was happening in front of her. What had she said? What had she done now?

Jonathan cleared his throat. 'My Lady, we didn't make a bad character application before because we believed Ms Williams to be of good character, but since she has now asserted, under oath, that she has never handled poisons before and we believe this not to be true, the Crown would like to apply for Ms Williams's school record to be put in front of the jury.'

Her school record? Adam was confused.

'Objection,' declared Morris loudly. 'This should have been

applied for much earlier in the proceedings. Much, much earlier! How is this relevant?'

'This is relevant, My Lady, to rebut what she has just claimed: that she has never handled poisons before.' Jonathan was barely capable of containing his excitement. 'This is new information that has come to light from one of Ms Williams's teachers, who has been following the trial and has furnished the Crown with this new evidence, which we shall, of course, immediately serve to the defence, and which I present to you now.'

He handed a file to Raquel who presented it to Judge Peters.

'This is most unusual,' replied Judge Peters, shaking her head. 'It really is.'

'The defence objects, My Lady. In the strongest terms,' Morris stressed. 'The very strongest terms. We have not had time to consider this evidence, neither has my learned friend applied to admit this material in a lawful way.'

Judge Peters sat at her desk, deep in thought for a few minutes, as she leafed through the pages of the report. The whole of the court was silent, awaiting her response.

'You can take your instructions in due course, Mr Brown. I am going to admit this. The matter needs to be put to the defendant that she has allowed herself to be portrayed as a person of good character, and this is evidence to the contrary.' She looked up at the rest of the courtroom. 'I think this might be a good time to break for lunch, and we can resume back here at two p.m.'

Forty-Five

Morris was furious, Lexi's parents were weeping, and Nisha was frantically poring over the school report. Adam felt his head was about to explode. He needed fresh air. He needed to clear his brain and excused himself for a walk around the block.

Outside, the steps of the Old Bailey were heaving with over-excited journalists, cameramen and radio reporters, who were all buzzing around, high on the scent of the story, all jabbering into their telephones, telling their desks to expect something big, huge, truly exciting later from the court.

'Poisons.'

'Previous!'

'Bad character.'

'Some sort of record, no reporting restrictions, we've heard it's bad.'

Adam could hear snippets of conversation, as he walked through the fug of cigarette smoke and occasional cloud of a fruit-flavoured vape. The Stop the War protestors were mostly eating their lunch on the steps, talking among themselves – they were not so vocal now that their poster girl was on the ropes.

Two p.m. Back inside court, the stage felt very much set for Jonathan. The press were ready.

'All rise!' said Raquel, as Judge Peters walked in and nodded towards the prosecution to resume.

'Now . . . your French teacher, Miss Davis?' Jonathan threw the grenade and paused, waiting for the name to hit home.

And it did. Lexi looked immediately up to the gallery to catch her mother's streaming eyes, which she dabbed with a tissue. She looked back at Jonathan and swallowed. Her face turned the palest white and shone with a sheen of sweat.

'Poor Miss Davis and her ketamine overdose. Tell me, Ms Williams – what do you know about what happened to her? It was a tragedy, no . . .?'

Jonathan picked up a fat red file. Lexi looked on in horror. What else did this man have on her? Her eyes were round with alarm. Then Jonathan put the file down; it was clearly empty, thought Adam. He'd seen him use such a trick before. Although quite why he felt the need to do such a thing to a terrified 21-year-old girl who was already on the rack was beyond him. Jonathan really was a prize shit sometimes.

He then flapped out a lengthy piece of paper, as if to indicate quite how long her record of misdemeanour might be. Very long indeed, according to his sheet of paper. The bottom half of which, Adam noticed, was blank.

'Shall I carry on? Poor, poor Miss Davis, spiked – is that the word? – in front of the whole school. She went mad, danced across the stage, tried to take her clothes off, claimed she was aboard a spaceship on her way to Mars. How everyone giggled to see her so humiliated in front of all those nice grammar-school girls. She was a laughing stock. And the drug . . .? Well, that was administered by you, wasn't it, Ms Williams?'

'It was meant as a joke! It was just a joke!' Lexi declared. 'A funny joke.'

'A joke that was so funny that poor Miss Davis ended up in hospital, terrified, in fear for her life even – and you, Ms Williams, *you* were expelled. Were you not?'

'I was,' Lexi whispered.

'I am sorry, I didn't quite hear that.'

'I was!' Lexi yelled, thrusting her chin in the air.

'Indeed, you were.' Jonathan paused and ran his finger down the lengthy piece of paper. 'Can we discuss the ketamine? You can't buy that in a shop, obviously. It has to be "scored". Purchased,' he explained to the jury. 'On the streets, doesn't it, Ms Williams?'

'If you say so.'

'Well, it's an illegal drug, so you can't be prescribed it. It is a class B drug, up there with amphetamines, and just below heroin and crystal meth. Not something one can pick up at Boots, or any other chemist. So did you buy it off the streets? Aged . . .' He checked the paper in front of him. 'Aged seventeen. That's a very confident thing to do at that age. Buy drugs on the street. How did you buy the ketamine, Ms Williams?'

'I had contacts.'

'Contacts! That's impressive. Contacts, aged seventeen. And when you purchased the drugs for the unsuspecting Miss Davis, were you aware of the side-effects of ketamine? A horse tranquiliser, so I am reliably informed.'

'I don't know.'

'Shall I run through them? Unconsciousness? Slow breathing? Hallucinations. It's a drug that is often misused in sexual assault. What the poor unsuspecting Miss Davis had done to warrant such a spiking is anyone's guess. Too much homework? Did she care about her class's future too much? Wanted them to do well? Poor, poor Miss Davis.'

'We HATED her!' Lexi shouted suddenly from the witness box.

It was as if she'd been backed into a corner and had come out fighting like a rabid dog. The whole front row of the jury recoiled. As did Jonathan, ostentatiously shocked at her outburst.

'Almost as much as you hated Max Bruce?'

'Objection!' Morris leapt to his feet.

'Sustained! Mr Taylor-Cameron, you know better than that.'

'My Lady, I can't apologise enough, I just can't. No further questions.'

And with that Jonathan sat down and smiled across to an impassive-looking Georgina – just as Lexi burst into tears.

The court was adjourned. Lexi was taken back down to the cells, and the Stop the War protestors took up their position on the steps of the Bailey, shouting their slogans, with the television reporters all standing in front of the glare of their camera lights, reporting every gripping, salacious, gritty little detail to their viewers at home.

Forty-Six

After the court adjourned, Adam and Morris returned to Stag Court together for an emergency meeting in Morris's room, where they sat up until gone midnight drinking tea, coffee and eventually a couple of stiff whiskies, while running through the options and possibilities they had for the following day.

Morris was irritable and clearly annoyed with himself that he'd allowed Jonathan to play such a trump card, with such flamboyance, especially when there was so little he could do about it. He paced his room repeatedly.

'There must be something else . . .' he said, over and over. 'You must have turned *something* up, Adam . . .?'

'Well, I might have something,' Adam said eventually, 'but it's not very clear.'

'Why didn't you say?' Morris stopped and stared at Adam.

'I didn't want to disappoint you.'

'Disappoint me? Don't ever say that to me again,' said Morris, shaking his head. 'I am not that intimidating, am I?'

Adam did not reply but instead told him about his meeting at the gallery and the footage that Sergei and Steve had shared.

He had some of it on his phone which he let Morris watch. And slowly they hatched a plan.

The first person Morris called to the stand the following morning was Cosmo Campbell from Stop the War.

Wearing a red striped shirt with a blue blazer and a navy tie, Cosmo Campbell appeared so establishment that he looked like he might drive a racing-green Mini and upsell 'gorgeous duplexes' for Foxtons in Notting Hill. Ironically, Adam thought he was the just the sort of boy the Williams parents would have liked their daughter to have brought home for Sunday lunch.

'So how did Stop the War manage to recruit the defendant, Miss Williams?' asked Morris.

'If I may say so, sir, we don't actually recruit people. We're not like MI5, or some sort of cult; we have volunteers. Unpaid volunteers. Our cause sort of speaks for itself, so we simply attract like-minded people, people who care about other people, who simply want the world to be a better place. We don't need to recruit. Volunteers come to us of their own accord.'

Cosmo Campbell was a good-looking young man, with a mellifluous voice. Adam looked around the court. He was charming if not the birds out of the trees, then certainly quite a few young ladies in the public gallery.

'So Miss Williams came to your group of her own accord?'

'Well, yes, that's correct.' He smiled. His parents had clearly sent him to an expensive orthodontist. 'She started liking our stuff during lockdown across all our socials, I suppose, and then she met some of our group while at uni, and then, well, then she started attending some of the meetings in town. London. Our main base is in Fulham, just off the Fulham Palace Road, and she turned up there. Offering to help.'

'How did she strike you at the time?'

'She didn't really. That's why initially I couldn't remember her – she was a bit of a loner, with not many friends, as far as I could see; but, you know, we weren't really mates.' He shrugged. 'I've only really found out more about her recently.'

'But she was an active member of your organisation.'

'She was, yes. In fact, she offered to help with the Blue Face protest.'

'Was this before or after the attack on the Home Secretary?'

'Oh, way before. But, to be fair, she didn't know anything about that, as she was interning at the Royal Academy at the time and was not part of the planning process, which, of course, by its very nature was top-secret.'

'I am sure.' Morris nodded. 'So, then . . . Max Bruce? Why did you choose him?'

'Well . . . he's famous.'

'He *was* famous,' corrected Morris. 'Any other reason?'

'No.' Cosmo shrugged. 'It's all about headlines and hits. Fame, that's it.'

Adam stared at Cosmo Campbell. The randomness and the arbitrary nature by which they'd chosen their victim was baffling.

'And Miss Williams followed the same protocol as with the other Blue Face protests?' asked Morris.

'Yes.'

'Could you explain this for the court?'

'Well, it's always the same paint, the same colour, otherwise there is no continuity of action. You spray your target and then you don't resist arrest. It's simple.'

'And your home computer?'

'Oh, you wipe that clean. We teach you how to do that at our HQ in Fulham. It's just to protect the group, and your contacts and all that.'

'So not the tactics of a professional terrorist organisation then? Not the protocol of a professional hit?'

'No!' He chuckled. 'Just common sense.'

'And cyanide? Was that a new direction for the campaign? A way of upping the stakes, getting a few more front pages?'

'No.' Cosmo shook his head and frowned. 'We're anti-violence. We are against the war; we've never killed anyone. We're Stop the War!'

'Stop the war!' shouted a lone voice in the gallery.

'Stop the war!' Cosmo Campbell yelled back, his fist in the air.

'Mr Campbell! If you do not behave, I will have you and your supporters removed!' Judge Peters barked. 'This is your only warning!'

'Apologies,' he said.

'No further questions,' said Morris.

'Mr Taylor-Cameron?' asked Judge Peters.

Jonathan looked up from his desk, and looked Cosmo Campbell up and down, as if he were inspecting a horse before a race, a horse which he clearly found lacking, as he waved his hand, suggesting no questions at all.

'Oh,' he said suddenly, leaping to his feet. 'It's normal practice, then, to wipe the entire computer history before a hit?'

'Yes, it is good practice for us. We always do it before a protest.'

'Good practice for a murder as well, I would suggest.'

'Order!' commanded Judge Peters. 'Mr Taylor-Cameron! I expect better of you.'

'Your Ladyship, Your Ladyship!' Jonathan grovelled, bowing and all but genuflecting, with full-on namaste hands. 'I apologise profusely. I don't know *what* came over me.'

Adam knew exactly what had come over him: he'd seen an opening to score a cheap point and had gone for it. Georgina did not look at all amused. She glanced across at Adam, a genuine look of mortification across her normally serene face. Georgina was scrupulously fair. She disliked showmanship and showboating and show-offs, all of which described Jonathan. She was not enjoying sitting by his side.

'The defence calls Steven Graham.'

The name sent Jonathan scrabbling for his papers. Who was this? He'd been basking in the glory of his final riposte and had not been entirely concentrating.

Steven Graham walked into the courtroom dressed like an undertaker: black shirt, black tie, black suit. He looked not that dissimilar, thought Adam, to a middle-aged member of a nineties boy band on a night out up West. Steve walked slowly across the courtroom, taking in the packed gallery, who were leaning in, about to hang on his every word. He appeared to be enjoying his moment in the sun, as he swore on the Bible and told the court his full name – Steven Eric Andrew Dexter Graham.

'Mr Graham,' began Morris, 'how long have you worked at the Royal Academy?'

'Just over ten years and six months now, give or take a couple of weeks.'

'As a guard?'

'In security, yes, sir. My job is to liaise with the public and make sure that none of the priceless works of art get touched or ruined or destroyed or stolen in any way.'

'And you were on duty on the night of the incident?'

'I was. It is my job, currently, to be in that part of the gallery guarding the Max Bruce masterpiece painting – *Primal Scream* – literally twenty-four/seven.'

'A full-time job then,' Morris said.

'You could say that.'

'Can you explain to the court what happened in the gallery on the night in question?'

'There was a party, speeches, all that, and then Max Bruce got up to speak and Miss Williams said she felt a little faint, so I offered my chair to sit on, underneath which there was stored a can of paint, which she used to spray the artist in the face.'

'And you saw all that?'

'I did. I had the best view in the house.'

Georgina looked across at Adam. Her arched eyebrows were frowning.

'How long had the paint been there, do you think?'

'Objection!' said Jonathan. 'Speculation!'

'Overruled. I presume this is going somewhere?' asked Judge Peters.

'It is, My Lady.'

'I did think that perhaps Miss Williams had placed the spray-can under my chair that day, or perhaps the evening before, but I was proved wrong.'

'Proved wrong?'

'By the CCTV.'

'Is that the CCTV that the prosecution has not shown us?'

'I don't know what you've seen, but this was not watched by the police, that's for sure.'

'Oh?' Morris feigned surprise. 'And why is that?'

'They weren't interested. They didn't go into the security room, and they didn't watch the tapes. They didn't see when the spray-can was placed under my chair and what happened after that.'

'Perhaps we should have a look at these tapes?'

Morris nodded over at the court technician and the TV screens flicked on, showing the empty gallery, with a viewing bench, the security guard's chair and a view of the *Primal Scream* painting.

'Since this is quite grainy footage, Mr Graham, perhaps you might talk us through it?'

'Sure.' Steve nodded, smoothing down his tie and pulling out a large pair of thick black-framed glasses, which he put on the end of his short nose. 'Here's the gallery, there's *Primal Scream*, and here's Lexi, Miss Williams, walking into the gallery, at 7.30 p.m. on the Saturday before the party. If you look at the clock on the tape it quite clearly says that date and time. If you watch closely . . .'

And every single person in the court did. In fact, you could have heard a pin drop; almost no one dared breathe.

'. . . she looks up at the camera briefly, and then slides an object underneath the chair, sticking it with what looks like giant Scotch tape.'

'So that's it. Miss Williams hiding the spray-can of blue paint under the security guard's – indeed, your – chair?'

'But that's not all of it,' Steve said.

'Is it not?'

Jonathan rolled his eyes at Morris, and Georgina smiled. Morris's acting skills were not quite up to RSC standard.

'If you look closely, you'll see someone else comes into the gallery the following evening. They're a bit more savvy about the cameras. If you see, they don't look up, but they move the chair around the room, if you look. It goes right and then left – it's like they are picking a spot. And then, if you watch closely, they slide their hand underneath the chair and we can see them fiddling around with the chair and taking something – a spray-can – from a bag and placing it under the chair.'

'Is this footage of someone swapping the spray-cans? Taking the one Miss Williams had put there and replacing it with something different.'

'It certainly looks that way to me. That person is taking one thing away and putting something else back.'

'So the spray-cans were swapped?'

'They were.'

'No further questions.'

Judge Peters looked over the top of her desk.

'Mr Taylor-Cameron? Your witness.'

'No questions, Your Ladyship.'

Morris had done well, and Adam suddenly felt a slight sense of relief that Nisha's trust in him had not been in vain, and even if Morris had not been enamoured by his digging around and his amateur sleuthing, at least he had found something. There was a scintilla of hope at last. Even Lexi's mum had stopped dabbing her tears, and Lexi herself was sitting up a little taller.

'The defence calls Natasha Fitzjohn.'

There was murmuring and mumbling in the court. Why was

the curator being called by the defence? Even Jonathan looked a little perturbed, and the smirk he'd worn for the past few days slowly faded from his face. Although it had to be said, his face did perk up a little when Miss Fitzjohn strode into the courtroom.

Wearing black patent heels, with bare tanned legs, a tight split black leather skirt and a cream silk shirt, open at the neck, she also had plenty of gold jewellery, a dark glossy lip and a killer blow-dry. She'd certainly worked the Old Bailey catwalk before she'd come into court. She exuded glamour, sophistication and spectacular confidence. As she was sworn in, Georgina had to lean over and quietly remind Jonathan to close his mouth.

Morris started gently, asking her questions about the retrospective and how much of a shock the 'whole thing' must have been.

'Especially when you realised that the assailant was your assistant.'

'I know . . .' Natasha smiled, adding, with a swing of her bobbed hair, 'Especially as I had seen the spray-can in her desk.'

'I read that in your police statement,' confirmed Morris.

'I wasn't the only one, I don't think. But I remember it being there.'

'Did you not find that odd? Did you ask her about it?'

'I was busy.' Natasha shimmied her shoulders to emphasise her busyness.

'But surely someone with an eye like yours would realise the spray-paint was cerulean blue, the colour of the Blue Face protest? The attack on the Home Secretary had been all over the news. The colour had been discussed endlessly. Why would you not stop her? Call the police? This was your big moment.

The end of years of work, the opening of the Max Bruce retrospective. You wouldn't have wanted that to be ruined, surely?'

'Blue is blue,' she said tartly.

'And cerulean is cerulean,' replied Morris. 'You have a keen eye – you're a curator.'

'Who am I to stop someone's creative process? This is the art world. We all work other jobs to support ourselves. The paint could have been for personal use. She could have been the new Jean-Michel Basquiat for all I knew! Temping in a gallery by day, creating in the evening!'

'I wonder if we might see the CCTV footage again?'

Natasha swung her head round to look at the TV screen. From the expression on her face she appeared to be surprised at what she was being asked to watch, but still she managed to keep her cool.

'Do you recognise the room, Miss Fitzjohn?'

'I do,' she confirmed. 'It's the Royal Academy and that is the masterpiece *Primal Scream*, painted by Sir Max Bruce OBE.'

'Correct.'

The court watched in silence as the footage continued. There was Lexi planting the can under the chair, there was her glance up at the camera, which confirmed it was her. Next came the shadowy figure who kept their face turned to the floor, but it was obviously a woman in high heels, with sleek bobbed hair. The outline of the figure matched the one in the witness box – very much so, since she'd made the mistake of wearing the same black shiny shoes, which glinted in the bright gallery lights.

'Is that you changing the can under the chair?'

'It is not,' Natasha replied with a gentle laugh, as if the mere thought was risible. 'I mean, the footage is so grainy.'

'But we can see with our own eyes you're fiddling with the chair, moving the can around underneath. We can see you take something out of your bag and replace it.'

'If it were me, and it isn't, then I would be moving the chair to better protect the painting, and I would have no idea what was underneath it.'

'Did you murder Mr Bruce?' Morris asked.

Natasha laughed as she played with the necklace around her fine neck.

'The man whose exhibition I'd fought for, and whose precious painting I'd returned to the nation?' She was impossibly cool under pressure. 'No!'

Forty-Seven

The following morning, after another white night during which Adam had had visions of blue cantaloupes, hardcore drug-taking and glamorous women in black high heels, all exacerbated by the wailing screams of the urban foxes who patrolled his Islington street at night, helping themselves to next door's bins, he arrived at the Old Bailey feeling exhausted, but quietly optimistic.

Surely he and Morris had managed to find enough doubt – reasonable or otherwise – to make the jury think twice about convicting someone so young and without a previous criminal record? Although he did acknowledge quietly to himself as he climbed the steps, past the placards and the press, that Jonathan, much as he annoyed him, had done a surprisingly good job.

But that was undoubtedly down to Georgina. And there she was. He found himself smiling at her despite himself.

'How are you?' She smiled, standing in the security queue. 'Morris had a good day yesterday, don't you think? That Natasha woman was something else. Jonathan couldn't take his eyes off her. If I hadn't intervened, he'd have ended up salivating all over his own shoulder. Gross!'

'How are you?' He smiled again.

'Tired.' She puffed out her lips. 'I was up at four a.m. on a phone call with a client, can you believe, and then I had to run through the closing speeches with Jonathan. Have you spoken to Nisha yet?'

'Not yet.'

'The CPS have dropped the terrorism charges apparently, which is good news for your girl.'

'Really?'

Adam stopped in his tracks. He suddenly felt overwhelmed with relief. In fact, he was surprised by how much it affected him. What a weird job this was. Sometimes you became emotionally involved in the fate of your client; sometimes you really wanted to fight for them, to be on their side, to battle the injustice; and sometimes you felt very little at all.

But this one felt personal. Maybe it was because he and Nisha had been to see Lexi at HMP Bronzefield before the trial. They'd both seen her implode, collapse in front of them – from an arrogant, angry young woman forced to face her demons to a broken soul crying in a cell. Hubris. Nemesis. The question was – would there be catharsis? Would she be proved innocent in the end?

An hour later in court, Jonathan stood up and adjusted his wig. He was a barrister who enjoyed a closing speech, mainly because all eyes were on him and he could not be interrupted. He walked into the middle of the courtroom, standing right in front of the jury, and rested a hand, gently, on the bench. The gallery above was packed. Camilla, Elisa and Loughton were sitting there centre-stage. Jonathan acknowledged them as he drew breath. Adam wondered if he'd asked them to attend, a timely reminder that Max Bruce wasn't just some abstract celebrity who'd been poisoned at a party, but a real person, with wives and children.

Jonathan began by describing the party, the champagne, and the people there and the reason they had gathered to celebrate what should have been one of the happiest days of Sir Max Bruce OBE's life – but which had in fact ended in his murder.

'The facts of this case are simple,' he continued. 'Max Bruce was murdered in cold blood. In front of his friends, his family, his children . . . his loved ones. He was killed, poisoned by the defendant for a political cause. Alexandra Williams, Lexi, or @lexluthor189, as she likes to be known, is an activist. She was part of a political movement that wanted to create as much chaos, publicity and noise as possible.'

He looked up at the public gallery by way of example. A couple of the older jurors nodded in apparent agreement that the rabble had certainly and constantly slowed down the court process.

'And what was Max Bruce to her? He was nothing but a pawn in her game, her publicity game. You have heard how Williams didn't even know Sir Max. You have heard from the leader of the protest group himself how Sir Max was simply chosen at random just because he was famous. How many famous people had they chosen and rejected, one wonders? Who are those that got away? But Max Bruce wasn't just famous; he was a national treasure, who is now forever lost to this country. Our country. This isn't just the death of an artist we are talking about, but the death of a movement, an idea, the end of an era. And for what . . .? A few front-page stories and a Twitter storm?'

Jonathan shook his head and looked profoundly sad, before breathing in and bravely carrying on.

'When it comes to the facts of this case, ladies and gentlemen of the jury, things could not be clearer. You have seen the film footage, taken by the deceased's eldest son. Where you can clearly see Ms Williams spraying the can of blue paint – the toxic blue paint that poisoned him to death – full in Max Bruce's face. You have seen her determined expression on the film, her rictus grin, you have seen her determined practice as well – and this shows true dedication – on the twenty or so "scalps" in her own flat. This was no accidental crime; this was planned. It was intentional. It was planned to such an extent that Ms Williams took an internship at the Royal Academy so she could be nearer her victim. Three months beforehand. The internship was unpaid, but Ms Williams didn't care about being remunerated – her rewards were not financial. Her job was not organising a retrospective, it was murder. This attack was planned, very carefully planned, and executed to perfection. Ms Williams's only mistake was to leave a forensic trail. A trail that led right back to her desk and to the ladies' lavatories.

'Ms Williams will claim it wasn't her, but then . . . she did also claim that spiking her French teacher, poor Miss Davis, with drugs so strong that she ended up in hospital and left the teaching profession for good afterwards was just . . . "a funny joke".

'Alexandra Williams is a dangerous young woman with form for poisons who was radicalised during lockdown, and the Crown has clearly produced evidence that can be ratified. You can be sure that she murdered Max Bruce – you must find her guilty as charged.'

Jonathan sat down swiftly and leaned over to thank Georgina. She nodded slightly, glancing across at Lexi who stood in the dock, her eyes glazed, as if she was unable to take in what had just been said about her. She looked like she might vomit as she rocked back and forth, her face growing paler by the minute.

Morris stood up and wearily shook his head. 'Ladies and gentlemen of the jury, I am not sure how we have all got here . . . This case . . . this case is so flimsy, so full of holes, it is like a sliver of Swiss cheese. The Crown appears to have found the easiest suspect and presented the facts to you as if this were an open-and-shut case. As someone suggested to me the other day, it's like they're playing Cluedo. They have Alexandra Williams, in the gallery, with the blue paint. Job done. Except the law is not a game of Cluedo in this country; it is for the prosecution to prove its case. It is not down to Miss Williams to prove her innocence, but for the Crown to prove her guilt beyond reasonable doubt. All the evidence we have here, ladies and gentlemen of the jury, is circumstantial. The police themselves admit that the only person they tested for poisons was Miss Williams. The only desk they swabbed for poisons was Miss Williams's, the only footage they consulted was filmed by Loughton Bruce. They clearly wanted an easy life, and they took the easy route. They found their suspect at the scene, and did not so much as look left or right or under a chair, or even at further CCTV footage to see if anyone else might have been in the gallery with the blue paint at the same time.'

Morris paused and turned to face the jury head-on. 'The defence is not asking you to *like* Alexandra Williams. The defence is not asking you to understand her politics, or why she might have joined Stop the War. The defence is not asking you to forgive a lonely teenage girl who was locked up in her bedroom and wandered down the wrong path. But the defence *is* asking you to find her not guilty. The defence is asking you to look at the evidence. Dispassionately. There is no cyanide trail to the flat, there is no evidence that she bought the poison, paid for the poison, or laced the can of paint with the poison. A can of paint that was left in the gallery for five . . . whole . . . days. A long period of time. A long period of time during which anyone could have tampered with it – and anyone did. We saw that with our own eyes. That evidence. But there is *no* evidence, at all, that Alexandra Williams is guilty of this crime. There is doubt, there is very reasonable doubt, and where there is doubt, you must acquit.' He stopped, smiled and slowly nodded. 'Thank you.'

Morris was the opposite of Jonathan. He was solid and exuded trustworthiness and justice. He was significantly less charming than Jonathan, but it looked as if he'd managed to convince the jury. That the truth was the truth. Lexi's parents appeared perhaps a little less anxious than before. All eyes were now on Judge Peters for her summing-up of the case. Although a judge was not supposed to influence a jury either way, her observations would be critical.

She took her time, she jotted down a few notes; the rustle of the paper and the scratching of her pen were audible over the microphone. She began addressing the jury with her legal directions, and then moved on to a summary of the cases presented by both Morris and Jonathan and their teams, and then, finally, she spoke.

'The issue at the heart of this case is a simple one. Was Alexandra Williams the only person with the motive and the opportunity to poison Sir Max Bruce? As you know, it is not for the defence to prove the innocence of Alexandra Williams; it is for the prosecution to prove her guilty. You have to ask yourselves: have they done that? Have they produced enough evidence that you are sure? Miss Williams must be the *only person* to have poisoned Max Bruce. If you are not sure, and you think it could possibly have been someone else, then you have to acquit.'

The case was adjourned, and Lexi was taken down to the cells below. How long for was entirely dependent on the jury. She went quietly, without protest, which was something of a relief. Who knew what the twelve good men/women and true would have thought if she'd been dragged down kicking and screaming, waving at her supporters (who in fact were equally taciturn up in the gallery)?

Adam and Morris cleared up their papers and left the courtroom.

Nisha announced she wanted to go down to the cells and see how Lexi was feeling, and Morris said he had to meet a client in town but would go and reassure her parents first.

Adam walked alone away from the chaos and the mayhem outside of the Bailey. The protestors were out in force. He saw Camilla, Elisa and Loughton being interviewed by a very chatty-looking reporter in a scarlet jacket, talking about justice for Max Bruce.

And then he turned the corner, and it was quiet.

He walked towards the lane and Stag Court, listening to his own shoes hitting the pavement as his mind churned over the evidence, the argument and the counter-argument in his head. Which way the scales would tip was anyone's guess.

'Ah, Adam,' said Tony, as he walked towards the post room to see what fresh hell was in his pigeonhole. 'I see the court reporters have said you've closed.'

'We have,' replied Adam, sounding distinctly jaded.

'What do you think?'

'It's hard to tell.'

'Biggest case of the year.' Tony grinned. 'It must feel good to have finished.'

'Let's see if justice wins,' replied Adam.

'Doesn't it always?' said Tony. 'Anyway, glad you're back. I've asked Stacey to swing by and put some files on your desk. The botched chin doctor? We've got a date for the PTPH – it's the end of next week. There's no peace for the wicked, Adam. Just a lengthy prison sentence!'

Adam was sitting at his desk when Stacey arrived.

'Knock-knock,' she said, poking her head around the open door. 'I bring files,' she added, proffering up a stack that she was hugging to her chest.

'Hello, Stacey! How are you?' asked Adam, sitting back in his chair. 'I feel I have been remiss in my mentoring, what with all these cases. Pull up a chair.' He gestured in front of him. 'How's it going? How's the pupillage? Jonathan?'

'Well, that's kind of you to ask,' she said, remaining standing as she put the files down on his desk. 'But I've just handed in my resignation. Well, not just – two days ago.'

'You have?' Adam was astonished. 'What's wrong? What's happened? Why didn't you come to me?'

'You were in court. Everyone's always in court. I like the law and all that, Adam – I do – but this life is not for me.'

'Why do you say that? You're clever. You're talented. You beat four hundred other candidates to get this pupillage.'

'I'm sure you'll find someone else to fill my shoes.' She laughed. 'But you know, this is not what I want. The hours are too long, the work is relentless.'

'Everyone thinks that to start off with. But you get used to them, and the money will be great – eventually . . . at some point . . .' he added enthusiastically.

'I'm not interested in money. I'm interested in people. And here I'm lonely . . . Very lonely. I have no friends, no life. I'm afraid I'm out.'

'Are you sure?'

'I've never been more sure . . . See you, Adam.' She walked towards the door and then turned. 'See you around, I hope. You're one of the nice ones.' She smiled briefly. 'Don't ever forget that.'

Forty-Eight

Adam spent the best part of two days plagued by acute anxiety, listening for the Tannoy at the Old Bailey. He and Nisha were taking it in turns to babysit the jury, waiting for the announcement and those simple words: 'All parties to Court Number One.'

It was one of the things that Adam disliked most about being a barrister. The wait. It was obviously imperative to keep busy doing something else – other case notes, emails, letters, anything – while drinking prohibitive amounts of coffee in the mess, but all the time keeping half an ear out for the Tannoy. And every time it crackled into life, Adam's stomach plunged down to the soles of his feet. Nothing made him feel more sick, more anxious, than waiting for the voice of God – which was exactly what it felt like.

Finally, they were called. The Tannoy had announced that the jury had come to a verdict, and Court Number One was full to capacity to hear it. Clearly the tom-toms had been working overtime as well. For every news reporter was crammed into the court, sharing seats, perched half-buttocked at the end of a bench, notepads open. Up in the gallery was equally as packed. The wives and Loughton and Lexi's parents and anyone and everyone who'd managed to push and shove and squeeze their way in.

The whole place was airless and still, as if all the oxygen had been sucked out of the room, as Lexi was led in, still wearing her white shirt and blue skirt, her mouse-coloured hair slicked back into a ponytail. She looked anxiously up at her mum, who nodded encouragingly.

The jury came in next, led by their foreman – a tall, skinny forty-something man who was wearing a poorly cut suit and had the weary air of a desk-bound accountant.

'Have you reached a verdict on which you all agree?' asked Judge Peters, her voice popping as she spoke too closely into the microphone.

'We have, Your Ladyship,' he replied, bowing his head.

'Would the defendant please stand,' requested Raquel.

This was it.

Lexi got slowly to her feet. She looked up at the gallery and then imploringly across at Morris and Adam as if they could magically pull something out of the hat at this late stage. Something. Anything that could stop this from happening.

'On the count of murder, how do you find the defendant – guilty or not guilty?'

The question hung in the air. All eyes were on the accountant. He simply stared at the judge.

'Guilty.'

There was silence. After all they had heard and seen, no one had expected that.

A cry, one cry, came from the gallery above. It was lone and deep and visceral; it developed into a scream that was cacophonous and echoed about the courtroom. It was primal.

Adam's heart stopped. So that's what it sounded like . . .

What a terrifying noise. He looked up at the gallery and there she was, standing, her arms hanging limp by her side, her mouth raised towards the heavens, wide open in agony. The cry came from Lexi's mum, and it was enough to chill the soul.

Others soon joined in, shouting their protests, calls of 'No!' 'Fix! Fix! Fix!' and 'Free Lexi!' came from all corners of the court. Up in the gallery some of the protestors had managed to smuggle in handmade cards with STOP THE WAR scribbled in capital letters, which they waved above their heads before being dragged out by the bailiffs. It was chaos on the verge of hysteria. The wives and Loughton swanned out with a contented flourish, while others in the gallery started throwing screwed-up balls of paper that they'd clearly been making for a while, hurling them down on the press and other members of the judiciary.

Meanwhile, Lexi just stood there, as if in a dream, a nightmare, waiting for it all to stop, for it all to be over.

Adam was shocked. He went numb. He could barely hear what was going on above the wild heartbeat that was pounding in his ears. How had this happened? How had they found her guilty? He should never have insisted on putting her in the dock. He looked over at Morris, who was sitting in his seat, turning over page after page of his notes, trying to find something he might have missed.

Finally, after over five minutes of outburst, during which the bailiffs removed the most verbose and troublesome and Judge

Peters repeatedly shouted for everyone to sit down, the court was called to order.

Jonathan stood up. 'My Lady, it is quite clear that there is only one possible sentence available to the court in this case.'

'This is a young woman,' intervened Morris, standing up. 'A pre-sentence report is respectfully requested.'

Judge Peters did not reply.

'Alexandra Emily Jane Williams,' she began, 'you have been found guilty of the murder of Sir Maxwell Bruce OBE, that on the sixteenth day of June this year you poisoned him with cyanide. I see no reason for a pre-sentence report in this matter. There is only one sentence I can pass in this case, due to your lack of remorse, the premeditation involved, and indeed the public interest. You are sentenced to life imprisonment, and I recommend that you serve a minimum of thirty years before you are eligible for parole. Kindly take the prisoner down.'

Two policewomen edged towards Lexi, who turned to face them. She went quietly. Docile, submissive, she put her wrists together to be handcuffed. Adam watched her leave, led out by the policewomen, and he realised he preferred it when she was defiant and angry and full of spirit, fighting the patriarchy with her fists in the air. He found her compliance disconcerting, heartbreaking even. Judge Peters thanked and dismissed the jury, and immediately after, Morris stood up swiftly, snapped shut his notebook and walked straight out. It must have been the first time in over a decade that he hadn't prevailed in a high-profile case. Nisha too gathered up her things.

'There's always an appeal, Adam,' she said gently. 'I shall start putting things together for that. I'm going to talk to the parents now.'

'Do you want me to come?' he asked.

'No, no, you get off. Let me deal with this.'

Adam wandered out of the Bailey in a daze. On the steps, as predicted, he spotted Jonathan, his new cufflinks glinting in the sun as he granted interview after interview with pushy journalist after pushy journalist.

Adam walked on, blinking in the sunlight, past various groups of protestors. Some were openly weeping, their placards and posters discarded at their feet, some were still defiantly shouting slogans, but their numbers were decreasing by the minute. This cause was lost, for today at least.

Standing at the side of the road, Adam sighed loudly. How could this have happened to such a young woman, someone who was clearly innocent? There was something wrong with the system. He felt angry and exhausted at the same time. He did not want to go back to Stag Court to have Tony console him by giving him another hefty legal case, or to catch the wandering furious eye of Morris as he contemplated why on earth he'd agreed to having Adam on his team in the first place.

Next to him, by the traffic lights and the crossroads, Adam spotted an electric Lime bike and leapt on it.

He didn't know where he was going, and he didn't care. The freedom, the wind in his hair, his buffeting robe as he cycled through the traffic made him feel a little better. His phone rang in his pocket. He pulled it out. It was his mum. He put his earphones in and answered.

'Oh, Adam, Ads, those poor people, that poor girl – it's all over the news. How could that have happened? I am just about to go and see Lesley, for a set, and I thought I'd call you first. You will appeal, won't you, Adam? I know you need new evidence for that, don't you? But you have to appeal . . .?'

On and on she talked. Poor this, poor that. What were her parents going to do . . .? What a tragedy . . .

It wasn't until she drew breath that Adam realised exactly where he was.

'Mum,' he said. 'I'm going to have to call you back.'

Forty-Nine

It was late afternoon when Adam walked into the Royal Academy and paid his £24.50 to have one last glimpse of the Max Bruce retrospective. Naturally he didn't bother with the rest of the exhibition, and he went straight to the rubberneckers' room to see *Primal Scream*. It was surprisingly empty. Maybe the verdict had put people off coming to see where a now-proven murder had taken place, for Adam was the only person in the room. He went and sat down on the viewing bench to stare at the painting. This image would haunt him for the rest of his life, he thought, gazing at it.

What was this all about? The image of Natasha Fitzjohn came into his mind. What was she looking at when she returned evening after evening just to sit and stare. He stood up and slowly walked over to the painting. He paused. He walked closer still, straight to the corner she'd seemed obsessed with. 'No touching the canvas,' he heard Steve's voice in his ear. There was the signature. The big brash name – MAX BRUCE – painted in a thick, aggressive black. And then . . . he looked closer. In the tiniest, smallest writing down the side, tucked into the frame, on a bare bit of canvas, in pencil, as if written by a mouse, Adam made out the words: BABY TASH. It was faintly written and easily overlooked, especially if no one had seen the painting in over forty-two years.

Baby Tash . . . Baby Tash . . . Baby Natasha. Forty-two years. What did Natasha Fitzjohn see in this painting? Adam smiled. She saw herself.

'Mr Green.' His blood ran cold. She was standing right behind him. 'What are you doing here? Straight from court, I see. Can't bear to be torn away?'

'Well, it is a wonderful painting, painted by a wonderful man,' replied Adam, turning around.

'I wouldn't go that far,' Natasha replied, standing in the same black patent stilettoes she'd worn in court three days earlier.

'Why not . . . *Tash*?' Adam smiled.

'It's Natasha, actually. Always is . . .'

'Not "always has been", though. You weren't always called Natasha, were you, when you were little? When you were a baby? Baby Tash? This is you, isn't it?' He pointed towards the painting and she laughed lightly at the absurdity of the hypothesis. 'You're the missing eldest child? That's why you sit and stare at it. Max Bruce was your father!'

'I wouldn't really call him that.' She smiled tightly. 'To be a father you have to be there, you have to love someone. To be a father you have to give a shit.'

'But he was your father?'

'You know, I have always loved this painting. I saw it as a tiny baby, but after Bruce left me and my mother, I never saw it again. I have made it my life's work to get it back for the country, just so that I could see it once more. See my name, see that I did exist. Once. That he did love me. For a second. My image was in his head. He did think about me. Even if it was just for a few days.'

She sat down on the viewing bench and stared straight ahead, seemingly lost in thought.

'Why did you have to kill him?' ventured Adam, his mouth dry.

'I didn't.'

'You're not still saying it was Lexi, surely? Lexi's not clever enough to have done that. You have to be super intelligent, super smart, to pull that off. She isn't any of those things . . . But you are.'

She didn't reply, so he carried on.

'You spotted the spray-can. It was an opportunity too good to miss.'

'You think you know me, but you don't.' She looked him up and down, the contempt in her voice and on her face writ large. 'My mother was an art student who had an affair with Max Bruce, she got pregnant, he left straight after I was born. His family hated her – she was poor and not well connected, and they ignored her completely. She took her own life when I was fourteen. You have no idea what I have been through, the sadness, the pain, the rejection. Bruce laughed when I tried to contact him, my letters were returned unopened. He sent me a cheque. Once. Out of guilt, for ten thousand pounds. I never cashed it.'

'It must have been hard?'

'You have no idea what hard is!' she spat. 'I'm glad he's dead. He spread nothing but misery and pain.'

'I can see why you did it. But how did you manage it?'

'I'm not that foolish.' She laughed, standing up and beginning to walk away. 'Have you got a tape recorder in your pocket?' Her voice was mocking, her head shook from side to side. 'Is your phone recording?'

'So you don't mind letting a young woman take the fall?'

'Oh, please!' she retorted, putting her hands on her hips. 'It's a big, bad world out there, Mr Green. It's dog-eat-dog. We're all collateral damage to one person or another. Governments, systems, relationships, parents . . . Someone always wins.' She laughed dryly. 'And someone always takes the fall.'

Fifty

Adam walked into the Wig and Pen to order the stiffest and strongest drink he could think of. He wasn't sure why he'd elected to come to the pub just around the corner from Stag Court. He was just sure he didn't want to drink on his own. What a day, what a verdict, what a damaged human being that woman was.

Walking through the door his heart sank immediately. This had been a terrible idea. Jonathan was at the bar, clutching a whisky. The last thing Adam needed was to have him crowing with victory, his nostrils flared with superiority, and his breath laced with the claret-soaked spoils of triumph.

Yet when he approached the bar, the man looked positively downcast.

'You alright, Jonathan?' asked Adam. 'I expected to see you brimming with Pol Roger, riding the shoulders of champions.'

'Oh, it's you,' Jonathan replied flatly.

'What's the matter?'

'I can't bear it,' he said, flashing his WhatsApp at Adam by way of explanation.

'Bear what?'

'Pippa's just told me she's pregnant.' He shook his head in abject horror. 'Pregnant! I am going to be paying school fees, Adam – school fees! – until 2044 at the very least. Twenty forty-four! Will I still even be a-bloody-live then? Another child! I've seven already! What am I going to do? I'm going to be playing football in the park when I'm sixty! Either that or collecting from ballet lessons with my Zimmer frame.'

'Babies are a good thing, aren't they? You should be happy. My mother would be over the moon if I told her news like that.'

'I don't know what to do. What do I do?'

'Celebrate – you're going to be a father!'

'Again,' Jonathan said, rolling his eyes.

'Again,' confirmed Adam, giving him a fat pat on the back. 'Come on. Let me buy you a drink.'

'Oh, no, no, no,' said Jonathan, scrabbling around for his wallet. 'I can't let you do that.'

'Jonathan, please, stop. It's fine,' said Adam. 'Remember – I'm not your pupil anymore.'

Lexi Williams is currently in HMP Holloway, waiting for the appeal that has been lodged by Adam and Morris. No one yet knows when it's coming to court. Meanwhile, Natasha Fitzjohn has recently received an OBE for Services to Art. She is still running the Royal Academy. For now . . .